Praise for *Rose Nicolson*

'I loved this book' Richard Holloway

'This novel is full of surprises, rich in delights. Greig writes with rare authority and understanding. Sometimes it seems as if he was behind a heavy tapestry or curtain listening to everything being said, then keeking through a gap to view the action' *Scotsman*

'Exceptionally enjoyable . . . Greig very skilfully combines a gripping adventure story with an exploration of the dark forces that shaped Scottish history' *Sunday Times*

'Prepare to be pitched back in time in this visceral and passionate novel set in 16th Century Scotland' *Sunday Post Dundee*

'Andrew Greig's novel is written in archaic Scots; the result is an immersive reading experience, helped along by a glossary. This is a meaty, satisfying novel and the character of Rose, a strong woman trapped by her circumstances, will linger long' *The Times*

'[N]ever allows the narrative to flag. William Fowler is his perfect alter ego, a poet, a gowfer and a natural raconteur' *Literary Review*

'[A] highly entertaining historical novel' *Independent*

ROSE NICOLSON

ROSE NICOLSON

Andrew Greig

riverrun

First published in Great Britain in 2021 by riverrun

This paperback edition published in 2022 by

riverrun

An imprint of

Quercus Editions Limited
Carmelite House
50 Victoria Embankment
London EC4Y 0DZ

An Hachette UK company

A CIP catalogue record for this book is available
from the British Library

Paperback 978 0 85705 486 9
Ebook 978 1 78429 245 4

10 9 8 7 6 5 4

Typeset in Monotype Fournier by CC Book Production
Printed and bound in Great Britain by Clays Ltd, Elcograf S.p.A.

Papers used by riverrun are from well-managed forests and other responsible sources.

To Judith, David, and Sandy,
for all we have shared from the start.

A glossary of Scots dialect words and their approximate English meanings is placed at the back of this book.

ROSE NICOLSON

Memoirs of WILLIAM FOWLER of Edinburgh:
Student, Trader, Makar, Conduit, would-be Lover
in the early days of our Reform

*It is a hard thing to speak of, how wild, harsh and impenetrable
that wood was, so that thinking of it recreates the fear. It is scarcely
less bitter than death: but in order to tell of the good that I found
there, I must tell of the other things I saw there.*

William Fowler, translation of Dante's *Commedia*
(Hawthornden Collection, Edinburgh)

BOOK I

THE SONSIE QUINE

(St Andrews, 1574–1578)

A tale I have for you. Ox murmurs,
Winter pours. Summer is gone:
Wind high, cold . . .
Ice-frost time: wretched, very wretched.
A tale I have for you.

William Fowler, draft of 'The Amra of Colm Cille'
(Hawthornden Collection, Edinburgh)

The Doo-Cot

W E HAD BECOME NEAR-ACCUSTOMED to the farting thud of small cannon, the prattle of musketry, the yelled orders and clashed steel, swirling about our city's tenements. Then followed the clatter as a sortie of Queen's Men from the Castle swept through the barricades, down the High Street to confront the King's Men.

At the first explosions, my father would sigh, go down the winding stair to bar the entry to our close, then latch-key our nail-studded door. He would return to our refuge, solemnly count our heads, place the key on his work table, then go back to writing inventories and bills of sale. *Mon Dieu!* my mother might mutter, not breaking off from sorting haberdashery pledges.

That work room was most the solid and siccar in our house, its hidden heart. My father in a rare flight of fancy cried it *The Doo-Cot*. Not that we kept doves in it, but rather scrolls of contracts, receipts and undertakings. These roosted together within the wooden cubbyholes that lined three walls of the room, from knee-height to ceiling.

My father made them himself from ornate panelling ripped from Blackfriars following one of Preacher Knox's inspirational sermons on Christ cleansing the Temple. Most of the ornamentation had been prised or slashed off the panels, but the occasional serpent, Tree of Life, sheaf of corn and mild ox remained, to my delight as a bairn. They became part of his filing system. *You'll find the Mar papers lying down next tae the Lamb*, or, with relish, *The Archbishop's accounts are to the richt o the Gates o Hell*.

Fragrant with ink, parchment and sealing wax, steeped in peat smoke in winter months, the Doo-Cot was my favoured place in our home. My mother cried it the Counting House. How their marriage, as the Reform gripped and even the most cautious took sides, is laid bare in that divergence!

For months now the Queen's Men had held Embra Castle and the surrounding tenements of the upper part of the town, including our Anchor Close. The King's Men, led by the Earl of Morton, held the Canongait, Holyrude and Leith. Our Queen Mary had fled, but might return with a French army. Her son and heir Jamie Saxt, said to be a poorly made bairn, was held 'under protection' in Stirling Castle, and who kenned what he wanted?

So the Lang Siege ground on with parleys, shootings, cannon thuds and clatter of hooves. When it was quiet, we nipped out for food supplies with the rest of the populace. Otherwise we shut ourselves in the house, retreated to the Doo-Cot and waited it out.

One dreich May morning, our lives changed. Unknown to us, Drury's English troops – our gallant allies in the Reform (my father), or heretical enemies of the True Church (my mother) – had drawn a score of big cannon through the night up towards the Castle. When the familiar skirmishing started, we shut ourselves in the Doo-Cot. Around midday came a much louder BOOM, then a deep thud felt in the gut. Dust and plaster showered from the ceiling. The scrolls and papers shivered in their nests.

Silence, and a cold draught coming up the winding stairs and under the Doo-Cot door. My father hesitated, picked up the latch key. *I'd best hae a look*, he said, and was gone.

Our close door had been blown off its hinges. As my father stood baffled, someone fired from the mouth of the courtyard. Upstairs, we heard the bang and a cut-off cry.

We found him collapsed in our doorway. Mother and my big sister Clemmie dragged him within, the cook and I struggled to bar our door. He died on our entry slabs, looking puzzled as Drury's big cannon started up outside. The smell of warm blood and stone dust burns in my nostrils yet, and sudden bangs still render me an affrichted boy.

MY MOTHER BELIEVED THE Reformists had killed him. Neighbours said it was one of the Queen's Men, during a counter-attack. Some claimed it was English forces. I knew only that my father was dead from the religious wars. The stain on the entry slab took weeks to scrub away. I still saw it in my mind's eye, each time I left or entered our house.

When Drury's troops poisoned the well, took the Forewarks defences and brought the big cannon closer, after twelve days of house-shaking bombardment the Queen's Men surrendered the Castle and the Lang Siege was over. Their lives were guaranteed by the English leaders. But they were soon handed over to the King's Men, and Kirkcaldy of Grange and his brother James were sentenced to be hanged at the Merkit Cross, just as Preacher Knox had prophesied.

My mother sobbed in the Counting House, not so much for the men as the death of her hopes. Grave-faced, our neighbours went out to witness the hanging. I followed on but lost them in the crowd. A man with burning eyes hoisted me high. *Ye maun see this, laddie!* Against my wishes, I saw them, fleetingly, from the back of the crowd, those blood-engorged faces turned golden masks as they spun towards the sun.

That marked the end of that phase of our uncivil war. Soon after, my elder sister Clemmie grew a sickness within her gut. I closeted myself in the Doo-Cot while her howl and retching diminished to cough and whimper, then a silence that echoed long through the house.

Those were hard times. They weakened and hardened us, as such times do. Our front door never closed rightly again.

CHAPTER I

A Student Departs

I HEAR AND FEEL IT yet under my scrieving hand, the scrape and shudder of our door as I forced it open into the Embra dawn. I stood a long minute neither fully in nor fully out – a lifelong position with me, I suppose. The wind through the Castle Gait rugged at my cloak. It would be a rough passage.

I suppressed signing the Cross, gripped my pack and stepped out. A hard yank and the door grunted like my father's last breath. Then I was out in the not-quite darkness, heading for Leith and whatever life would bring.

THE WATCHMAN AT THE Canongait port stood forth and barred me with his lance, more from boredom than alarm. The odd scuffle, shooting and stabbing apart, old Embra had gone quiet as though taking a breather. In any case I was a stripling and likely unarmed.

'Where mak ye and wha are yer people?'

I gave him back as boldly and well-spoken as I could. 'I am William Fowler of Anchor Close, as well you ken. I am commencing to be a student at St Andrews.'

He spat in the mud. 'Lazy bastards aa. What's in yer pack?'

'Bread and cheese for the voyage.' I made no mention of the brandy flask lest he confiscate it. 'Also paper and writing materials.'

'Little good they'll do ye.'

'You might be right there, Master Morrison.'

He chuckled and lowered his lance. 'Your faither was a good man, for a money-lender.'

'He was an honest merchant who advanced credit against surety,' I corrected him.

'Your mither will be looking for anither.'

'She has o'er much sense than to marry again.'

We looked at each other, John Morrison and I, in the mingled lights of dawn and watch-torch. 'Sorry aboot yer big sister, Willie. She wis bonnie.'

My feet yearned to turn back home, though there was no place for me there. My mother and remaining sister Susannah shared women's grief I could not take part in.

'She was that.'

'And your big brither John wis a fine, strapping lad.'

'So I am often told.'

We stood, heads lowered in that chill wind. 'Pass, wee man.'

With as much conviction as I could muster, I went through the port we cried World's End.

'Good luck to ye!' he called. Then, more faintly, 'Ye'll be needing it.'

AND SO I LEFT wind-tossed Edinburgh, that high-masted, tight-bound vessel of some three thousand families crammed within its walls, gaits and wynds, who all kenned or guessed each other's business, where kindness was delivered with a rough tongue, where sweetness came wi salt, and justice and injustice alike came swiftly, at dagger point or rope's end.

I see myself in the growing light, clutching my pack, passing the ailing Preacher's house, sniffing the orchards and gardens of the Canongait in the morning air. Mid-September 1574, a fine, if challenging, time to be young. My mother would have been at a clandestine early Mass, or already in the Counting House. She did not see me off, whether out of indifference or too much feeling, I cannot know. The night before, she had passed me a packet of papers, receipts and pledges, to carry out business for her in St Andrews, and help pay my fees and lodging.

Within the bundle she had slipped a wee gold garnet-pointed Cross, enough to rouse Preacher Knox from his sick-bed. Seeing my hesitation, she held up her hand.

'Please,' she said, one of few times I remember her using the word. '*Pour ton âme, mon petit*. It will only grow in value.'

Such were my mother's twin passions: finance and the True Church. I had accepted the crucifix, knowing it balanced by my father's Reformed Bible – plain, severe, in the vernacular – uppermost in my trunk sent on ahead.

FULL LIGHT AND HIGH tide at Leith. My future beckoned through of a thicket of swaying masts. I had never been to St Andrews, nor even sailed outwith the Firth of Forth. The world would never be so fresh and fair and queasy-making as when the *Sonsie Quine* sailed on the ebb that morning.

I stood on deck, clutching the foremast. At first exhilarated by the pitch and toss out on the estuary, as we tacked by Cramond Island I was beginning to feel distinctly off. A skinny boy with long red hair and white face abruptly emerged from a hatch. I had seen him on the quayside, flanked by two men who quickly took him below. Now he staggered to the starboard rail to eject his breakfast. Which set me off, and for a while we were companions in misfortune.

We got down to bile about the same time, and keeked across at each other.

For the first time I saw that strong beaky nose, his stubborn squared-off chin and blue-green eyes. He wiped drool from his pimply face and I realised that though taller, he was a year or two younger than me. Gentry was in his dress and bearing as he leaned closer.

'Friend, a loan of your dirk,' he muttered, sour-breathed.

How had he noticed it, pouched within my jerkin? His voice was low, hoarse, of the Western Borders.

'The need is great,' he said. I hesitated. His long-fingered hand grasped my sleeve. 'I am asking nicely. *Sois gentil*.'

For a moment we looked each other in the eye. My free hand went automatically – my mother habitually commanded me in French – into my jerkin.

'Quickly!'

I slipped the dagger from its pouch, then it was gone within his cloak. He turned back to the rail to vomit again just as his escort appeared, one on either side. The taller one stared hard at me, saw only a short boy of no account, then took my companion's arm.

'Best come below, Master – we don't want you falling overboard!'

They led him away. As he turned to descend the ladder, he glanced up at me, nodded. That swift hard nod nailed his face to my memory.

THE *Sonsie Quine* ROLLED into the lee of Inchcolm Island and the seas calmed somewhat. The Abbey, one of the oldest in the country, had been cleansed with all the others in the tumultuous year leading up to my birth. The stout church was roofless, and birds passed in and out the vacant windows. The cloister and chapter house appeared uninhabited but more or less intact. The stone was blackened around the windows of the scriptorium, which must have burned well.

Preacher Knox's sermon at Burntisland in the autumn of 1559, against Idolatry and the distractions of Beauty, had had its customary effect. Anything of high value left in the Abbey would have gone to one of the Lords of the Congregation; the less fancy items to the lairds of Fife; the practical items of wood and dressed stone to the Burghs.

A couple of monks, wild and unshaven, emerged from a rough shelter by the shore and stared as our ship rolled by. By their tattered robes, they had once been Augustinians. They looked as feral as their few sheep, wild as their vegetable garden. The Reform had decreed that all monks and friars convert, or leave for whatever countries would have them. They might live on within the ruins, but hold no Masses, receive no income, have no books or novices, give no Sacrament. A merciful settlement, some said.

The mate told me that due to *a bittie blaw*, we would no longer be picking up timber in Limekilns, but instead crossing direct to Fife. We sailed out of the lee of Inchcolm, and the wind and swell rose to new extremes. I clung to the rail and the rigging as we tossed and plunged but I was sick no more. As we tacked further out into the Firth I surrendered myself to God's Will.

I became aware of a new urgency. The captain was on deck, following the mate's arm pointing out towards the Bass Rock. The sea had changed. The waters ahead were green, white, dark, leaden, all scurrying and shifting, strangely lit. Then the full storm hit us. The great trees of the masts bent and groaned. Our vessel slewed, leaned over so far the upper yards snagged in the running wave.

The mate screamed above the wind at the two hands as they

struggled to further reef the sails. They lost control of the mainsail, which flew wide, smashed into the jib rigging and the boom cracked.

A hand thwacked my back. It was our captain – a Dutchman, my mother had said. A year earlier she had advanced him credit to buy a share in the *Sonsie Quine*, thus my free passage. His face was red with drink and weather, but he seemed sturdy and untroubled amid mayhem.

'Help take the wheel!' he shouted in my ear. 'We need a man free.'

I gaped at him. I was practically a child.

'On ye go! Hold on to me!'

I clung to his broad leather belt, felt his strong arm round my shoulder as we zig-zagged across the tilting deck and slammed into the wheel. A rope lashed me to the wheel-stem. The smaller steersman adjusted my fists round the spokes, then reeled away.

'Watch me, laddie!' the steersman at my side cried.

The captain and the hand had gone to fight with the rigging and straining sails. Tipping into a huge on-coming wave, the ship slewed over, water rushing across her decks, those spars caught in the passing wave strained and snapped. The whole boat groaned as though slain.

The steersman bared his teeth, gave a great cry and forced the juddering wheel over as I too heaved with all my strength. The wheel and its stem were shaking so hard I thought they would split. We forced again, the bow came round, our ship shook free of that devouring wave. Then we were down, down in the abyss, veering into the next roller.

We took it straight on, rose up and up. I could see over the white and black sea, all the way to the Berwick Law and those green fields we would never reach. My lofty resignation of minutes before was succeeded by black dread at being taken by the sea, sinking down into nothingness or worse. What if God were not a Protestant? What if He were? I was damned either way.

We spun the wheel as the bow dropped and we slid down off that great wave. A bawling in my lug. I looked at the steersman, his face streaming water, and he grinned his few yellowed fangs.

The Lord's my shepherd, I shall not want!
He makes me down to lie!

We bawled it out together, the old Psalm in new language, vernacular and raw, as we rose up, plummeted and rose again. The wheel shook and strained against my hands, but it held.

At last the mainsail was saved and reefed, then we tacked hard over and sailed by the jib for St Serf's castellated tower at Dysart. My heart was high, my head rang clear as a bell. I was drookit, clothes ruined, but have never felt so light and fearless as that afternoon we skidded and furrowed our way across the tumult.

Some would say that our cry was heard and answered from Above. That may be, though more devout men than I die each year in the unruly Forth. All I know is that *we* heard it, our hearts heard it and were made strong. That day I learned the power of sung words.

As the storm abated, the steersman turned to me, water and saliva still running from his beard. His eyes were huge and dark-shining.

Perhaps he was a religious man and had just had the revelation he was justified.

'Weel, yon wis fuckin rowdy,' he said.

CAPTAIN WANDHAVER PASSED HIS flask. I took a swig, gagged at its fire, swallowed and drank again. We were moored for the evening, off Dysart. I had gone below and changed into dry hose and breeches, but still could not get warm.

'Some storms come sudden-like,' he said. It sounded near-apology. 'Your mother would have been put out if I'd lost her investment. You did well.'

I handed back the flask, feeling his words and the brandy burn down to my toes. That let me speak my mind. 'Weren't you feart?'

He looked back at me, that red-faced, rough, clever man. 'Surely I was. Your mother is a forceful woman.' He showed a good set of teeth in his round turnip head, then shrugged. 'The sea is what it is, and I am used to it.'

'So you are carrying valuables for her?'

'I am carrying you.' He paused. 'And will return with further timbers from the Cathedral.'

We stood silent, amidships, in the half-light. A pale rent flared above the rounded paps of the distant Lomond hills.

'I was sore afeart,' I confessed. 'The sea is so . . . deep.'

'You have not the face for drowning, lad. I have never been wrong about such things.'

Captain Wandhaver was no plain dealer, but he said this so casually, as if it were simple fact, that I did not think he was joking me. Though there were no reasonable grounds to believe him, his words have lodged in my brain these many years.

'Hanging, mind you,' he added with a chuckle. 'That is another matter. I cannot say you'll not hang.'

'I'm o'er wee and unimportant to hang,' I replied, basking in our manly badinage.

He grasped my shoulder with his mighty paw. 'Master Fowler, you are too unimportant for the axe, and I wish you the good fortune to stay lowly. But any man may hang – aye, and some women too.'

Intrigued, part in jest, I enquired after my fellow-steersman, the one with the skelly eye, who had bellowed the mighty 23rd Psalm into the storm. Did he have the face for drowning?

The captain made no reply. He took another swig, stoppered the flask, and sombrely folded it away within his coat. The gesture reminded me.

'That boy with the long red hair and the two men – who is he?'

His face and favour turned from me. 'Never ye mind,' he said, and stomped off to check the anchor ropes were sound.

Though the *Sonsie Quine* still kicked and rolled, I was able to eat below with the crew. It seemed I had passed beyond sea-sickness, and indeed it would never return. The red-haired boy and his escort did not reappear to eat with us, though I noted plates and glasses being taken from the galley to some for'ard cabin. The mate saw me watching and shook his salt-crusted head, so I returned my attention to beef and bread.

A SHARP CRY WOKE me in the dark. Through the planking I heard a muffled groan, a thump, then silence. The crewman bunked beside me did not stir. He was either asleep or made a good show of it. Across the way, another snored.

I listened in the rolling dark. Perhaps someone had tripped and banged their head? I lay on my bunk, listening through the slap and mutter of water through the hull. There might have soon been voices, but very low.

I lay awhile on my back. *In pastures green he leadeth me, the quiet waters by.* I saw again the view across the tumultuous sea to the green fields of the Lothians, felt uplifted out of abyss. Is that how Preacher Knox had felt as a French galley-slave when he gripped the oar, buoyed up in his faith, seeing far ahead and beyond? And what did he see in recent months, aided up into the pulpit by his young wife and the elders of the kirk of St Giles? Judging by his visage, what he saw ahead was not to his taste.

In my narrow bunk, safe for the moment, I rolled onto my side and sank deep down.

GREY LIGHT THROUGH MY tiny window. Still uneasy and excited, I went early up on deck and so witnessed a flat-ended boat move away through the dawn, its course steady on St Serf's tower. Two men in unfamiliar livery rowed, and at the stern, back turned, was the red-haired boy.

I cursed. To have given away my father's dirk! It seemed a wretched start to this adventure. And yet the course of my life was set by that moment's impulse.

Fair winds took us up the coast of Fife. The sun had some autumnal warmth in it, enough for me to sit for hours against a hatch-cover. I day-dreamed great deeds and achievements, sketched out a future, a degree, a lassie's face turned my way.

And I thought about the boy, my comrade in vomiting, how deftly he had hidden away my father's blade, and those noises in the night I might have dreamed but suspected I had not.

'So we are sailing into Anster?' I said to the mate as he passed. Our ship was heading straight on a squat church spire. 'Not going on to St Andrews?'

He hunkered down. 'First rule of sailing, laddie,' he said. 'Where yer pointing is seldom whaur yer bound.' He furled the lead-line round his gnarled fist. 'Five-knot ebb tide. Tonight I'll be in a Kilrymont alehouse and ye'll be in yer cosy college bed.'

RIGHT ENOUGH, WE PASSED a roofless priory at Crail, then rounded Fifeness well into the afternoon, standing off from the foaming skerries, then rode a backing wind by a high sandstone cliff, then for the first time I saw the spearing spires of the ruinous Cathedral of St Andrews, red-tipped in the late sun.

My trunk was carried off the ship. I waited for the red-haired boy's escort but they never appeared. I asked Captain Wandhaver, 'Are those two men not still on board?'

He turned his big, round head, gazed impassively on me.

'They left the ship.'

'Not with the boy. I saw him being rowed towards Dysart.'

'They had left afore that.'

'Oh,' I said. I shook hands with the captain, said he had taken good care of my mother's investment.

'*Gut*. Keep your head down and mind the boom, lad. The wind in these parts changes with little warning. No doubt we'll see you on the *Sonsie Quine* again.' He slapped the mainmast as if it were an old friend. 'She is well named, for she is both a queen and a lucky ship!'

I FOLLOWED THE CART carrying my trunk up the brae, through a corbelled eastern port and into the town. Soon enough, in a daze of novelty and fatigue, I sat on the sole chair in the monastic bareness of the chilly room – my *bunk*, as the porter cried it – under the eaves of the house off Merkitgait that was to be my home. The college was not in a fit state of repair to house me.

I got out my key but the padlock on my trunk opened of itself. I lifted the lid. On top of my clothes, next to my father's Bible and my crossbow, lay the dirk.

Faint with relief, by the yellow light of a creusie lamp I inspected the note.

I thank you for the loan. In time I shall make good. ℬ.

THE PAPER WAS QUALITY French. The writing was young and forceful, a cursive italic script, blot-free, its line level as a blue-black horizon. The magnificent initial was a ship in full sail, a veritable galleon of pennants, flourishes and trailing lines. My hand itched to copy.

The dagger's blade seemed shinier and sharper than before. Not a spot of blood or gristle on it.

I sprawled on my hard pallet and stared at the ceiling. My father's blade lay on my work table. The oil lamp flickered. The floor still rocked me from the voyage. I blush to write it now, but I was awe-struck at my own life as it sailed into the unknown.

CHAPTER 2

The Scorch Marks of the Martyrs

I WOKE FEELING OLDER. I had helped steer a two-master through an autumnal gale. I had perhaps given a red-haired boy the means of his liberation, though best not think on that too closely. I had exchanged worldly saws with Captain Wandhaver, and been assured I would not drown though I might hang.

I pouched the dagger and slipped it under my clothes in the dresser. Found a space behind the wainscot for the little crucifix. Stacked paper and writing materials on the scarred table: ruler, pen-knife, travelling ink, quills and calfskin-bound notebook. *Elements of Fine Handwriting* by Johann Bedansk, a parting gift from kindly Dominie McCall, now sat on the creusie-lamp ledge. My father's vernacular Bible announced my religious soundness to any visitor.

I looked around. My bunk was as bunks are – ascetic, comfortless, ill-presented, draughty, damp, fit only for students and mice and numerous small things living in the rafters. But it was mine and I liked it well.

MISS WHITTON, MY LANDLADY, looked me up, she looked me down. She shook her head.

'They will be sending me babes in airms next,' she said. 'Will ye grow?'

'If you feed me richt.'

'You'll get your gruel and bread in the morns. Cheese if I like the look of ye, which as yet I doubt. Meat weekly, herring on Fridays, salt cod Tuesday. Sweep the stair, put out yer ain unmentionables. I don't hold wi wine nor strangers in this hoose.'

I soon learned Miss Whitton abided by Knox's *regulative principle* on household and social matters: anything not explicitly sanctioned was forbidden. She was heavy-set, sharp-eyed and sharp-tongued. Her bosom rolled like the sea. She wore a black wool bunnet indoor and out, at all times and seasons. She complained of the wind from the east, the west, south, and particularly hated the north. *Naething guid e'er cam frae the north! Drunken Hielanders! Papists!*

'And crazed Anabaptists,' I suggested.

She glared at me suspiciously, slapped down the gruel. 'You think I tak in students for my entertainment, laddie? Wi'oot pilgrims or monks, friars, Cathedral and benefices, this toun is broken. We're skint, the University likewise.'

To call her crabbit would be uncharitable to crabs. 'Do you have milk?' I asked after my first spoonful. 'Honey?'

'Believe me, laddie, this is not the Promised Land.'

SHE WAS RIGHT ABOUT that. Walking into the wide Merkitgait, I was impressed and downcast in equal measure. Many of the houses were fine ashlar stone, windowed generously, corbelled, and a few even slated. Coats of arms of the gentry, the Council chambers, the grand Market Cross – there had been prosperity here.

But the market itself was poor and shoddy, the booths near-empty. The midden spilled out along the street. Folk looked half-starved. Some stared at the stranger, more averted their eyes. Even in that bitter climate, many went barefoot.

The air smelled of salt, fish guts and peat smoke. I passed the place of executions, by the Market Cross. A man pushing his cart of seaweed took one hand off the shaft to tap his bunnet in respect as he passed, but he did it discreetly, and two older men picking at the midden scowled and spat in his direction. Anyone over a certain age here had seen men die publicly and horribly. Some would have had a hand in those deaths.

I found the fousty shop in Merkitgait that sold scholars' gowns. A new one hung darkly red in the window, trimmed with ermine, leather-cuffed. Not for me. I pawed through the old gowns, looking for the heaviest, for the wind was nipping. I lifted one to my nose, sniffed. Evidently its last owner had favoured pipe smoking over washing. Another was slick with fish oil, which I knew from my mother was the devil to get out of wool.

I found one that would do. It had been patched at the elbows, the collar was greasy, but the wool was weighty and sound.

'I hear there are few scholars this year,' I suggested to the owner waiting hungrily at my side.

He stared at me, torn between contempt and avarice. The latter won. 'There are mony! Mony, young sir! Mair than ever!'

I looked around the deserted shop, the piles of gowns like crimson tattie-sacks. 'So I see.' I made him an offer on the gown. He recoiled as though struck, then came back with three times that. I shook my head, waited.

My father had been a mild, sociable man who liked to be liked, and he negotiated by conciliation. He had become a burgess of Embra because folk liked and trusted him as a merchant and sometime advancer of credit on surety. But I had also witnessed my mother in action, and she was hard as the setts that paved the High Street. Shopkeepers paled as she approached. Booths might as well have put up their shutters.

'Ah weel.' I shrugged. 'I am told the other place is in Southgait. I bid you good day.'

He caught my arm at the door and came down by a third. I went up, a little. He dropped his price again. I shook my head. 'That is half my fee for Martinmas Term. I need to eat.'

I thanked him for his time, said he had a fine large selection of gowns, and doubtless plenty new students would soon get out of their beds and beat a path to his door. This was, after all, their last day to matriculate.

His mouth twitched. 'Yer no green as you look.'

'Learning is one thing, sir, business another.'

He did not disagree. We looked at each other, each weighing the other's need.

'Throw in a fur mantle to keep my neck warm, and these gloves, and we'll settle,' I offered.

He glowered back at me. 'I'll warm yer neck for ye, or the hangman will.'

We shook on it. If he had lost on the deal, he would not have settled. I kenned that, and he kenned I kenned it. Even my mother did not negotiate to humiliate but to win.

I walked out onto Merkitgait, lighter in my purse but warmer around the thrapple, with the smelly but serviceable ermine stole that would be my best friend that winter, and the old scarlet goonie worn high on my shoulders.

In that flaming gown, all could see I was a scholar, subject not to the Burgh or even the King's laws, but to the University. Its authority was ecclesiastical, conferred by Papal Bull (somewhat out of fashion of late). Some respected that independence, others detested it. Miss Whitton had already warned me not to walk alone in Fishertown at night, and avoid the narrow wynds around the West Port.

But those who judged me by my gown were misled, for in mind I was as much a burgess as a student. Though my heart rang to

Henrysoun and Dunbar, high romance and Petrarchan sonnets, I kenned well that coin and credit underwrote my interests.

I intended to plough both the fields of learning and of commerce, yoking together the dark horse and the light. Seen from high abune by the eye of God or the laverock, it is evident my life's furrow has repeatedly veered one way, then the other, as though the ploughman was unresolved or dimwitted.

I EMERGED ONTO BROAD Southgait. It looked braw in morning sun, gracious in grey ashlar, set off by trees and gardens behind the tall houses and Burgh chambers. The sound and smell of the sea was in the air. This town was bright and open after the tall, dark, walled-in city of my birth.

I looked along the street and for the first time saw the Blackfriars Priory. It was a thing of beauty, so elegant, so of the Renaissance, my heart near stopped. Yet it was the corpse of a building, the windows empty, shot through with sky. Raw niches where the statues had been ripped away. The great doors had gone, doubtless to a Lord of the Congregation. The roof remained, though with many missing slabs. The Priory gardens were a tangle of roses, brambles, seeded herbs.

The Great Reform came at a cost. Some said it was just a necessary phase in building the New Jerusalem in my country. Others saw back-sliding and Papists everywhere, my own mother being one of those. Two girlhood years in service to the Guise household had secured her loyalty to the Old Faith, and she still wore her hair coiled up in the French manner. I felt this was an unnecessary provocation, given her profession – or perhaps that was tolerated, in a way it wouldn't be in a Reformist?

I turned away, followed along the Southgait to pass into the courtyard of St Leonard's College, host for my formation through the next four years. Weeds and small trees grew from the arches, the eaves dripped moss, but at least it still had a roof and recent plain glass windows to its chapel.

A stout red-faced man wearing a biretta and short black cape stood in a doorway. Above him in crumbled lettering: *HEBDOMADAR*. He took one look at me, saw by my gown worn high that I was a bejantine first year, pointed wearily to the next door along.

My admission hearing with Dean Jarvie was brief. I handed him the note of certification from my wee Embra school. He glanced at it, nodded. 'I studied at Glasgow with your Dominie McCall,' he said. 'A man thick as Henry Tudor's warships.'

He flicked my certificate onto the low fire. A pause, a flare, then eight years of labour rose and wobbled up the chimney. *Sic transit gloria scolistica.* 'According to our esteemed if somewhat inexperienced Principal Wilkie, and also the Burgh Council, though it is no damn business of theirs, this is a Reformed University. So let me hear your Catechism and Creed, in the vernacular.'

I gave forth my Confession of Faith, in my father's mild yet fervent voice, feeling him inhabit my throat. Jarvie sat in his carved chair, looking out the window at the leaden horizon. He grimaced, waved his hand.

'Enough. Now in Latin.'

I duly intoned. He sighed when I had finished. 'You are your dominie's pupil and no mistake.' He switched back to the noble tongue, which he spoke with a keening whine, and asked for my opinion on Pliny.

We were now into my Grammar interview, to establish my suitability for admission. Though the matter was in dispute, my education would be entirely in Latin. So I stammered out that Pliny was a great scholar, the foremost Roman historian, but not necessarily to be relied on.

We exchanged a few tags, then he outlined the structure of the teaching, college discipline, cluttered with terms I could only guess at.

Dean Jarvie sighed, dipped his quill. 'I dare say you'll pick it up by the time you graduate,' he murmured, then scratched out a note. Blotted and rolled it, tied it with green ribbon, handed it to me.

'Take this to the Bursar,' he said. 'St Leonard's eagerly awaits your money. We need a new roof.'

I took the scroll and made for the door. He coughed, I stopped. He swivelled one jaded eye in my direction.

'*Gaudeamus igitur,*' he intoned. 'Life is all downhill after this, believe me.' He flapped his pale hand. 'Bugger off, work hard, avoid the pox. *Exit!*'

THE WELL-FED, POX-MARKED BURSAR eagerly undid the green ribbon, read the scroll.

'Good, good. Excellent!' He rubbed his fat fists. 'Now we discuss the fee for our ancient and honoured University. A degree from here will get you into Paris, Bologna, Padua!'

Perhaps I'd have done better to have gone straight there? The Bursar's face fell when I produced not cash but my mother's promissory note. Still, her name was good, and he filed the note on top of others, in a flat wooden box, then patted it affectionately.

'We may seem a bit agley and run-down here, and our numbers are few though select,' he said. 'But things will pick up soon.'

I left St Leonard's quadrangle and emerged into a keen coulter blade of a wind off the sea, ploughing strips across the grey liquid field beyond the harbour. It would soon strip my scholar's gown of its fousty, sweaty odour. Despite the Bursar and Dean Jarvie's efforts, I felt high-hearted and lichtsome, for I was young and they were not.

I took a detour to look better at the Cathedral, where I stood and gawped. Even in ruins and roofless, it dwarfed anything we had in Embra. A few townsfolk pecked like corbies among the rubble. Two men with a crowbar coaxed another block from the wall, tipped it onto a wooden sled.

The far high window gave onto the sky. It must have once been magnificent. Even my father said the stained glass in St Giles had been *richt bonnie* – yet it was better to let in the clear light of Scripture and Reason. Being born in the year of the great destruction – the Great Foundation, as my father cried it – I had never seen coloured glass to judge for myself.

Some wooden booths remained intact, leant to against the cloister wall of the Cathedral. Three students exited from one, red robes slung so low down their backs as to be round their waists. They seemed very tall and grand, in their final year, judging by the robes. They glanced at me, saw a mere bejantine, and passed by, still arguing intently.

And so I went on to the Scaurs, to call on my future tutor, Charles Abernethy.

I WORKED THE GREAT knocker enthusiastically till a housekeeper appeared.

'Whit are ye wantin here, bairnie?'

I was a man who had steered *Sonsie Quine* through great storm, so I gave back boldly. 'I am here to see my regent Abernethy!'

'Are ye now?'

'Aye,' I managed, for she was fierce and minded me of my mother.

'Bide here, chiel,' she commanded.

I waited on the chill step, looking along the Scaurs to the Bishop's Castle on its headland. Cardinal Beaton had burned George Wishart there, from midday to dusk. My father said someone stuffed a musketball in the martyr's mouth to muffle his screaming. Soon after, Wishart's supporters broke into the Castle, dragged Beaton from his mistress's bed and dangled the corpse out the window by his ankle, still in his bloodied nightshirt. During the following siege they salted the Cardinal in the cellar to hold back the decay. Finally French cannon smashed the Castle into submission, and the survivors, Knox among them, were taken as galley-slaves.

My father planted these horror stories in my mind, where they had grown tall and frightful, but standing now in the very place was another matter. The struggle that had killed my father had had its origin here, in this windy street. The *locus classicus* of our Reformation. Holy Jesus.

'Glaikit laddie!' The housekeeper made me start. 'Ye maun come by.'

I was led down a dark-panelled way into a chamber to meet my regent. A stir in the corner, and a corpse sat up on the couch. Joints cracking in stick-like legs, he stood up full height, lifted his gaunt skull.

'Are you Plato or Aristotle?' it croaked.

Sarcastic Dean, grasping Bursar, now a delusional Tutor. 'I am just William Fowler, sir.'

'Ah, but by what means are ye *justified*? Some say that is the question.' He clicked his teeth, extended his arm towards me. A long finger, flesh sunk on the bone, shook direct at my heart.

'I am justified by Faith alone, sir,' I said obediently.

I'd been taught to say those words long syne. Did I believe them? Could one decide to have Faith because it would be politic? Would I indeed be saved? There was no way of kenning, which kept our consciences alert and anxious.

'But on what grounds rests your faith, boy? Reason, authority, tradition – or the evidence of your senses?'

An acrid, heady smoke drifted from the low fire. He had switched to Latin, adding to my confusion. He was taller, thinner and closer to death than any living man I had seen. Tiny tufts of white hair clung to his dome. His eyes were fireless pits.

'So,' he said, '*think*, William Fowler. You have four years to answer: do you hold to Plato or Aristotle? Will ye be Divine or Humanist?'

It seemed my tutor for the next four years was eccentric, but not actually mad.

SCUNNERED BY A SURFEIT of Latin, I wandered back along the Scaurs, drawn towards the Bishop's Castle. I was vaguely aware of walking through a dark patch on the cobbled way.

'Get aff yon, Papist bastard!' Two furious men muscled me back against the wall. One grabbed my stole and jerked the ends tight about my throat. They shouted in my face that I had walked through the blackening left by George Wishart's pyre.

Choking, I spluttered out that I was new here.

'Ach, he didna ken, Alec,' the other one said. 'Let him alane.'

His pal loosed the stole. As I choked and coughed, he spat on the pavement. The other man gripped me by the arm, pointed at the ragged darkness imprinted on the cobbles.

'Never step on the scorch marks o the martyrs, son,' he said. 'Dinna forget.'

I did not forget. I came to know several such marks in the town, dark ragged circles as though Hell itself had leaned from the Pit and spat on the cobbles.

Still rubbing my throat, I carried on towards the harbour. The dwellings here were lowly cottages, turf-roofed, each with its tiny window. *Fishertown*. Behind them towered the vast shell of the Cathedral. Impossible to miss the poverty of one and the ruined splendour of the other.

'As you sow, so shall ye reap,' my father had commented when news came that our Queen Mary had signed surrender to the Lords of the Congregation and set sail for England.

My mother rounded on him. 'You quote Scripture as a parrot, like that brute Knox! The truth of it is *As you reap, so shall you sow*. What calamities shall our children harvest?'

I winced, recalling, wrapped my gown tighter round myself and sat on a bollard at the edge of the Green. Creels and crab claws, fish heads and guts, nets hung out to dry on poles. Two elderly fishwives, bent as those claws, picked weeds off the netting while a younger lass deftly began repairs.

I watched in the cold sunlight, absent-minded at first, then with interest. The girl flicked her wooden shuttle in and out the gaping rip, across and back, knotted her cord with a flick of the wrist, across again, looped over, then down. She paused to knot, tighten, inspect, then more quick diagonal passes and the net was whole again. Would one could repair a rent world so!

One of the old women called in incomprehensible Fife. The young lass looked up, shuttle in her skeely right hand, twine in her left. Thick brown curly hair poked from her bonnet, her lips were full in laughter. Her head turned and eyes of deep dark blue lighted on me.

She nodded, neither docile nor wanton. Just a direct look, as to acknowledge she was here and I was there. Then she smiled. Sitting on my bollard, wrapped in my student gown, I smiled back for she looked fine as Life itself.

You might say she took me in. You might say she roped me as neatly as a Border reiver snags a neighbour's beast. Yet she did it without effort or intention, her thoughts certainly elsewhere.

One of the wifies laughed. I flushed red as my gown and the quine turned back to the net. She opened up another tear with her left hand, inspected it. She made a knot, paused, tightened, then *flick turn flick knot cut*, her shuttle hand made good the gap.

If only my Grammar could be filled in so! She appeared deft, quick in understanding, stood so sure on her ground. I envied her untroubled youth – then looked more closely at the stout, weathered, bent women around her. She would be like them soon enough, unless she were very fortunate in marriage.

The door of one of the low dwellings about the Green opened, and from the darkness within emerged, improbably, a student. The red gown was drawn around his shoulders, not worn high about the throat like mine. A second year, then, all of seventeen. He was sallow-skinned, too thin for his height, like a seedling grown in the dark. His hair stuck up wildly above a thin hooked blade of a nose. His gown was coarsely patched. A Poor Scholar, I guessed.

He glanced at me – a flicker of alert interest – as he limped up onto the Green, aided by a long staff clutched in his right hand. Then he ducked among the netting and straightaway curled his arm round the girl's waist. The boom of the *Sonsie Quine* might as well have swung and hit me in the chest.

As she prodded him with her shuttle, laughed, then carried on working while they talked, her smile was all for him. My fine romance had been conceived and died within one minute.

When I was able to look again, the tall student with wild hair was limping through the gateway towards St Leonard's. I sat cold-arsed and alone on my bollard. The town was hostile. The University was a farce, packed with grotesques. I lacked Grammar and intellect to make good here. It was a waste of my money – be honest, my mother's money. I would do better to find proper work. A seaman, perhaps, sailing to the Americas, grasping the wheel in steady hands, my true love a fisher lass in New Scotia, wielding her shuttle like Penelope . . .

But I was no bold sailor man. I was a wee podge with insufficient Grammar, marooned on a cold bollard far from home. I could see no good reason to be here. Better to be a merchant burgess like my father before me.

The girl carried on her work but I could not bear to watch her. Instead I looked up where the empty Cathedral windows towered against the sky. The age of Idolatry was gone, with all its splendours and corruptions, and we lived in its dour aftermath.

High in the blue lift, a gannet rose on the wind. It held its position by the highest window arch with a mere flex of its wings. Its head turned this way and that. Without apparent effort it glided forward into the gale, passed through the window-space like a pale thread drawn through the needle-eye.

A second gull, its mate perhaps, followed it through the high window, then both were out of sight, behind what was left of the side walls. They must be passing up the roofless nave of the Cathedral, above where the altar had been, and the relics of the saint, where the pilgrims had paid and queued and knelt to kiss the casing. Such Idolatry! Such reverence! Such income for Church and town!

The two birds reappeared over the walls at the far end, tilted sideway to the wind, were borne speedily away over harbour, fisherwomen and the bonnie lass.

Just two gulls passing through a high window in the teeth of the wind, yet that released me to rise and walk back through the stricken town, to the sanctuary of my bunk.

CHAPTER 3

Exit the Great Rebuker

FEW FORGET WHERE THEY were when that news came. It was November, still dark in our bare and comfortless college chapel. We stood to pray, then sat to intone the Psalms, the better to avoid Idolatry. It was damnably cold and I had missed my breakfast gruel. Virtue and suffering were pew-neighbours in our Reformed Kirk.

Our dire keening of the Psalm tailed off, for Dean Jarvie had entered the side door and was now crossing in front of where the grand altar had once been. This was not the way of things. He took the minister's arm and whispered in his ear. That fervent apostle went paler in the gloom.

The lame Poor Scholar across the aisle, the beau of my bonnie fisher lass, snagged eyes with me as the Dean ascended the pulpit. He surveyed us. He glanced out the vacant slit window, still unrepaired, then grasped the rail.

'A great man has gone to stand afore his Maker,' Jarvie announced.

For once there was no drawling sarcasm in his voice. 'Pastor John Knox is dead. May the Lord have mercy on his soul.'

A Swiss student to my right keeled over, then another. It might have been shock, piety, or simply lack of food and the cold. It felt as though the solid flagstones beneath our feet had given way.

On some instinct I looked to the Poor Scholar. He was staring back at me as if only we two knew what to make of this change. He nodded somberly, giving nothing away as we shakily sat to sing the great complaint of Psalm 88.

WE FILED OUT OF the chapel. Outside, the gulls still haggled over scraps, but for us the ground had shifted. Our lectures had been cancelled for the day, though it's doubtful Knox would have approved. He had made it known he wanted no memorial other than a New Jerusalem erected amid the corrupted ruins of Auld Scotia.

I carried within such mixed feelings about him and our times. That flinty, passionate man had prayed with the martyred George Wishart, survived the French galleys, rewritten the Prayer Book in England under Queen Bess, honed his Calvinism in Geneva and returned to Scotland with his purpose clear and sharp. While I was still carried within my mother, his raging sermons against Idolatry roused mobs to cleanse every kirk, abbey, priory and Cathedral of our country. It was said not a single piece of stained glass remained intact. He was believed to have the gift of prophecy, which tended to see the defeat of his enemies, and he saw a lot of enemies.

My mother loathed the Preacher. My father revered him and once shook him by the hand in the Canongait while I stood aside in awe. His new wife Margaret was very young. More contentiously, she was a Stewart of the high gentry. Yet he seemed easy and affectionate with his family, more than most men, and they with him. What to make of such a man?

'So we are unmoored again amid life's storms.' It was the Poor Scholar from Fishertown, standing by me.

'It is a great loss of something certain,' I said cautiously.

'Aye, he was maist certainly certain,' my companion said. 'It is not a quality for a philosopher or a Humanist scholar.'

'But essential in a Divine?'

'Maybe, maybe.' A pause. 'You wish to be led?'

I was not used to being probed so, in this eager manner. 'Only where I wish to go,' I said slowly. Then I blurted, 'I do not as yet know where that is.'

He looked at me. My father would assess the worth of furnishings so. He shifted his stick and held out his right hand. 'Thomas Nicolson,' he said.

'William Fowler.'

I watched Nicolson's long back erratically tick-tock like a pendulum away towards Fishertown. We had done little more than exchange names, yet already his good opinion was one I sought, despite his closeness with the fisher girl.

THAT EVENING, WE STUDENTS congregated in The Langside, the only howff that would have us. The older students, gowns low across their backs, held sway in the back room known simply as The Byre. We younger ones chirped and scratched in The Bog. We began to drink and get to know each other.

Life without the Old Faith, then life without our Mary Queen of Scots, now life without John Knox. We were unmoored and lurching broadside to the swell. A queasy excitement slopped among us. Cheery, curly-haired Charles Ogilvie, already our class clown, announced he asked for nothing in life but good drink and bad women.

'Ye shouldna be in St Andrews without greater ambition than yon,' Claud Hamilton sneered. He was a long-nebbed, angry-looking fellow, somewhat older than most of us. His eyes gleamed like wet slate. His older brother John looked scornfully over the rabble afore him. The younger brother David glared so skelly-eyed no one could be sure who he was glaring at. All three had the the haughty, hungry stare of raptors. The Hamiltons had been a power in the land, and might be so again if the wind changed back to Rome. I resolved to give them a wide berth.

'I ken!' Ogilvie raised his glass of dubious porter. 'So here's to making do!'

As we toasted making do, Tom Nicolson ducked under the lintel. Instead of going through to The Byre among his peers, he lurched down onto our bench, black staff in hand. 'A momentous day,' he said neutrally.

'A grand day!' Ogilvie cried. 'No lectures! I went tae the gowf.'

'Are you not here to learn, friend, rather than bash a ball about the Links?'

'I'm here to get letters after my name, then be done with study,' Charles Ogilvie responded. 'Who has ever been made happy by learning?'

'So is Happiness your goal, or Truth?' Nicolson speired.

We were familiar with Disputation. It was a branch of Rhetoric. The aim was to win, to carry the day. But Nicolson seemed only curious, intent on knowing.

Ogilvie looked at him, at us, down at his glass. 'Well, both. I should like both!'

'And if you could not have both – what then? Would you prefer happiness based on untruth, or a less pleasant life that sought the truth of things?'

Ogilvie looked to us but found no help there, for we were busy asking ourselves.

'Well, what do you say, raggedy smart-arse?' David Hamilton scoffed at Nicolson.

Nicolson sipped his brandy. 'I am asking what Master Ogilvie thinks,' he said. 'I am asking him *to* think. Nothing else matters here.'

Ogilvie raised his eyes to the smoke-stained roof. Shrugged. Chuckled. Fell silent. 'I dinna ken,' he said at last.

Nicolson rapped his staff on the floor. 'Honest man! So you choose to tell the truth though it makes you uncomfortable. As, in his own way, did John Knox.' His eyes were shining as he raised his glass. '*Slainte var!*'

We drained our glasses, unclear whether we were toasting Knox or Ogilvie or both. The latter at least looked pleased, if baffled.

Sour beer was followed by sweetened wine. A fiddle scraped and keened. In the corner two students struck up with their lutes. We thumped on the ceiling to beat out *The Lousin Time o Hairts*. And then *The Hangman's Bonnie Daughter*. As we bawled out the choruses, the Hamiltons' scrawny cousin Billy Hay pushed past us, clutching his jewelled purse in one hand and an oaken cudgel in the other.

'Doubtless Knox will be with his Maker,' one of the Divinity students remarked piously.

'Aye, and doubtless setting Him right,' young Ogilvie quipped. One tried to cuff him, others laughed.

I said my father had kent the Preacher, and once sold him a writing case. I had asked my father why the Pastor was so gloomy in speech and visage – were we not now a Reformed country? Had his party not carried the day? And I told the company my father had replied, 'Aye, but not the richt part of his party. That is still in doubt.'

'His labours are over. I wager ours have but begun.'

This from Nicolson in the corner, by the low fire. He had been drinking hard as anyone.

'I wager ten to one Knox is roasting in Purgatory!' Claud Hamilton jeered.

The room went very quiet. Some were open-mouthed, tankards stilled. Nicolson rapped his staff on the stone flags.

'Calvin teaches we are justified or we are not,' he observed calmly. 'God has no need for Purgatory, friend.'

'I am no friend of yours, Poor Scholar.'

'The Reform teaches we are all brothers in Christ.'

Claud Hamilton spat into the fire. He could not safely deny it. He switched his ire to me. 'What think you, wee Fowler, smirking sae smug?'

I had downed the best part of a bottle of claret. 'I'm thinking *The snow lies deep on glittering Soracte*.'

Tom Nicolson had a wee grin to himself.

'Well, there's nae fuckin snaw here,' John Hamilton grunted.

'Nor on Soracte,' I replied. 'Yet Horace's line endures when Knox no longer does.'

The Hamiltons and Billy Hay glared at me, suspecting cleverness.

'They say the Preacher left nae money,' Ogilvie said. 'The parish will hae to look after his wife and bairns.'

'So he was an honest man,' Nicolson said. 'I never doubted that.'

'Aye, but where are his fulminations and teachings now?'

'In us,' Tom Nicolson murmured. 'In us, friends. For better and worse.'

James Niven, who drank only ginger water, stood and glowered at us all. 'We won the argument,' he declared. He was a big, powerful man, amid a group of burly Fife lairds, Kirk supporters all. 'This is now a Protestant nation. Dissent will no be tolerated!'

The Hamiltons went pale but dared not openly disagree for, if reported, that could have them expelled. Some students murmured agreement with Niven, the rest looked elsewhere. Such were the times. A Reformed Kirk indeed, but of what kind? And who would limit its reach? The King?

Tom Nicolson dragged himself to his feet, grasped his stick. 'Weel, I dispute on Aquinas in the morn. I bid you goodnight.'

The Hamiltons stood between him and the door. Nicolson looked them in the face, then made to step around. Claud Hamilton stuck out his boot and tripped the stick. Quick as an adder, Nicolson drove his staff down hard on Hamilton's toes.

It was near-comical, the round O of Claud Hamilton's mouth. His legs quivered, he swayed, a hissing came from his lips. The boots were expensive and soft, the pain must have been excruciating.

The door closed on the night and Thomas Nicolson was gone. The rest of us were left fractious and uncertain, amid our still unfinished New Jerusalem.

THROUGH THAT FIRST MARTINMAS Term, I never truly stopped shivering. The east wind forced its twisted auger through cloak, thatch and classroom wall. Dominie McCall had ill prepared me with his praise – my Latin was not up to the daily use the college insisted on. My speech and rank were too common for the gentry, while being o'er Frenchified for followers of Calvin.

I had felt some affinity to Thomas Nicolson, but the Poor Scholar was a year ahead of me and we did not often meet. I saw him twice with the fisher lass, talking closely as they crossed the drying green above the harbour. It had been a foolish dream of a lonely boy. After that, I walked mostly on the West Sands, nursing my horn and my loneliness.

St Andrews was a place of ruins and gaps. Every altar, rood-screen, statue, bright window and carving had been destroyed, and a new world had yet to be built in its place. Stripped of lead, the roofs leaked, then slumped. Anything of use was carried away. As in Embra, the poor remained poor.

At my mother's direction, I cashed in two sureties with the Burgh Council, one at good increase. Her note bade me keep my eyes open for more such opportunities. As her sole surviving boy, I was more the recipient of her losses than her love.

When fellow students heatedly argued religious affairs, I inclined my head in some ambiguous mid-point between consideration and agreement. I dreamed of achievement yet remained lowly. My aspirations swithered like a compass needle set near iron. Would I be scholar, merchant, poet, lover? Amount to anything at all?

Shivering in my bunk one afternoon, I considered how that alarming boy from the *Sonsie Quine* had signed his magnificent *B*. Close study revealed the order of the marking, then my hand adopted his emphatic slant. You might say I learned the cut of his nib. Thus began my lifelong interest in imitating others' handwriting.

On other solitary evenings, hunched by the creusie lamp, I took poems to heart. Long-dead Henrysoun and Dunbar became my closest companions. This led to early attempts to translate the poems of Horace into our vernacular, which brought some comfort and heart-warmth, as though his words were swallows on a sixteen-hundred-year migration from his sunlit villa to my frigid room off Merkitgait.

That passion, that quickening, that fascination with translation and plausible imitation, has never entirely left me. If I am true to anything, it is to this. The rest is fear, flesh, necessity and dross, of which I am compounded.

THE FIRE SMOULDERED, THEN died in our tuition hut at St Leonard's. There were no funds for coal. We huddled in little scarlet mounds of misery and incomprehension, scratching out Abernethy's Grammar and Rhetoric.

Latin, how I hated it! It seemed I was trying to tunnel into a citadel, armed only with my horn christening spoon. Leaving the lecture, I trudged head-down across the quad, sick at heart.

'You took no notes today, I see.' Thomas Nicolson lurched to my side. 'You have mastered the art of memory?'

'Scarcely. My ink was congealed and my hands were numb.'

He nodded. 'Try mixing in a little fish oil.'

'To a fisherman's son, fish are always the solution.'

'To a merchant's son, the world is a business transaction.'

I looked at him. Wild, salt-stiffened hair, wide dark eyes lit by life within. 'I hope it is not, but fear it is so,' I replied. 'What do you make of Plotinus?' I asked. 'Abernethy lost me.'

'Plato's ghost,' Nicolson said confidently. 'Hostage to Byzantium. You would do better among the pre-Socratics.'

I stopped at the gateway port that gave out onto the brimming sea. 'I have absolutely no idea what you are talking about.'

He laughed. 'Give it time!' he cried. 'Keep the faith.'

'Aye, but which Faith?'

We stood there, wind grabbing at our scarlet gowns. I already knew some of my fellows were fanatical Reformists, testing and haranguing at every turn. They sought certainty, not scholarship. The rest of us kept our beliefs and doubts to ourselves.

'God knows,' he said at last.

'I expect He does.'

On that canny, unresolved note, we parted, he off to Fishertown for haddock at his family's lowly cottage, and me to my bunk to look at the ceiling for a while.

NICOLSON SLID ALONGSIDE ME during the sermon in the Holy Trinity, the town kirk. 'I've brought ye some fish oil,' he whispered. He passed me a tiny leather flask. 'Twa-three drops should keep your ink flowing. The smell wears off.'

After the sermon, which dwelt much on Hellfire and little on a loving God, Nicolson and I walked back together towards Fisher-town. The Hamilton brothers and one of their circle, Tam Anderson of Lindores, the towsie-headed son of a Fife laird, were commenting behind us. Nicolson's fist whitened on his staff as we passed Deans Court.

Rapid footsteps, then a clip at my ankle and push to my shoulder. I fell hard on the blackened stone where Walter Myln, aged eighty-two, had been burned at the stake for heresy. He had been condemned by

Archbishop Hamilton, whose great-nephew and his pals now stood laughing as I pushed up to my knees.

Tam Anderson grinned at me. 'Sorry, friend. I didna see you down there. Are ye looking for some trinkets for your mother tae sell?'

I stared at him, flames rising in me. Anderson looked to the Hamiltons, then, encouraged, turned to me again. 'They say she is a wad-wyfe tae all and sundry. Whit else does she do for money?'

My head-butt caught him full on the thrapple. He fell clutching his throat, then I was on him, battering with my fists. We rolled and scuffled in a flurry of gown till Ogilvie and Jeb Auchterlone dragged us apart.

The Hebdomadar waddled up, grinning in his Sunday best. 'Fechtin?' he crowed. 'There'll be fines! Double for a Sunday!'

NEXT DAY, LEAVING THE chapel with our morning prayers and sombre Psalms dispatched, I went direct to Tam Anderson. He saw me coming and made himself ready, but I held up my open hands and apologised for my quick temper.

'In truth, my mother is hard pressed to carry on my dead father's affairs,' I said. 'She but helps folk carry on, with loans against surety.' This was partial truth. He stared, looking for the catch. 'She is a political innocent,' I continued. This was blatant untruth. 'I worry for her, and it made me o'er quick to take offence.'

His face grew red as his gown. He muttered his regrets at his sally, and at our family's loss. I felt him eye me. Though short, I was barrel-chested and strong-armed for my age, for I had fetched and carried in my father's warehouse from earliest years. I had surprised him with my head-butt and flying fists. Surprised and shocked myself.

'My father's land is held in surety,' he said gruffly. 'He invested unwisely in Queen Mary's cause, and now the lender bears down on him.'

'Times may change for the better for our absent Queen.'

He looked me in the eye. To even admit the possibility was seditious, but there were many who wished it, and many more waiting to see the next airt of the wind. I nodded fractionally, to suggest where my allegiance lay.

'It seems your father has borrowed on bad terms,' I ventured.

'I am damn sure of it!'

'My mother could cover that loan with one at better terms.'

He stared at me, then clasped my hand. 'It could not be on worse! Please look into it.'

I wrote to my mother, offering her this business and asking her to make it good for my sake. She did so, promptly and with adequate margins. After that Tam Anderson and his circle of other Fife laird's sons, such as Lindores and Ogilvie, were my best protection against the Hamiltons and their ilk, whose spite I was able to hold in check as that first term ended.

CHAPTER 4

A Shoogly Handcart

THE WORLD'S WHEEL SPINS. The soft clay of the self spins with it, awaiting shaping hands.

John Stout the Hebdomadar was notoriously an interferer in our affairs. It was said two bottles of brandy delivered to his office could bring one of the very few available women of the town to a shed in the college grounds, and another bottle would secure access to the arduous medical treatment that often became necessary a month or so later. Not for me, still in thrall to a twice-glimpsed fisher girl, and some Provençal high dream of romance.

Catching me outside the Porter Gait in our second term, the Candlemas, Stout passed me a note with a look of a man denied a drink on the Sabbath. 'Frae the Dean,' he said grumpily. 'It's sealed.'

Sealed for good reason, I discovered back in my bunk. Through a haar of chilly Latin, I discerned that the Dean knew I sometimes acted as an intermediary for my mother. Perhaps we could meet discreetly in his lodgings off Southgait?

I went in the back way, as instructed. Dean Jarvie hastily led me within, offered brandy. A pipe? I accepted the former, rejected the latter, which I had already discovered made me feel I was back in rough waters off Inchcolm.

Jarvie, his customary hauteur mislaid, fumbled out a key and opened a stout door under the stairs. I was in a storeroom, daylight seeping in around heavy shutters, windows barred.

When Jarvie held up the creusie lamp, I was looking at a stack of rolled-up tapestries. Also two open chests stacked with silver bowls, platters, two claret jugs. A large Communion plate in chased gold and blue enamelling – Italian, I fancied. A dozen solid silver candlesticks, still encrusted with tallow, with the stamp of the Blackfriars. I noted a clutch of very fine small saints, wood-carved, finished in lapis lazuli and unstinting gold leaf. Marked to the Greyfriars, unmistakeably from the Low Countries.

I slowly picked up the sole chalice. My mother believed that on occasion this contained the blood of Christ. My father said that was rank Popery, wizardry and superstition. With slightly shaky hand, I turned it over, took in the mark. Reims. The craftsmanship was remarkable, but so was the weight it would melt to.

The Dean and I looked at each other.

'Your need must be great, sir,' I said.

He hastily drank from his cup. 'I have incurred debts that have lately been sold on to others who are not of my . . . persuasion. They seek to break me, or force me to resign.'

I nodded. It was no secret that Kirk and State and Burgh Council all sought to control the colleges. 'So you wish these . . . items . . . sold? Or held in surety, redeemable in bond?'

'I want them sold and far from here,' he said. 'I only held them for safe keeping.'

'Of course,' I said. 'For a better time.'

The Dean nodded gratefully. 'Indeed.' He drained his cup. 'Though that will not come in my lifetime, if ever.'

In the silence between us, for the first time I believed that true. 'So – to be moved and sold?'

'At a fair valuation.'

'Of course,' I assured him. 'That can be arranged.' Inside I was singing *Gaudeamus igitur*!

'Removal as soon as possible?' Jarvie asked anxiously. 'Discreetly? You can arrange that?'

'I know just the man,' I said. 'He sailed yesterday for Embra, and intends to return within a week.'

'A week!' The Dean's face glistened in the lamplight. 'That is too long! My enemies could raid the morn. This very night!'

Thus does opportunity present itself. 'If it were done so speedily, that would affect the price,' I said. 'Thirty per cent below agreed valuation.'

'Ten?' the Dean offered.

'Sorry,' I said. 'The risk, as you acknowledge, is considerable.'

I picked up the plate, gauged the weight. Lovely working, but it would have to be melted down. 'Thirty per cent. I can authorise a promissory note that holds good. All this off your hands tonight.'

He thrust out a clammy hand, as I knew he would.

'Make me an inventory,' I said as we shook on my first deal of significance. 'If possible, witnessed and agreed.'

With pounding heart, I slipped out the back way.

QUICK WORK, THEN, MY mind now sharp as a whetted dirk. I wrote to my mother, informing her of what I was about. I needed her authority and blessing after the fact. There was no time for her to do other than trust me. I told her the man I needed to help get the goods away. The final valuation and disposal were up to her.

I was pleased to see my hand was steady as I sealed the note. My regent's lectures always felt like hard passage into a headwind of Latin, but this was with the breeze. I hurried through the dawn streets to the mailing stable. Next call, Fishertown. There was no one else I could call on.

Few philosophers are quick-witted in practical matters, or can be relied on in a fight. Most peer vaguely at the world, as though Reason were cataracts. But from the moment I first set eyes on Tom Nicolson bending to emerge from his mother's hovel, I sensed he was not one of those dreamers. When he drove his staff down on Claud Hamilton's foot the night of Knox's wake, I knew he was also unafraid and sharp in response.

The question remained: could he be tempted?

I chapped on the low door in Fishertown. A bent, stout woman opened, recoiled slightly at my scarlet gown. I asked for Thomas.

'Ye'll be a freen o his?'

'Yes,' I said. 'Aye.'

'Haud on, son. He's at his buiks.'

When Nicolson appeared, he closed the door firmly ahint him and looked at me enquiringly.

'I have need of a handy, discreet man,' I said. 'A friend would be even better.'

IN THE LEE OF the Cathedral wall, I laid it out to him direct. I told him of the goods held by the Dean, and the deal I had struck. I needed a helping hand, a witness, and a secure and secret store. And it had to be tonight.

I said it would be well-paid employ, but didn't press the point. I sensed he was proud and touchy about his poverty.

'Well, well,' he said at last. 'Our revered Dean? It is a wicked world.'

'Perhaps.' I couldn't stop grinning from embarrassment, or excitement, or both. 'But we can have sport and profit in it.'

'This ploy could go agley.'

'For certain,' I admitted.

'A siccar and secret store?'

'Just for three or four nights, till the boat comes.'

He raised dark eyebrows at that. 'You hae a ship?'

'I ken a man who does.'

'And you can trust him?'

'We have had dealings,' I replied. 'A rogue, but I would swear to him.'

He chuckled, looked up at the ruined St Rule's Tower against the last light. 'There is a bound manuscript on Heraclitus that I covet, and my hose is more hole than hose. And I ken such a storage place – the gear-cellar of my mither's brither.'

'He'll not be using it?'

'My uncle drooned aff Craster in the August gales.'

'Ah,' I said. 'I am sorry to hear that. So you'll do it?'

'By these pickers and stealers,' he said, and held out his hand.

WE SET OUT AFTER the last curfew, pushing a covered handcart along the muddy track that ran above the shoreline, by the Cathedral and St Rule's Tower. We were both dark-cloaked and cowled like true villains.

It was late March. The wind off the sea broke the moon-trail, and the waves on the harbour wall covered any sound we made. We took a cart handle each, he hobbling on my right, stick strapped across his long back. We did not speak, though when we stopped at the highest point to change sides, his teeth gleamed. It was a fine, foolish ploy.

Our cart just fitted through the narrow passage by the Dean's. I chapped lightly on the rear door. The Dean was pale as he let us in, all of us breathing fast.

Two creusie lamps burned in the storeroom. Our cargo had been sorted out. The tapestries were rolled and tied. The lovely carved saints were nestled in an open box, their lapis eyes glittering in the lamplight.

'I think I ken you by your limp,' the Dean said to my friend.

'And I ken you by your office,' Nicolson replied.

We were all extremely nervous, trust in such dealings being rare as a Pope at the General Assembly. 'I brought a helping hand, and a witness,' I said to the Dean, who did not look best pleased. 'To be sure all goes soundly. You have the inventory?'

The Dean shook his head. 'I am advised it is safer for all parties to have none.'

'Advised?' I didn't like that. 'By whom?'

'By me, young friend.' The voice from behind made me jump. Nicolson gripped his stick as a man stepped forward. 'To make siccar all goes soundly.'

He was bare-headed, plump, with a beard trimmed square in the Flemish manner. Smiling slightly, sharp-eyed. He had a short sword in a hanger, and his hand hovered over it as he inclined his head to us.

'John Geddes, *à votre service*.'

I bowed back. My father's dirk remained pouched inside my jerkin. If there were to be ill business, it would come later.

BETWEEN US WE LOADED up the cart, then secured the cover. We argued about documentation. The Dean wanted none, for obvious reasons. I needed something, for myself and for my mother. My father had suffered before from sales made and then disputed. Eventually John Geddes reluctantly wrote out *Assorted Cleansed Goods in wood and metal. Twenty-seven items.*

'I will need it signed to be sold at valuation, less thirty per cent commission. By yourself,' I said to the Dean.

He didn't like it. I assured him it would be destroyed once the goods had gone through my mother's hand, but I must have it for now. The Dean signed. Then the invoice was signed as witness by John Geddes, in a notably fine script. I produced the promissory note of payment in what appeared to be my mother's hand, at which I had become adept, finished by the seal she had given me for occasions like this. Then by creusie lamp I wrote out a separate receipt of the goods, then signed it.

Geddes took the receipt, studied it carefully. 'You write a goodly secretarial, for one so young,' he said to me.

I was absurdly pleased. 'It is one of my interests,' I said.

'Mine too,' he replied. 'And you make a hard bargain.'

'The risk is considerable, and largely my friend's,' Tom said.

'Indeed it is,' Geddes said, and smiled.

WE PUSHED THE LADEN handcart onto the track for Fishertown while the moon vanished and returned. We flinched at shadows, then stumbled in the dark. For a while I believed there were some sounds behind us, carried in the wind. I had not foreseen John

Geddes. He seemed intelligent, able, unaffiliated to any cause but his own.

With much sweating and lurching, we eventually gained the roofless church of St Mary of the Rock, said to be much older than the Cathedral. Nicolson called for a break by the precinct wall. As I blew on my blistered hands, the darkness shifted.

I fumbled for my dirk, but my arms were pinioned from behind. Two figures came from in front, all in black, cowls up.

'No,' Nicolson said firmly. 'Dinna resist.'

I had been a fool. I was about to be robbed of my new possessions. Tossed over the cliff, found face down in the sea, days later. It was not uncommon.

Nicolson turned to our assailants. '*Pax vobiscum, fratres.*'

The taller one reached out and took him in his arms.

THEY WERE OLD, THOSE former monks, tottery and thin, but they shepherded us surely along the way. They took us past the Cathedral, helped us with the cart over deep ruts, then into the lane of storage cellars behind Fisher Row. Tom Nicolson produced a latch key, opened the door into the dark.

We manoeuvred the cart inside and left it there. Tom pulled the door to, worked the latch. Stacked a couple of fish boxes against the entrance, dropped some rope and a creel in them.

He embraced the former monks, whispered with them, then they faded into the night and left us alone.

The wind cooled sweat against my chest. The stars were now bright overhead. Below us the waves broke on the beach. There was an amphitheatre of cloud round the moon.

'Old friends, Culdee monks,' Nicolson said softly. 'They live in the ruins and teach me forbidden philosophy. In return I make sure they are fed.'

That might explain some of his odder ideas. 'Can we trust them?'

'Of course. They are the last of their kind. They have no connection to this world.'

We shook hands, then bade goodnight as the first light of day broke above Fishertown.

I MISSED MORNING PRAYERS, then sat distracted through the first lecture of the day. Nicolson passed me in the quad, nodded, then limped on. I took this to mean his uncle's cellar was still siccar.

My stomach troubled me with sharp pains, as it always would at such times. Stealing Church goods was a capital offence. But these items came from a *cleansing*, urged by Knox, quoting his beloved Isaiah as he roused the mob. Lawyers could make a lifetime's living arguing over their ownership.

For all his craven fears, the Dean had received these goods to preserve them for a better day. Yet when he had said, 'That will not come in my lifetime, if ever,' though raised on my mother's fervent hopes and my father's fears, I had felt it to be true. The Old Church was not coming back, nor would our Queen Mary return from

England with an army. The Dean needed money for his old age, for his family (haughty wife and two irritating boys), for his other family and extra child (said to live in nearby Dunino).

Why shouldn't the Dean sell what, after all, no one owned? And why shouldn't an enterprising young merchant facilitate, do well by the risk? It all helps the world move on. Trade greases the squeaky wheel of the shoogly handcart of Time.

I was still savouring the phrase *the shoogly handcart of Time* as I turned the corner and saw John Geddes standing outside my lodgings, hands in the deep pockets of a heavy blue serge coat and looking straight at me. In that moment I wished I had confined myself to Plato and Aristotle, for this could not be good.

GEDDES INVITED ME TO join him in herring and small beer. At his expense. To celebrate a good night's work. I did not dare refuse him.

We sat in Hogan's Loft, ate pickled herring with dark bread and weak porter. 'So,' he said, 'I trust your gear is well secured?'

'On its way to my agent as we speak,' I replied.

He lifted an eyebrow at that. 'So soon?'

We cut our herring and our bread, munched in silence for a while. I knew him to be local-born, graduate of St Leonard's, now a leading young scribe and draughtsman, maker of fine documents and maps of estates. He came, like myself, from mercantile classes.

'Flanders? The Baltic?' he casually enquired.

I shook my head. 'Ships sink,' I replied. 'My father – God rest his soul – did not trust ships for trade. Nor do I.'

Geddes looked at me closely. I looked at him back. 'My father likewise died when I was but a boy,' he said eventually.

'I am sorry for your loss.'

'Thank you. It is hard, is it not, to be without an older head, a guiding hand?'

He put his skeely fingers on my arm.

'Yes,' I said. 'It is.' To my shock, my eyes filled with tears.

He patted my shoulder. 'There, there.' He got to his feet and looked down at me. 'I feel kin with ye, young Fowler. When you have time, come by my little scriptorium in the West Bow.'

'Thank you,' I said, half rising. 'I must work on my Grammar and studies, but writing skills are of interest to me. I will come in time.'

He seemed pleased. 'My regards to your friend Nicolson of Fishertown,' he said. Then hesitated, but it was too late to take it back.

'I scarcely know him,' I replied casually.

Then John Geddes was away towards the Scaurs. I watched him go, then straightway hurried in search of Nicolson. I found him at Mathers the printer, flipping through old abstracts. I took him aside and said Geddes knew his name and where he lived. Nicolson listened closely, eyes dark and hair wild as John the Baptist after a rough night in the desert.

AS WE SAT ON the cliff-top, Nicolson's nephew came to report that two unkent men were passing through Fishertown, looking in windows, walking round the backs, poking along by the gear-cellars. When asked their business, they said they were in search of storage space, but the lad said both had pouched dirks, and one had a pistol-shaped bulge under his jacket. Nicolson whispered in the lad's ear and he ran off.

Soon enough, three burly Nicolson cousins found and offered to help the two strangers in their quest for an empty cellar. They all went down the brae towards the harbour, where a couple more fishers joined them. The two strangers were admitted to inspect a lowly storage cellar.

Once inside, there was a brief flurry, and the inquisitive fellows were relieved of their weapons.

Five burly fishermen exited the cellar, made good the door. There was no sound from within as creels were stacked around. The tall, thin student with his patched cloak and stick passed by, had a word with the fishermen, then limped away back up the brae.

'AYE – *We keep oor ain fish-guts for oor ain sea-maws.*' Nicolson grinned as we lifted the handles of the fish cart. 'Besides, my uncle was held in high regard, even if his nephew is thought a bittie touched.'

We heaved the cart laden with our goods wrapped in an old sail, crossed the road in darkness, then set back on the track for the Cathedral.

My hands stung from last night's blisters, and there was no moon, which was to the good. Fine mizzle drifted off the sea as we traversed the grassy precincts. Nicolson seemed sure where he was, but even at that we rammed into the occasional stone block along the way. We cursed in whispers, backed up and went around. I winced at every faint clank from inside the cart.

We passed St Rule's Tower of blacker black, then Tom nudged me and we swerved off down a decline, panting to stop the cart running away.

Then down below, in the bowels of the Earth it seemed, a flicker of yellow flame. We stopped. Two cloaked figures joined us. Together we carried the goods down worn steps. We were in a cramped underground masoned chamber. The lamp glimmered on a black circle of a well. On a ledge above it a finely carved snake was devouring its own tail.

'Older than the first Kilrymont church,' Nicolson whispered. 'They say Columba himself blessed it. And that it is haunted. I have my doubts on both counts, but it serves to keep folk away.'

A shivering grue passed over my flesh. There are no ghosts in my philosophy, but the place smelled of ancient presences.

The monk's hand was tight and bony on my shoulder as he guided me back up the steps. It was good to be back in the rain and breeze and the faint sough of the sea. We wobbled off towards Fishertown, our cart and hearts much lighter now.

THREE DAYS LATER, AS a bleary sun was setting, the *Sonsie Quine* grated up against the harbour wall, and I was there to meet her. I made arrangements for my shipment, shook on it with Captain Wandhaver.

'You are growing a little, I think,' he said. 'Your mother will be pleased with this dealing.' He winked and went below.

The following day, a group of young fishermen opened the old cellar by the harbour and dragged two sorry and staggering specimens into the light. Out of pity they were given water, then sent on their way.

That afternoon, passing by the Fisher Cross, I met with John Geddes. He looked me over, then inclined his head. 'You are a quick student, Master Fowler,' he said. 'I doubt I have much to teach ye.'

'I am sure you do,' I replied. I had no doubt as to who had employed the two men the Nicolson cousins had incarcerated. 'I will come to your workshop by and by, if the offer still stands.'

I set off for St Leonard's, my stomach easier now that the *Sonsie Quine* with my goods in the hold had rounded Fifeness, bound for Leith. I passed under the archway towards the lecture shed, clutching my notes on Aristotle's *Nicomachean Ethics*. And how, indeed, should men best live?

CHAPTER 5

This Giddying Idolatry

O<small>UR FRONT DOOR STILL</small> caught and scraped. I heaved it to, set down my satchel, feeling the ground still shifting. My mother and I embraced cautiously, sensing some reckoning was due. Now more girl than child, Susannah hugged me tight.

'You've grown, brother mine!'

'Aye, maistly sideways,' my mother observed.

In the Doo-Cot I was given claret unwatered. I felt much older, two terms survived, and still rather pleased with myself from the dealings with Dean Jarvie.

I sipped the leathery claret and looked around a familiar but changed room. The cubbyholes still lined the walls, but where my father's desk had been was a kneeling prayer stool, and the Holy Mother simpered in a niche.

'You must be feeling siccar,' I said. 'Is this wise?'

'It is a necessity of my soul,' she said. 'In any case, I do some business with the Burgh Council. Chancellor Atholl also has need of me, and he shares my persuasion.'

I looked through the window slit down the High Street. No guns, no cannon, no barricades, not a soldier in sight. A sole pikeman at the Canongait. Quiet times under Regent Morton, his predecessors silenced. Folk will put up with a lot for quiet times, for a while.

'Smartly done with Dean Jarvie,' she said. 'You will be a financier yet.'

Praise indeed, by her lights. 'I would rather to be a scholar and poet,' I retorted. 'But did we not do well by my dealings?'

'Well enough,' she granted. 'If there are more opportunities to purchase sacramental goods of the True Church, take them.'

'They were not all melted down?'

'Some have gone where they will be rightly appreciated.'

'Ah.' I drank a little more, felt the warmth. 'Please be careful.'

'The day will come again for True Religion,' she said.

'Yes, but which one?'

She was on her feet, standing over me. 'Mind your tongue! You're not too old to put across my knee.'

I put down my glass with only slightly shaky hand. 'I think you'll find I am, mother.'

We stared each other out. She moved away to the window, gazed down towards Holyrude. 'You are your father's child,' she said softly. 'Afore the Reform, I greatly cared for him.'

'I am glad to hear it.'

'I miss him yet.'

'As do I,' I replied, and my voice slipped a moment. 'Will you be marrying again?'

She kept her head turned from me. 'I think not.'

'You may need protection.'

'I can buy protection. The Kirk, the Crown, Regent Morton, all use my services.'

'Ah,' I said. I reached for the bottle. 'This is good.'

'Help yourself,' she said, and nearly smiled. 'Trading as an honest merchant is one thing, William, and not to be despised. But finance is better. They hanged the Duke of Norfolk for trying to overthrow the heretic Elizabeth, but Roberto Ridolphi who funded the scheme lives comfortably yet.'

Now we were nearing the heart of it. I stretched out my legs. 'So Heaven must be as full of bankers as it is of martyrs.'

A flush bloomed on her temples, below the first grey hairs. 'Your cynicism is very foolish.'

'As is selling Indulgences to ease wealthy souls in Purgatory.'

'You would, like Calvin, deny Free Will and Good Works?'

'You aim to buy your way to Paradise?'

We glared at each other. Behind her, the kneeling stool, the forbidden Mother of God in pink and blue. My heart and mind were kicking down their stalls. 'So the University has not yet dulled your wits,' she said.

'We sharpen them every day in disputation.'

'Take care not to cut yourself.' She looked more closely at me. 'Time you decided whether to shave or no.'

I blushed. I had rather fancied a slim Italian moustache, as in portraits of Petrarch, hoping it might make me more poetical. 'Did you keep back the saint I requested?'

She opened her keepsake chest and handed over the little carved statue I had asked her to reserve from the Dean's hoard. Lapis-eyed, cloaked in gold leaf, white-lead cheeks with a dab of rose; quietly ecstatic, smiling inwardly as she fingered her lyre: St Brigid, patron of musicians and poets, warming in my palm.

'Thank you,' I said. 'I couldn't bear to sell her with the others.'

My mother's hand closed round mine. 'In the end you must trust in Beauty,' she said. Her breath was sweet on my cheek. She lightly fingered the tiny face. 'This is in part pagan,' she said, 'but sacred for all that.' She kissed the fingertip that had touched St Brigid, then crossed herself. '*Ora pro nobis*,' she breathed.

She went to the door, brisk again, for Grizel Sempill was calling up the stair. She was a lively woman with children by Archbishop Hamilton, the same who had burned old Walter Myln and been hanged in turn in Stirling. Grizel cared little for the Kirk's opinion, and our house was more lichtsome when she came by.

'Still, in this world don't neglect business,' my mother said, and went down the stair to greet her old friend from Guise days. Our interview was over. I paused to give remembrance to the Doo-Cot that had been. My father's hand on the latch key; *I'd best hae a look.*

I followed on down the winding stair, stroking St Brigid with compromised thumb.

BACK AT ST ANDREWS for Whitsun Term. I called on the Dean, presented him with a hefty leather purse, my share deducted and duly accounted.

'Let that be an end to it,' he said.

'Yes indeed,' I said. 'But I shall require a receipt.'

I stayed until he wrote it most reluctantly. I kept it safe, and though Jarvie returned to his usual supercilious hauteur, he flinched whenever he set eyes on me.

I found Tom Nicolson near St Salvator's and gave him his fairing, plus a bittie more. I could not have done it without him.

'I will buy new hose, and a codex of Heraclitus our Bursar is flogging,' he said. His eyes shone. 'Thus my legs will be warm and my thoughts enlarged by the philosophy of India!'

'We may share more such enterprises in future,' I suggested.

He shook his head. 'Once a philosopher, twice a businessman.'

For a while we studied the ancient elegance of our rival college. They thought themselves very superior; we thought them conventional and stuffy, *vieux jeux*. The cobbles at our feet were still darkened from the fire that had consumed another martyr.

'There are many lessons one can take from martyrdom,' Nicolson remarked. 'What is yours?'

'That it is not for me. At least, not for any cause I have met with yet.'

I did not feel proud of this, but it felt like a truth-mark, scorched into what passed for my soul. He chuckled, laid his pale hand on my sleeve. 'Perhaps our friends Ogilvie and Auchterlone have the right of it. We should content ourselves with bodily pleasures, gowf, and a good laugh, and then die. But what of the Hereafter?'

We stood in silence as the wind speired for a weak spot in our cloaks. I supposed this exchange was the kind of thing I had come to St Andrews for, though I wished the winds were less bitter and the fees more modest.

'Then again,' he added, 'if there is nothing you would die for, what weight has your life?'

'At this moment I'd die for coney stew,' I said. 'Though my mother opines I am already too weighty.'

He sighed. 'Lord, you are so stubbornly shallow, *mon ami.*'

I clipped him with my boot. He reached down to pull my hood off. We happily tussled along the street to the Fisher Cross.

'Ah, ye great gowks! Have ye nothing better to do on a fine morn?'

It was the lass I had watched mend nets on the harbour green on my first day, who had talked and cuddled with my friend. I had glimpsed her since, sometimes with him, but always looked away for it pained me to see her.

Now she stood planted firm on Merkitgait. Her smile quirked as though we entertained her. She wore not her work apron but a simple dark green dress, a grey mantle about her shoulders.

She took his arm. 'So, brither mine, wha's your new scholar pal?'

The day grew brighter, the great sea brimmed. As Tom introduced me to Rose Nicolson the fisher girl, I was hooked by the heart, and dragged aboard most willingly.

We three talked and laughed awhile. I noted she treated my ever-thinking friend with affection but not awe. An elderly woman, swollen hands taped with bandages, called from the wynd.

'Jist a minute, Auntie Jean!' Rose replied.

Apparently the midday meal was spoiling in the pot. Rosie asked me to join them, but Tom Nicolson compressed his lips, so I said it was time to go and get a grip on some slippery syllogisms. Rose lightly touched my arm. 'I hope you can mak my brither mair normal.' Her eyes were deep blue and strikingly alert. 'Come by the Green onytime.'

I walked away in joyful daze. So this was it! The grand thing poets wrote about, that singers loosed their thrapples for! This painful unsettling, this restless picturing of she who has just left, who talked and laughed, erecting the day into something splendid as a pre-Reformed Cathedral. A radiance in the air like stained glass! This giddying Idolatry!

MY PROFIT FROM THE dealings with the Dean allowed me to seek an additional Latin tutor, ideally one who also taught speedwriting for note taking. I found the long-retired Nicol Burne, a man seemingly composed of chalk and ink, skin across his cheeks yellowed as taut vellum. It was said he had once been secretary and scribe to the Greyfriars, whose priory was rapidly dissolving into air. The Burgh Council could no longer afford constables, and let such pilfering pass.

In his dim room off the Fishmerkit, Nicol Burne lay stretched on a pallet, head propped up on a reading-stool, a worn cloak wrapped about him like a winding-sheet. The smell of fish guts drifted in from the street outside. I explained my difficulties following lectures and disputations, my deficient Grammar, my struggle to take notes at sufficient speed. He rolled his desiccated head on the reading-stool.

'Young James Melville had the same difficulties. He was almost greiting when he came to me as a bejantine.'

'You taught Melville!' James Melville was a coming man in a Kirk desperately short of bright young Protestant Divines. His stern uncle Andrew was busy reforming our Universities to make them more Kirk-wise. The Universities were busy resisting those reforms.

'A bright boy and able, once he had abandoned the lute.' He showed a few long yellowed teeth in what might have once been a smile. 'Are ye of his persuasion, might I ask?'

The coins in my pooch gave me courage to respond. 'Yes,' I said. 'You might ask.' We looked at each other, he reclining and me standing.

'I am no lacquey, cheeky-breeks,' he growled. 'Shut the door ahint ye.'

'In truth, sir, I am of no persuasion, but I remain persuadable.'

My voice went out and died in that chill room. Outside in the merkit someone was crying *Fresh saithes! You'll ne'er get a better wan!*

'A true child of our ruinous times,' Burne said eventually. 'Sit ye down.'

I sat on the sole stool. The room was silted up with manuscript papers and books. Many were uniform-bound, possibly from the sacked priories. That apart, all was most simple and drear. The grate had not seen fire in a long time.

'How is your mother Janet keeping, boy?' I stared at him, open-mouthed. 'Stop gaping like a codling,' he croaked. 'Ours is a small country and she is of the Faith.'

THANKS TO OUR SESSIONS, my Grammar improved no end, and Burne also taught me shorthand note-taking to better record lectures and disputations. Over the years secretarial scrivening would prove a marketable skill, and in time entangle me among the plottings of the high heid yins.

You might say Nicol Burne was money well spent. He was also mentor and friend to a lonely boy. I came to greatly look forward to my twice-weekly visits, bearing my fee and some small sweetmeats from the market stalls below. When the days were bitter I would also bring peats, and coax a glow from his grate. The aromas of pastry and peat mingled with the watered wine we sipped from small wooden cups – another country, another age!

Burne was also the first to suffer my early poems – expressions of exile, longing and aspiring adoration, as derivative as they were heartfelt. I knew no one else to take them to, poetry not being to Tom

Nicolson's taste, for it advanced no propositions. I feared my verses were of no account, while secretly hoping Burne might hail them.

Nicol Burne, lying propped on his pallet to ease his back, laid aside my pages. 'You have done Horace no favours by transporting him to our wintry Scottish Hell,' he muttered. 'Leave him be in sunny Italy.'

I was downcast, embarrassed at my presumption. I apologised for taking up his time. He waved his hand as though he had long ceased to see his time as valuable.

'You would do well to read something closer to our times,' he said. He reached out and reverently handed to me, as if it were the Sacrament itself, three volumes bound in dark red leather, the *Commedia* of Dante. 'It begins in Hell,' he murmured, 'so you need do no more than look around ye, to better comprehend. I shall not need it again.'

I stammered out my thanks, knowing I had been handed on something much more than a book. However heavy, fousty and battered, in my arms lay the Renaissance.

'You will need to learn the Tuscan dialect,' he said. 'Fortunately for you, I have nothing better to do.'

Unaware of the consequences of this offer in my life to come, I stammered I could not pay. Again, he waved his mummified hand.

'I shall enjoy your advancement,' he said. 'Better not tell anyone you are reading this most lamentable Papist work.'

One ancient leathery eyelid winked. Another knot of my Fate tightened.

ON MY WAY HOMEWARD, clutching my *Inferno*, *Purgatorio* and *Paradiso*, at the corner of Southgait I collided with a wifie bearing a weighty cooking pot. She was bent by life, the pot likewise scorched and battered. I fixed on it, each dent, the blackened streaks, the fresh copper rivets that fixed the handles grasped in her podgy, reddened hands. The smell that rose from it was Life itself, in the form of mutton stew.

Instead of scowling, she smiled. Instead of by-passing I nodded, acknowledging the pot, its weight, her effort in carrying it. She lowered the pot onto the cobbles. 'A sair fecht!' she said. 'Would I had less mouths tae fill!'

'Aye', I said, and thought, *But each is precious to you.* Her shift and mantle were widow-dark. Her arms strong and plump. Her face pox-marked and weary-cheery. 'Let me gie you a hand.'

Together we carried the laden pot down Castle Street, the sweet smell of it rising from under the lid. And once in her kitchen, she scooped me a bowl, and I ate it with rough bread sitting at the door in the warm day, reading the opening lines of Dante's *Inferno*.

> *Nel mezzo del cammin di nostra vita*
> *Mi ritrovai per una selva oscura . . .*

THE WORDS POURED OFF the page like molten gold. *Half-way through the road of our life, I found myself in a dark wood . . .* Gravy-laden bread in one hand and book in the other, my happiness brimmed like the tide.

CHAPTER 6

But Does He Bloody Care?

Subdued by a glacial Sabbath wind, Tom Nicolson and I turned to walk back from the pier-end. Ahead of us rose the empty arches of the Cathedral, ribcage of a gigantic corpse. I was thinking of my chilly bunk, the lecture notes that needed reworking before the morn. With Burne's help I could now better write, read and converse in Latin, but I had not yet learned to think in it.

My friend was silent, brooding. As we passed through the postern gate, two men hurried into us. We gave way. The bearded young man nodded to us curtly – he came on occasion to our lectures, standing aloof in a swish green doublet. Today a French rapier jutted at his hip.

But what made me stop and stare after them was the boy. Long-limbed, fox-red hair pushing out under a black fur hat, he had fixed eyes on me, hesitated, then hurried on with his companion's arm secured round his shoulder. He was taller now, but I knew I had last seen him being rowed away from the *Sonsie Quine* at dawn.

'You ken yon laddie?' Tom Nicolson asked.

'He once had something of mine,' I replied. 'But he gave it back, good as new.'

'And who was that other mannie wi the big dangly thing?'

'Just some nob or other,' I said, straight-faced.

'Shame on you.'

In the distance, man and boy hurried onto a black barque as the mainsail jerked up the mast.

We walked up the brae, then turned into the Cathedral precinct. The main doors had long gone for timber, grass grew wild where the Augustinians for hundreds of years had laboured to save their souls, praise God and train more Augustinians. In the open nave, where had been tapestries, rich cloth, carved stalls and radiant windows, was now mud and a few sullen men working with wheelbarrows and ropes, though it was the Sabbath.

'You dinna have to be of the Old Faith to find this a dismal sight,' Nicolson said as he clambered onto the plinth where the High Altar had once stood. 'Are you truly of the Reform?'

It was the most personal and dangerous question of the times. 'God knows,' I replied.

'Indeed He does,' Tom said. He looked up into the grey-blue sky, and yelled at the ever-present, ever-passing gulls, '*But does He bloody care?*'

The labouring men looked up.

'Come down fae there,' I hissed. 'Are you insane?'

79

He shrugged, but jumped down from the plinth. 'Dinna heed me,' he said. 'It's just something my sister says.'

'*Rose?*'

'She has a queer mind.'

Together we peered down into the darkness of the under-vault. St Andrew's casket had once lain there. On High Days, pilgrims could pay extra to kiss the viewing-glass. The saint's relics had vanished, no one knew where – chucked into the sewer, or perhaps in some very private collection?

'Did ye ever hear Knox preach?' Nicolson asked.

'Twice. I felt my soul fizzle like spit on a stove. He sounded English from his long exile, but he rebuked like a man of Haddington, coarse as you like.'

'Aye, he was the great rebuker,' Tom Nicolson said, and we passed out through the Western Gate. 'It's a sair fecht, to keep men rightly building our New Jerusalem.'

The sun went in, the wind was cold. I wrapped my gown about me. Out in the bay, the black barque had rounded the cliffs of the Scaurs, heading northwards, bearing the armed man and the boy to their Fates.

A WEEK OR TWO later, as the Hebdomadar was locking up, I asked after the young blade in the green doublet, who had not reappeared at our lectures.

'Kerr of Allertoun is cauld as a landlord's hairt,' he said

with relish. 'Fell doon the stair o his ain tower. Broke his neck, they say.'

'Gracious Heavens,' I said.

He glared at me. 'Common Justice, laddie! They say it was he slipped poison to Regent Mar at the banquet in Dalkeith.'

'Regent Morton must be sorry he is gone,' I ventured.

The Hebdomadar scowled, spat on the pavement setts. 'Morton! That man will get his fairing. If not for him our richtful Queen would be with us yet.'

The Hebdomadar locked the lecture hut and set off, keys jangling, in search of his next drink. I went home to the sullen fire of Miss Whitton to brood about that lad with the grand insignia $\mathscr{B}$, hoping and fearing we might meet again.

WITH THE THOUGHTLESS ARROGANCE of youth, I had assumed Burne was a long-extinct volcano, a curiosity whose loneliness it pleased me to cheer, though in fact he cheered mine. After the last disputation of Whitsun Term, I mounted once more his narrow stairs, chapped on the door and entered his shabby room.

He was fully dressed! Sitting up! Flushed and smiling!

Just as remarkable was the other old man in the room, standing silently by the window, hands clasped, bare-headed with heavy grey whiskers. I had seen his portrait in our college hall. No mistaking the gravity of his mien, those deep grooves down his reddened cheeks, the great nose like the haft of an axe buried in his forehead.

'Geordie, this is my current meal ticket, William Fowler. He has begun to write verses, and has a fair hand.'

I bowed to George Buchanan, the greatest Latin writer of our age, formerly tutor to our long-exiled Queen, for many years tutor to our stripling King. Buchanan argued that in the Scots tradition kings ruled by consent of the people, and could be deposed. Jamie Saxt had lately dispensed with his services.

'All young men write verses,' he said as he inclined his aged head to me. 'Most grow out of it.'

'I hope rather to grow into it, sir,' I said. 'Given time.'

The grooves down his cheeks deepened. The prospect seemed to depress him. 'Then I advise you compose in the vernacular,' he said. 'Latin composition is dying.'

'I thought your *Somnium* was so fine,' I said. Ogilvie had put it my way, and I had enjoyed its satire on the life monastic. 'It was really . . .' I floundered. 'Funny.'

Buchanan almost smiled as he turned to Nicol Burne. 'You see, Nick, I am not entirely forgot.'

'*Somnium* was a knavish piece of work, Geordie.'

'Aye, we were young men then.' He turned to me. 'We were once as you, Master Fowler, foolish and high-spirited, as befits youth.'

Nicol Burne cackled as he buttoned a cloak about his scrawny neck. 'You were never young, nor foolish. Not even when we were students at St Leonard's, in 'twenty-five.'

'I was so!' Buchanan protested. 'Mind those poems I wrote in praise of the Principal's daughter?'

morning, still reeling, I tottered on board the *Sonsie Quine*. Captain Wandhaver clapped me on the back, offered me garlic sausage.

Perhaps my life would have taken the same course without that gaudy evening with Burne, Geddes and Buchanan, but I doubt it. I was ill all the voyage back to Embra, and never again could I tolerate oysters, smoked or otherwise.

CHAPTER 7

The Wholesome Broth of their Company

JEB AUCHTERLONE DID NOT appear at our matriculation for Second Year. On my way to lectures, my patched red gown now worn carelessly about the shoulder, I met him on the Northgait. He wore a carpenter's apron, and seemed the better for it.

'I sold the goonie,' he said happily. 'I am apprenticed tae a cleek maker wi a bonnie daughter. You play at the gowf?'

I did indeed. It had been my father's sole recreation, down at the Leith links. I would carry his cleeks, then learned to swipe the stuffed feathery ball with him. When playing with pals in Brunt's Field over the past summer, he had still been my ghostly cadet, murmuring caution and encouragement in my ear.

Auchterlone invited me to play with him and his new friends from the town. We shook hands and I went off to my extra Grammar with Nicol Burne, and he to the carpenter's workshop.

I watched him go, plump in his apron, greeting townsfolk he

passed. He had found his best line in life, and well may he be content who has discovered that! His talents dwelt in his hands, a healthier dwelling-place than the mind's unsanitary hovel.

FISHING FOLK WERE THE first to settle around the rough harbour between the skerries. Then the first chapel was built nearby a sacred well, giving the settlement its name, Kilrymont. There followed monks, then merchants, trading through the port. Norse ships and fighting men arrived, they became the gentry and farmers. The great Cathedral built to house St Andrew's relics became the religious centre of the entire country. Kings and archbishops visited, lairds grew wealthy, artisans were employed. Their guilds' leaders were elected to the Council.

Through all this, the fishing folk went down the brae to their boats. When the Reform came, with its stern, salty cleansings, most took to it. After all, they could never buy Salvation. They could only place themselves rightly into the on-coming wave, pray for the best and bow to the worst. An implacable, unpredictable God matched their life experience.

St Andrews had the Toon and the Goon, with much trade and scorn between them. But the fishing folk lived apart in Fishertown. They did trade with the town, but were not of it.

My point being? That though Tom Nicolson and I had become friends, and though I gaped like a codling when we passed time with his sister at the nets above the harbour green, he had not invited me within their lowly cottage. It might as well have been the inner sanctum of a Cathedral, glimpsed behind the rood-screen but never entered.

Then one fine late autumn afternoon Nicolson hailed me as I came from crossbow practice (the archery medal was coming up and I had hopes of finishing in the top five). I dangled the bow across my shoulders and waited for him to unburden, small talk not being his forte.

'It has been pointed out to me my family now eat better and dress more warmly, thanks to you and . . . that dealing we had.'

'Good,' I replied. 'It was exciting and profitable.'

'It was morally dubious and fraught with danger,' he said sternly.

'Such is life,' I said, very man-of-the-world.

'Mither has asked you to eat wi us,' he muttered.

'Thank you,' I said. 'I am honoured.' He looked at me suspiciously.

'Truly,' I said. 'I look forward to seeing more of your family.'

'Good. Next Saturday.' He turned to go, then swivelled on his stick. 'I should say my sister Rose already has an understanding.'

'I'm sure she has a very good understanding,' I replied, then made off.

'She does indeed!' he called after me. 'Tak tent!'

MRS NICOLSON LOOKED WIDER and shorter than before, with no need to stoop as she came to their door.

'Come awa in, laddie, and mind your heid.'

I ducked under the lintel and passed within. Warmth and smells of food, fragrant bedstraw, nets. The room was simple and very clean. One large rough table was prepared for eating. A smaller one, by the window, lay strewn with Tom's books and papers. Opposite the open fire I made out stone box beds, straw, blankets. Cut flowers in a rough vase, all yellow and pink and sweet.

It felt like home in a way my home had not since my brother's then my big sister's death, and my parents sundering over the True Faith. Peat smoke brought water to my eyes as the various cousins' and nephews' names were called out. Rose turned from the fire, smiled on me and made the day complete.

I sat by her and Tom by the wee window as we waited for food to arrive. Amid bairns' squabble and laughter, and the low, rapid, husky voices of Fishertown, I took my fill of the wholesome broth of their company.

Mother Nicolson asked me, as their guest, to say Grace. All round the table heads bowed, eyes closed. Silence but for wind whuffling in the smoky lum and the sea out back. Unsure of their specific Faith and not wishing to offend, I improvised a Thanks Be to our Creator, Guide and Saviour, who brought us to be in each other's company to eat and talk together, and be sustained body and soul for another day, by His almighty hand.

As I spoke, my eyes inadvertently flickered open, and I saw Rose had her eyes open too. Alone among those devout downturned faces, she was looking straight ahead, and her expression was so unexpected I stumbled in my Grace. I hurriedly closed my eyes and concluded *Let the Lord be thankit*, then we fell to leek soup, herring and tatties.

TOM AND I SAT at the little table, looking through his few precious books. Rose joined us. I learned she had parish school reading, the vernacular Bible, the Catechism and sermons, and her Grammar had been augmented somewhat by her brother.

'Aye, he's practising tae be a dominie,' his mother commented proudly from her straw-backed chair by the fire.

It was soon evident Rose Nicolson had quick understanding, a good memory, and could argue well. 'I havena time to keep up wi Grammar,' she commented. 'But I think tae masel while guttin and makin good.' So we talked in the vernacular when she was present, and her jibes and objections were often challenging.

She could also do her numbers and write, but her hand, like her brother's, was poor. I held up Tom's notebook, flicked through its pages. 'Your line wobbles like a carter on his way back frae the pub! And these the blots where he falls blootered!'

She laughed as I had hoped. Tom protested these were but notes done in a hurry, for his eyes only. I held up a fair copy of his essay against Ramus the logician.

'And this is your brother's best writing! The matter may be fair, but its manner is foul.'

She took it from me, turned to the light coming in the little

And that was how come a fisher lassie, daughter of a line of fishers that went back to the Flood, could read and write both in Latin and the vernacular, to tolerable standard, while her mother – a shrewd, insightful woman – could not. And that was how come I could sit beside Rose Nicolson and improve her hand, and argue and laugh over the broadsheets and issues of the day.

For those giddy, joyous hours, I owe the Reformed Kirk of my country, however improbable that may seem.

THE COLD, BRIGHT AUTUMN morn held out the prospect of Psalms in the chilly chapel, then hours sitting by the cathedra of our regent, flailing away with our quills. We had embarked on the syllogism, that device so seeming-irresistible. Major premise: *All men are mortal*. Minor premise: *I am a man*. Conclusion: *I am mortal*.

Looking down from my attic window I saw my fellow students striding by, all cocky, as youth is. All anxious, as youth is. Why wait for the world to begin? *Carpe diem!*

I left my satchel of papers, ink and notes on the table, ran down the stairs. Bumped into Miss Whitton with a besom in her hand.

'You look cheerful,' she said suspiciously.

'And why not!' I replied. 'Another fine day in God's creation!'

'It is a *fallen* Paradise,' she cried after me. But I was heedlessly bound towards the harbour green and Rose Nicolson.

I found her there, at some distance from the other women, her arms full of wet linen from the Bishop's Castle. I gave her a hand getting sheets up on the lines where they flapped and cracked in the wind. I said they minded me of sails on the *Sonsie Quine*.

'Except these are going nowhere,' she commented. 'Like masel.'

I glanced at her, but she kept her face from me as we carried heaped-up crab-stinking nets across the Green. 'So whit are ye studying of late?' she speired.

'The syllogism, and *The Great Chain of Being*.'

'Mmm.' She nodded, shifted the nets in her arms. 'What's that when it's at hame?'

I hesitated. 'There was an Ancient Greek philosopher cried Plato,' I began.

'Aye, heard o *him*. And his wee pal Plotinus.'

I blinked. 'Well, yes. Though that's much later.'

'Seven hunner years.' I stared at her. She shrugged. 'We had a good dominie at the wee school. And my brither talks to me of his studies. On ye go.'

As she spread and examined the nets over the poles, I tried to regurgitate, in the vernacular, my half-digested learning. The Great Chain is a vision of all forms of being as on the rungs of a ladder, each ranked in order of their complexity and potentiality. Everything from the ground we were standing on, to fish in the sea, that barking dog, the gulls overhead – each had its place in the hierarchy. Birds rank above fish, but below useful animals like kye and sheep.

'Maist ingenious,' she commented, and plucked her mending-spindle from her waistband. I tried to remain undistracted as she reached up.

So everything is ranked in its class, I explained, and within each class is another hierarchy. For example, lions and suchlike come top in the class of animals, being untamed and free. Then the useful and smarter animals, like dogs. Then the silly sheep and the kye. Then hedge-pigs, mice, frogs and so on.

'Midgies at the verra bottom?' she enquired.

'Aye! Then below them trees, crops, all things that grow but cannot move of themselves. And then down to the purely material, minerals, rocks, then earth.'

'You've got to feel for earth,' she murmured as she secured her twine. 'Sae lowly, yet aathing grows from it.'

I looked at the side of her cheek. That wee crease by her mouth. Was she interested or baffled or taking the piss? Lasses did that, but not usually in matters of Philosophy.

'The upper levels are pure Spirit, free of matter,' I persisted. 'Angels and suchlike, with God at the top.'

'Well, naturally.'

'Then below Him, but still pure Spirit, come the angelic orders.'

'And they'll be ranked, I expect?'

'Aye! Nine ranks of Angels – seraphim and cherubim and the like.'

'Nine! Glory be! Who counted them?'

'I don't know,' I confessed. 'Some are in the Scriptures. I think they added more later.'

Her spindle flicked, turned back on itself, looped another knot, then moved off across to close another gap. I loved watching her hands, so quick and skeely.

'So your Great Ladder gives painters fairlies tae paint, and occupies the minds of monks wi o'er muckle time on their hands.'

'Maybe,' I said. 'But I am no theologian.'

'Guid!' she said. 'I've never met one wha smiled.'

The things she came out with — as if metaphysics were a game, not a serious, near-incomprehensible matter I had sweated Latin over. She let air into my over-stuffed mind.

'And below Angels?' She leaned forward, gripped the twine between her white teeth and pulled the knot tight.

'You and I. We are a blend of Spirit and the Material, sharing both realms.'

She snicked the twine with her fleshing knife. 'That must cause difficulties,' she said.

'It does that!'

She turned and smiled. I blushed. Her physical presence was causing me difficulties indeed.

'Man is flawed by his materiality,' I mumbled.

'And women more so, doubtless! Lacking Reason, puir things.'

She had already turned away, hands busy again. I did not know what to make of her. She turned back to me, spindle in one hand, knife in the other.

'This Ladder of Being,' she said. 'Could there be missing rungs? Ones we dinna ken of?'

'I suppose so.' No one in our tutorials had ever brought up such a question.

'I mean, is there a *logos* to this ordering, or do you look at what you see and then order it?'

My mind was starting to wake up. 'That depends on whether you are with Plato or—'

'Aristotle,' she said. I stared at her. 'Well, it's aye one or t'other.' Who was I dealing with here? She shrugged. 'Tellt ye I had a good dominie. It gies me something to ponder while working. Tell me mair.'

She turned back to the net, spread a rent across her left hand, looked at what was missing or broken.

'It's a grand vision,' I said. 'It helps comprehend and order all things.' The stray hairs on the nape of her neck shone as she inclined her head. I was sore distracted. 'It sounds more convincing in Latin,' I concluded.

'Nae doot,' she said. 'No doubt.' I noticed she sometimes started repairs by cutting, making a shape of hole that could better be repaired. The same with her language. She was about to knot her yarn, then she paused and half-turned to me. 'This Great Ladder of Being – whit does it lean agin?'

My mind stopped. Nothing came. A great shining nothing.

She smiled, not cruelly but companionably. 'I mean, surely it would fall over otherwise.' And her hands flickered across the gaps, turning and weaving and making the morning whole.

I would have said more, asked more, but a gaggle of young fish-wives came across the Green, and one shouted a comment, and Rose responded in impenetrable Fife. I made my farewell and walked off towards St Leonard's. I understood that throughout our conversation she had been translating for my benefit, as I had tried to do for her.

I LAY ON MY pallet that evening, looking at the ceiling and thinking of her. Her full, clever lips, the way she stood so securely on the Green, how her eyes looked at me and past me. The things she said. *It gives painters fairlies tae paint, and occupies monks wi o'er muckle time on their hands.*

Spirit and Matter, a ladder propped on nothing.

I lay recalling Rose Nicolson opening my mind with her words, my heart with her quick hands. I imagined her fingers tracing my lips, and mine on hers, meeting in our original tongues, translating our heart speech, *oor hairt-leid.*

I threw the blanket off, went to the table. Trimmed the quill, stirred ink, then began to scratch out my first Scots sonnet, *Tae a Fisher Quine Divine.*

Truly, it is execrable. If you come across a copy, once triumphantly written out in my hand and pressed upon friends, please commit it to the flames. I am clear-sighted enough to know its deficiencies, vain enough to wish to keep what little remaining reputation I have.

My essay on the Great Chain of Being did not go down well. My tutor noted *wild and irrelevant speculation, with possibly blasphemous tendencies. Not without interest – to some.*

CHAPTER 8

Gin Ye Accept the Premise

I WOULD FIND CAUSE TO call by the Nicolson cottage – a book to loan, some notes to return, more fish oil to pick up. If I timed it right, Tom was out and Rosie was in. She was aye busy, but we could talk if I lent a hand. I hung my scarlet goonie on the hook, rolled up my sleeves. Give me a good blade and I could skin and joint a coney, re-set a wonky dresser, or re-wick and trim a sputtering lamp wi the best of them.

She was quick to smile and quip, but as quick to withdraw inwardly. She was my age, my height, our eyes met on the level. She knew the University, its characters and tensions, through her brother, but of course had never set foot in the lecture rooms.

She wore lilac gloves on High Days and Holidays, to cover hands already cross-hatched with scars. She liked to sing (not particularly tunefully) ballads of drowned fishermen and ill-starred lovers strangely unable to recognise each other after an absence. Once in a while she would hum Hieland melodies, then catch herself and stop. When she sat at my side to practise her writing, her lips moved and the tip of her tongue showed as she wrote *italic script*.

We became friends. I had grown up among lasses, and in the cottage it was easy to be with her. Meeting her outside on the Green, or unexpectedly in the street, would confuse me utterly.

I came to know the seasons when she was staying with relatives down in Eyemouth or Craster, at the herring gutting and curing. Rose would be away for weeks, then like a returning bird she would abruptly reappear at the nets. Then I would stroll by where the fish-wives gathered like scolding gulls. The older ones mocked me but kindly, adjudging me hairmless and knowing me Tom Nicolson's friend. The younger ones kept their distance, glancing over at us, not entirely friendly. She did not seem to talk much with them.

I met few in that lowly, snug house who were not extended family, and came to understand how unusual my presence was at that table. I was grateful to be there, aware how reluctant Tom Nicolson's invitations were.

After the lonely chill of my bunk room, the Nicolsons offered warmth and sustenance. I sat gownless, my natural self, among the throng of children, cousins, and thrawn widowed aunties, not understanding much of what was said but deeply comforted. When I was spoken to, even the bairns used our common tongue. I likewise amended my Embra speech. We offered translations of ourselves, and so more or less understood each other.

Of the father, never a mention. That puzzled me. As I knew all too well, early death of a parent was normal. Desertion was not uncommon. Many fishermen had second families in a seasonal port. It was a matter for gossip, laughter, shrugs, disapproval, envy or regret – but not this absolute silence that made enquiry impossible.

Then came an afternoon on the Green, when the other lasses had gone to the caulking shed, and I was holding the rent net open while she mended. We were concentrating on the work at hand. Perhaps that was why I felt able to talk of my father. I told Rose that though he was a Reformist, he was a gentle, kindly man. And my mother, for all that she was of the Old Faith, was hard-headed to a fault. How strangely and unexpectedly mixed folk are! Is that not a blessing?

I found myself telling her of the Doo-Cot, of the manner of my father's death, that of my brother John when I was but a bairn, and then my elder sister's. The acrid stench of dried fish caught in my throat. Rose put her free hand on my arm, left it there for two long beats, then returned to work.

'And your father?' I asked, casual-like. 'What happened to him?'

Her hand stopped with the spindle. 'He is awa,' she said.

'Away? I took it he was—'

'Deid?' She looked right at me. 'My Da isna deid, though he might as well be.'

She went back to work, her face pale, lips set.

'I'm sorry,' I said. 'I mean I'm glad he's not dead.'

'Has Tom spoken of him?'

'No,' I said. 'Never.'

'Guid,' she said. 'Better thon way.' She gave me a tight smile, finished her knot and cut the line. Then she quietly added 'He was awfy clever but.'

'Like Tom. And yourself!'

'Aye, maybe,' she said. 'But my faither wasna always in control of himself.'

'*Unlike* yourself,' I said, trying to make light of it.

'That's richt,' she said. She moved on to the next gaping rent and went back into herself like a whelk into its shell.

'They say George Buchanan writes Latin better than any in Europe,' Rose said eventually, re-emerging. 'Yet he still believes, on theological grounds, that the stars and planets all circle round our Earth! If I cannot trust him on this, why should I trust his Calvinist views on bishops or Free Will? Eh? Have you read his cosmology?'

I shook my head. 'There are not enough hours in the day.'

'Or are there *exactly the right amount*?' She held up her spindle, her eyes suddenly outshining the day around us. 'Gin you or I die the morn, would our lives not hae been brimful?'

I considered it. The sea was full to the horizon. The day that had been bright now seemed brighter. 'You may be haivering, but it feels braw.'

She laughed, lifted the next net from the pile. I helped her spread it out along the poles. She assessed the nearest rent. 'Haivering is what folk cry an unfamiliar notion.'

'You get your ideas from Tom?' I asked.

She smiled to herself, then pointed down at the pier where students took their post-kirk walk. 'Are they no a straggle of red ants, carrying their crumbs of learning?'

As when passing through a doorway one misses a step and falls forward, for a moment the world was not where I expected it. 'A striking image,' I managed.

She laughed. 'You may have it.' (I did, I did! One of the more successful lines from *The Tarantula of Love*.) She looked down at her reddened hands. 'Tom is skeely at picking up ideas frae books,' she said. 'Perhaps he has o'er many, and they make his mind murky.'

She spoke with affection, as one might of a clever child. She shrugged, made her first knot and continued her repairs, and spoke no more of it.

WALKING WITH TOM NICOLSON by Swallowgait one morn, I waved to Jeb Auchterlone. He was hurrying towards the Links with an admiring quine on his right and a caddy carrying cleeks on his left. 'There goes a happy man,' I remarked.

Nicolson shrugged as he hirpled along. 'The unexamined life is not worth living,' he said dismissively.

'Auchterlone doesn't think so.'

'He could be said to think?'

I stopped dead. 'Tom, your studies are doing you harm.'

'How so?'

What do we owe our friends? Support and approval, for sure. But sometimes something more risky. 'Ye are becoming awfy arrogant.'

He opened his mouth like a herring gull. Looked down, tapped at the cobbles with his stick. 'Is that why I have no freends?' he said quietly.

'Could be,' I replied.

He looked at me, his long face doleful. 'I thought it was because I am a Poor Scholar.'

'Haivers! You are the best scholar in your year, they say the best since James Crichton. But man, do not look down on the rest of us!'

'I take ideas seriously! They are our only gait through a world of stupidity and greed.'

He looked crestfallen. I put my hand on his arm. 'Not the only way,' I said. 'For the rest of us, there is laughter, the lute, poetry, family, archery and gowf. And friendship, even wi those who smell of fish.'

His hand closed on my arm. 'Fair enough,' he said. 'I'll ease up on the philosopher kings.'

We walked on by the Cathedral, spectral in the morning haar, to our respective chilly lecture huts. We never spoke of it again, but our bond was stronger for that exchange, like a dab of glue hardening within a mortise joint. It would in time be tested.

TOWARDS THE END OF next term I was at my favourite place in the world – the Nicolson table at dinner time. Warmth, laughter, steam from the kettle, food coming off the stove. Rose was in disputation with her older brother.

'Even you canni square Free Will and Divine Omniscience, Tom!'

Tom looked vexed. 'To ourselves, we seem to have Choice. But from the Creator's viewpoint, we do not. So we are at once moral agents, and we are not.'

'I've seen mackerel twist better on a hook,' Rose commented as she passed the tatties.

'It's jist Logic!' Tom said, taking a redder. 'God is omniscient, which must include the Future. So what is going to happen must be already fixed. But in our ignorance, we feel we have choice.'

'Our Ignorance I can live wi,' she said. 'But how could you, or any man, ken God's nature and powers?' She set down her knife with a clatter. 'Maybe God has little interest in us. What of fires, floods, earthquakes, the diseases that kill randomly? The honest lasses that die birthing, the guid men that drown? God could be flawed, limited, even wicked!'

'Then He wouldna be God,' Tom said curtly.

'How can you ken?' she exclaimed. 'The Divines crawl at His feet, pleading their Understanding is weak. If it's so weak, what can any man – aye, or woman! – ken of God's attributes? And what –' her voice soft, under her breath, in the rising steam of the tatties and herring – 'what surety is there of His existence at all?'

Her mother slammed down the big pan. 'Your faither wouldni hae ye talk so.'

'And whaur is he, mither? Does faither even live, any mair than oor Lord?'

No one spoke. Tom clasped his stick, his face pale as peeled willow. One of the wee cousins started to sob, silently, snot and tears dripping on his plate.

Rose stood up, looking at us all. Then she ran to the door. 'Ah, you're aa sae glaikit!' she cried, and was gone.

I made to follow, but Tom put his stick across my way. 'Best leave her be. She gets het up. Our faither was the same.'

He rose, put his arms round his mother and murmured in her ear. Then wee sister Mary dished up the herring and tatties, salt and kale. She put one portion for Rose in the range. Tom said Grace, we murmured *Amen*, then ate in silence.

Rose returned a while later. Face averted, she ate her dried-up food. Nothing was said, nothing was done, save her brother's hand on her shoulder, gently, in passing.

I walked home thoughtfully through the gloaming. Rose Nicolson was not just a bonnie fisher lass, any more than she was the Virgin Mary.

IT SEEMED TO ME Rose was fast becoming less temperate and more frustrated by her life. One day remains in my mind, when it became undeniable.

I see, as from above, Nicolson and myself walking upon the West Sands in bright, hard light. It must have been a Sabbath afternoon for Rose was with us, for once not working. We came upon young men playing futeball, their shouts and cries carried out to sea by a brisk westerly.

We cooried down in shelter under the dunes, watching them sport unburdened by thought. Rose sat between us, wind agitating her hair and scarf, dark blue eyes set on the horizon, her mind removed from us.

'The young and free at play,' I said with some envy.

'Ah, but are they really free?' However radical his thinking, Nicolson still clanked the chains of Calvin. I groaned inwardly. 'The future is already kenned in the mind of God. So Free Will must be an illusion, however cherished and natural. The sun appears to go round the Earth, though we ken now it is not so.'

'The logic is compelling,' I admitted.

'*Gin ye accept the premise*,' Rose said. She said it low but clearly. Her weathered arms were close to mine. I could see pale hairs lean and quiver.

'Hey-ho! Rosie!' A young man came running from the futeball, breeks rolled up and feet bare. He was nearly tall as Tom but more hefty. 'You been watchin the gemm?'

'Oh aye,' she said calmly. 'Ye scattered them like Goliath did the Philistines.'

'Maist certainly did!' He glowed with life and energy.

'Aye, John,' Tom said.

'Aye aye, Thomas.'

Rose's Intended stared down at me, took in my gown. I looked him back, saw vigour free of reflection. We nodded cautiously to each other.

I watched her and him walk away along the sands, back towards the town. She took his arm. Their shoulders met. Their hips and all.

'I tellt ye often enough,' Nicolson said gently. 'She has an understanding. He will do well by her, and she by him.'

'You can't mean that!' I cried. 'She has a brain! He just has hands and feet!'

He gave a wee smile at that. 'Now his faither's deid, Johnny Gourlay owns a sea-going boat and a netting skiff. He is literate enough, though puts it to little use beyond reading Holy Scripture in the kirk. He adores her without using long words.'

'But she could do better for herself!'

'With a penniless student?' He looked along the beach, at the two distant figures moving up onto the Links. 'My sister has a queer, deep mind, but she is not free, any more than Gourlay, or you, or I. These are the lives God has chosen for us.'

Then God is an eejit rose to my lips like bile, but I could not spit it out. I jumped up and set off in a huff, in the general direction of Leuchars. He caught up with me, pegging along with his stick. He put his free arm round my shoulder.

'You were more fun when reading Heraclitus,' I said. 'I pray in time you digest Calvin, then let him pass in the usual manner.'

He chuckled but said nothing. Behind us the players picked up their jackets and went home to their labours. I turned and saw one throw the ball up high for another to catch, and faint laughter came by on the breeze. *Gin ye accept the premise*. Meaning: the existence of an all-powerful, all-seeing, benevolent God.

I could deny no longer the way Rose's intellect inclined. It was beyond heresy, near-unthinkable. She might as well jump off the Bishop's Castle and expect her skirts to bear her up.

CHAPTER 9

Heresy and Necromancy

I WAS BACK IN EMBRA at the end of Second Year, scribing for my mother and learning her accounting systems, when Tom Nicolson wrote about hearing James Melville preach at the Holy Trinity kirk, and again at St Salvator's. His uncle Andrew Melville was in the mould of Knox and Calvin, a stern, admonishing, fiercely bearded figure fighting to establish a pure Reformed Kirk, but his nephew was *a young man of our times*.

Tom's handwriting became more agitated. They had talked together afterwards, taking a lengthy philosophical walk alone out the West Sands. Young Melville was clean-shaven, full of laughter, open of countenance, the light of life in his eyes. *He has a ready wit and love in his heart. You would like him – he values poetry, and was a dab hand on the lute. A fine singing voice and such good company!*

I was immediately jealous and dubious of such a paragon. Still, Tom had finally met someone of his own intellectual ardour, who was also seemed full of fun and good humour – not a defining trait of the Calvinist wing of the Reform.

James Melville had been made temporary minister for Ainster, a wee fishing port over the hill from St Andrews. But they still found time to meet and walk and talk together. Apparently Melville even got my friend out onto the Links, where they vigorously debated while swiping their way round the course. *Such fine instruction! I feel I have missed the very point of the intellect, which is to guide us to know God's Will and submit to it most willingly.*

I stood at the slit window of the Counting House, looking over Embra towards the Fife hills happed in shawls of rain. What can we do about the rain, or God's Will, I wondered? It falls as it falls. The only lassie who interests me is spoken for. Submission and acceptance are essentially drainage ditches.

Our hearts yearn for things to be otherwise – *exempli gratia*, a girl with deep intellect and all the curves Creation bestows, who ought to be one's mate for life. Yet the rain keeps falling, turning all to mud, and she has an understanding with a well-set fisherman. I put Tom's letter aside.

Then wonderfully a letter came from her, in much-improved cursive script. *He is infatuated, I fear. All talk is of Melville this, James that. My brother the former Humanist, who dangled Heraclitus before my mind, now expounds on Justification by Faith Alone! I admit JM is a fine-looking young man, most attentive as he and his cohorts talk with us simple lasses at the Green. I shall soon be to the Eyemouth drave with spindle and blade and tape for my hands, far from friends and the provocations of philosophy (barring my own homespun musings amid gasping gills and falling scales). Pity me but pray do not pray! RN.*

I sat in the Doo-Cot and wrote to her about family and business life in Embra, my new acquaintance John Drummond of Hawthornden, with whom my sister Susannah was already exchanging amorous glances. I wrote to amuse and entertain, for I sensed behind the humour Rose was in poor spirits. I did not woo her, but suggested she might commit to paper some of her musings, to clarify her thoughts and so I would better understand her.

The briefest of replies came, dispatched from Craster. *If wishes were fishes, men would swim free. Alas I am but a fisher lass and cannot swim. Your busy friend, RN.* The paper bore a faint bloodstain in one corner, and a spattering of silvery scales like stars. My mother came into the room, stared at me then sniffed.

'Your correspondence smells of fish,' she said. 'Surely you could do better.'

'I shall reply with the smell of coinage on my fingers,' I replied. 'Siller for siller.'

'I doubt she will reward ye,' my mother said icily. She sat at her table to commence her monthly accounting. How did she know about Rose? But she was correct – I wrote but received no reply.

FRESH OFF THE *Sonsie Quine*, ready for my Third Year, heart high as a buzzard circling in the updraught of my dreams, I turned into

Fishergait. By the Cross I straightway saw Nicolson, so tall, so thin, waving his stick. Not to me but to his two approaching companions.

So it was I first met James Melville. We call such meetings *fateful* in retrospect, yet I felt something tug in my breast as I approached, as if I were being pulled forward by an unseen hawser.

'Master Fowler,' Melville said. His grip was firm, his look direct, his wide brown eyes clear. Clean-shaven and fresh-looking, he appeared more cheerful farmer's boy than rising Divine of the Reform. His full mouth had yet to acquire the grimmer furl of his uncle Andrew, whom I had lately seen admonishing the citizens of Embra from the pulpit of St Giles.

Too good to be true came to me, though that may have been jealousy at his good looks and his being my friend's new hero. It was churlish to take against a man on account of his good manners, enthusiasm for Reformed Religion, and evident pleasure in the world and his place in it.

The fellow at his side was staring at me with hot, dark eyes, shifting restlessly from foot to foot. Dressed in severe black, with grey bonnet worn across his narrow head, he minded me of a half-starved hoodie craw.

'This is Nathaniel Pow,' Melville said cheerily. 'He is a rising star in our Kirk.'

I had seen Pow on occasion emerging from St Mary's College, talking fervently at the centre of a group of acolytes. Now he nodded curtly, as though I had already displeased him. I withdrew my handshake and nodded Pow back. Perhaps he was merely blate and shy.

He was certainly skelly-eyed, which was disconcerting. One dark iris fixed on me. The other seemed to wander off over my left shoulder. Tom raised his stick in greeting and I looked round. Approaching us, basket balanced on her head, came a strong-legged young goddess bearing an amphora of ambrosia. That is to say, Rose Nicolson was carrying the day's catch to the market.

'We are debating Predestination!' Tom cried.

'I suppose that was inevitable,' she replied. She smiled on me, put her free hand lightly on my arm, then on Melville's, before putting her basket down. I saw Pow frown at her familiarities.

'Mistress Nicolson, this is Nathaniel Pow,' James Melville said. 'He is a coming man, and sound.'

'You mean he aye agrees wi you?' Rose said.

Melville chuckled. Pow stared at Rose and sternly intoned, 'He means I cleave entirely to the Word in all things.'

'Aye, but which words? There are so many to choose among.' She began laying out haddock and saithe on the slab by the Fisher Cross. 'Aa fresh the day! Straight frae yer ain guid sea!'

'That the scholar must elucidate and the minister inspire,' Pow said. His eyes were fixed on her as she moved. The turn of her head, the swift lift of her arms, her curls drifting from her casually coiled kerchief, all were lovely. I did not like the way he regarded her.

'Indeed,' she said. 'So is it going to be this one – or this one – today? Your choice is already been determined, but which shall ye choose for your sermon, which for your dinner?'

'You speak with levity of the revealed word of God,' Pow said.

She turned to face him directly. 'I never joke about fish at the Merkit Cross,' she said. 'I leave the Word to you in the Kirk.'

Pow flushed. Melville seemed entertained. Her brother looked both concerned and indulgent. 'She doesni mean harm,' Tom said. 'She sometimes speaks at random.'

'There is no random in God's eyes,' Pow intoned. 'She is of the Elect or she is not.'

'Ah, yes,' from Nicolson. 'The Law of the Excluded Middle.'

'Excluded Middle – *c'est moi*!' cried Rose Nicolson. We all turned to look at her. She leaned back agin the fish slab, folded her arms. 'We're aa equal in the sight of God, yet I canni study. I canni teach, even at the wee school. I might teach in a nunnery but they hae been abolished.' As we gaped at her, the largest cod twitched, flapped its tail on the marble. 'I may not take part in public Disputations. I canni be an elder of the Kirk – unless things have changed greatly among the Presbytery.'

Melville laughed. 'No, they have not changed that much. Ours is a reform, not a revolution.'

'It is God's Will things are ordered so,' Pow insisted. 'There are many instances in Scripture—'

'I dinni doubt it, Master Pow,' Rose said, one hand holding up a rock eel by its gills. 'It is your destiny to deal wi souls. Mine is tae deal wi the denizens of the sea, pair wee ignorant beasties.' She looked to me. 'Will, can ye gie me a haund wi the lave o the catch, fetch them up frae the harbour?'

Pow and Melville may have been startled by her abrupt shift of register. I knew, as did her brother, she was contemptuously cutting them out. As I went off willingly with Rose – Plotinus could wait – I heard James Melville say, 'She is a lass of spirit, Nicolson.'

Tom mumbled something. I heard Pow intone, 'She is in need of Salvation, as are we all.'

Rose and I went through the port, me carrying the empty basket, she humming to herself as she did when vexed. 'Yon Pow mannie,' she said abruptly. 'Aye preaching to us lasses at our work. Fair gi'es me the creeps.'

THAT SABBATH, JAMES MELVILLE conducted the service at the town's kirk. I went out of curiosity and because it was politic. And because Tom was taking Rosie.

To pass time during *longueurs*, I did a rapid head count of the congregation, then took a guess at the population of St Andrews. The kirk was fairly busy wi pained penitents, but by my rough calculations they still only made up roughly one in six adults of the town. This at the height of our Reform! It seemed many folk were indifferent, or otherwise engaged (it was a fine morning for the gowf), or believed themselves damned anyway, without a priest to absolve their many sins. Who knows? The believers made so much passionate clash that it was easy to forget they were not universal, not even a majority.

The Reform might have laid the foundations for our shining city-state of God, but judging by the faces around me that morn, there was as yet little joy in it. *The Truth is not intended to comfort you but to set you free*, Nicolson had declared the day before. He was losing what weight he had. His shaved cheekbones were like razor shells, blue-tinged. I preferred his Humanist phase.

To be fair, Melville preached well and enthusiastically on Justification By Faith Alone, quoting Scriptures of James, Romans, Ephesians, warming the hearts of women and men alike. I did my best to be amiable when we met up with him afterwards. Nicolson regarded him with glowing eyes. Pow patrolled at his side. Rose wore her lilac gloves but kept squeezing her fingers. 'Salt in cuts,' she said quietly. 'They are the very De'il.'

As we all walked together out along the pier, Rose enquired whether, given that our Creator already kenned if we were to be saved or damned, there was any point in virtue. If all was already decided by God, what use in prayer, chastity, kindness or honest dealing?

James Melville looked startled, then laughed and explained that Good Works were often the *marks* of the Just, though not the *reason* they were Saved. Man was a fallen being, and could not save himself by his own efforts. Only God could justify him.

She nodded, then looked up into his eyes. 'So when Martin Luther translated our Bible into his vernacular, and to the Apostle's words *We are saved by Faith* added the word *alone*, this was not what might, had he been a fishmonger not a Reformer, have been cried putting his thumb on the scale?'

'My sister knows not what she is saying,' Tom hastily said. 'She means not to be sacrilegious.'

James Melville smiled kindly. 'She has a point, strikingly expressed. But had she studied the original Aramaic, she would see that the construction clearly implies *alone*. The great Reformer *restored* rather than *added to* Gospel Truth.'

Rose flushed. 'I must go to the Fishergait the morn and acquire some Aramaic.'

Tom frowned. Melville looked at her with interest, Pow with disapproval.

'Then I shall accompany you,' Melville said, 'for I am also lacking Aramaic! It is my learned uncle has a good supply.'

'So you take his word for it?' she asked. Then she added, in part under her breath, 'We are indeed saved by faith alone.'

'Very good!' Melville laughed. Other walkers looked concerned at laughter from a minister. He flung his arms out, nearly dislodging Pow's grey bunnet. 'Very good indeed! Fortunately my uncle is an honest monger, and would never dream of putting his thumb on the scales!'

Rose opened her mouth to retort, but Tom put his hand on her arm. She paused. I saw her mind withdraw like sun behind a cloud.

'I must leave you all,' she said. 'I hae work at hame.'

She turned and hurried off back to Fishertown. We watched her diminish.

'Remarkable lass,' James Melville said at last.

'But much in need of instruction,' Pow added, staring after her.

'She has an understanding,' Tom Nicolson said. 'Her beau is like to become an elder of our kirk.'

'Capital!' Melville exclaimed. 'A Reformist education has not been wasted there.'

If you kenned her better, I thought, you'd be alarmed rather than amused.

IN THE FAMILY HOME, Rose was at ease, indiscreet, surrounded by laughter and flyting. But I had come to notice that outside the house she was seldom in company, save that of a few older women. My first glimpse of her mending on the Green, alone but for a couple of old biddies, turned out to be typical. At the nets, the creels, the curing shed, she worked largely alone, her lips moving with her silent thoughts. The other young lasses went by in chattering groups, glancing her way.

Nathaniel Pow was increasingly among the lasses at their work. Fishing for souls, doubtless. On the whole they seemed pleased by his interest, but they giggled when he was gone. Their leader was Bella Muir, a solid three-master of a girl, aye joking, but you wouldn't want to cross her. I noticed that when she and Rose met in a narrow wynd they would pass like cats, slunk agin the walls.

I was heading down to the drying green after morning lectures. In the distance Rose was sitting on her own by lobster creels, her sleeves rolled up. Bella Muir approached with some followers, paused to stand tall over her. I could not hear the words, but the faint laughter did not sound kindly.

Muir made some final quip as she moved on. Rose threw aside

her spindle and jumped to cling crab-like to her back, her hands clawing at Bella's face. At the first screams, I broke into a run. The two lasses were now scrapping on the turf, the others in an excited ring. I got there same time as Nathaniel Pow and we pulled them apart. Bella's face was bloody from scratches, Rose's cheeks were bruised. Pow's eyes shone.

'Unbeliever!' Bella yelled. 'Hielan hoor!'

Rose broke free and clawed for her eyes. When Pow grabbed her arm, Rose turned and smacked him in the face. Blood bloomed a rose at the end of his long beak. Rose seemed possessed.

'*Witch!*' Bella Muir hissed as she backed away. '*Pagan! Necromancer!*'

Shocked silence among us all. Rose lifted her skirts and ran off homeward. Pow wiped the blood from his nose and stared after her.

WHEN I WENT BY Fishertown next day, there was a crowd clustered outside the Nicolson cottage. Excited folk were peering in the tiny windows. I pushed through, chapped on the door and gained admittance.

Pow was at the long table, vernacular Bible open. Another man in severe black was taking notes. A third had legal tomes. At the other end of the table Rose sat glaring at them, half-hidden by her weeping mother.

'Go fetch Tom,' I told her wee brother Bobbie. 'And John Gourlay if he is not at sea. Now!'

I cleared a space and sat down beside Rose, claiming to be her advisor, here to help clarify the charges and her defence. I established this was a preliminary kirk inquiry, not a court of law. There was a statute against witchcraft, but only one prosecution I knew of, and that had collapsed.

But necromancy was potentially a serious charge, one levelled against Catholic priests – after all, they claimed to turn wine to Christ's blood, wafers to Christ's flesh. Necromancy was a catch-all that included practices of the Old Church, the cures of the old wives, rags tied to wishing trees, curses, speaking in tongues and fainting fits.

It seemed Bella Muir had already given her testament. She was silent now, shifty and not a little scared. Under oath she had accused Rose Nicolson of murmuring spells and curses. ('*I was quoting rude bits of Catullus at her!*') Several Muir kye had sickened, there had been a spate of miscarriages in the toun. Rose Nicolson had been heard to deny the divinity of Christ, and mock the handiwork of the Creator. ('*I said it was a hellish day, and that the sea didni care if fishermen lived or died.*')

The hearing was malevolent and worrisome, but any competent defence lawyer could point out it was common knowledge that Bella Muir had set her kerchief at John Gourlay and been outraged when he had chosen Rose Nicolson over her. Nathaniel Pow spent too much time wi the fisher lasses, had gotten a slap for his cheek, and in any case lacked authority to call an investigative session.

Rose was about to speak again, but I caught her eye and shook my head. With the witness recording, I wanted to be sure she said nothing incriminating, nothing clever. This was not the time for sarcasm or wit.

I demanded to hear what the charges were precisely, and on whose authority. Pow grew heated but I kept him at bay with cod-legalese. Mother Nicolson huffed and wept in the background. Rose stared at the table, stirring crumbs with a bandaged forefinger. I feared they would push her into indiscretion, so I haivered on.

At last the door opened and Tom Nicolson lurched in. I was on my feet, tugged at his arm, got myself between him and Pow.

Then Johnny Gourlay arrived with two of his pals. The quasi-court broke up. Pow and his two aides were ejected, still clutching their papers and Bibles. Bella Muir and her cronies screeched like gulls over a fish head. The neighbours had a good gawp. The only one silent was Rose. She sat still, staring at the table, fingering scraps of bread as though an answer lay there.

In the street, Pow threatened he would call a Session and constitute a Satanic Inquiry. Gourlay threatened to knock his head off. In time they dispersed, still muttering malevolences. Gourlay went within, took Rose by the arm and gently raised her to her feet. I saw he cared for her deeply, and was better placed to protect her than I.

As she left, she touched my arm. She mouthed *Thank you*, then she was gone with her man.

THE LIGHT WAS GOING, the leaden horizon ruled as though ready to be writ upon. We came to the end of the pier. Tom looked down into the sea, tapped the stone with his staff.

'You hae seen how it is,' he said at last, not looking at me. 'You did well, but Gourlay can shelter her and you cannot.'

'I will make something of myself!' I cried. 'I will be a scribe, dominie or some such. I can carry on my father's trade and my mother's affairs.'

'I tellt ye, Gourlay is of our folk. It is the difference between salt water and fresh. Mix them and what you get is brackish, nae use to man nor beast.'

'I don't see you going out wi a fishwife. Or any lass at all.'

When vexed, Nicolson pursed his lips to whistle tunelessly. 'I am peculiar,' he conceded.

He stood at the edge of the final stone block of the unfinished pier. The Burgh lacked resources to extend the pier further and give the town a sound harbour. The swell curved round and broke below us.

'She likes me,' I said. 'You ken right well she does.'

'She likes you well enough,' he said. 'But she is not for you.'

'Who says so? You, as head of the household? Or your absent father?'

He flinched as though I'd flicked a whip at him. 'My sister is not at my command, even if I wished it.' He wasn't whistling now. 'Rosie may laugh and smile and be very clever – I know none more penetrating – but she is realistic. What do you want wi her?'

I knew only I wanted to be in her company, see her lips move and hear her mind.

'Nothing dishonourable,' I managed. I looked down at the gurly sea, the dark weed flexing in the swell. 'I don't know . . . Perhaps to marry.'

'Marry! Dinna be ridiculous!'

I charged at him and we went over the edge in a swirl of red gowns.

THE WATER WAS COLD, then very cold. But it was deep enough to break our fall and not enough to drown in. It seemed Captain Wandhaver was right, I had not the face for drowning though I might yet hang.

Nicolson's arms were tangled in his low-slung gown. The sea was up at my throat as I stooped and grabbed him to his feet. We staggered back alongside the unfinished pier, through weed and over skerries, then fell enfeebled on the shore.

The passing town lads found us hilarious. We pretended our plunge had been a wager. They did not believe us and strutted off sniggering. A small boy offered to swim out and fetch back Nicolson's staff, for a fee.

We squelched back up from the harbour, through the East Port past the Hebdomadar.

'Fines!' he hissed triumphantly. 'There'll be fines for fechtin!'

We got as far as Southgait where we would each go our way.

My sodden cloak weighed a ton, and cold had stripped my limbs of strength. My jaw scarcely worked.

'I'll pay the fines,' I managed. 'My fault.'

'Na.' He looked down, then up at me. 'Mither aye says I hae a mouth like a haddock. Ma fault tae.'

The immersion had stripped him back to his mother tongue. He reached out, clasped my arm. A froth of salt water ran over his fingers.

'Win her if ye caun,' he said, and almost smiled. 'Ye're no ridiculous at aa, jist young.'

He limped away towards Fishertown. I shook myself like a water-logged hound, then squelched back to my bunk.

CHAPTER 10

A Sermon on Calumny

THE TOWN HAD BECOME agitated and charged, as if the Creator had rubbed amber across His celestial sleeve and passed it over St Andrews. Rumours fizzed and crackled. Spaniards had poisoned the Castle well. Witches had been seen at the pier-ends of fishing burghs, raising storms. A French army had landed in Berwick to restore our Queen Mary in place of her son. Another Bartholomew Day's Massacre of Protestants was planned.

In the midst of this febrile stirring, Jeb Auchterlone stopped me by the Links to warn me of a petition demanding that Rose Nicolson be brought to account for blasphemy, atheism and necromancy. It had many signatures and marks, some of them from Fishertown.

On my way to lectures, I glimpsed Tom with James Melville in the distance, walking out on the West Sands. Nathaniel Pow glowered at me outside the ruins of Blackfriars. Rose stayed indoors. Her mother, embarrassed but unyielding, would not let me in to see her.

Through a bribe of candies for the younger Nicolson brother, Bobbie, I managed to arrange a meeting under cover of darkness. I chapped on the door of the gear-cellar, the same one where Tom and I had once stored the Dean's church goods. Rose let me in, barred the door, tended the sole candle. She sat on a fish box. I sat by her on a heap of nets. We had never been so close alone before.

The candle wavered, chasing shadows across her face. 'Thank you for the other afternoon, Will,' she said. Her hand closed warm on my arm. I put my hand on hers. 'I'll no forget.'

'You are lovely beyond measure,' I blurted.

Flushed in the candlelight, she looked into my eyes.

'So that's the way of it,' she murmured.

'No syllogism has ever been as certain.'

She smiled a little at that. Put her other hand on mine. 'And I thought ye just loved me for my mind.'

'Your mind astonishes me and worries me,' I replied. 'It has got you in trouble deep.'

'I ken,' she said. 'I try to keep my thoughts tae masel, but sometimes . . . Had I Faith and no desires, I'd enter a Sisterhood, if any remained in this dour country.'

'I'll protect you!' I exclaimed. 'I can make a living by scrivening or trading. We can live anywhere. Money kens no borders!'

She reached out and touched my face. Nothing important had happened in my life before we stared at each other. 'You think you are so hard-headed,' she said softly. 'My wee dreamer.'

'I love ye, Rose Nicolson.'

She put her fingers to her lips. Without taking her eyes off mine, she gently touched her moistened fingers to my mouth.

'I'm protected among my ain folk,' she said. 'Johnny is a guid man and strong, and he leaves my mind alane. He has standing here.'

'He is no equal for you!'

'And you are?'

'I will try to be so!'

'Besides,' she said softly, 'I sair fancy him. That counts for a hundred philosophies.'

I felt a dirk had been planted in my heart. I made a final plea. 'I have a fuller understanding of you, Rosie.'

She stared back at me, looked down at her hands. 'Understanding is over-rated, Will. See where it's brought me.'

'Kiss me and we'll ken where we stand.'

She stared at me. The corner of her lip lifted. Her eye brightened. She began to lean in.

A sharp crack on the door. 'Rosie! Oot o there!' Tom Nicolson's voice, hoarse and low.

She jumped up and unbarred the door. He limped in, staff in hand. Glared at us.

'This isna helping,' he hissed. 'Awa hame!'

Out in the lane I met two of Pow's acolytes with a shuttered lantern. They muttered most un-Christianlike as I pushed by. I got home like a blind man, by feel alone, lips tingling where her fingers had touched.

THAT SABBATH JAMES MELVILLE preached again in the town kirk. Myself and Tom Nicolson were there. Rose stayed at home. The place was full, for young Melville had a growing reputation and his uncle was leader of the Calvinist wing of the Kirk.

After the keening Psalms, James Melville climbed into the pulpit. He paused and looked around, handsome, humble, assured. He let silence bind us, then he spoke. His voice was calm and clear, not hectoring, not *de haut en bas* but as among equals. He took as his text Titus 3:2. *Speak no evil.*

He spoke of our tumultuous, divided times. He enlarged his reference to 2 Timothy 3:3, where Paul lists the sins that characterize such periods, including *false accusers.*

I glanced at Tom Nicolson, saw a small smile flicker. In front of us, Pow's neck reddened. With reference to further Scripture such as Corinthians and Ephesians, Melville spoke of Malice, Jealousy, Envy, Vengeance. *Do not revile. Look into your heart when you speak against others.*

I sat back, well content to be on this voyage.

'Timothy and Titus urge that we require evidence, proof, and reliable witnesses when we speak against others. Otherwise it is but slander, and slander is sinful. Surely, friends, Satan is the ultimate slanderer!'

Melville was leaning forward into the sunlight beams through the new clear glass windows. I thought of my father, how he would have welcomed this passionate communing, the Holy Book in plain vernacular, the minister but a man among men and women.

'In Scripture we have infallible revelation, but in life we are often mistaken, sometimes sincerely, sometimes in Malice. Look into your hearts, friends.'

I did, and saw much that was tawdry there. James Melville leaned back, spread his hand tenderly over the Book before him, and whispered the finest words therein: *Be still. Fear not. God is Love.*

Who would take issue with that? I wished my mother were here, instead of intoxicated by her Latin Mass in some secret place. Still, I blessed her inwardly, and felt some healing in what passed for my soul.

Melville announced Psalm 141: *Set a guard, O Lord, over my mouth; Keep watch over the door of my lips.* As we intoned, though I was dubious of some articles of the Faith, and keenly felt the absence of beauty, uplift and mystery in our cleansed and sober kirk, I sensed myself a Protestant doubter.

We shook hands with Melville outside the kirk. I thanked him for his teaching against Calumny.

'The teaching is not mine, Will, but Holy Scripture's.' His eyes shone. He was, among other things, a performer sailing on the backing wind of his performance. Tom shook his hand, fervently gripped his arm as they arranged to meet again soon at his lodgings in Anster Wester.

Nathaniel Pow shuffled past with his followers, eyes down. Perhaps he was contemplating his heart. Still, I took care to avoid him and his entourage, until in time events made this kerfuffle as nothing.

A FEW DAYS LATER, I found Rose walking on the beach below the Bishop's Castle.

'Thank you,' she said. 'My accusers have gone back into the shadows of the wynds.'

'Thank Melville,' I replied. 'And the Scriptures.'

'I'm sure Pow could find a dozen contrary ones.' I rather agreed, but begged her to mind her tongue for her own safety. She shrugged. 'Young Melville has as keen an eye for a lass as Pow, though a better heart. He advises I marry soon for my reputation's sake, and set up hame some distance from here.'

'What think you of this?'

'I think my brither is excited about going to see Melville in Anster. They'll play gowf! They will have such conversations! James has promised to bring his lute out of retirement!'

'Melville has done us a service,' I replied, aware she had abruptly changed the subject.

She pursed the lips I had once been within a heartbeat of kissing. 'I'm soon awa to Eyemouth for a while,' she said. 'Safer yon way.'

'You'll no forget what I said in the cellar?'

For a moment she looked me in the een. 'How could I?'

My heart rose like a laverock in the morning. I went on my way to morning prayers, whistling *O I loved a lass* – an unreformed faith, but my own.

MELVILLE'S SERMON, TOGETHER WITH his standing among the Reformers, seemed to have done the job. Though Pow looked dirks whenever I passed him in The Pends, and Bella Muir still queened it among the fisher lasses on the Green, for the time being there was no more talk of pursuing Rose Nicolson for heresy, atheism or necromancy.

I thought constantly on our meeting in the gear-cellar, her hand on mine, my blurted love. I did not regret saying it. I called at the cottage but she was already gone south following the herring, and her brother was still away visiting Melville in Ainster.

Then he was back, limping through the West Port, eyes down. I seized him by the arm. 'How went your stay?' I asked. 'Did you resolve the great questions of the age?' He shook his wild salt-stiffened hair. 'Play gowf?' No response. 'At least, drank long into the night?'

Nicolson flushed and looked away. He seemed to wish only to escape me. 'Drink was taken,' he said at last. 'Perhaps o'er muckle.'

What had happened? An argument? About Rose? On some point of doctrine or doubt? Tom shook his head and limped away, clamped shut as any barnacle.

The next time we saw James Melville in the street, one man flinched and the other went pale as chalk. They nodded to each other, eyes not meeting, then walked on.

There was no more talk from Tom of the glories of Calvin, which was something of a relief.

IT WAS A RARE soft afternoon towards the end of Whitsun. I had come from a formal disputation with Saltine and Reekie where we argued the toss between Faith, Good Works or Happiness as our best aim in life. Saltine promoted Good Works, tried to reason that they were an attribute of the Elect though in no way interfering with God's choice in the matter. He rather tied his bootlaces together over Free Will, and a quick push brought him down.

Reekie attempted to cast Aristotle as a proto-Calvinist who, somewhat contrary to the tenor of the *Nicomachean Ethics*, held that we are justified by Faith alone. In response I had aired that Luther, when translating the Bible into German, had added the word *alone* to 'saved by Faith' in Romans 1:17. I suggested that, assuming we were having a scholarly debate not a theological one, this addition of *alone* could be said to be putting one's thumb on the scales. The argument was entirely borrowed from Rose, expressed less saltily.

I moved on quickly, to avoid the wrath of the fundamentalists, but saw Regent Abernethy smirk behind his ancient hand, and Nicolson nodded approvingly.

After the debate, Tom shook hands with me, bade farewell for the summer, added his family's best wishes then limped away. Then he paused and turned.

'Rosie returned from Eyemouth this morn,' he said. 'You may wish to see her afore returning to Embra.' He nodded and was gone.

THE AIR WAS WARM and salty, loud with gulls. I stravaiged along the beach below the Castle, idly looking into tidal pools. I picked out a small flat oval stone and let it dry in my palm. It had one round hole at the centre, and another, smaller, off near the edge. Some accident of the sea? An ornament from old, old times, worn by one of the first fishers of Kilrymont?

I wiggled my little finger through the small hole, then tried to fit my ring finger through the other. It would not quite go.

'Haud by, Will!'

I turned to see Rose Nicolson hastening my way, in bare feet and work apron, still clutching her mending-spindle.

'I hoped to see you afore you're off hame!' she cried. Her voice broader Fife than I'd remembered. Her hand on my goon was reddened and chafed, her wrist scarred from the gutting knife. 'Are ye weel?'

'Well enough, thank you.' I shrugged, and added, 'Probably no wiser. And yourself?'

She opened her mouth to the air as she had once opened it to me. 'Doin' awa,' she said at last. Then she grimaced, added: '*Semper fidelis, semper felicitas.*'

'You haven't forgotten your Horace, then.'

She smiled, a little sadly, I thought. 'Those fish have swum. You look older.'

'I expect so,' I replied. 'Here – a keepsake for you.'

I held out the stone disc. She looked down at it, then up at me. A smile began to furl along her lower lip, a breaking wave. She took a step towards me to take the stone. Then her mouth opened on mine and mine on hers.

It was not like the practice kisses from my dear dead sister. Nor was it the poetical kiss of Petrarch's verses. Nothing had prepared me for this, so far removed from my romantic day-dreams and my nightly shameful horn. This was warm, moist, entirely bodily yet soul-opening. Her lips and being melded into mine.

That profound kiss lasted but a minute and has lasted me a lifetime.

Chattering voices on the evening air. She pulled back. I let her go. She took the stone from my hand, and smiled. How many nights would I ponder the import of that smile?

'I shall keep it wi mine,' she said.

Her name was cried from the harbour. John Gourlay was hurrying our way.

I went up the brae. As I gained the crest, a clod whizzed by my head, splattered against the archway. Gourlay was standing by her. He was laughing scornfully, she did not look best pleased. Had I been carrying my father's dirk, I would have run back at him and used it.

Instead I walked away, back to my bunk to pack my gear for home. I rotated my head, as though that would clear my mind, let my shoulders drop, as though that would release my heart.

What a piece of work I am, that can encompass fleshly desire, tenderness, sorrow and soul, and the impulse to violence, all within one afternoon? Did Aristotle know of this? Did the risen Christ?

CHAPTER 11

The Skelpit Dug

How that summer in Embra dragged out, like the ray of the setting sun across the Firth. I could not confide in my sister, nor my mother who seemed wholly caught up in dealings with the French estates of her exiled Queen. Fantasies, I thought, fantasies of return and restoration. Morton's grip on the Regency was greedy but still seemed sure.

Meanwhile I lived with my own imaginings. I thought much of that kiss, Rose's parting smile, her lips shaping *Sorry*. I thought to write to her but that was no way to propose, and in any case what could I offer? Day and night I ached, inflamed as though poisoned. I wrote some less bad poems that would one day be recast within *The Tarantula of Love*.

On a less exalted plane, I did some trading in recent carving from the Low Countries – Lutheran and sombrely glowing – with some notion of having prospects to lay at the feet of my beloved when next we met.

And there was gowf at Brunt's Field, with John Drummond of Hawthornden, to bring relief. Drummond proved both lichtsome and scholarly, and a dab hand with a niblick. He was a Reformist, but one more Humanist than Calvinist. When I brought him home, my sister Susannah's eyes glowed. He glowed back. When he played the lute in her company there was little need for candles, such was the brightness in our kitchen.

My mother, seeing the way of things, herself loving music, and taking to his open-handed ways and good looks, chose to overlook his religious loyalties: *A man so kindly and melodic must be a Papist at heart* – which I thought a slur on my father. In any case, Drummond was a gentleman of modest estate. He would do well. My sister thought so too.

I saw their eager happiness, and ached for my own. Aching for my future when I would be someone of substance and achievement. Aching for my childhood when my father was alive, our Queen still in Scotland, and the Castle still intact.

And aching of course for Rose Nicolson. That kiss. Her vexed look at Gourlay. On these slender pegs I hung my hopes.

THIS TIME I DISPENSED with the *Sonsie Quine* and rode post horses from Embra to St Andrews. I felt this to be more grown-up, and I had money in my purse from the Lutheran carvings. Less remained after I had gone to the Bursar and paid my exorbitant fees for an education I could now see was patchy at best – like the cloak of Tom Nicolson crossing the quad towards me.

He told me he had been accepted for a doctorate on Averroes, the Arabian philosopher. 'He defends philosophy against the dictates of religion!' he exclaimed. 'How wonderful!'

He enthused about the synthesis of Islam and the Greek masters, and how the times were ripe for Averroes' reappraisal. '*The Incoherence of the Incoherent*!' he exclaimed. 'What a title!'

'You might as well cast your shoe at a cloud to knock it from the sky, as engage with such vapourings.'

Nicolson chuckled, undeterred. Then he grasped my arm, leaned in closer. 'Claud and John Hamilton are back in town wi their mad cousins. Don't go wandering around at night.'

My stomach began to emit sharp pains. 'What are they here for?'

'Politics and mischief, what else?'

'I'll ca canny,' I promised.

We watched a couple of dazed and wide-eyed bejantines being led by the Hebdomadar into his rooms. They were sending children now.

'And your sister,' I said casually. 'She is well?'

'Well enough, for one gutting and salting in Craster.' He glanced at me. 'So you didn't meet any fine lassies in Embra?'

'The only ones I met were awfy dour or awfy silly. My heart's unchanged.'

'Will,' he said gently. 'My sister is a fishwife fae a long line of fishwives back to the making of the world. That she can read and write and reason well is grand, but she is going wi a man with a half-share in a boat, and a quarter in two others. She's kent Johnny Gourlay since they were bairns.'

I chewed my new attempted Italian moustache, near to tears of frustration. 'I will study and scribe,' I cried. 'I will trade. I shall win her!'

I stomped off to my lectures on Aristotle's Natural Philosophy, the study of the world as it is.

IN OUR THIRD YEAR my peers and I wore our gowns wrapped across our backs, signalling our sophistication (or our decline). By now we took the cold for granted, as we did thinking in Latin, ever-rising fees, grasping landladies, the railings of fanatics, and weary teachers clinging to their meagre salaries.

Regent Morton still held sway, though the Calvinists had concluded he was the wrong sort of Protestant, while the Kirk and town councils fumed at Morton's collaring a share of their benefices. A fresh bout of unrest was running through the country like the plague. Rumour walked abroad, dressed up as News. I heard a man in Merkitgate insist Jamie Saxt had died when still a child in Stirling Castle, and the lad with the unsteady gait had long been an impostor – to what end was left to imagination. Some scoffed, but as many walked away infected, for what could disprove such a claim?

The fever reached new heights some weeks into the term when it was announced Regent Morton was coming to St Andrews.

I emerged from my bunk, walked along North Street. A lively crowd had gathered to see Morton ride with his followers and guards along the Scaurs and into the Bishop's Castle, clutching a fine fringed hat against the gale.

'Aye, he is getting fat, right enough.'

'So would you be if ye had the Kirk's benifices streaming into yer pooch.'

Morton was a big-shouldered, full-bearded, meat-faced man. I got a glimpse of red hair, coarse complexion, a gap-toothed smile. His broadsword looked too large for use, but those who flanked him seemed handy, heads turning, their hands ready on swords and pistols. Ever since Regent Moray's assassination in Linlithgow, and then Regent Lennox being shot dead in a street scuffle in Stirling, public appearances of our high heid yins had become edgy affairs.

Still, no one attempted to shoot or stab Regent Morton as he and his red-haired entourage rode by, up the drawbrig and with a gracious wave disappeared within. Assorted lords and earls followed on. Argyll, Atholl and Erskine of Gogar, Catholics all, blank-faced or joking, deep in thought or waving to their people. George Buchanan went by on foot. He noticed me, nodded gravely, then walked in alone. There were some boos, some cheers, jostling and scowling, but no fatalities.

The folk of the town, some doubtless disappointed, dispersed to their business. John, Claud and David Hamilton turned away down The Scaurs, too absorbed in their conversation to do more than scowl at me.

When we emerged from lectures, the town was further agitated. There were more men with red hair, swords and pistols, and their followers, some in livery. It was said Regent Morton was closeted with the Dean and the Principal, then meeting with the Kirk session, going on to dine with the Burgh Council and assorted Lords and Fife lairds. Keeping his head on his shoulders had become full-time work.

'I trust our Regent has brought his own food taster!' Ogilvie said as we ate at the Whins, our latest favoured howff near the Links. I liked it less when the Hamiltons and Billy Hay plonked themselves down nearby.

'A tasteless remark, considering the fate of Regent Mar,' Hay declared. 'It would be divine justice if Morton drank a fatal glass!'

It was common knowledge that Mar had died in agony after a banquet *chez* Morton. It was also dangerous to voice aloud in a crowded house. We looked at our plates.

'In our Scotland it is safest to humble oneself before God and remain insignificant,' Jimmy Motion opined. He could be relied on to offer up dull pearls of piety.

'You'll be safe enough then, Jim,' Tam Anderson said, and we all cracked up, even the Hamiltons. Then we toasted the term to come, with wine that was rough but at least not actively poisoned.

OUR IRON-LUNGED TOWN CRIER proclaimed a public holiday, the University included. At noon in the Merkitgait, the Burgh Council announced that Morton had granted funds for extending the harbour wall, which would be good for the fisher folk and skippers and supporters of Morton, and bad for what remained of the Cathedral, which was becoming more skeletal with every passing month.

Tom Nicolson was much cheered by this news. The Hamiltons and their followers – there seemed a lot of them strutting around – looked sour and angry, but then they often did. As the day wore on and more drink was taken, scuffles began breaking out in the streets and howffs. I noticed a number of troublesome faces kent from Embra – Kerrs, Johnstones and the like.

Tom and I went down to the Links for some peace and safety. Sheep grazed, fishwives mended nets and aired their laundry, while gowfers played intently, for it was a fine day and almost warm. I watched our former fellow student Jeb Auchterlone going down the fifth with Tam Anderson (a handy player with a baffie), plus the new Earl of Mar I recognised from Embra at his father's funeral procession, and a laird with a very large hat and a hacking swing that pained me to look on.

'Yon's Kirkcaldy of Grange's son,' Nicolson said in my ear.

Straightaway I was a boy, watching three hanged men turning slowly in the late sun flooding the Market Cross, below the half-ruined Castle, just as Preacher Knox had once prophesied. The execution of Kirkcaldy of Grange had been Morton's doing, the supposedly final defeat of the Queen's Men.

I turned away, unable to look at that terrible swing.

And looked into the bonniest face I knew. The day grew brighter as Rose Nicolson smiled on me. She was dressed in blue, her Holy

Day clothes, two shades lighter than the autumnal sky. Dove-grey pointed shoes, mud and grass on their tips. White gloves, stretched and baggy around the wrist. The lovely curve of her dark brows above deep blue eyes. The curve of her lips, that had parted for me. I saw the whole of her in one, as one might see the good Earth on Creation.

She turned to the man on her right, and the day grew dark again.

'Johnny, you'll mind Will Fowler, that keeps my brother from his books. And at one time helped me with mine. Will, you ken my fiancé.'

John Gourlay stared at me. He was strong-shouldered, dark-faced. He did not like me or my gown. Why would he? We lived in the same town, but under different regimens.

We talked awhile, the four of us, on the sunlit Links by the Swilcan burn. Her blue holiday dress, her man in dark serge, and our red goonies, all ruffled by the breeze. We spoke, I think, of the movement of the herring and Morton's visit, while I dangled from her smile and voice and shining eyes, helpless as Kirkcaldy of Grange turning on his rope.

In truth I heard little she said after *my fiancé*. I had thought there would be time to change her mind, and now there wasn't.

Gourlay was in his best gear. His tight-fitting jacket had dark blue trim around the collar and cuffs, most like done by his mother or his wife-to-be. He looked proud and uncomfortable, as I once had in my scholar's gown. I could not take my eyes off that trim, a simple double zig-zag. The work of it. The time. Her time. The hungry pride with which he looked on her. It all moved me near to tears.

'WHEN WAS THIS ENGAGEMENT decided?' I managed as we passed into The Scaurs.

Nicolson glanced at me, looked a bit shifty. 'Some days back, down in Craster. Gourlay was on the line boats, and she was salting on the pier. They have set a date for the end of the autumn drave.' He sounded both rueful and proud. 'I'd have thought to say once she tellt me, but Averroes has been much on my mind. I feel I am being shown the nature of the universe.'

'How pleasant for you,' I said. 'And what if it is an ill nature?'

We bumped into a group of town lads warming up for trouble. Fortunately they recognised Nicolson as one of their own, and let us pass in favour of shouting insults at a group of Johnstones, some armed. We hastened through Butts Wynd, past the two uneasy pikemen there, and took the long back way to the college.

At last Nicolson spoke. 'Will, Rosie likes you fine but she was never for you.'

'Not part of the nature of the universe, then?'

'Not the real one. Johnny Gourlay is dour but decent, they have long kent each other. When he is elected to the Presbytery, he can protect her from further interrogations. We canna call on James Melville's aid again.'

I still wondered why not, but for sure it left Rose more exposed.

I enlisted the Cynics – after all, a girl is just a girl, a piece of flesh that touches your heart for an hour. A kiss is just a meeting of lips. I summonsed the Stoics – after all, we are all going to die and soon enough, so no point getting het up about anything.

Neither consideration helped a jot. We crossed the Kinness burn, came up the brae to St Leonard's, and distraction appeared in the tubby frame of the Hebdomadar.

'I hae glad tidings for you twa buggers.'

He announced that Nicolson had been awarded a scholarship, following his routing of the Ramists at the disputation at the end of last term. And I had won a prize of three pounds Scots for best poem in the vernacular (four were submitted, one of which was obscene and another ill-spelled – but still!).

The day set on a fresh course, though the disturbance from meeting Rose and her man still sloshed murkily in the bilges of my heart (an image I intended to work on later). We resolved to celebrate our good fortune. We reasoned that it would be best to avoid the town, which was in raised, hectic mood. Nicolson proposed the most out-of-the way and least popular howff, The Skelpit Dug, out by the old Lepers' Hospital. We would be untroubled there.

I wonder still what difference it would have made had we gone elsewhere. I see Rose Nicolson's hand pausing with the shuttle among the rent threads of old nets. Pausing, taking in the shape and structure of the whole, seeing what needed done and then doing it, tightening and making good under grey sky and ceaseless wind.

WE RESOLVED TO GO out incognito, without our gowns. This was in part canniness, given the restlessness of the town. We too were in a thrawn, rebellious mood. I kept warm in my father's old sealskin weskit, coarse cloth breeches, and a greasy leather Dutchman's cap, courtesy of Captain Wandhaver of the *Sonsie Quine*.

Waiting for Nicolson in my bunk room, I looked in the keeking-glass by which I had begun to shave. I did not see a scholar, nor a burgess's son. I looked like someone I would rather not meet in a narrow wynd, which was exactly how I felt.

On impulse I opened my trunk and took out my father's blade, pouched it, then tucked it away within my weskit. Yes, I was a cack-handed poet rejected in love, but at least I looked like one you would not wish to cross. I aimed to invoke Catullus on the prowl in Rome's midnight piazzas.

Miss Whitton bawled from below. I descended to find Tom Nicolson improbably flirting with my landlady. He was grinning in some patched garment apparently made from sacking, a villainous black hat perched high on his mad hair, gripping his stick.

'Aye, you weel deserve each other,' Miss Whitton said, shutting the door on us. 'Dinna wake me coming in.'

We were in hectic mood and no mistake. The town likewise. We kept our heads down as we hurried through the shouty streets and packed wynds, heading down to the harbour, then with relief emerged onto the empty beach.

Stars were coming out in the dim blue, a yellow rind of moon ducked in and out of clouds. It minded me of that long-ago, when

Tom and I had pushed our handcart with the Dean's church goods to their hiding place. Since then I had been a mostly sober student, keeping out of trouble, working on my shorthand and Italian with Nicol Burne. Over the terms I had progressed through Grammar, Rhetoric and Logic, to Plato and Plotinus, all the way to Aquinas, and was finally being initiated into the more wordly Aristotle. I had taken notes, sweated through presentations and stammered through disputation.

I had been industrious and a little dull. In all likelihood I would remain so. I would write some poetry, though none would ever truly express what lay in my mind. I had done what my father had hoped for, and my mother had expected. I had laboured by day and into the night by candlelight and creusie lamp, imagining a time I would lay it all at the strong fine feet of Rose Nicolson.

My youth had passed in dreams and delusions. Rosie was to be married. It was o'er late to unmake. Pale breakers to our left, dunes to our right, the sand spurted under our feet as we hurried on through near-darkness towards the feeble light of The Skelpit Dug.

TWO BUNDLES OF RAGS stirred at a corner bench as we entered. The man at the bar flinched as we came in. He was stooping but strong as he stared at us. His big hand strayed over the cudgel on the counter, then relaxed.

'Ah, young Nicolson,' he said. 'Whit are ye wantin here?'

'Fine food and strong drink, Scobie.'

'And a couple of dancing quines,' I added.

He fixed on me, eyes dark in their pits. 'There are nae dancing quines here, son.'

'I have been sorely misinformed.'

'Weel, ye'll no be sorely missed when ye go.'

Standard repartee, but the man seemed ill at ease. The two men in the corner muttered, then bent over their jars.

'When she is sober, Scobie's wife maks the best fish stew in Kilrymont,' Nicolson informed me. 'Is she on form the nicht?'

'*This nicht, this ae nicht, every nicht and aa, Fire an salt and candle licht, And Christ receive thy soul*,' the landlord intoned, and something in his tone made my flesh crawl. Then he shrugged. 'She is aye on form,' he said. 'Since last Candlemas she is sober as a kirk minister when the bishop calls.'

He tapped out a brandy each, then hurried us up the stair and into a little room on the left.

'How about the room wi the fire?' Tom asked.

The landlord shook his head.

'Taken. They want left alane.'

I heard voices through the wall, a burst of harsh laughter, a young voice. Scobie hurried off and left Tom and I alone. We toasted each other's good fortune, knocked back the brandy. *Here's tae us! Wha's like us?* Heat rose from the belly into the mind.

'The cudgel? A little extreme.'

'The clientele here can get a bittie rough,' Tom said. 'He seldom uses it.' Next door voices rose, then subdued. 'It's not usually quiet as this on a holiday. Strange.'

The fish stew came in pots, set down with harsh rye bread. It was good. The wine was the kind best knocked back before the taste registered, so we did.

We toasted each other's success. We talked – he talked – of Parmenides and Averroes, of flux and flow and change. We talked of Plato's eternal forms, by which cats and dogs, trees and tempests, he and I, are as they are. Can that be so? Is the theory consistent with itself? Does it explain anything at all?

When Nicolson's mood took him, he made philosophy seem not a dead debate but something vital, as though Understanding was within our grasp if we persisted. Unlike every scholar I had encountered, bar Rose, he seemed to have little interest in reaching a position, building a fortress, and then defending it. Like her, he wanted to think and talk and see where it might take us.

We did not talk about his sister and her husband-to-be. I did not say she had kissed me, full-hearted and without reservation. Had she kenned full well she would marry Gourlay? Or had I been o'er blate and so missed my moment?

The voices next door had fallen silent. The wind must have dropped, for the night was exceeding quiet. Quiet enough to hear a faint jingle-jangle and an exhalation of horses.

I went to the window and looked down. The tavern door was open, and light spilled onto two men who had just dismounted.

One leaned forward, removed his hat and then I knew him. Claud Hamilton. A sword glimmered at his belt.

I gestured urgently to Nicolson. He limped to my side, looked down. Our landlord had his hands raised as if to ward off or deny. They must be talking low because we could hear nothing. The other man – thin, all in black, bare-headed and bald as a gowf ball, short rapier at his hip – reached out and put his finger on Scobie's lips as if rebuking a foolish child. Our landlord stared ahead as though turned to stone, and that frightened me more than anything.

'His name is Pate Wilson,' Nicolson whispered. 'This is not good.'

The group stepped inside. How quickly one's head can clear. We heard the first soft creak on the stair and knew that the horsemen had not come to drink. I fumbled within my shirt and drew out my father's blade. Tom's eyes widened. He nodded approval, then pointed me to the hinged side of the door.

Stationed at the far side of the doorway, Nicolson clutched his staff in both hands. He leaned forward as feet mounted the stairs. They gained the corridor. We must strike first and hard to have any chance.

Silence outside our door. The knife haft was sweat-slippery in my fist. In the lamplight Tom's pale face was intent, calm, ready.

Slither of boot and creak of floor, moving past, further along the corridor. Then a door banged open. Shouts, a boy's scream, a crash. On the instant we were out in the dark corridor, stairs down to the left, the lit doorway to our right.

We went right. God may ken why. Perhaps the youthfulness of the cry. In any case, that moment in the corridor of the shabby howff – not even a decision but an impulse – determined much that came thereafter.

We were in a room where an unarmed lad held a stool before him, screaming defiance at a tall man closing on him with sword and dagger. Claud Hamilton stood a little back with a pistol in his fist. The man called Pate Wilson paused, then turned towards me with a rapier and a smile from Hell. Hamilton cursed and raised his firearm at Tom. As Wilson closed on me, I glimpsed a blur of staff and Hamilton screamed, jumped back clutching his arm, his pistol falling.

Tom's staff whirled again and smashed the hanging lamp. Burning oil fell, then all was dark. Someone was muttering *Fuck fuck fuck*. I dropped to my knees, felt some material drag over my head. In sudden fury I stabbed and slashed upward. Felt my blade jar. *Christ!* A gasp, groan, whimper, a thud on the floor.

Someone rushed past down the stairs, knocking me to the ground. Small flames flickered on the floor beside a slowing body. By their light I saw Wilson hesitate between Nicolson and me. He chose Tom, who whirled his staff as he backed away. Wilson grinned, flicked rapier and dagger, and came on, practised and sure.

Behind him, the red-haired boy darted to the dying stranger on the floor, plucked the dagger from its hand, then whacked it into Pate Wilson's back. Wilson twisted and fell. The terrifying, terrified boy knelt across him and with both hands drove the dagger to the hilt.

CHAPTER 12

A Fellowship Sealed in Blood

A LAST EXHALE FROM WILSON, then silence but for our heaving breath and Claud Hamilton's horse galloping away into the night. Small flames flickered on the floor, not quite catching. Two dead men and three still living.

The laddie rose from his knees. His face and jaw had filled out and he had the first wisps of a moustache and he was now taller than me, but there was no mistaking the boy from the *Sonsie Quine*. Lamplight bloomed and the landlord Scobie stepped cautiously into the room.

'Oh man,' he said. 'Man!'

He stamped out the flames that licked the dead stranger on the floor. 'I didna think it would come to this,' he said. He turned towards the boy. 'Honest.'

'Aye, sure,' the boy said angrily, and stepped towards him.

Nicolson limped forward, hand up. 'No,' he said. 'Enough of that. He'll not clype on you.'

'*Certes,*' Scobie said.

'None of us will inform on each other,' I said. 'We are all inno-cent, all guilty here.'

The lad stared at me. 'I am indebted to ye yet again, friend.' He wiped his bloody hand on his breeches, held it out. 'I am Walter Scott,' he said grandly, 'retoured heir to Branxholme and Buccleuch.'

'Will Fowler of Anchor Close, Embra,' I managed. His palm was sticky against mine as he unpeeled it.

'And I am Nicolson of Fishertown,' Tom said. 'Master of phil-osophy, lord of fuck-all.'

Scott gave him a sharp look, then nodded. 'May you forget what you have learned tonight,' he said as he took my friend's hand. In this manner our . . . what shall I best call it? Fellowship? Long friendship? Bondage? – was founded and sealed in blood.

'Best clear up afore licht,' Scobie said.

'GOOD STICK WORK,' WALTER Scott said to Nicolson as we loaded the bodies of Wilson and the unknown man into the boat. 'You're a bonnie fighter, friend.'

'No, I'm a philosopher.'

'I had not dreamed of such a philosophy.'

'The great Socrates fought in the Spartan wars.'

'How many did he kill?'

'None, so far as I know.'

Scott bound a sackful of stones to the unknown man's legs. 'Lucky him.'

He worked quickly, with a certain swagger, but I had heard terror in his young voice and his grunted sobs after. He knew fear like the rest of us, and he knew that I knew – for which he never entirely forgave me. Only during our last meeting in Antwerp, so many years on, would that change, before he bravely passed beyond bravado.

I asked about Pate Wilson. Who he?

'He used to kill people,' Tom said.

'A soldier?'

'A hired man. A specialist.'

Scott looked up from lashing a stone slab across Pate Wilson's bloody back. 'Some say it was he shot Regent Mar in the street in Stirling,' he said. 'And Regent Moray in Linlithgow.'

'Nah,' Scobie said. 'Aabody kens that was Hamilton of Bothwell-haugh, from ahint the washing.'

'Believe that and you'll believe the sun goes roon the Earth,' Tom muttered.

'Does it not?' from Scott, innocently or otherwise.

'Not in my book,' Tom said.

'I must read your book when I have the time,' Scott said.

'You can make the time,' Nicolson suggested.

'Na, the times mak me.' Scott giggled. 'Bothwellhaugh kent as much about using a carbine as my arse does about mathematics.'

We were chattering away like we were born to this, though it was nerves and bravado. The light was already coming in fast. Scobie went off to bury the swords, though I suspect he kept the fine pistol to sell. Scott and Nicolson rowed the boat with the two bodies out to deep water off the point and came back with it empty.

I went into The Skelpit Dug to scrub dried life blood from my blade and hands.

SCOTT ABRUPTLY LEFT US. He shook hands, told us to wait by the inn till he returned. In truth we were exhausted and incapable of going anywhere.

We watched him hurry away across along the beach, heading for town. His red hair flamed in the low winter sun. He seemed a brand on legs, the world caught fire around him.

'I doubt we'll see him again,' Scobie muttered. 'Yon lad is dangerous to ken.'

'Dangerous not to ken,' I said. 'What if Claud Hamilton comes back?'

Nicolson shook his head. 'You cut him, and I broke his arm.'

'But his brothers and followers? Can we ever go back?'

Something like a chuckle from Nicolson. 'According to Heraclitus, no.'

'God give me strength! What are we going to do?'

Nicolson's stick rolled from his knee to the ground. He left it there. His head dropped. 'Dinna ask me,' he said. 'I'm a philosopher. I can only tell you how best to bear it.'

We sat there, staring at his stick. It would have made a fine allegorical etching, two shocked young men staring down at a staff neither has the energy to pick up. It could be titled *The Limitations of Philosophy*.

SCOBIE PRODUCED PORRIDGE AND brandy, muttered '*Get awa hame*', went inside and barred the door. Nicolson and I sat astride the dyke, ate and drank.

'Pate Wilson?' I said at last. 'How do you ken the likes of him?'

Nicolson made to speak, had another swig of brandy. 'Through my faither,' he muttered.

'How so?'

'Pate killed people by whatever means, for whoever paid. My faither . . .' He struggled, looked out at the horizon as though its emptiness made speech easier. 'My faither did too, but not for money. He thought of himself as a soldier, only without uniform.'

'In whose cause?'

'For Mary of Guise, then our Queen Mary. He was a Hielander of the Old Faith.'

'You said the fisher folk don't marry out.'

'My faither is an instance why.' His left hand scraped livid furrows across his right arm as he spoke on. 'At Regent Moray's killing, my da prepared the balcony and the washing. Wilson made the shot. My faither held the horse for Hamilton of Bothwellhaugh's escape, then he and Wilson fled. They took ship to France. I have not seen my faither this seven years. It would be death for him to return.' Nicolson paused, then added bitterly, 'In any case, he has undone our family.'

Tom and Rose had always been sceptical, verging on scathing, about high politics. I began to understood why.

Out of nowhere, hoofbeats came thudding up the brae. Five, no, six horsemen, fully armed. We slowly got to our feet. Like good Stoics we awaited our Fate.

The horses paused some distance off, then young Walter Scott rode on alone. He jumped down from a fine Borders cob, now cock of the walk in a blue velvet cloak and a gleaming rapier at his hip.

'We must leave, friends,' he announced. 'Atholl, Argyll and the Hamiltons have called off their attempt on Regent Morton. Most have fled with their injured kinsman – congratulations, lads! – but men are out looking for you.'

Nicolson and I gaped at him. *Attempt? What attempt?*

'We are students,' I managed. 'Harmless students.'

'As of last night you are mair than that. Your names have gone out and cannot be recalled.'

Tom Nicolson and I looked at each other. Had we turned left last night, run down the stair and into the night, instead of right and into that fatal room, we would be free men. We had done this to ourselves.

Scott waved behind, indicating the armed horsemen. 'These are Hepburns, my new stepfather's kinsmen, and can be trusted. We will get you to Branxholme in Teviotdale till this stushie is sorted. A couple of weeks at most, then you can resume your studies – though best stay armed at all times.'

'I'll need to go by my bunk to collect my gear.'

Scott shook his head. 'I'll have it sent on later. We'll pick up fresh horses at Dysart.'

Nicolson and I looked at each other, hesitated.

'You can surely ride?' Scott asked.

'Can you sail an open boat?' Nicolson retorted.

'I've never had the need to,' Scott said grandly.

'Likewise.'

Clinging on to the biggest Hepburns, we left The Skelpit Dug, avoiding the town. Though only a boy, Scott rode ahead as leader, and none challenged him while we moved west through the afternoon.

I WAS ACCUSTOMED TO the slow sway of my father's pack-mules, or a well-schooled hire horse, but this Borders cob was a fighting beast. I clung on to my rider, a tough older man, as we hurried westward through Fife, watchfully skirting the villages of Dairsie and Cupar. At times I felt elated to be riding in armed company, with laverocks and peewits wittering in the lift and the distant sea agleam. Free from the lecture room, free from books, free of complexity! The leaves against the sky were sharp enough to cut the eye that saw them.

We made it without incident as far as Windygates. My guts were shoogled from the bouncing of the horse, but that scunner was naught when, on this side of the burn, a troop of horsemen emerged from the trees, bristling with lances.

We slowed. Looked behind where another dozen or so came over the brae. We stopped.

'Oh bugger,' the man I clung to said, and reached for his crossbow. 'Kerrs and Maxwells.'

Young Walter Scott looked round at us. His face was pale, his red hair spilled out under his hat, his blue cloak caked in mud.

'Haud here,' he said. 'If they kill me, ride like fuck.'

He trotted towards the main group of horse, very upright, his gloved right hand raised well clear of his sword. He was, I reckon, but fifteen. It was the boldest thing I ever saw.

The horsemen closed round him. He seemed to be talking with them. I peered around my horseman, inching my dagger from its sheath. On the back of the cob to my left, Tom Nicolson clutched his staff. His lips were moving but I couldn't hear.

The horsemen behind us stayed back, hands poised on crossbow or lance. Down by the river, the parley went on. Then, faintly on the breeze, laughter. Scott leaned forward and shook hands with the two riders at the centre, then he turned and waved us on.

We rode slowly through the gang as they parted for us. Eyes met mine. Hardened men. One nodded curtly. Another smiled, friend-ly-like, as I went by. Some looked regretful at not killing us, others relieved.

Our horses forded the burn, Scott at the fore. My back prickled, waiting for a crossbow bolt that did not come. As we left the stream and went on into the trees unmolested, I felt warm wet in my breeks.

'For God's sake, dinna mess my saddle,' my rider said over his shoulder as he let his crossbow drop back into its hanger, but he said it kindly enough.

'WHAT DID YOU SAY to them?' I asked Scott as we took a break above Markinch.

'I tellt them the coup had been called off, that Regent Morton is still alive and free with two hundred of his supporters, the King is guarded still in Stirling, and the Hamiltons have left the county. We agreed that sometimes it is better to live to fight another day.'

'Why did they laugh?'

'I invited them to join me on a raid into England next year. See if we can get ourselves some better breeding stock.'

Nicolson stirred from his thoughts. 'Yon was bold and braisant, Buccleuch,' he said. 'I've never seen the like.'

Walter Scott smiled, perhaps even blushed. 'Bold Buccleuch,' he murmured. 'I like that! Has a ring to it.'

So he would be, for the rest of his life, *The Bold Buccleuch*. If the ring fits, wear it – as my wife used to say, sometimes in scorn, sometimes tenderly.

Then we rode on for Dysart. Scott said our lodging there was held by the Douglas family, his mother's people. The sun levelled over the fields, our shadows lengthened. The air was dew-damp, then salty as the coast grew nearer, and for those last hours I knew nothing but drying breeks, the jolt of forward going, and freedom in my surrender to it.

IN A SOLID HOUSE by the harbour we three lay on straw by the fire, letting wine and heat ease our bruises. Empty-headed, I watched the flames. Nothing was certain now, other than that Rosie Nicolson was getting married and I might have killed a man.

To my right, Tom twirled his staff between his palms, contemplating Lord knows what.

'Back in Windygates,' I asked him, 'were you reciting the Lord's Prayer, or Hail Mary?'

'Seneca. *Life, if well lived, is long enough.*'

'Did that help?'

'Not as much as I'd hoped.'

Young Walter Scott laughed as he hunkered in the inglenook, quivering and restless. Long blade of a nose, lips slightly rolled back onto his teeth as though snarling or amused at some joke. The thin beginnings of a beard. High wide forehead, red hair dragged back to his shoulders. The blazing energy of that boy.

'You have helped save my life twice, Master Fowler.' He stared at me and I felt myself nailed to the wall like a pilgrim's plaque. 'I shall discharge that debt when time and Fate allow.'

Nicolson stirred, sensing debate. 'You believe in Fate?

Scott held out his right hand, turned it in the firelight. Wide in the palm, broad-fingered, weathered and scarred already. 'I save myself by this hand. Such is my Fate.'

When he acted, all was calm, strong, certain. But I learned silence and inactivity made Walter Scott strain like a falcon on its leash. 'Last night I killed another man,' he continued at last. 'My grandsire died with his Papal Indulgence safe in a drawer. Now it is Hell or Purgatory for me.'

'Not so long ago, everyone believed the sun went round our Earth,' Nicolson said. 'But that did not make it true. Purgatory is rot.'

Scott looked at us. '*Mon Dieu*,' he said. 'So this is what you get up to at University.'

'We learn a multiplicity of teachings, and how to argue between them,' I said, somewhat pompously.

'And have you come to a conclusion?'

'Not yet,' I admitted.

'And you pay fees for this?' Scott bounced to his feet and bundled more logs on the fire. 'The money I save by not going to University, I will use to buy an Indulgence, just in case.'

'If you carry on in your profession, it would be worth having a sheaf of Indulgences in the drawer,' Nicolson murmured to the flames.

Scott chuckled but did not disagree. As we drank he told us more of the plot to overthrow Regent Morton in St Andrews. Erskine of Gogar had agreed to hand over protection of the King to the new alliance. The Kirk had been squared, for they had had their fill of

Morton. At a private meeting in the Castle, Atholl and Argyll would charge Morton with Darnley's murder. He would be smuggled out through the old underground tunnel, while his followers were locked within the Great Hall. He would likely be killed in a scuffle with persons unknown.

'Such as Pate Wilson?' I asked.

'Just so.'

'But why seek to kill you?'

Scott nodded. 'It seems my title and estate were promised to the Hamiltons. I was a little *entrée* before the main course.'

'A *bonne bouche*.'

'A tender morsel to the falcon.' He stared into the fire. 'But thanks in part to you, Morton will be Regent a while yet.'

'Only for a while?' Tom asked.

'If the King lives to take control, my great-uncle cannot remain Regent.' Scott shrugged. 'He is losing authority. This attempt was but a symptom.'

This was high politics, not the student world. Yet it had brushed against ours and nearly killed us. High politics had killed my father, caught in the cross-fire between the Castle and the Town. I meant to have nothing to do with it, yet in some part I sought advancement and adventure. Now our names had gone out.

'The other man who died at the inn,' I blurted as we settled down for the night. Tom was already snoring by the door, staff across his chest. 'Who killed him? Was it me?'

Scott looked at me across the dying flames. 'This weighs on you?'

'Of course,' I said. 'I mean . . . Hellfire.'

'A stranger's death is a heavy thing to have on one's hands,' he said quietly. 'One crosses into another country.'

'Yes indeed,' I muttered.

He looked into the fire-lit darkness. 'Friend, I'll tell ye a tale.'

And he did. It came from within, spoken formal and grave beyond his years, as though a Confession from the Old Faith. I treasure having been perhaps the only one to ever hear it. May its telling have brought him some relief.

I WAS TWELVE, but big for it. My father had taken much pride in his long-clock, shipped from the Low Countries during the religious wars. It ticked in the gloom at Branxholme, at the far end of the hall. When he died in Moffat – pleurisy or poison, who kens? – as eldest son I took over its Sabbath winding.

That morn I had reached inside the case and in a dwam cradled the lead weight, cool in my hand. Then at my back, between one tick and the next, I heard a faint brush, such as clothing might make. My mother was in Hawick, seeking guidance from her uncle the Earl of Morton. Stock was vanishing from our fields. Our followers were few, her suitors many.

I hunkered down, head bowed, against my father's clock, as though in deep thought. I had lately been retoured sole heir to our estate. I was unarmed.

The lightest creak from behind, not far off now. My right hand lifted the lead weight free from its hook. As something brushed over my hair, I turned and struck out with all my power.

He stood, swaying, eyes shut, mouth open, the garrotte dropping from his hand. My recently arrived riding master. I hit him again, the lead weight in both hands, full on his left temple. Crunch! His eyes went wide, then he dropped. I knelt over him, struck twice more.

One can feel it, the passing of a man. On the floor lay a gut line with finger loops at either end. His feet were unshod, to better creep. He had been a Crozier, recommended by our helpful neighbour Chas Elliot.

I thought: So this is how the world runs.

At length I got off my knees, hooked the lead weight back inside the clock. I fingered the pendulum and set it swinging. It was clear my mother must marry again, and soon.

He was my first. Some say it gets easier thereafter. Not true, though their faces become less distinct.

SCOTT TURNED ON HIS back and stared up blank-eyed at the ceiling, a stone effigy. I wished to offer him absolution, but I was a boy without training.

'If I should scream in the night,' he murmured, 'take no heed. It is but a passing disorder. By day I remain the Bold Buccleuch.'

'I am still thinking of Hellfire,' I confessed.

'Fear not,' he said. 'You cut Claud Hamilton, but I killed the other, then Pate Wilson.' He rolled himself in his cloak, sighed heavily and was asleep.

Some believe Scott of Buccleuch, later Sir Walter, in time our first Lord Scott, to be *au fond* a killer without conscience or tender feeling. This was not so. His version of events at that dreadful inn brought me some comfort, as he intended.

CHAPTER 13

Don't Be Below him if He Falls

NEXT EVENING, WIDE-EYED AND arse-weary, we rode down into Teviotdale. This was foreign territory indeed. Folk had harsh rapid guttural speech, as though their throats were clogged by shouting. The air was thick, moist and mild. The grazing seemed poor compared to our Lothians.

Scott and our Hepburn escort relaxed and packed away their weapons as we followed the burn past Hawick, towards Branxholme. The morning was dew-soaked, the sun low and yellow on the hills that enclosed us. We passed two burnt-out steadings, then a broken peel tower, its door destroyed and scorch marks up all the lower storey. Nicolson and I looked at each other.

Scott rode up to us. 'You see what we have to put up wi,' he said. I smiled inwardly at that grand *We*. 'For a hundred and fifty years we've been playing beggar-my-neighbour, and now we are indeed beggars.'

We rounded the bend of the river and saw Branxholme Castle against the blue Borders sky. It was not small, with two fine towers, and much of the stonework looked new.

'You seem to have done well enough by it,' Nicolson remarked neutrally.

Scott gave him a sharp look, then nodded. 'For the moment. My father spent most of his short life rebuilding this. My mother's re-marriage will help. Till next time.' He frowned as we trotted past the walls. 'Reiving is all we ken in the Borders, but there's no stability in it, you see?'

'The Stoics say there is no stability in human affairs.'

'Aye, but surely to God we can do better than this!' He jumped down from his horse, was mobbed by a pack of grey lurchers. He smiled and stretched his arms wide, shaking off the stiffness of the ride. It looked as though he were embracing the whole castle, the surrounding hills. 'I intend to.' He glanced at us, almost secretively. 'There is a solution, you know.'

Then the main doors of the castle opened and out stepped Juno.

Lord knows my mother was formidable, but she was at least constrained by being only a burgess's widow, and no taller than I. But Scott's mother was Lady Margaret Douglas, niece of Regent Morton, and she was tall, strongly built, with her fair hair plaited and wound-up high in the French manner, adding further inches to her stature.

I slid down from my horse, my knees shaky as I hit the ground. Standing proud and upright in the sunlight in a dark velvet cloak trimmed with blue, she was a goddess, a Hera, a proud Juno.

Scott briefly kissed her on the lips, then indicated towards us. 'Mother, these are my friends Nicolson and Fowler. They saved my skin in St Andrews.'

She looked on us. She had her son's pale green-blue eyes, compelling assent. 'Truly my boy cannot be left alone,' she said. 'You will be aye welcome here.'

She held out her hand to be kissed, so we kissed it, in a clumsy, fervent way. Her skin was soft, with some indefinable scent of woodland. She smiled down at me, her mouth full and fleshy as her son's.

There was a shout from above us. We looked up to see a youth walking high upon the parapet, dark against the light.

'My madcap new husband is at it again,' she said. 'Bothwell really is *de trop*.'

Francis Stewart, newly made Earl of Bothwell, had got back to Branxholme before us. Now he was walking the narrow parapet of the Nesbie Tower, arms wide, seventy feet up, wind streaming his long hair. Then he grasped the ivy of the keep, pulled up onto the new slates, padded up like a wolf till he gained the roof-ridge.

Scott's mother stood beside us, shaking her head but her eyes were shining. Her hand tightened on her son's shoulder. I heard her murmur: *You are still heir, Wattie. We will be safer now.*

Bothwell made it to the great chimneys. He waved down – *Hullo there, young coz!* – then squeezed between the two stacks and began forcing a way up between them. Just by pressure, I supposed. I had not seen the like. I thrilled to his boldness.

Francis Stewart, lately married in a handfast ceremony to Scott's mother, not yet sixteen and supposedly still banned from his new wife's bed, approached the top of the chimneys. He reached up and groped in the great nest there. He held up his hand in triumph, something pale gleamed, then he began working his way down between the chimneys. He gained the roof-ridge, gripped the parapet, then lowered himself into the ivy and thus into the upper attic window of the main house, wherein he disappeared.

'Safer?' young Scott said. 'You are sure?'

She ran her hand through his fiery hair, teasing it onto his shoulders.

'His family are a power,' she said. 'This estate remains ours, but you will have some claim on his should he fall.'

Nicolson and I glanced at each other. They were talking as though our presence did not signify, as high gentry do. Or perhaps they trusted us. Or both.

'He is not dull like those Croziers,' Scott said. 'He will do fine.'

She smiled an inward woman's smile.

'I dare say he will,' she said. Then, as the youth himself came round the corner, brandishing his eggs, she quickly added, 'And if he should ever fall, don't be below him.'

(A WORD ON THIS young Earl of Bothwell. Not *that* Bothwell, as my son Ludovic assumes. Dear God, what passes for education these days? *Not* James Hepburn, the 4th Earl of Bothwell, who scandalously married – by ravishment, some insist – our Queen

Mary, herself recently widowed following her husband Lord Darnley's unfortunate death by explosion and strangulation. Not the one who fled Scotland, to die insane in the pitch-dark oubliette of Dragness Castle, Denmark, in the year I graduated. No, the Bothwell I watched performing simian feats on the chimneys of Branxholme was Francis Stewart, who had recently been made 5th Earl of Bothwell by his young cousin Jamie Saxt. Regent Morton had officiated at the ceremony, as he had at the handfast marriage of Francis Stewart to Margaret Douglas, Morton being uncle to Lady Margaret and guardian to Walter Scott. We are indeed a small country, particularly in our upper reaches!)

FOR THE MOST PART, Tom Nicolson and I were left alone at Branxholme. We gravitated towards the kitchens, amid the warmth and household retainers. Our status was debatable, being neither kin nor gentry, but the kitchens were where food and fire were, also laughter and easy manners, and a couple of forward young lasses, Annie and Mags. Annie seemed right at ease with Nicolson, whom she cried *Fishy Tom*, and they spent time quipping in the inglenook.

'Master Fowler, stop eyeing ma custard tarts!' Mags said, and set off Annie giggling among the pots.

'They look fresh and full to me, young Margaret,' I retorted. 'I have seen many worse.'

She slapped my hand away from her pastries. 'You'll no be touchin mine the day!'

'And the morn,' I said, making eyes at her, 'if I ask nicely, *s'il te plaît*?'

'Deep burns run slow,' she retorted. 'You are fast and shallow.'

'Aa the better to stride across,' I rallied, and won her laughter.

There would be no more sitting by Rose at the table, improving her hand, working through Horace or reciting Henrysoun together. Those had been hours set apart. The extraordinary things she said. Our one long, deep-souled kiss. Her parting *Sorry*. I was sorry too.

'Lost fancy for ma custards, fickle man?'

Mags smiled down at me. She was a sparky lass, bonnie enough. 'I'll settle for some wholesome bread and cheese,' I managed.

'Ye'll hae to ask nicely.'

'That I will willingly do.'

I had other things to forget, matters more weighty than my first boyish passion, such as the sound when a blade is driven deep into a man's back. For now, Branxholme was the place to be.

BUCCLEUCH AND BOTHWELL SPENT much of the time out hunting together with their horses and dogs. They had much to resolve. They were now kin, the only solid thing in a shifting world, and even kin were not always to be trusted. I thought it must be strange, having a stepfather no older than oneself. Still, they always seemed to return in high spirits, muddy and damp, hares, coneys and partridge dangling from their saddles, enough to keep Annie and Mags busy and bloody for hours.

One day Lady Margaret passed me on the stair, carrying a bunch of letters. The topmost was sealed with green wax. I complimented her on the impress.

'My first husband's ring-seal,' she said. She held out her right hand with its ring. 'Fine, is it not?'

'Yes,' I said. 'Very fine.'

'I use it for his affairs,' she said. She held up another letter, with a red seal. 'And this one I use for mine. I wear it on a chain round my neck.'

I tried not to look where it must hang. 'Do you never confuse the two?' I asked.

She laughed. 'Let me show you something.'

She took my hand and led me out the great door into the day. The high gentry seemed to do things differently. My own mother seldom touched me, and I certainly did not kiss her on the lips, as Scott did his mother.

Margaret Douglas pointed up the wall. There were two big armorial panels set up there, both in pale, new stone.

'That one commemorates my late husband's work, when he had the castle rebuilt from its last ransacking. The other one is mine, and will mark the work I complete.'

'So are you Douglas or Scott or Hepburn?' I asked, then regretted my forwardness.

Juno smiled down at me. 'All these,' she said. 'But what has issued from me is all Scott, and he is where my chief hopes lie. Do not stray far from him, and you may prosper.'

Hoofbeats thrummed behind the castle, then Scott and Bothwell rode round the corner at full pelt, thundered shouting past us down to the river, where they whooped and hollered among their dogs, then let the steaming horses drink. Margaret Douglas-Scott-Hepburn regarded them fondly.

'Laddies,' she said. 'They have their swords and crossbows and pistols. But we have marriage, and it is by marriage and heirs a family rises or falls.' She smiled as she turned away from looking at her husband and son. 'I understand you make poetry?'

'On good days,' I confessed. 'Which do not come that often.'

'Do you scrieve epics, ballads or love sonnets?'

'Love sonnets. In the mode of Petrarch, or sometimes in our native metrics.'

'Good, that is as it should be. Love, always love! It lifts our spirits, does it not?'

'Love is a tarantula,' I replied. 'Mostly it stings.'

'Well,' she said, ducking slightly as I opened the main door for her. 'Love and suffer exquisitely by all means, young man. But remember this . . .' She paused till I had followed her indoors. '*Marry cannily*,' she said, and pulled the door to. I believe I did, in the end.

ONE AFTERNOON TOM CALLED out as I crossed the courtyard. He gestured me over and folded away a note. He was sitting on a bench and his face was grave, but then it often was. I remained standing.

'My sister Rose . . .' he began.

'I seem to mind her,' I said. 'The one with the fisherman fiancé.'

'Husband,' he said quietly. 'As of three days back.'

'My, that was quick.'

'There were compelling reasons.'

'I am sure there were.'

We looked at each other. He fingered his staff. 'I am sorry,' he muttered.

I whistled *I Loved a Lass*, caught myself at it, then ceased. 'Congratulate her frae me.'

I left him to go for my fighting lessons with Buccleuch. I wished folk would stop saying *Sorry* to me. It wasn't as though somebody were dead.

'You have a greitin face today,' Buccleuch said when we met by the river.

'I'm sick,' I replied. 'Sick of the world and sick at heart.'

He sat on a bough, his favourite lurcher, Big Peter, solemnly at his side. With his long legs on the ground Scott bounced up and down, then he laughed like a boy. Well, he was a boy.

'Never mind,' he said. 'Worse things happen at sea! I have another salutary tale for ye.'

I sat on the branch beside him and listened closely while he made his confession.

IT WAS AGREED I should be sent to Great-Uncle Morton's house in Pittendreich, for my better protection and further tutoring. The Croziers were unhappy about their kinsman's disappearance — to France it was rumoured, but I kenned our Blackden mire held his body fast. They proposed Sir Cammie Elliot for my mother, with an offer to merge our estates. She negotiated, offered and excused, prevaricated deftly, as Queen Bess long has in England.

Great-Uncle Morton was busy in Embra being Regent, securing incomes from the Kirk lands, trying to appoint allies, and so on. He wrote that he would send two of his household to escort me to Pittendreich.

I met them in Leith. They smilingly said they were from north of Dundee, but they did not sound it. Together we boarded a serviceable barque. The captain, a red-faced Dutchman, blinked when he saw them, then I was hurried below.

As the barque rolled into the Firth, I blethered with my escort about the joys of Pittendreich, the famed twin towers in the French style, the sophisticated gardens. They assured me it was all very wondrous and I would be comfortable there, which struck me as unlikely for there were no towers in that wan fastness, and the gardens grew mostly cabbage and neeps.

The storm increased. The men became yellow-grey, and I insisted on going on deck to spew. They reluctantly assented.

A wee plump sturdy lad was voiding his stomach on the port side. I staggered towards him, and we shared our moment. He was shorter but older than I, said he was going to be a student at St Andrews. 'Fowler by name, fouler by nature,' he gasped as he retched. I liked that. I also liked the protruding haft under his doublet. While my escort vomited also, we made the transaction. I was escorted below decks with an ally inside my shirt.

The first man died as he slept, the second as he woke. One cry, then my hand over his mouth as I cut and stabbed like he was pig. It was very foul. Yon night I learned that to kill in cold blood is much harder, like jumping a burn without taking a run-up.

When I had gained possession of myself, I went to find the captain. I had a purse but he would not take it. We weighted the dead with ballast and slipped them o'er. In first light he signalled to my kinsmen in Dysart. They sent two men and a boat, for which he did take coin, and fair enough.

I cleaned the stout lad's dirk, left him a note, then clambered down into the boat and away to live another day.

I HAD GRUNTED APPRECIATION at Scott's *jumping without a run-up*. That apart, I listened in silence and not thought of Rose's lips on mine, nor her man Gourlay. I stared at the ground under the branches, feeling it pitch and roll. How strange to hear this story, with myself not at the centre. So familiar yet so different, as the shared world must be for each of us

'I am glad to have been of assistance,' I said at last. 'Not so keen on the *stout*, but.'

'You have since grown upward but not out,' he conceded with a grin.

'Thank you for returning the dirk,' I said. 'It was my faither's, and is most dear to me.'

He slapped me on the shoulder. 'I put it to good use, eh?'

'I don't have the stomach for these doings,' I said. 'It seems to come naturally to you.'

Young Walter Scott whistled between his teeth, we watched a kingfisher flash upstream. Then he turned back to me. '*The Bold Buccleuch* your friend cried me, and I glory in it. But I'll tell you this – my head ached thunderously that day, and my hands were shaking as we pulled for shore.' He sprang from the branch, which leapt up free. 'Let's go eat!'

I sensed the confession, if such it was, was over. 'And do you still trust your great-uncle?' I asked, and regretted it as he stared back at me.

'I trust my good right hand,' he said at last. 'And I trust you, for ye didna ken me when we met.'

LADY MARGARET DOUGLAS LEANED on the turn of the stair and called me to her day chamber. Within, she poured wine, held her Venetian goblet high. 'To better days gone, and better yet to come!'

'Amen,' I said, and drank. The wine was not the leathery claret to which I was accustomed, but richly, sweetly, warmed the throat with a whiff of summer herbs.

'This is Italian,' Scott's mother said. 'We have a vineyard near Padua. A branch of our family endowed a collegiate convent there, and they daily pray on our behalf.'

'May their prayers be answered,' I replied politely, thinking the practice scandalous.

She ran her tongue across her lips, considered. 'My son is shaping up to be one in need of many prayers. I travelled there when I was a girl, in my grandfather's time. It is a rare city, and the wine is very fine. I may retire there to warm myself in the sun.'

'That will not be for many years,' I said. 'By which time a fine wine may be a great one.'

She blew a languid kiss that made me blush. 'You flatter well,' she said. 'You must have had practice in St Andrews.'

'Practically none,' I said frankly, and drank again. The wine spread its warmth through my body. This was my first encounter with Padua and I liked it very well. 'St Andrews is not that kind of place.'

For a moment, Rosie's mouth opened again on mine. The memory, or perhaps the presence of Lady Margaret, give rise to the usual stir-rings. I lowered my goblet to my lap.

'Our girls here are somewhat lively.' She flourished an oatcake as though it were a fan, then popped it in her mouth. 'Perhaps it is the air of Teviotdale, or that our young men are gone. You may find your stay here educative and enjoyable.'

She took a hearty swig of wine. I watched her long throat con-vulse. Like her son, she made whatever room she was in seem small. I heard boisterous voices coming down the passage.

'But I urge you to take sufficient care, young man,' she added. 'We would not want any *issue* from your time with us.'

I DID INDEED TAKE sufficient care with Mags. More accurately, she took sufficient care with me. She first furthered my education on a warm afternoon deep in the woods of beech and oak. There was some awkwardness, but soon laughter and sweetness.

Over those days at Branxholme she as it were *lowered my gown*, each occasion encompassing more worthwhile learning than an entire year at college.

I shall not forget a hidden ledge above where the burn flows into the Teviot.

Another prolonged tutorial followed in the powder room in the Nesbie Tower, amidst kindling and old blankets, a chair angled up against the door.

When we left a dell in the hills above Ettrick, sun in our eyes as we brushed heather and thyme from our clothes, I had knowledge to better please my giggling tutor.

At the end of the afternoon in the byre by the furthest pasture, amidst bouts of sneezing from the stoor, she capped me with her own bonnet, and pronounced me ready for the world. She added I minded her of a lad who had gone.

It was a quick aside, in faltering voice. I brushed away her tears, and felt my own gather.

She sat up, pulled straw from her hair, laughed. 'There was anither syne, but he is gone tae Kirk Yetholm, which in my opinion is to be as good as deid.'

'DON'T WAVE IT ABOUT!' Walter Scott instructed. 'Unless you mean to distract. Place your thumb, here.' He adjusted my hand on the haft. 'Strike upward.'

With wooden dagger, then my father's dirk with bated tip, every morning Scott and I trained in the courtyard. I learned to stand side-on, keep my weight forward, head still but keep the body moving.

Bothwell, passing, called out, 'Man, even Wattie's sister could fight better than that!'

Nicolson sat in the sunlight, reading a book, staff across his knee. Scott had adjudged he was so deft with that stick that no further training was required. *Do something queer wi your free hand*, was all his instruction. *Your enemy's eye will follow it.*

Then he came at me with bated rapier, showed me what to expect and how to dodge it. *Get inside their strike, then your short blade holds advantage.* I could not carry broadsword or rapier, not being a gentleman. Facing a sword with only a dagger, one feels at a loss. But I learned if one slipped inside the sword strike, the advantage is yours. The greater weapon becomes a liability. I liked that.

Scott taught me to watch my assailant's eyes, not his blade, and to jalouse his intent. *Man or woman signal intent wi their eyes, gin ye attend.*

Whatever the weather, Scott drilled me every morning, while Tom read out choice passages of Henrysoun's *The Testament of Cresseid*, the sole book that had survived the last burning of Branxholme.

Ane doulie season to ane careful dyte
Suld correspond and be equivalent . . .

HERE IN MY ROOM in Shoreditch, casement open to the stinking street, I intone those lines to foreign air – England has never become home, and I never truly prospered once the Court moved south – and once again breathe in that sunny courtyard deep in muir-fragrant Teviotdale.

Tom Nicolson chants the lines and turns the page. Wattie Scott, still unmaimed, slim and gout-free, comes at me again. Our blades flash in the sun and I breathe freely from uninfected lungs. His mother, a woman at once fleshly aglow and fashioned from teak, pauses to scorn and approve. Bothwell, who would die penniless in a Naples bordello after somehow finding the time among his raids and rebellions to father eight children by Lady Margaret, lopes by, grinning and panting like a young hound. Mags leans out from the upstairs window, yellow duster in hand, and the world feels brimming full, as Rosie Nicolson ventured so long ago.

All this is taken from me. All this I have had.

CHAPTER 14

An Education Resumed

CAME A MORNING NICOLSON and I were in the courtyard, bantering with Annie at an upper window, when a horseman arrived in Hepburn livery. Lady Margaret hurried out. She broke the seal on his letter and read with care. Then she smiled.

'You may return to St Andrews and resume your studies in safety. The Hamiltons have been exiled.'

As we cheered, above our heads the shutter closed and Annie was gone from sight. As I made to follow Tom Nicolson within, Scott's mother tightened her hand on my wrist. 'Does your mother prosper?'

'You know her?' I said, astonished.

'We met in Holyrude, in better days.' That signified Queen Mary's rule. 'We have had dealings since – rebuilding castles does not come cheap! Send her my salutations.'

'I will when I see her next.'

She still held me by the arm. I waited, having learned she said little casually. 'Janet Fockhart is a canny woman,' Lady Margaret said. 'She has chosen not to re-marry. But pray tell her that, while I applaud her loyalty in religion, she should not back a horse that will not finish the race.'

In time I would recognise that horse.

NEXT MORNING, AS WE prepared to leave for Fife, Annie stopped me by the stables. She led me by the hand into the big barn full of furniture and furnishings freshly collected from God knows where. I said surely Nicolson would mind. She laughed at that, as though it were likely as a swallow on a spit. She assured me Mags would have no mind either, and put my hand upon her sweet fork.

They knew what they were about, those lasses. There was no issue, beyond mutual pleasure, laughter and affection. I think of them now, all lust put by, and smile.

WHEN TOM AND I returned to St Andrews, we were summoned to see Dean Jarvie. He welcomed us back, said some *notorious parties* had left the University, and that he wanted Regent Morton to know he had the college's *fullest support*. There would be no penalty for our *understandable absence*. Perhaps we could now return to our studies and avoid further trouble? We assured him that was our sincerest hope and intention.

Some things had changed, though. Fellow students gave us a

wider berth. I seldom went out without my father's blade hidden but handy. I avoided taverns and wynds at night. Nicolson or other trusted fieres like Anderson and Ogilvie would walk me back to my bunk, where I installed a stout bar on my door and took care to use it. Miss Whitton pursed her lips but made no objection, which by her lights signalled approval. She must have heard something of our doings.

Meeting me by the West Port, John Geddes winked but made no further comment. We began occasional sessions at his workshop where, in exchange for unpaid standard scrivening, he undertook to educate me in hand-imitation, the use of authentic paper, correctly watermarked, aged with powder. And he introduced me to Eugene Duboisson in Newport, a man skilled in making duplicate seals.

I was flattered and wary, both of which came all too naturally to me.

He also introduced me to the practice of snuff-taking, and I got in the way of carrying small twists of it with me. When stuck for an answer in disputation, it allowed me to pause, snort, then, when the impact hit, deliver my riposte. An affectation, no doubt, one that suited a version of myself, the young blood and slightly *outré* man of fashion.

ONE DAY I TOOK a scunner to morning prayers, and went to the harbour in hope of delivering a long overdue fairing.

And there she was, walking alone in work apron but with her

blue shawl happed about her against the wind. We stopped a few feet apart. I looked about. There was no one close.

She asked after me. I said I was quite well in body. She hesitated, then thanked me for looking after her brother in our recent difficulties. I said we had looked after each other, as friends do.

I looked at her and saw a bonnie girl become a woman, no more, no less. Whatever mystery remained was not the same one as before. Thanks to Mags and Annie, I knew how she was made. Perhaps that was what made her blush as I stared at her.

'So you are marrit,' I said at last.

'Aye. So it seems.' She held up her hand, looked wonderingly at the gold that encircled bone.

'Approved by the Kirk, and part of the Gourlays. You will be siccar now.'

'There were many pressing reasons,' she said.

'I have no doubt.'

She flushed. 'In truth, I do not feel so different.'

I realised that though much deeper in intellect, she was as new to matters of the heart as myself. I reached within my gown and held out the package, intended for her before her engagement. I had thought to keep it for myself, but that seemed churlish and ungenerous.

'This is for you,' I said. 'Congratulations and good fortune in your marriage.'

She slit the wrapping with her ragged nail. Nicol Burne had given the book to me, insisting he had little use for it now. It was a bound, well-thumbed manuscript copy of Lucretius' *De Rerum Natura*.

Her face quickened. She eagerly turned the yellowed pages, lips moving as she murmured the Latin verses. 'A joyous book in a joyless time,' she murmured. Then the light died. She closed the book and held it out. 'I hae nae time nor use for this, Will. There's little call for uplifting metaphysics in a fishwife's life.'

I put up my hand against taking it back. 'Uplift helps us endure,' I replied. 'We both have much to endure, and surely more to come.'

She looked me over. 'You've changed,' she said. 'It is a good hardening.'

'Me? I'm soft as a Shetland shawl.'

She laughed quietly. 'Put that in one of your poems.'

'You think I have not?'

She abruptly leaned forward and kissed me, lightly, on the lips. A breath passed between us. 'Thank you,' she said. Then quietly added, 'Sorry.'

'Nothing to be sorry about,' I replied, and discovered I meant it. 'I wouldn't have missed our friendship for the world.' I stepped back while I still could. 'And for the Lord's sake keep your alarming thoughts to yourself.'

'I will try.' Her hand alighted on my arm. 'You have aye been a friend in my mind's loneliness.'

When I looked back, she was still standing there, eyes deep as the sea behind her.

AT THE FAR END of the netting green I encountered Bella Muir. She scowled at me. 'I aye kent yon lassie wis a hoor,' she said as we passed each other.

In my pain I went too far. I whirled and seized her arm. 'Gin you repeat that calumny, Johnny Gourlay and I will hae the Kirk session on you.' She went pale. Her hand twitched but she did not strike me. 'For the Christ's sake, Bella,' I added, 'get down frae your pyre.'

'Pox on ye baith,' she muttered, then stomped off.

Bella Muir was not alone in needing to step out from the martyr's fire. The college bell was ringing, I hurried up the brae, back to the life scholastic.

IN TIME OUR GOWNS descended from neck to shoulder to upper arm, and were now wrapped about our waists as my peers and I swanked through our Final Year. The end we had long yearned for was thundering towards us like a runaway Clydesdale.

Through the Dean, I received an offer of the post of dominie in Arncroach, where the school was a lean-to shed against the parish kirk.

'Weel out of harm's way there,' Tam Anderson commented. 'Nothing happens in Arncroach.'

I nodded but thought, *Well out of Fortune's way too*. It was the kind of post I had once fancied being able to offer Rosie Nicolson, where she would be my love and we would raise sturdy-legged bairns together, and of an evening I would dash off simple yet ravishing *Fife Bucolics* to please my friends and depress my rivals.

That future was as out of the question as a woman entering the gates of St Leonard's. We scarcely saw each other after she'd moved from Fisher Row to the Gourlay cottage by the Kinness burn. I had weaned myself off going by the Green.

I pondered the dominie post. Or should I return to Embra and live like my father, as an honest, industrious merchant? Then again, there was Paris and the Collège de Sainte-Barbe. I had not forgotten Nicol Burne and George Buchanan, half-cut, happily recalling their years there. Why not? There was nothing now to keep me here.

I swithered atween selves, as I have all my life, following the dark horse and then the light.

ALL THROUGH MY UNIVERSITY years, despite the rumours, tensions and alarums, we had known a comparative stillness in the wind, a lull, under Regent Morton. Few truly believed it was anything more than that, and so it proved.

Springtime in St Andrews in my final year. Sleet was dissolving like sea-foam agin the clear glass chapel windows as we groaned, some with zealous hearts, all with numb feet, through Psalm 57:

> I am in the midst of lions; I am forced to dwell among ravenous beasts,
> Men whose teeth are spears and arrows, whose tongues are sharp swords . . .

WE TRAILED OFF, FOR Dean Jarvie had oiled in through the side door and crossed to the steps where the rood-screen had been. This had not happened since the announcement of John Knox's death. The Dean had been pale then. Today he was flushed.

'Scholars and gentlemen of St Leonard's,' he announced, then paused. He had not entirely lost his gift for pomposity. 'Regent Morton has resigned from government. He has surrendered Holyrude, the Castle, and the Great Seal.'

Collective gasps. The sleet slid from the windows. Nicolson and I looked to each other. Jamie Saxt was but a boy of eleven or so. Who was in charge now?

'At last a changing of the guards,' Anderson muttered on my right.

The Dean waved the paper in his fist. 'The regency is dissolved! There will be no more regents. God save King James the Sixth and his loyal Kirk!'

Behind me someone cried *God save Queen Marie*, and there was the sound of a fist on bone, and a scuffle broke out among the pews. The hardened Protestants were crying *Heresy! Save our Jerusalem!* Tam Anderson and his pals clambered over the pew into the row behind and laid about them.

A full-scale riot threatened till the Dean waved in the stewards, the Proctor and Hebdomadar. Eventually the factions were held apart, and threatened with Expulsion by the Dean, and with Hellfire by the minister.

For the only time in my years at the University, the service was abandoned. Eventually Nicolson and I stood alone in the empty chapel.

'What happens now, Will?'

From boyhood, we had known only Regents. Moray, Lennox and Mar had been killed off in turn, but the institution itself was some kind of stability. Now with Morton's departure, it felt as though our world had lurched to the edge of the cliff, with nothing to catch our fall. Would the King and the moderate Reformists prevail, or the Calvinists, or the Catholic Church return again? Nothing was clear apart from our division.

'It may be to the good,' I said. 'My mother at least will be well pleased.'

Nicolson looked around the empty, frigid chapel, then he sang in sardonic fashion a line from the Psalm:

I will take refuge in the shadow of your wings until the disaster has passed.

BUT HIS GAUNT FACE was still troubled. I knew something had been on his mind the last few days, but did not ask.

'That's all very well,' I said, 'but I have Finals to sit.'

NEWS AND RUMOURS SWIRLED in from Embra. The Catholic lords Atholl and Argyll had forced Morton out and they now led the Privy Council. Jamie Saxt was again warded 'for his own safety' in Stirling Castle. Morton had retired to Loch Leven and apparently was spending his time planning gardens to ease his old age. My mother wrote me a jubilant letter to say Mass had been openly held in Holyrude. Queen Mary would return from England to reign jointly with her son. *The tide is on the turn!* she signed off, then added a post-scriptum: *Extend the Anderson loan against surety.*

I read the letter twice, then burned it. My mother was needle-bright in business, but religion sometimes made her unwise.

I tried to keep my head down and concentrate on bringing four years' study to a profitable conclusion. Through the last months, Natural Philosophy had been well to my taste. We lived in a world without Church magic, open to being surveyed and understood. No more priestly conjuring of holy water, wafers transubstantiated into Christ's flesh! No mumbled chants, no holy spells, those things that so lifted my mother's heart.

Yet stripped of the supernatural and the authority of tradition, it appeared that in matters of observable fact, even Aristotle was being proved wrong. Could it be our current age was superior in some knowledge? Let us count a horse's teeth, anatomise the body, map the movement of the stars and planets, rather than argue it all from first principles! Grind better lenses! Think afresh! Dizzying prospects, to live in such times.

One afternoon I pushed away my papers, strapped my dad's dagger against my chest and went out into the muddy street. I needed to consult Tom Nicolson on St Anselm's ontological argument. But he wasn't in the college, or the printer's, nor on the Links with Auchterlone.

I walked on to St Salvator's, for once in a while Nicolson went there to sharpen his mind on the whetstone of orthodoxy. I turned the corner off Merkitgate, and saw four figures striding into our rival college. As they unbuckled their swords for the guardian, I ducked back into the vennel, heart up in my neck. I peeked again. Claud, John, David and the youngest boy Arthur, waving his sword and exclaiming in the sunlight.

I hurried homeward to my bunk, barred the door and sat on my pallet clutching St Brigid. The Hamiltons were back.

EVENTUALLY I NEEDED AIR. I replaced St Brigid ahint the wainscot, alongside my mother's wee jewelled crucifix. Then I adjusted the dagger under my shirt and slipped down the stair in my red goonie.

I called by Fishertown as dusk came on. A dim yellow light glowed in the Nicolson window, so I chapped on the door. Mother Nicolson tried to welcome me cheerily, but something was not right. She said she didna ken where her son was, and her distress made me believe something was afoot. *My lass lives wi her man noo.* I said goodnight and headed on down Fisher Row.

The wind from the sea was laden with salt and weed. I realised I had come to love that chilly guff, that and the gulls' cry, passing ghost-like in the dimness at the cliff-edge. Then faint bird calls became human shouts. I heard pounding feet, coming up behind me.

I turned, hand inside my shirt, bracing for combat. Tom Nicolson lolloped gownless round the corner and thumped into me. As we steadied each other against the wall, he thrust something into my free hand.

'*The auld Well,*' he hissed. '*Later!*'

He lurched off into the darkness of the Cathedral grounds. As I passed the letters into my gown, three men rushed down the close. I put my hands up.

'Whoever you're after, I am not he. I am a student.'

Three men I did not know, two heavily bearded, the other with rapier drawn. Even in that poor light, they saw I was not their quarry, and I saw their pursuit was fatal in intent.

'Which way?'

I pointed down the brae. 'To the harbour,' I said. They cursed and sprinted off.

I GROPED MY WAY to the Cathedral and hunkered down at the foot of the old Night Stairs where once monks descended from sleep to their devotions. I waited till the night had entered my joints and the distant shouts had long gone. Then I moved on cautiously towards the darker dark of St Rule's Tower. Paused there, taking my bearings. Something pale streaked by me, a ghost, an avenging spirit, a gull.

I drew my dirk and moved slowly across the grassy brae. My cautious foot found a masoned step. Then another. I made a not entirely convincing mew of a gull. Waited till a faint reply seeped from the ground below, then the rasp of a stone moving. I stepped down.

In the little underground sanctuary, by wavering creusie flame, I gave Tom back the letters. He grasped me fervently by the hand. I waited for the explanation we both knew he owed me. And finally, in a low, hoarse voice, he talked.

The letters were his father's. Well, not written by his father but given to him in France, to deliver privately. *From?* The Duc de Guise. *To?*

A long pause. 'The Duke of Atholl. And Argyll.'

'What do they offer?

Nicolson showed me the seals still unbroken. 'Money, probably. Troops, maybe. A marriage offer? Perhaps all three.'

I shivered. This was far beyond my competence. 'But you don't believe in their cause? Or even approve your father?'

'No. But afore they captured him, he passed me the letters and I ran off.'

'Where is he now?'

'I do not know.' And then, more brokenly, '*Ah dinna ken.*'

As he blurted out his story, I put my arm round his thin shoulder and tried to reason it out. Tom had received a note from his father, asking for a *rendezvous*. Even as they embraced by the darkening pier, four armed men had set about them. In the rammie, Tom's father slipped him the letters, then took a cudgel to the head. As two kept Tom at bay, the other two searched his stunned father. One of them was John Hamilton.

'They were definitely looking for letters?' I checked.

'Yes.'

'So they kenned he was coming?'

'Aye!' he sobbed.

'Wheesht, wheesht,' I murmured. 'They took care not to kill him?'

Tom nodded. 'I suppose so. They could hae easily. I cracked heads with my staff, then ran.'

I weighed the two letters in my hand. The Guise seal I knew from my mother's papers. One was clearly addressed to His Most Excellent Duke of Atholl. The other to Argyll. Our two new leading Privy Councillors. From the foremost Catholic family in France.

I tilted them closer to the lamp. Fine secretarial script. I made to open the larger one, then paused and left the seal unbroken. *Think, man!*

'We must find him!' Nicolson whispered. 'They will kill him.'

'I doubt that. They want the letters.'

'But won't they expect me to destroy them?'

I assumed there was a subtle mind behind this scheme. Indeed, I banked on it. 'Not if they reason clearly and believe you do too. It is generally known you are no Papist conspirator.'

'Then they will torture him!'

'To what end? They want *you* now. For the letters. And he is all they have to exchange.'

A long silence. The tiny flame guttered. I thought while my friend suffered.

'Let them hae the fuckin letters,' he said brokenly. 'I want my faither back.'

'So do I,' I replied. That could not be, but perhaps I could make good for my friend. And, though she was lost to me now, for his sister.

But the consequences of returning these letters? It wasn't hard to guess. Missives so fiercely sought would not be about the weather in Paris and the latest dance in Lorraine. I was sure as *oeufs* is eggs that these letters, if revealed in the Privy Council, would do for Atholl and Argyll.

Perhaps that was the point of them?

Yet this did not smell of forgery. I believed these letters were sincerely seditious – otherwise why would loyal Catholic Nicolson *père* risk his life to deliver them? Something more devious was going on. Someone had known about these letters and had them tracked all the way from France to Leith. It seemed ex-Regent Morton had not been spending all his time designing new gardens at Loch Leven

'I can see a way,' I said at last. 'It is laborious and crooked, but I can see no other.'

And then I put it to him. He stared at me as if I was *fou*. But he listened. And eventually assented.

We left the ancient sanctuary before dawn. He went to ground with his Culdee friends among the ruins of their church. In ragged cowl, unshaven, dirt applied to his face, he looked as half-mad as they did. And I went to call on John Geddes, knowing him devious, to commence the most desperate act of my life to date.

WAS IT FOR OR against the Reform that I undertook this counter counter-plot? Though my father's last sigh had been a bewildered *Jesu!*, there was nothing I could take from that beyond a hatred of cross-fire. There was much to detest on both sides of the religious divide, and much to admire. Beauty against Clarity, that old set-to.

No, this was personal, to aid Tom Nicolson and, through him, his sister. And perhaps in part it was my own vanity. I believed I had grasped what was going on, and that I was clever and capable enough to outwit it, and that was a great excitement in my brain. The whole plan presented itself before me as *To Thaliarchus in Winter* might have unrolled within Horatius Flaccus, probably to his own astonishment.

This was high politics and very dangerous. And my Finals were due within weeks. Still I chapped quietly on John Geddes's door and woke him up, knowing well I could not trust him, but there was no one else.

Geddes's eyes widened. His fleshy lips pursed as he listened. In the end he agreed with my plan, though he would not have a hand in it. If it came to light, he would say I had stolen the materials.

We sat at his work bench and he delicately slit around the seals, and together we read the Guise proposals for the restoring of the Old Faith in Scotland. It was everything we might have expected: money, troops, a Guise wife for young Jamie Saxt. It might even have worked.

'Ye'll hae tae pay me,' Geddes said at last.

I nodded. 'I don't have much, but there's those that do. They'll pay.'

He thought about it. Smiled a little. Of course they would pay, and well. Yet I suspect it wasn't just about the money with him, though he'd auction his grannie were she still alive. For both of us it was the ploy that is too fine to resist.

He held the paper to the light, passed his finger over the watermark. Yes, he could get his hands on this. Made by Nicolas Le Beau at Troyes, used by the Guise family. Very good stuff, smooth and not too absorbent. He would need to blend the ink. The nib would be special cut. The seals would go to Duboisson, though odds were he'd have the die already. At least there was only one hand in the writing, bar the signature.

'Let's see if I taught you well.' Geddes pushed scrap paper towards me. 'Copy. Practise. Then do it freely, as if it were your own. Don't strive for complete consistency, for only a liar or a fraudster is consistent. The Guise signature's the thing – start wi that.'

Then he went out to get us breakfast. I slid the bar to behind him, then got to work, beginning with a note of my own, calling in a long-standing debt.

'AYE, NO BAD,' GEDDES said on return. 'Work further on the signature. Make it more slanted, and more uneven. It looks like a forgery!' He chuckled at his own wit, picked up one letter and sniffed. 'Seems I maun smoke,' he said. 'Best tobacco a Frenchman can export,' he said. 'Details!' He lit up his clay pipe and blew a perfect smoke ring across the papers.

'Don't get too comfortable,' I said. I picked up my note. 'This must go by the fastest post horse this backwater possesses, and I can't be seen on the street.'

He sighed but took my packet, glanced at the name on it. Raised his eyebrows but made no comment as he headed for the door. I took a peck of snuff, flexed my wrist and fingers as though about to pick a lock or play the lute – both handy life skills – then got to it.

CHAPTER 15

Better than a Casket Letter

I HAD TWO LETTERS OF the same size, paper, folding and script as the originals. I had slept little, and that on straw on Geddes's workshop floor. My friendship with Nicolson was common knowledge, so the college and my bunk were to be avoided. Fortunately, I had been discreet about my connection to John Geddes. Duboisson came good with the duplicate seals, and his messenger handed over a stick of French green sealing wax along with them.

We lit the candle, dripped wax, imprinted the seal.

Geddes held up the letters, turned them over, sniffed. Then he dropped them on the floor and lightly scuffed his shoe over one, then the other. He picked them up and looked at me. His smile was one a master craftsman might bestow on a promising apprentice.

He battered the letters against each other, then scrunched a little.

'Fit to go, loon,' he said. 'Better than a Casket letter.'

I never got to speir about those celebrated forgeries (were they his, I wonder now?), for hard on his words came a banging on the door, a yelp from the street. I slid back the bar and let in Tom Nicolson's nephew Eck, panting like a fresh-landed mackerel.

He had just run from Fishertown, and the story he had to tell was much as I'd banked on: armed men at their door a day back, claiming authority from the Constable, searching for the student Thomas Nicolson, son of the Hieland traitor. They had searched the cottage, enduring the rough edge of Mrs Nicolson's tongue, found no one and nothing.

They had gone away. And had returned this morning, led by *a sleekit, skelly-eyed arse o a Hamilton* – that would be David – and made the offer I had anticipated: the man for the letters.

SUCH SWAPS ARE DELICATE, intricate. Each side anticipates the other will cheat if at all possible. Indeed, thinking of my adversary, he would be suspicious if I did not attempt to.

I now needed a man of broad sympathies, who could be trusted by all parties and not easily frightened or bullied. Whose integrity was beyond question. Who was beyond being bought off or threatened. Who was at hand in St Andrews. Who was known to me, but not too closely. One who understood both human emotion and the necessities of State. An intermediary, with an *entrée* to both Court and Council.

So it was on the third night, the letters prepared and hidden,

Geddes went out to find George Buchanan. He brought him back, stooping and thin-shanked, but bright-eyed.

'This is nothing tae dae wi me,' Geddes said. 'I'm off to The Langside for a bottle and a pipe.'

He left hastily. Buchanan looked at me without comment, loosened his stole. I bade him be seated, offered him brandy. He shook his aged head. 'Yon gaudy night with Nicol Burne is one of many things I shall not do again.'

He regarded me gravely. This man had been tutor to a young Queen Mary, then to Jamie Saxt, also to Michel Eyquem, or Montaigne, whose curious project of *enquiry without destination* Nicolson had lately alerted me to. Committed Protestant, yet Humanist, Calvinist of the moderate sort (if such can exist), the greatest Latin stylist of his age – the coulter blade of Buchanan's life had ploughed deep furrows down his cheeks and below his sunken eyes.

Yet he had been young once. He had had loves and dear friends. He had presumably once had a father.

I laid out the entire situation as I guessed it to be, complete with the original letters from the Duc de Guise. Buchanan read them with care, held close to his face in unsteady white hands. His old lips whitened.

'An invitation to Treason,' he said. 'Many have gone to the scaffold for receiving less.'

'But *cui bono*, sir? I asked myself who would want to intercept these letters and bring this about. To what end? And what limits are there to his ambition?'

Buchanan rubbed the side of his long neb but made no comment. There was no need for names. Then I set out my surmise as to what was going on here, the scheme behind the scheme.

His eyes widened at that. He hesitated, then decades of understanding and experience came to bear. Inside that shrunken skull, the different salinities of the Renaissance and the Reformation had met and mingled. Those eyes had witnessed plots, forgeries, martyrdoms and assassinations. He had been present in Paris during the St Bartholemew Day's Massacre, and had never forgotten that slaughter. He had known duplicitous men, and some sincere ones, no less lethal.

The history of Scotland he was writing would lead a mind to despair of men and women. Yet he had had a father. And he knew our ex-Regent Morton still had ambitions that went far beyond laying out his gardens.

'Young man, you know I am irrevocably for the Reform.'

'The Reform it must be, sir. Absolutely!'

His stare went through my flippancy like a pitchfork through a straw bale. 'I sense you are not truly convinced.'

I opened my mouth and to my surprise spoke as I had done to no other, scarcely even to my own soul. 'Sir, in truth I do not think about it often. I am a shallow youth with a youth's other interests . . .'

'Lassies, poesie, gowf, advancement,' he grunted. 'I was young once.'

'. . . But I hold our Reformation is the least bad option currently on offer.'

He thumbed his nose thoughtfully. Half-hidden by his hand, I thought his mouth might have twitched a smile.

'Our boy King,' he observed, 'though a lazy, wilful, clever whelp, and neither well-made nor a complete man, is better by far than any who would replace him.'

That was it. The oracle had spoken.

'High politics are not my concern,' I said. 'I wish they would let me be. My concern here is the father of my most dear friends, as well as seeing Justice done. Or at least Injustice not done.'

I got the ghost of chuckle. 'Indeed.' He leaned forward closer to me. The night was quiet, just the whispers from the grate and the distant sea. 'So what do you want of me?'

I picked up my apprentice forgery work. His eyes flicked to the letters, then back to me. He nodded. His brain was still quick.

'Only you can make it happen,' I urged. 'Serve your country's good one last time.'

I sensed George Buchanan's weariness, his wish to just be left alone to write his History of Scotland. I was offering him one last chance to put his shoulder to the wheel of the world rather than just record its revolutions.

'I will have that brandy, boy,' he said at last, and his voice was firm and whole again.

I fetched it eagerly, put another peat on the fire, and then suggested how this ploy might be accomplished. We talked about it. We refined it. We looked at all eventualities.

Finally Geddes came home, chapped on the door to be admitted.

I slid back the bar and he reeled in, wine-breathed, and together they went back through the midnight streets to Buchanan's lodging, the drunk leading the old on their valiant dance. And I, the choreographer, laid me down to sleep on the straw.

THE FEW TATTERED MONKS who still lived among the ruins of St Rule's were rudely awoken that night by four armed men. Their cowls were jerked back, but all were adjudged too old. They were cursorily beaten for refusing to talk except in Aramaic or Greek. When the intruders left, one of the search party hung back, apologised, and quickly crossed himself before returning to the night.

After attending to their injuries, the least-ancient Culdee monk was sent to rouse their new recruit from the sunken well sanctuary. Tom Nicolson hurried away while it was still dark, through the dreels, backways and wynds of the town he knew as well as anyone, till he softly chapped at the postern door of Jeb Auchterlone's lodging. They had once attended the same college. More to the point, they had played the Links together since boyhood, and only the other week had relieved two members of the gentry of their prize purse over a foursomes.

Together they slunk through gardens off North Street, crossed by the end of the Scaurs and down onto the Links. The young cleek-maker opened the decrepit green-keeping store among the gorse, used only by sheltering caddies on the worst of days. As a cold April dawn came creeping over the North Sea, the cleek-maker unlocked the sunken gear-cellar at its rear, passed down blankets and food to the philosopher, then locked up and padded home whistling. No more siccar place in St Andrews.

AUCHTERLONE CAME TO GEDDES'S door to pass on the news of Tom's relocation.

'Yon letters are in much demand,' Geddes commented to me, his head appearing above the hatch as I cowered in the attic. 'I want you out of here *summa cum celeritate*.'

I nodded, knowing this arrangement was unsustainable. 'They're going to get their letters soon enough.'

Buchanan had agreed to be the go-between and guarantor, and was out and about all day making arrangements. All concerned were *very* keen. The choreography was agreed. The prisoner would be handed over in exchange for the letters. The seals would then be broken in front of a select audience of witnesses and interested parties. Those invited *must attend*.

The venue? Now remodelled following the demolition by Strozzi's cannon and John Knox's removal to the French galleys, Archbishop Beaton's death, and the martyrs' pyres still warm in living memory, this would be played out at the Bishop's Castle on its headland by the Scaurs, where I had stood and gawped on my first day in St Andrews.

I WOKE TO HOOFBEATS clattering on the cobbles outside sound returned my childhood, the small cannons' whuddering father's blood spreading across our doorway slab.

Shouts from outside. A fist hammering on the door. I slid back the bar.

Hepburns, fully armed, faces I recognised from our days at Branxholme. And at their head, Bothwell and Scott, raised and excited as if setting out on the hunt, and Tom Nicolson on foot, pale as a gull, links grass on his dew-soaked boots.

'Let us do this prompt!' Bothwell cried, as though the whole ploy were his. Walter Scott looked down at me and winked.

'So you got my request,' I said to him. 'Much obliged.'

'Wouldn't miss this for the world!'

Tom and I walked to the venue, surrounded by horsemen. Curious faces turned our way as we struck up Merkitgait, turned through Castle Gait. We were not many, but we had purpose. All morning weel-kent faces from Court and Council were being been admitted to the Castle. A small crowd gathered, for the word was out something momentous was going on, though no proclamation had been made.

As we came out the end of Castle Street, many armed men closed in on us from left and right, directed by a few on horse. Douglases of course, of Morton's party.

Then the Castle doors opened. George Buchanan stood alone, all in plain black with close-fitting fur hat and gloves, unarmed and empty-handed. Behind him were the Dukes of Argyll and Atholl.

Claud and John Hamilton and their kin were already crowding about the Douglas men. Stalemate.

In his Paris days, along with writing passionate love poems to his viperous *amour* and toying with the lute, George Buchanan must have developed a taste for theatricals. He strode down the drawbrig onto the cobbles. The crowd parted around him as he took up position by the scorch marks of Wishart's pyre. A sigh as of cold wind coming off a sea of infinite regret. All that was missing was a roll of drums, a trapdoor and smoke effects.

Buchanan gestured to a knot of Morton's Douglases. They rode through the crowd, parted to reveal a tall, once powerful Hielander, bruised and battered in a tattered plaid. Nicolson's father had his son's deep brooding eyes, but with the mottled face of a drinker and the stance of a fighter. He looked like one who has lost badly and is only now learning the extent of his defeat.

Tom Nicolson limped forward to hand two letters to Buchanan, who made a show of examination. Nicolson did not even glance at his father, who looked to him longingly. Then ex-Regent Morton, wrapped most humbly in a plain heavy brown cloak, smiling, swept past Argyll and took the letters. He had a close look at them, then nodded. These were the ones he had sought.

The Hieland man was immediately taken into custody. Buchanan had warned me this was likely, for Nicolson *père* was still proscribed. Still, better in care of the State than held by Morton.

This concluded the scene *Man exchanged for letters*. All the principal players went within the Castle. Whatever happened next would be for a select audience.

The crowd loitered, conjecturing and getting cold, then dispersed, unsure what they had witnessed, only that they had witnessed it. At the back of the crowd I spied Rosie standing by her husband Gourlay. I looked again, took in how her right hand lay on her belly. She sent an anxious smile that flew like a swallow from her to me, then turned back to her life now.

Accompanied by Tam Anderson and a couple of sturdy Fife lads with cudgels, I set off back to my bunk. I had not been invited to the next scene. Buchanan had stressed neither I nor Geddes should be seen to be in any way connected with this affair, because rumours existed about his abilities with a pen, and, for all I knew, about mine.

Up in my attic bunk, I barred the door, sat and waited. I thought about Rose, broadened with child, irritated that it still meant much to me. Then I wondered how the scene was playing in the Castle. Then I tried to revise, but my notes might as well have been written in Aramaic. I took out my St Brigid statuette and lay on my pallet stroking her tiny, radiant face.

A PITY I WAS not there to witness my script read out before such a select and attentive audience! But that evening, as we sat down to shellfish and Rhenish wine at Bothwell's lodgings, half a dozen Hepburns keeping guard outside, the scene was recreated for me by Bothwell, Scott of Buccleuch, and Tom Nicolson.

The gathering at the Bishop's Castle was not a Privy Council nor a court hearing, yet after being contacted by George Buchanan, many high heid yins were there. Chancellor Atholl in his gold cloak and chain of office. Argyll only a little less splendid. Morton dressed in humble brown, mud still on his boots, the loyal former servant of the State, come to lend his experience if called upon. Also present were Archbishop Adamson, both Andrew and James Melville for the Kirk, and the Chief Justice.

All had to give up their weapons as per protocol, but once all were within, a dozen soldiers quickly ringed the room, and the main door was barred. Atholl and Argyll looked to each other. Morton studied the wall tapestry of stags surrounded at the hunt. Now came Act Two: *The Reading of the Letters.*

It opened with a Surprise Entrance. The boy King Jamie Saxt lumbered in with his current guardian Erskine of Gogar. All bowed as he took his high seat, dribbling a little, his feet not quite touching the ground.

Morton's lawyer presented. These letters had come from the Duc de Guise, with his signature and seal, his messenger being Angus Nicolson, the wanted Catholic rebel. He had been intercepted with his son at St Andrews harbour by kinsmen of Lord Morton, who had received intelligence of his coming. The father had been held, then the son had fled with the letters. *These letters. Unopened. Addressed to the Lords Argyll and Atholl.*

The King swallowed saliva and grunted. Atholl and Argyll went pale and their robes seemed too big for them. Tom Nicolson was brought forward to establish he had escaped with the letters his father had brought, and then hidden in caves before finally contacting the honourable George Buchanan, in the hope of arranging the release of his estranged father.

As the guards waited, hands on hilts, Morton's lawyer broke first the seal of the letter addressed to Atholl – *Oh, man, he was pale as pork!* Bothwell cried – and began to read aloud.

After the customary felicitations, the lawyer read of the unseasonable weather, the new dance everyone was doing, the duchess's condition . . .

But now to the purpose, dear friend.

The lawyer paused dramatically, read on. *We commend your continued loyalty to King and State, alongside loyalty to the Holy Father . . . In good conscience, know you must remain honest servants and wise advisors to His Highness . . . We hear he is proving most learned and indeed a manly poet of real ability . . .* Morton's lawyer tailed off, baffled. Then his eyes read on, and his voice firmed up. *But the additional purpose of this letter is to ask you to . . .* (Dramatic pause.) *. . . promote the charms and suitability of our own dear daughter . . . would be happy to see her married to such a wise and broad-minded King as he will prove . . . peaceful friendship, religious tolerance and burgeoning trade between our Kingdoms . . . Yours ever . . . Guise.*

The lawyer coughed, stopped. The boy King nodded, seemingly amused or perhaps bored. Morton examined the cornicing, his face blank as stone. Argyll strode forward and took the letter addressed to himself, broke the seal and read aloud . . . much the same bilge. *Loyalty . . . wise, talented young King . . . possible marriage.*

Jamie Saxt held up his hand. His voice had recently broken but not yet healed.

'Why . . . why intercept such tender, wholesome letters?'

'Why indeed, Your Majesty,' from Erskine of Gogar, a man who recognised well the airt of the wind. 'Perhaps to deny your honest counsellors, the Lords Argyll and Atholl, such loyal, sound advice?'

SCOTT SEIZED MY SLEEVE as we raised our glasses to my forged letters. '*A manly poet of real ability!*' he cried. 'Our wee King's face! Very good, my friend!'

'Thank you,' I said modestly. 'I may have gilded the lily somewhat, but I judged it worthwhile. You may question a man's parentage, but praise his poetry and he is yours forever.'

AND THUS THE HEARING'S theatricals were concluded. Morton quickly excused himself – his gardens were calling, his dear wife was not well. (It was well known his wife was not of sound mind, and his three daughters likewise declared insane and prodigal. His five illegitimate children kept him busy enough.) He kissed the King's hand, and left while he still could. Atholl and Argyll withdrew for words with Buchanan. Erskine of Gogar took Jamie Saxt for a good meal and some minstrelsy, courtesy of the Archbishop and the Burgh

Council. Nicolson senior was taken into custody, still looking back at his stony-faced son.

'Buchanan anticipates my Da will receive Royal Pardon,' Tom assured me. 'After all, at great personal risk he delivered letters of friendship and loyalty – though he will be advised to return to France.'

'And that is what you wish?'

Tom looked me in the eye. 'There is nae place for him here.'

Then Scott, Bothwell, Nicolson and I toasted our successful ploy. Bothwell quickly drained his glass, then hurried off with his kinsmen for *some fun in the toun*. (In *this* town? Surely not.) Tom, Scott and I filled our glasses again and sat looking at each other, waiting for inspiration. We three had not been together in St Andrews since the night at The Skelpit Dug. What would our toast be?

The pause lengthened. Tom shook his head as he stared at his glass. It was one of those occasions when the dead return, unwelcomely. Scott looked at him close, then at me.

'Mind yon sleekit Kerr of Allertoun?' he said softly.

Tom shrugged, did not look up from his black thoughts. 'I've often wondered,' I said.

'Time that apple fell from the tree,' Walter Scott said, then began.

Kerr of Allertoun had been first among my mother's suitors, even afore my father's headstone was cut. His foppish lisp irritated me, though that was not why he had to die. Nor was it because my grandfaither had

213

been butchered by Kerrs in Embra High Street twenty-five years earlier. I was learning to pause, think on, just as my mother would consider well her options before agreeing to marry young Bothwell.

Kerr of Allertoun brought me to Newburgh with tales of hawking and bawdy girls. Great-Uncle Morton had approved the trip. (In what Eternity will his head be reunited with his body, eh?)

Under an archway in St Andrews, we had passed the lad from the Sonsie Quine, *the one whose dirk I had once borrowed — still tubby, if a little taller, almost a man. It put me in mind of my escorts last time I had sailed on that ship.* Trust nane but yer mither, *had been my father's frequent admonition.*

So I watched Kerr of Allertoun closely as our barque wallowed north. I took care not to stand in front of him on deck. I ate only dry bread and cheese, pleading mal de mer.

I was still not sure, all through the following afternoon with his falcons, hunting over the reed beds of the Tay. Was that pity in his steward's eye? Was there something bothersome in the practised way Kerr slid the hood to blind his young raptor?

The evening's entertainment brought no quines, wanton or otherwise, but mine host's fine singing might have served to relax my care. Afterwards the luthier, then the waiting-boy, then the steward slipped away. Kerr pressed me to more wine, but I declined. Did his face stiffen? Was it just natural irritation? I wasn't sure. But the absence of others, the guttering of the creusie lamp, made hair rise up my nape.

Kerr smiled, suggested I was now old enough for some braw cognac. He slid two glasses from the shadows, produced a sealed bottle and waved it before me. I gazed at his hectic face and nodded. He opened the seal with his blade, went back at the sideboard, leaned over the glasses as he filled them.

He turned back to me, proffered my glass in his right hand. I took it, sniffed, made a face.

'You'll come to like the taste,' said Kerr. 'There is no finer.'

I lifted the glass to my lips, but slowly, as if wary of this novelty. I smiled, paused my glass. 'Can we quaff this up in your tower? I want to drink whilst looking at the stars.'

His smile seemed hard work. 'Bien sûr,' he said.

I led the way, holding the creusie lamp. He followed, bottle in one hand and our full glasses in the other. The long blade on his belt scraped the walls at each turning of the stair. First-floor landing. Second floor. A small door at the top of the third stair. And there I turned. Head down, he panted upward. With all my fear and rage, I kicked out. Tumbling down the stone spiral he went, the glasses breaking and then, with a crack, his neck.

I checked he was done, then went hollering for the steward.

SILENCE AT THE END of his tale, Scott of Buccleuch raised his glass. His confession had bound us tighter to him, as if we were complicit. He waited till Tom and I had lifted ours.

'The toast?' I asked.

Scott and I looked to Tom. 'Tae the mighty dead,' he said softly. 'Lang may they lie still.'

'*Lang may they lie still!*' we chorused, and drank.

After all, who wants Pate Wilson back among us? Deep into my next glass, amid our bold and hectic laughter, I saw my dying father wink.

We drank into the night till we declared our loving fealty to each other, deep as the North Sea, only warmer. And in the morning, with a head that felt someone had hit me from behind with a horseshoe, then replaced my brains with sealing wax, I got back to the small matter of my Finals.

CHAPTER 16

A Scrimshaw Snuff-Horn

ONE NEED NOT BE a Stoic to know life holds no lasting triumphs.

When I went to see Burne for our last session on the Florentine dialect and the *Commedia*, I let myself in through the street door and hurried up his dingy stairs, looking forward to revelling in my recent ploy. I didn't doubt he knew something of it from George Buchanan.

I chapped on his door. No answer, which wasn't unusual, for he was commonly in deep thought or simply asleep. So I went in.

Nicol Burne lay stretched on his pallet with his head twisted back like a broken crab claw. His mouth gaped, his eyes wide and blank. I didn't need to put my hand on his wrist to know he had gone. Hunkered down by him, I looked round and saw that his room was in extreme disorder. Papers everywhere, books scattered and opened, chests ransacked.

Despite the chill, he was beginning to smell. He must have been here for a few days, back to when Morton's men were still looking for the letters. Now that quirky, brilliant brain was stilled. I knelt and wept.

WE BURIED HIM TWO days later, me and George Buchanan and a few other skeletal scarecrows from the old days. It was cold, it was raining. I was the only young person there.

Buchanan looked weary unto death, though he would stagger on a while yet, long enough to finish his dolorous History of Scotland.

At the graveside, he crossed himself. That Papist gesture, maybe for Paris when he and Burne were young and foolish. When he lifted his gaze from the dismal trench, our eyes met. For people like myself and Buchanan, there can be no Confession, bar the arduous to-and-fro of written words scratching towards truth.

I TRAILED WEARILY UP the stair to my bunk, mud of the grave still on my boots.

'Ye had a visitor,' Miss Whitton cried up accusingly after me. 'Yon marrit lass frae Fishertoon. And tak aff thae boots!'

There on my table lay a short, curved tusk. Pale grey, scrimshaw work along one side. I tilted it better to the light. Carving of a walrus, two men clad in furs, a three-masted ship, icebergs.

I flipped open the silvery lid at the wide end and took a pinch of high-quality snuff. Thus fortified, I read the accompanying note, written in a hand somewhat deteriorated through lack of use.

I thank you for my father's life. His father made this. Your sincere and grateful friend, Rose Gourlay (Nicolson).

I ISOLATED MYSELF FOR those last weeks of study. There came a point when I gained an elevated position from which I could see the entire landscape of four years of studies laid out. All the hedges, ditches, burns, tracks and outcrops, the unexpected short cuts and connections, were now revealed in their relations.

Grammar, Rhetoric, Logic, Natural Philosophy, Moral Philosophy, Metaphysics, all these fields fitted together, more or less understood. I saw the roles of Music and Mathematics and Theology within them. The provocations of Rose's highly original mind had a place there. I surveyed the sweep of the thought of the ancient world, then its medieval commentators, right up to the most contemporary thought (courtesy of Nicolson), Averroes and Erasmus and Montaigne, the Humanist tradition that had brought about our Renaissance, and then in time produced the Reform.

There was the rub, because I sensed Humanism and the Reform were brothers locked in deadly embrace, for one was destined to destroy the other. Socrates, Plato, Aristotle were our teachers' saints, but no amount of neo-Platonist gilding could pretend they had known Christ. Their teaching was Reason, Evidence and Debate, not Faith.

They had no Hell or Heaven, only the darkness in men's minds and the brilliant light over the Ionian Sea.

Troublesome thoughts in the night nipped like bedbugs. *We are saved by Faith alone.* But are we saved? Are we Fallen? Is God necessarily good, and how would we ken? *Gin ye concede the premise.* Are my times and place, so pressing and convincing, any more than a passing phase, even an aberration?

At times, walking the streets at night for relief, I felt myself slightly mad, a disconnected moon cut loose to wander about the Heavens at random. I began to glimpse what it was to be Tom Nicolson, with only family, gowf and me to tie him to this Earth. And I understood better the choice his more brilliant sister had made, to keep her thoughts to herself, and try to live, safe and sane, as a married fishwife.

Being myself, and not Tom Nicolson or Rose Gourlay, and the weather being too dire for gowf, in desperation I went to the Hebdomadar. He took me to the only orderly brothel in the town, used by respected clergy, merchants, Kirk elders and University staff. It did not make me more cheerful, but it did release me from thinking for an evening.

The following week, the Hebdomadar slyly suggested another outing, but to his surprise and mine, I turned it down. I did not want to obscure the wholesome pleasure and laughter once shared with Mags and Annie at Branxholme, and wished to keep the shreds of romance I had known with Rose, however painful to remember.

Instead, when I began to fear for my sanity amidst the realms of thought, I went down to the kitchen and sat of an evening with my landlady. She provided sweet pastries and I brought sloe gin, which she held to be medicine rather than alcohol.

Inspired by her medicine, Miss Whitton treated me to stories of ghaisties and gruesome martyrdoms, of local characters, noted fornicators and memorable deaths. (One yarn stays with me yet, about her neighbour Thomas Butts who had been part-crushed when demolishing the great altar in the Cathedral to get at the saint's relics, and his two friends in trying to save him had been themselves *squished flatter than flounders* when the whole structure collapsed.)

Now I was soon to be leaving, she became almost kindly. Anyway, it was better than the brothel.

NEWS CAME TO ST Andrews, so stirring that even I had to pay attention. Morton was back in power! With John Erskine and his brothers, and the agreement of Erskine of Gogar, our ex-Regent had entered Stirling Castle and taken guardianship of Jamie Saxt, claiming the King needed protection from pernicious influences (i.e. Atholl and Argyll) in the Privy Council.

When I went to his lodging, George Buchanan confirmed it. He had just been to Stirling, seen the boy King who seemed bewildered and helpless. Morton had now accused Atholl and Argyll of corresponding with Spain, seeking its financial and military assistance.

'He says there are incriminating letters, and I don't doubt it.' He stared at me. 'Do you know anything about this?'

I hotly denied it. I was preparing for Finals and didn't care who ran the country.

'And John Geddes?'

'I haven't seen him. I've scarcely seen anyone these last weeks. Enough harm has been done.'

The death's head of Nicol Burne floated between us.

'Morton has the right of it,' Buchanan said. 'But he is as hard to like as he is to dislodge. I fear the whole country will come to trial of arms.' He held up his thumb and forefinger, white and red and gnarly, like a lobster claw. 'My history cannot yet be concluded. We are this close to civil war.'

I wandered home to my bunk, disturbed and obscurely annoyed. Hard to concentrate on the Humanities when your country is riven from top to toe.

FOR A SELF-DESCRIBED *retired has-been*, George Buchanan was remarkably well-informed. Both sides, each fearing a coup by the other, raised their allies and followers. Apparently my mother had been doing healthy business in loans, asset sales and securities. Her letter was cheerful, for she believed Spain would help the Cause, perhaps provide a royal wife. She closed, *All may yet be well*, which to my mind was an incantation to disaster.

On a rare warm and sunny afternoon, just days before my Finals, the two forces met at Falkirk. For once, calculation and canniness won the day rather than crossbows, swords and cannon. Each side looked at the other and decided neither could win, as yet.

So they signed a truce. Atholl, Argyll and Morton were now all in Council. A triumvirate, all pulling together for the country's good. That had a history of working! In the streets and kirks, most were relieved but none were satisfied. I could not engage. I was done with politics. The letters affair had chiefly been for Tom Nicolson's sake, for his father, for Rose. I just hoped the peace would endure until my examinations were over.

Selfish and self-absorbed? Yes indeed. I had no doubt our leaders were, too. Even the near-saintly George Buchanan admitted his most pressing concern was that his History wouldn't be rendered out of date by fresh events. He said he aimed to end on a gloomily optimistic note, with the secure resolution of Scotland as a Reformed nation, perhaps the only true one, painstakingly chiselling out our New Jerusalem.

'With room for Humanist scholarship, free thinking, and the joyful Arts?' I enquired. 'That'll be right.' I received no reply beyond an equivocal grunt.

When we parted, the day before my Finals began, in the street outside his lodging, he said, 'I regret we bequeath you young people such uncertain times.' Then he reached out and shook my hand.

'*Gaudeamus igitur*,' I replied. 'Anyway, it touches me not.'

'Oh aye,' he said. 'That'll be right,' Chuckling throatily, he tottered off down Merkitgait.

EXIT

A Fresh Tack

To my Fellows in Early Days of the Reform,
when Town and Gown alike were Threadbare

Aitken, Niven, Francis and Carnbee,
Anderson, Saltine and Struan,
Farquhar, Gillies, Peterson and Motion,
Watson, Chalmers, Flett,
Hamilton, Hay, Dubesque and Manson.
Did not graduate – Auchterlone (gowf),
Kelvin and Ramone (lost to Theology),
Chisholm (fever), Franks (choked on bread),
Charlie Ogilvie (discharge of own pistol to his head) –

Our fees were outrageous, our landladies rapacious,
The few lasses sharp-tongued as gulls.
Our tutors exhausted, the honest in despair,
The corrupt plotting in their rooms.
All envied us, even in their grandeur, for we were young and
*   they were not.*
Their day has passed, as ours will soon enough –
Now laugh that off, Charles Ogilvie!

'OUR DAYS IN THIS wintry Hell are done,' I concluded, raising my chipped goblet to the rudimentary tables of the howff, where we exhausted, drunken brothers celebrated our Graduation. 'A toast to an end to Learning! Now let Purgatory commence!'

BOLD, BRAISANT WORDS! STILL thick in head and heavy in heart from our final night's revels and fareweels, I supervised the loading of my gear onto the cart for the harbour. I had already sold my gown to a mere child, such as I had been. The sheaves of my essays and terrible poesie, my clothes, cleeks and crossbow and writing materials were all packed in my trunk. Weighty in the valise over my shoulder I carried my *lares et penates*, the portable household gods that told me who and where I was – the St Brigid carving, the walrus snuff-box, my mother's wee jewelled crucifix, my father's blade, my three precious volumes of the *Commedia*. I still clutched my graduation certificate in my hand.

Miss Whitton reached within her cloak and handed me an orange. 'I've had waur students,' she said. 'Mind and see me gin ye return. Fare ye weel.'

She set off down the wynd with her shopping basket. How hobbled she had become. A hand gripped my arm, and there was Jeb Auchterlone, his wife and bairn standing by.

'A fine cleek you hae there!' he cried, nodding at my scroll. 'May ye clout Life's featherie lang and straight!' We kent the differing ways we had gone. At times I envied what he had. I doubt if he envied me but it may be. 'May I haud it, Will?'

I passed him my scroll. He turned it in his hardened hands while his wife waited and my trunk was hefted onto the cart. He sniffed the parchment, the purple wax seal of my college, the red one of the University. He looked out to the harbour, the boats that fished near waters and those going out into the world.

'Aye weel,' he said, quiet-like. 'Sic is life.'

He handed me back my scroll, clapped me on the shoulder, then turned to take his son's hand. 'Heid still, slow back, and dinna press!' he bawled over his shoulder, and was gone into the life of the town.

Sound advice, on the Links and anywhere! I swished the air with my scroll and stowed it within my travelling coat. I munched into the orange which, like Life itself, was both sweet and eye-wateringly sharp, then strode towards the harbour where the *Sonsie Quine* lurched, ready for the off.

THEY CAME FROM THE lee of the warehouses. One gripped his black staff, the other was carrying a bairn shawled tight to her bosom. I congratulated Rosie on its luminosity and good health. She asked me to be godparent to Lucy, who kept her eyes shut throughout. I declined, on the grounds of my being not close enough to God or St Andrews. At that bitterest moment, some strange exaltation, the relief that she would never be mine and my heart would not be risked again. (Youth, your trials were but begun!)

'You'll tak the dominie post in Arncroach?' she enquired.

'No, Fife must educate itself without me,' I said, smiling my best.

'You will teach in Embra, then?' Nicolson asked.

'I fear I hae been spoiled for that life,' I said. 'I shall embark on another.'

We shook hands, we embraced. We part not just with friends but with versions of ourselves. His lips, then hers, drying cool on my cheek.

As the *Sonsie Quine* rolled clear of the harbour, they waved to me, she with her bairn and he with his crutch. They went up the brae, grew small and black against the light, then tiny below the vaulting ribs of the Cathedral, then gone.

Thus I bade farewell to St Andrews, to the boy I had been and the men I might have been.

'AYE, THE BREEZE FAIR catches the een, does it not?' Captain Wandhaver murmured beside me. He passed his brandy flask and bade me take the wheel.

Gulls swirled about our ship as the crew emptied the bilges and I left the place of my formation. A gannet passed, unwavering, stiff-winged. As it tilted then straightened, for a moment I glimpsed what it was to be borne high above the martyrs, to roam entirely hungry and entirely calm.

To a rising wind we rounded Fifeness, then took a fresh tack for the city.

BOOK II

NOT ABOUT THE HORSES

(Trading with the World 1579–1582)

. . . Winters long-toothed, savage.

Congregations frost-mantled,
Migrant labour found stiff in barns.
Surgeons whittled fingers like clothes pegs.

Brandy and poor coal. Peat smoulders,
Laughter and loving in the ingle-nook,

Always danger unwrapping . . .

William Fowler, verso note on his draft Machiavelli translation,
(Hawthornden Collection, Edinburgh)

CHAPTER I

A New Pair of Shoes

THE SHOES ANNOUNCE THE man, and surely these proclaim
Quality: best Flemish leather stained three shades of brown,
seams double-stitched in crimson, long padded tongues soft on the
shins. Not one brass buckle, but two! The concealed risers within add
an inch and a half to one's stature, in a way four years of strenuous
thought at University had failed to.

Those shoes cost more than I could reasonably afford, but no
more than I intended to be able to soon enough. My sister Susannah
had faked to swoon at the sight of them. My mother assessed, then
nodded approval. She too dressed slightly above her station – not so
much as to excite malice or derision, but enough to signal her worth
as she would wish others to take it.

I pulled our door to and stood a while in fresh May sunlight.
Raised above the mud, dung and detritus of the streets where I made
my living, I surveyed the High Street, our St Giles Reformed kirk,

the Netherbow Port with its lounging guards. Ayont that, the orchards and town houses of the Canongait fell away towards Holyrude, that viper's nest. In the distance mast-thatched Leith and the blue-grey Firth of Forth . . .

The city, my city! That morn in fine shoes I stood above my other attempted selves – scholar, poet, lover, scribe, forger. Not a gentleman, though my unborn children might yet be. *I am William Fowler and my trade is trade.*

I dealt in what folk seek once their immediate needs are met: fine-made furnishings, for those not of a Puritan disposition. Of late there was a growing taste for lightness, fancy, pleasure over dour function, in items such as candlesticks, embellished dowry kists, long-clocks, tapestries, and padded armchairs to ease the tender arse.

In our uncertain times, well-to-do folk could abruptly lose everything, be sent to the Tolbooth, exiled or dispatched into the next world. Their furnishings must then be valued and sold in turn to others who prosper for now. Occasionally there were ecclesiastical items which needed to be handled with discretion. Such was life under Regent Morton.

Trade makes the world turn, as lately some say it does, on its own axis around a fixed sun. I was my own master, profiting by my late father's honest reputation and my mother's contacts. My Grammar was complete, though less used of late. My French was good, German, Gaelic and Dutch all workable, my Florentine Italian adequate for reading and reciting among like-minded friends.

These breeches, waxed jerkin and bonnet were functional for

handling goods in changeable weathers. The shoes signalled higher hopes, more sophisticated possibilities and tastes, without being *de trop* . . .

Stocktaking of the self completed, I clacked down the High Street of Embra – young, unattached, with losses, regrets and deeds I kept to myself. A non-Calvinist God might look down and forgive the pleasure a young man took that morning in his footwear, in the early warmth of the day, and the smiles of the quines at the flower stall.

I raised my eyes to the Firth and distant Fife. Out there lay St Andrews, and within its walls worked my closest friend in the world, and a lass once loved and marvelled at. But now she was a wife and mother, her early bloom going even as her fingers moved nimbly among nets. I prayed she kept her dangerous thoughts to herself, and that once in a while she thought on me, her friend and confidant. As for our sole heart-blooming kiss . . .

I descended into the Lawnmerkit, humming *In Scarlet Town where I was born, There was a fair maid dwelling.* I turned into the shadow of the wynd leading to my storehouse. *And her name was Barbara Allen.*' As I lifted the latch, a blow to the head turned the world black and white, and then nothing.

MY HEAD A THUNDERCLOUD, with lightning flashing through. I am in my storehouse, sprawled on the blue velvet Parisian couch. The faces above me are my new workshop boy – whose name I seem to have mislaid – and Mitchison the clock-maker, and a pale-cheeked lassie with tight curls.

My next thought: I must not bleed on the couch. Blood is the devil to clear from velvet. I gasped and clutched my chest as I sat up. *Jesu!*

'Aye, they gave ye a right thrashing,' Mitchison intoned. 'They'll no be friends of yours, I'm thinking.'

Patrick Mitchison's premises were in the close next to mine. A superior carpenter and clock-maker, with a sideline in coffin-making. It has perhaps moulded his wit. After all, what is a long-case clock but a coffin with a pendulum for a heart and intricate cogs for a brain?

'Only my fellow writers hate me that much,' I replied, rolling my head gently, waiting for the room to settle. 'Did ye get a look at them?'

Mitchison grimaced. 'They ran off when I hollered!'

'One was that toe-rag Papist, Claud Hamilton,' the lassie said. 'They came frae their hoose in the Cowgate in an awfy temper, on account of the stushie at Holyrude.'

Mitchison looked uneasy, unsure of my allegiances. 'You shouldn't take heed of my daughter,' he said. 'Her een are no great.'

'They look fine tae me,' I said. Got a smile, and perhaps a blush staining the girl's wan cheeks, her determined mouth.

'Take no heed of my faither,' she said. 'He kens nothing beyond escapements and counterweights, bless him. Name's Marianne, by the way.'

The Hamiltons. I had thought to leave all that behind in St Andrews. 'So what's this stushie, Marianne?'

'You've no heard yet? The Duke o Atholl went for a banquet with Regent Morton yestreen!'

I nodded. The room swirled, then settled. 'Good for him.'

'No, really,' Marianne chirped triumphantly. 'He took ill on the way hame, and now he's deid! Seems the wine didna agree wi him.'

Mitchison nodded, his long lugs flapping. 'Word is Regent Morton will be made head of the Privy Council again. That leaves Argyll chief among the Papists.'

So Regent Morton got Atholl in the end. Small wonder the Hamiltons were incensed. 'I dinna ken why they had to take it out on me,' I complained. I minded John Geddes's words after The Skelpit Dug: *Your name has gone out and canna be recalled.*

Marianne Mitchison was practical and sympathetic as she took a damp cloth to my head. Her eyes were hazel-grey, like early catkins.

'Let's get you mended,' she said.

JOHN GEDDES HAD MOVED to Embra after my graduation, secured himself funding from the royal purse, working up an arithmetical compendium to enlarge our young King's understanding. He was also acting as researcher and helpmeet for George Buchanan while that revered scholar struggled to complete his *Rerum Scoticarum Historia* before our country changed yet again.

Geddes raised a well-plucked eyebrow at my bandaged head as he welcomed me into Buchanan's lodging in Kennedy Close. He barred the door, for the streets and alleys outside were agitated, as though the Duke of Atholl's death were a stick prodded into a wasp's nest.

Buchanan was within, hunched at his writing table. Wax-yellow hand to his forehead, propping up the weight of his brains. He didn't look up. Beside him was a stack of fresh unbound copies of his book *De Jure Regni Apud Scotos*. This provocative dialogue asserted that, from the days of Fergus, in Scotland the ruler was chosen by the people, and any subsequent king was bound to those conditions, and may be removed if he becomes tyrannical or incompetent – akin to the Presbytery having the right to choose a minister, and to remove him if he displeased.

Unsurprisingly, Buchanan's former pupil Jamie Saxt had lately condemned the book.

'Grand publicity!' John Geddes declared. 'The printer can't print it fast enough.'

'And if it is banned?' I enquired, sniffing fresh ink on the copy in my hand, the heady whiff of a life less ordinary than a trader's.

'Even better,' Geddes said. 'It becomes essential reading!'

'Very well for ye to say,' Buchanan murmured. 'It's not your head on the block.'

Still, he didn't seem that perturbed. Perhaps equanimity came with age – the man must be in his late sixties, heading for the exit anyway. Yet he kept writing, and took his seat in Parliament, despite being out of favour. A lesson in persistence.

'Keep yon copy, *petit* Fowler,' Buchanan said. 'Best not carry it openly near Holyrude! Still writing poetry, I hope?'

'Not so much of late,' I admitted, suddenly ashamed to have become so bound up with furniture. 'My *Tarantula of Love* sonnets seem to be hibernating.'

I stowed Buchanan's book in my satchel, to get it bound when I could afford to. Then I produced the parcels of best Flemish ink, a new sideline. Buchanan's eyes lit up.

'Grand!' he said. 'Time to advance my calamitous History of Scotland. It will claim to purge our history of English lies and Scottish vanity – words guaranteed to offend all!'

'A purgative, right enough!' Geddes enthused. 'It will make many boke, but in the end settle the stomach and clear the head.'

Oh Lord, that man. Brush against him once and he sticks like a burr to woollen hose. As Geddes laid out the fresh ink pots, I fingered the bundle of used quills, both italic and secretarial cut. Habit urged me to take my pen-knife and trim the blunted nibs, but it is the height of presumption to shape another's quill.

'I admire your resolve, sir,' I said. 'Is it not dangerous to publish such views?'

Buchanan's lips quivered in a near-smile. 'I am o'er old to be worth killing. If they but wait a year or two, Time will do it for them.' He looked down at his manuscript, then chuckled. 'Besides, James Stewart may drool, yet he is no daftie. He understands that making martyrs is both tempting and foolish. He learned that from me.'

He selected his quill. I looked down at that ancient skull in which two seas, the Renaissance and the Reformation, contended and mingled. As a Humanist scholar, George Buchanan was well-acquaint with martyrs, both Catholic and Reformers. He had barricaded himself in the English Ambassador's house on St Bartholemew's Day, while outside in the streets of Paris Huguenots were slaughtered in their thousands. He had walked with both Calvin and Rabelais, and knew men who had known Erasmus. On the shelf behind him, waiting to be discussed among trusted friends, was the latest manuscript from another former pupil, Michel de Montaigne, *That the Profit of One Man is the Damage of Another.*

My fingers yearned to stroke Buchanan's head, smooth down his errant clumps of white hair – to bless, or obtain a blessing?

'*Excusez-moi*, I don't feel rightly,' I said. My head felt very strange. 'I maun awa hame.'

George Buchanan turned and assessed me. 'Aye, you've taken a fair dunt. John – will you see young Fowler hame? Some ill-starred folk out there.'

Geddes nodded and picked up a heavy stick. He also carried a blade under his coat, was said to be handy with it.

'I hope to see you at the play in St Andrews,' I said, both reluctant and desperate to leave. 'Thank you for the invitation.'

'I'll be there, if spared.' Buchanan chuckled, then turned back to his unfinished page. He propped his forehead, dipped his pen, a man towards the end of his life, impatient to set down the truth as best he knows it. And what else are we to do in our closing days?

AS WE HURRIED THROUGH the Grassmerkit, turning into the vennels whenever we heard horsemen or raised voices, Geddes gripped me by the elbow.

'The Hamiltons have overplayed their hand. Now we may prosper!'

I nodded, then regretted it. My brain resembled the *Sonsie Quine* rolling on a rough day in the Firth. It was crewed by Captain Wandhaver, shouting orders at Marianne Mitchison. Rose Nicolson watched, bound to the mast, bairn in her arms, her husband John Gourlay at the wheel.

On the steps up to the steep West Bow, I stumbled and retched. Geddes was talking – Lord, how that man talks! – about the arithmetical primer he is completing for the boy King. It will contain operations that allow Jamie Saxt to calculate his incomes and expenditures, establish his lands, and follow the latest algebraic debates, the dizzying possibilities of cube roots . . .

I fell to my knees and retched to bile. Am I going to die here, in this pishy vennel below the Castle, but five minutes' walk from where I was born, with a man haivering about *imagined numbers*? I had hoped for more.

'Hame.' I gasp out the bairnie word. Not *domus*, *chez moi*, or *home*, but the one safe place. 'For the Lord's sake tak me hame.'

I AM HAME. IN my bed. Looking at that well-kent ceiling. My mother bends o'er me.

'Who did this?' she demands. 'Hamiltons? Why would they do that? They are good men!'

'Doubtless they mistook me,' I say, close my eyes.

SHE WAS BACK, WITH Susannah anxious at her shoulder.

'John, Claud and David Hamilton have gone into the Western March with their followers,' she said. 'Government troops pursue them. Good Atholl is dead and that fiend Morton holds the field again. *Mon Dieu*, is there no end to our troubles?'

'Apparently not,' I murmured.

My sister offered soup in my horn christening spoon. 'Marianne Mitchison and her faither ask after you. I said ye'll no be needing wan o his coffins just yet.'

I just about smiled, slurping broth.

'Mitchison is a leading light in his guild,' Mother said. 'A burgess to boot. I ken by the cut of his coat that he is of the Faith.' My mother claimed to know a Reformer by his gait or the angling of his beard. 'And the girl is healthy and realistic. I have asked them to call again.'

Oh God, my mother approves.

THREE DAYS LATER I cautiously sipped claret in the Counting House. My thoughts were still disconnected, but now I saw but one of everything. Word was, John, David and Claud Hamilton had sailed for France, their followers and kin dispersed. Argyll still lived but Regent

Morton headed the Privy Council again. Jamie Saxt's voice had broken, but he still stammered and drooled. He was not yet the complete man.

'I will journey to St Andrews soon,' I announced, casual-like.

My mother's lips twitched. 'That's pleasant,' she said, not entirely pleasantly. 'See your old friends and sweethearts.'

'I look to extend the Anderson loan, attend a play where there will be good contacts, and take delivery of assorted snuffs.'

'Filthy habit! All those handkerchiefs.'

'I think of going into partnership. Snuff and tobacco are the coming thing.'

My mother sniffed. 'A fad.' And here we go again. 'There is more money to be made in finance than goods. Ships sink. Goods are cumbersome. Finance ne'er goes out of fashion.'

I sipped the woody wine. 'I hear Morton has called down the silver content of the coinage again,' I observed. 'What is a Scots pound now? Half the English?'

She smiled triumphantly. 'I kenned from the Chancellor – a good man of the Old Faith – that was in the wind. So I changed my cash to English whiles back, then bought back the Scots. Fifteen per cent augmentation!'

I looked at her, flushed and bright-eyed like when she came from secret Mass. I stroked the polished arm of my father's favoured chair, in dark walnut, a twin-masted sailing ship carved on its panelled flank.

'You can't sit on fifteen per cent,' I said.

'Just watch me!' she replied. 'I've asked the Mitchisons for their tea the morn. Bonnie enough lass.'

A shrewd investment, in my mother's eyes. My sister hollered up the stair. 'It's Bishop Leslie! I'm awa to see Master Drummond!'

'Could you leave us alone, Willie?' my mother said.

'Surely,' I replied, getting to my feet. 'Business?'

'Of a sort.'

I passed the Bishop of Ross on the stair, got a formidable stare from under eyebrows the size and shade of bat wings.

'Hail Mary, Mother of God,' John Leslie intoned.

'Aye, you'll find her in the Doo-Cot.'

I headed on down the stair, stepping as always around the long-gone, ever-present pool of my father's blood. I entered the bright day, wondering what was important enough to bring Bishop Leslie, a man more full of plots than a skipper's charts, from the safety of the North to a city where the Protestant cause was supposedly firmly in the ascendant.

(We would learn in time what my mother's visitor set in motion that day. Much was hidden and would remain so. Some scenes were played out in tumultuous streets; others took place in councils where the doors were barred and guards stood hands on swords. In private quarters, there were flurried limbs and whispered confidences. Some of this was reported to me, not always truthfully. Some I saw with my own eyes. And there were a few moments when I was more than witness, and did what I believed – or was led to believe – had to be done. Those scenes rise and tilt again as the pale gull of my hand glides over the pages.)

Chapter 2

Skipper Lindsay makes a Prophecy

I STEPPED BRISKLY UP THE familiar brae from St Andrews harbour, unencumbered by books. All I required were the documents and writing materials in my satchel. The ruined Cathedral was more skeletal, the wind still piercing as an awl. Fish, salt and midden, a soul-stirring tonic! I ascended past the drying green, glanced out of habit, but no fishwives there today, just a lad moodily mending lobster creels, two doors along from where *she* used to bide afore her marriage.

I hurried on. The bunting was up for the King's visit. The Castle works looked near-complete, with a new tower and grand entrance across the drawbrig. The window through which Archbishop Beaton had once dangled by his ankle in a bloody nightgown had been clear-glassed. All was trig and sprush, the banners snapped in the wind.

My old friend stood waiting on the setts, hard by George Wishart's fire-scarred blot. Same long thin beak, dark eyes staring intently below wild hair. A man composed of angles, leaning on his staff, today in his best gear.

'*Salve, amice!*'

'*Salve* yourself,' I replied. 'I'm done wi Grammar.'

We clasped hands, glanced at each other, checking. It had been the best part of a year. Perhaps we now sailed in different directions, in time to disappear from each other over the horizon.

'Vernacular, then,' Nicolson said in that jerky way of his. 'Mither has asked ye for yer tea eftir.'

'Gladly! I aye liked your mother.'

'She still bears a queer fondness for you.'

John Geddes, our patron for the afternoon playing, beckoned from under the archway. Behind him stood George Buchanan, his patron in turn. I briefly visioned all of us as pendant from another, from beggar to Earl, all the way up to Jamie Saxt – who dangled from God's thumbs, yet was perhaps helpless as any.

As we set foot on the drawbrig, Nicolson muttered, 'Rose asks after you but she'll no be there. She's busy wi the bairn.'

That ship had long sailed. Just a topmost flag on the horizon, still fluttering.

GEORGE BUCHANAN GOT US through the grand entrance and into the Castle. There he greeted a clean-shaven man I recognized as the canny courtier John Maitland of Lethington, who had turned up at one of our informal Embra poetry gatherings. I raised my hand in greeting. Maitland turned away coldly. In this setting, I was being impertinent.

'Never ye mind,' Tom Nicolson muttered. 'Every man still sits upon his ain arse.'

We squeezed into the crowded hall. It was my first time within the Bishop's Castle, first time at a full-length play, playing being against the Law of our land. So many fine folk, so dressed up! Such a quantity of satin and bright-dyed cloth! Hats from the Hielands, from France and Netherlands, some that drooped languidly about the wearer's lugs, others sprouting feathers like shocked birds.

My travelling cloak was crumpled and stained from the voyage. I felt myself a peasant in that gathering, though Tom seemed more amused than awed. A flicker-memory of auld Knox and his young wife, a quick glance of care atween them as they entered St Giles, in what now seemed another age.

Fair or pox-marked, all were mortal men and women. *Aa equal in the sight of God*, my father's core belief, mildly held yet immovable. *E'en the King*. Nicolson nudged me in the ribs, nodded towards a plump, jerky boy in gold satin and blue hose, being led through the press. He tried to climb onto a raised dais, struggled, then accepted a pull-up. He sat in a painted chair, face flushed almost to the colour of his hair.

E'en the King. Next to him I recognized the Earl of Morton, a thick-lipped glowering mass of meat. The men in silver hose either side of him were lean as knives.

'Maist of the Privy Council are here,' Geddes whispered. 'Andrew

Melville and the Kirk men didna come, preferring sober truth to make-believe.'

'Yon's the chief wizard,' Nicolson said. He pointed out a wispy man, smiling faintly as if at a joke he alone heard. 'Sir Richard Divers, author of our play. Local man.'

'The play is put on by Maitland,' Geddes said, not to be outdone. 'It is cried *Philotus*. A comedy in the Italian manner, but in metrical Scots. The King is said to favour the vernacular, yet is in thrall to the Continental. So, a canny choice!'

At the last, Scott of Buccleuch and Bothwell pressed into the gathering. Bothwell saw us, nodded indifferently. Scott grinned across the distance of our rank. The Great Hall was shoulder-to-shoulder full as the doors closed. Two soldiers stood behind Jamie Saxt, wriggling in his seat like a plump golden trout. The room smelled richly of candlewax, lamp oil, and incense's heady notes over men's sweat. John Knox would be rotating in his grave.

There were but three women in the hall, discreetly in the far corner. The boy King had no wife, and so no ladies-in-waiting. His mother, our former Queen, remained secured 'for her better protection' in some stronghold in England, still with a claim on the English throne and her son's. If she returned, it would be with a foreign husband and army. Little wonder Jamie Saxt twitched and jerked like a fish on the line.

In swept the trumpets, followed by honking bassoons. A bass viol juddered low, then the river-gnats' wail of small pipes. Our boy King's mouth was open, rapt, drooling slightly.

Two pretty lads dressed as *Peace* and *Justice* (the signs on their false bosoms proclaimed them as such, for the slow of understanding) appeared on the stage. Their courtly dance accelerated, becoming excitable and inciting. Then priapic clowns rushed on and cavorted till they were chased away by men with long grey beards, surely ministers of the Reform, who then celebrated their victory with discreet but unmistakeable self-stroking as they exited.

Laughter, laughter with unease following this introductory masque. Many looked to the King. The boy was leant forward, his high barking laughter clear over the music. Most of the audience took their cue from him.

Tom Nicolson murmured in my ear, 'Naebody loses money under-estimating public taste.'

Fair point, but it was all new to me, and the Masque *was* quite funny. *Peace* and *Justice* – the latter alarmingly attractive – took a bow and slipped behind the curtain, leaving the stage empty for the Play proper.

We had no theatre in Scotland, on account of the Kirk. England also had a Reformed Kirk, yet I had heard plays were lately all the rage there. Not Buchanan's Latin plays, to be read in private among friends, not coarse masquerades, nor solemn enactments of scenes from the liturgy, but full-length poetical plays of History, Tragedy and Comedy, in the vernacular, in a purpose-built theatre, apparently to audiences in their hundreds, most days of the week!

I watched Jamie Saxt, excited, flushed, twitching away on his chair, eyes darting round the room as the wine circulated. If he lived to rule over the Kirk and the Council, he might in time redeem our dour, beloved backwater.

From the upper gallery, so muted the room had to hush, there seeped a two-string fiddle. Old music, a tune bared to the bone, the sound of wind keening across bare muir. I kenned the bleak melody and the story, as did everyone in the hall, for it was ours.

> *Oh dig me a grave and dig it sae deep*
> *And cover it o'er wi floors sae sweet,*
> *And I will turn in for tae tak a lang sleep*
> *And maybe in time I'll forget her.*

THE LAST NOTES WERE followed by long silence. The King was openly weeping. Morton looked like he'd seen the ghosts of his murdered rivals. Ancient George Buchanan stared off into space, thinking perhaps of a woman in Paris in his youth.

The hall was briefly bound in an accounting of souls. Then came applause and its release.

GEDDES SECURED WINE, PUFFED out his cheeks. 'Blimey, lads! Bring on the comedy!'

'It's good to know we can do something brawlie,' I said. 'Could I but make a poem like yon song!'

'When I was a bairn,' Nicolson said quietly, 'my faither would play the great pipes, so dismal it would mak a stane weep.'

Geddes lifted his glass. 'To our bonniest companie!' he cried.

In that moment, with wine-reddened lips and slightly bulbous eyes shining, he was buoyant, a barque in full sail. Years later, his sea-chest would be found on a gleaming beach near Calais. When forced open, the letters within were so incriminating to the Crown, their contents were never recorded. John Geddes would be pronounced dead, though his body was never found. Murder, accident, or self-harm?

We drank a toast and turned to the Play proper.

WHAT CAN BE SAID of *Philotus* that afternoon? Doubtless it was ragged, being a one-off performance. The leads were two men and a boy, real players borrowed from the Earl of Leicester. The others were retainers, bejantine students, and local laddies selected by Maitland with the King in mind.

It had awkward pauses, hesitations and pratfalls, only some of which were intended. The costumes – borrowed from the trunks of the great and good – and hastily painted back-drops, some not yet quite dry, served their purpose. The music was vigorous, sometimes drowning out the verse – no great loss there.

But for most of us, it was our first full-length play. A comedy, and in Scots! The wine, jokes, bawdiness and snacks kept coming, so for the first Act, all was jocund in the crowded hall.

As I mind it, the plot was a series of variations on the Old Rich Man, a Virtuous Daughter, and the Poor Young Man. The Old Rich Man is enamoured of a Panderous Father's Virtuous

Daughter. Poor Young Man falls in love with her and they run away together. But she has an identical twin, a brother! He is persuaded to dress as his sister, and no one is able to tell the difference. As such she/he marries the Rich Old Man, and they go off together to consummate the marriage.

At this point the comic became saucy, then rapidly declined (or ascended, depending on taste) from the bawdy to the disturbing. The King looked flushed and excited, as were a good proportion of the audience. I noticed the three women had left the hall.

To complicate things, the Rich Old Man *also* has a Lovely Daughter, who is seduced by the Twin Brother, formerly presenting as a woman, now presenting as a man. They engaged in on-stage bawdiness, then went behind some thin silk, lit to show their shadow-forms vigorously coupling.

Things rather went downhill after that.

'A COMEDY OF ERRORS?' Nicolson said as the players took their bow. 'Mair a farrago of lewd nonsense!'

'It was a bit close to the bone,' I conceded.

'*Bone* is the word!' Geddes laughed. 'Yon fair-haired laddie is a richt tart. He fair got them going!'

Many of the audience stayed for the wine and sweetmeats and useful contacts. The hubbub grew louder. The King received loyal greetings, kneelings, bowings. He looked still stunned by what he had witnessed.

Then a commotion erupted like a dust-swirl raised in the street. It became a short, wide man with an engorged nose, torrential whiskers and a very tall hat. His arms were raised as he birled through the parting crowd.

'It's Skipper Lindsay,' Nicolson whispered. 'He's having one of his turns.'

Lindsay came to the seat where James Douglas, the Earl of Morton, was still flanked by his silvery guards. There he spun to a halt. His eyes focused on Morton. His right arm extended. Two gnarled fingers jabbed at the most powerful man in Scotland.

'You!' Skipper Lindsay shouted. The room was deadly silent. 'James Douglas, your days are numbered, and that number is small! Small, I say!'

Morton seemed unable to move. He looked to the boy King as though in appeal to stop this nonsense, but Jamie the Saxt wiped saliva from his mouth and stared down at his fingers. Skipper Lindsay then uttered, in a cracked whisper from the depths of his being, 'This is my malisoun, Morton – *You shallna see your gardens green anither year!*'

Skipper Lindsay then fell to the floor. He was surrounded by friends and carried away before anyone else could get to him. The courtiers whispered. Morton shrugged his beefy shoulders and managed to smile, but some words, once out, cannot be gainsaid.

'Well bugger me to Rome and back!' Geddes said excitedly amid the emptying hall. 'Had Morton been cursed thus in private or in the street, he would have dispatched Lindsay on the spot. But this was at a play, and the man was clearly raving, so he was stymied! And what did the King do?'

'He wiped his drool and looked at his hand,' I said.

'And the rest of the Privy Council will have taken note.' Geddes rubbed his hands. 'So Morton is diminished, and the King aggrandised!'

'Aristotle wrote there is a tiny sharp-toothed fish,' Nicolson observed to the general air, 'that makes its living cleaning the bigger teeth of its masters.'

John Geddes considered his wine. 'Aristotle also notes that the little fish is itself seldom eaten, owing to its agility and usefulness.'

I laughed. It was not often I heard my friend bested.

'Then you had best remain useful and agile, young friends.' George Buchanan had silently joined us. 'I am too old and tough to be worth eating.'

We gallantly protested this was not so. 'What made you of the play, sir?' I enquired.

'It made me glad I will soon be leaving this place.' Buchanan took me by the elbow and spoke for my ear alone. 'It is time you met someone. Say your farewells and come wi me.'

He moved with surprising rapidity through the crowd. Two guards parted before a narrow doorway. Buchanan led down a chill corridor, up steps, then paused at a couple of massive boar heads. A florid script informed us that these vast beasts were killed by James IV on the same day in Holyrude Park.

'I hope you are as adept in the Florentine dialect as Nicol Burne claimed,' Buchanan said.

'There is not much call for it these days,' I replied.

Buchanan moved on, stopping at another guarded door. 'Well, there is now,' he said. 'He's mad for it.' He knocked, and we entered.

As I bent on one knee and bowed my head, gazing close-up at a crimson embroidered slipper, our King declared '*Nel mezzo del cammin di nostra vita!*'

His partially broken voice was as himself, ungainly but persistent.

I responded, '*Mi ritrovai per una selva oscura, Ché la diritta via era smarrita.*'

A seal-like bark passed for laughter. 'Stand!'

For a moment we looked each other in the eye, the stripling King and the young merchant trader with his redundant University degree. 'You are short and well-rounded,' James Stewart the Sixth of that line said. 'Are you endowed so?'

To the side, two courtiers laughed obediently. I sensed they had heard this kind of thing before.

'*Ahi quanto a dir qual era è cosa dura*,' I replied. How hard a thing it is to speak of more.

A stare opened on me like the night blooming. Then Jamie Saxt started to giggle. 'Very good!' he said. 'Excellent!' He gestured towards a stool. 'Sit!'

I sat, the wad-wyfe's son. *Aa equal in the sicht of God.* I reminded myself that my mother had administered revenues from this lad's mother's French estates. Mortgages and loans against security maintained what Court there was. They likely helped pay for the afternoon's entertainment.

Jamie Saxt waved the courtiers to leave, which they did, sulkily, with a little *moue* and tip of the hips. The sole armed attendant remained, alert, right hand poised on the hilt of his sword. George Buchanan stood silently at the window, the leaden sea at his back.

'So,' the boy King said, 'to poetry and *belles lettres*. I understand you have written Scots sonnets on the pains of love. Perhaps you would care to pass comment on these poor efforts of mine?'

Advancement opened up before me like a cathedral door, and I blessed the shade of Nicol Burne, turning to mush in his pauper's grave.

'SO YOU AND THE King are not as estranged as some say?' I ventured as we clacked down the wooden drawbrig back onto solid ground. My knees were weak and my brains had seized. I could hear my own voice speaking as from a great distance.

Buchanan chuckled as he wound his stole tighter about his throat. 'Lately we have been reconciled to a degree. As his rule approaches, the waters grow choppy.'

'I have noticed. Important people are losing their heads.'

'He trusts me, because I am near the end and have no ambitions beyond completing my *Rerum Scoticarum Historia*. He does not enjoy my views on Scottish elective kingship, but on account of them, the Kirk trusts me. So I can inform him of their current concerns, divisions and debates. The nobility also trust me, for I am not in competition wi them.'

'So you inform the King on them all.'

Buchanan inclined his head in assent. 'In times of division, we need conduits – underground, secret connections – more than ever. Even between the Two Kingdoms, there are conduits. Some call them spies.' He looked at me, chuckled in his ancient throat. 'Some of them *are* spies. The rest are bearers of information and hidden diplomacy. Some day you may serve as one such.' He abruptly halted in the shadow of the Swallowgait. 'Not a word of this meeting to your friends. Not even John Geddes.'

'Why me?' I protested. 'I am just a merchant with a degree I don't use, and more poems burned than copied.'

Buchanan leaned close, his eyes milky but unwavering in the dusk. 'Because I think ye are honest.'

'In business, maybe. As for the rest . . .'

Buchanan waved his hand as though wearily swatting away a midge. 'I am sure you serve yourself, young Fowler. Doubtless you are as vain, delusional and self-seeking as any other. *But* – correct me if I am wrong – I believe you may serve the least bad cause of our days.'

I would consider this conversation for many days and many years: the salty gloaming as we stood in the Swallowgait, the sense of things pulling together, the net of my life taking shape around me.

'I dinna ken the cause you mean,' I managed.

He poked me gently in the chest, somewhere about the heart. 'I think ye do. So did Nicol Burne.'

And I did, in some way. 'Sir, I am not a Calvinist,' I protested.

Buchanan shrugged. 'In the end that is neither here nor there.' He paused, looked at the shell of the Cathedral against the darkening sky, folk hurrying homeward below the hungry gulls. He looked at it all with softened mouth and haunted eyes, like a man saying farewell to it all. 'I expect you are now deep in the *Purgatorio*,' he murmured, 'in which our hero navigates the deceptive promises of the temporal world?'

'Since you put it like that – *Si, maestro. È vero.*'

He chuckled. 'My young friend, we shall see more dark times, yet in the long run we may see light again. What is a Morton or an Atholl here or there, even a King or a Pope?'

Buchanan stared at me fiercely, then began coughing fit to choke. I put out my hand, touched his frail shoulder. 'I'd best see you safely home, sir,' I said gently. 'The night is coming on.'

The legendary old man had just recruited me. My life as a trader and occasional makar was compromised, and would always remain so.

Now I stare out the window from my sick-bed in Spitalfields, and wonder if John Geddes died at sea at all, or was that whole scene, the locked trunk on the shining empty beach, the scandalous letters, his last and most brilliant forgery?

CHAPTER 3

A Stymie is Laid

IN THE MORN WE gathered at the St Andrews Links, and put cleek to ball for sake of old lang syne.

A flip of coin partnered me with impetuous Bothwell. Tom Nicolson played with Scott of Buccleuch, who brought all his physical prowess, dash and resolve to the game, but had no talent for it. His frustration was entertainment to all but himself.

Jeb Auchterlone accompanied the four of us as cadet, tutor, old acquaintance and dispute-resolver. The purse we played for was put up by Scott and Bothwell, Nicolson being skint as always and myself but a poor poet and young trader.

The day was bright, with a fresh onshore wind rugging at our coats as we embarked on the hole cried *Lang Whang*. Each played according to his nature. I thought long, took a three-quarter swing with my wooden cleek, and sent the featherie ball short but straight. I had been practising, when time allowed.

Francis Stewart, Earl of Bothwell, was well-made and long-armed. He swung freely, committed to the ploy and sure of his success. His ball flew high and long, was caught by the breeze and stotted into long grass. He laughed. He had come from a gainful season of Border-reiving, riding under Regent Morton's protection. Grass and whins would not impede his progress.

And Walter Scott of Branxholme and Buccleuch, that fast-developing boy? He selected a long-shafted cleek from Auchterlone, frowned at his ball, then took a mighty swipe. The ball skited off the toe and ended on the beach. Much laughter. Scott flushed. Then he controlled himself. 'I'll play anither,' he said.

As he teed up, Jeb Auchterlone spoke. 'Dinna press,' he said. 'Heid still and slow back.'

Scott glared at him. 'I ken that,' he said.

He surveyed his new featherie ball. This time he kept his head still, swung back with great deliberation – then rushed the downswing. His head came up, the ball stayed down. It scuttered off the heel of the club into the nearest gorse. None dared speak.

Tom Nicolson handed Auchterlone his staff and selected the shorter driving iron. Clearly he was going to have to carry his partner. This game could elevate a cobbler and crush a Lord of the Congregation. We valued it for that even-dealing. He murmured the words of Marcus Aurelius: *Confine yourself to the present task*. Tom's drive went well past mine, but stopped short of the burn.

We crossed the wee brig over the Swilcan burn, past the net menders and laundry women, on to whatever the day brought.

THE LINKS WERE BUSY, for all that it was the Sabbath. From time to time the Kirk tried to have the game banned altogether, but Archbishop John Hamilton had been a keen gowfer and currently the Links were open to the general.

'He cannot have been all bad,' Scott remarked on the green at *Lang Whang*. 'For a Hamilton.'

'Killing Regent Moray in Linlithgow was pretty bad,' Bothwell said.

'I'm not sure he did,' Scott rejoined. He looked at me as I prepared to hole out. 'What do you say, Will?'

Then I was back in that terrible room at The Skelpit Dug, with the squealch of the knife going into Pate Wilson. My short putt wobbled past the hole. Scott of Buccleuch laughed innocently. Bothwell pulled out his brandy flask, took a good slug, then holed out for the half.

Lang Whang was followed by *Agin the Wind*, so called because it aye seemed to be. Still shaken, I placed my ball on its cone of sand. I called on Seneca. *That which must happen, will happen. Only shallow minds grieve over it.* I made my swing, and the ball flew well enough, considering.

Coming the other way down the fairway we met John Lindstrom teamed with the young heir of Lennox, taking on Skipper Lindsay and his brother. No mention was made of last night's stushie at the play.

Skipper Lindsay was an utterer of random quips, a drinker. Yet folk thought he had the gift of prophecy. *Ye shall not see your gardens green anither year.* It could not be unsaid. Today he was just another stout, tattered, red-faced man.

'So who shall win out in the end, Skipper?' Auchterlone asked slyly. Meaning: Morton or Argyll?

'Nae idea,' Skipper said. He looked to the ground, subdued. Then he twirled his niblick high. 'I tell you this much – we shall win by four shots!'

Their party headed off homeward down *North Mid*, and our match went on to *Sawmill*, where Scott joined Nicolson by the hole. 'Dinna fash yersel, Wattie,' I heard Tom say. 'We hae the beating o them.' Such familiarity would have offended at yesterday's gathering, but here on the course, Walter Scott clapped him on the shoulder.

As we went all square going down the last hole, *Hame*, my partner Bothwell remained confident. I was trying to be merry, but I'd been failing to hole out and wasn't best pleased. As the end approached, I could see Nicolson's Stoic indifference was likewise becoming threadbare as his hose.

Bothwell hammered the ball. It went high, swithered about in the breeze, then bounced up near the hole. Auchterlone applauded. Myself and Nicolson were both out of it, having spent several shots in a sandhole. It was down to Walter Scott.

He stared at the distant flag, daring it to defy him, gave a great skelp with his mashie niblick. The result was a truly fine shot. His ball ran wonderfully well towards the hole and came to rest just inches short of Bothwell's.

We approached the green to find Scott had left himself a stymie, with Bothwell's ball blocking the line to the hole. He glowered, resolved to chip his ball over Bothwell's, and went about it before Tom could reason with him. After all, they had two shots in hand.

Scott muffed the shot and knocked Bothwell's ball into the hole. Scott's own ball ran off four feet away. He missed the putt. In a fury, he missed the return putt too.

Scott hurled his club into the whins. 'Stupid, stupid game!' he cried, and stomped off towards the Langside howff.

SOME SAY GOWF IS only a game. If it goes awry we may lose our ball, even lose the match, yet no one has to die (except on rare occasions in Musselburgh, where they take the game *very* seriously). Besides, it is a fine thing to see Earls and Kirk elders, Kings and Chancellors, foozle and fankle, out-played by fishermen and tanners.

It is a sport beloved of Presbyterians, who like their pleasures hard-won. Even Knox in his younger day had been heard to laugh on the occasion in Leith when his shot bounced off a creel, then shot like a rabbit into the hole. He had exclaimed, *The Lord moves in mysterious ways His wonders to perform.*

When we arrived at The Langside, Scott was gazing into a stoup of wine. He looked up and grinned ruefully. 'Sorry about that,' he said. 'Gowf is fine exercise, but the greater exercise is self-control.'

He reached into his pooch and plonked his purse on the table. 'I've been having words wi my father.'

'Surely your faither is deid?' Tom said.

'That doesn't mean we can't have a guid conversation,' Scott retorted.

And I thought to myself, *This man may go far, if he lives to see his middle years*. I had thought Walter Scott was merely fearless, but he was braisant, something else altogether. Add a capacity for reflection and self-control, and an ambitious small-time laird may go far. As indeed he would. His investiture – I was there to see it, in a neuk below the gallery stair – sealed a progress begun long afore.

Bothwell scooped Scott's prize purse from the table, assessed its weight in his hand, smiled happily. Bothwell could be charming when the world went his way, as it had been of late. He already had his first bairn by Buccleuch's mother, the stables at Branxholme were well stocked, and he had the King's ear. (More than his ear, it was rumoured, but the Court produced rumour like Fife exported salt and coal.)

'Here, laddie,' Bothwell said, and tossed the purse into my hands. 'Order the best brandy all round, and keep the lave for yersel!'

ON THE WAY BACK to town with Nicolson, we ducked into a wynd and divvied up the prize purse, as arranged. A share was put aside for Auchterlone, who had called the toss aright at the start, as arranged.

'I'll gie him *laddie*,' I muttered. 'I will make burgess in time.'

Nicolson laughed. 'You will aye be a laddie to me, Will.'

'That's different,' I replied, stowed my coins away. 'You're a philosopher, and Bothwell is but an earl.'

Tom clasped me by the hand. There was a hint of moisture in his eyes before he lurched away on his black staff. 'You'll find Rosie at the nets this evening,' he called back. 'She asks after ye.'

WITHIN THE TOWN CHAMBERS later that day, I shook hands with Tam Anderson and we exchanged contracts and promissory notes. The Fife coastal ports were booming in salt, hides and wool to the Low Countries. Anderson was borrowing to invest further in land and trade. Putting on weight too, by the look of him.

'I hear Skipper Lindsay prophesied against Morton,' Anderson said. 'And the King said nothing. Can I safely favour Argyll and the Catholic cause?'

'I am just a trader,' I replied. 'I take no interest in politics.'

'That is not what I hear.'

'I'm just trying to get by.'

'So was Pate Wilson.'

I took a pinch of snuff, felt the lift in my head. It gave me time to consider. 'Who he?'

'His bound remains were lately found washed up on the shore at Fifeness. Friend of your enemy Claud Hamilton. Mair knife wounds in him than Julius Caesar.'

I shrugged. 'Wilson? Never heard of him.' I slung the satchel over my shoulder. 'I have an errand afore catching the boat home.'

ACROSS THE DRYING GREEN, nets bulged from the lines. Gulls wheeled above, the air was heady with rotting crustacean. Three fishwives worked the nets but none was her. One looked closely at me, then silently pointed to the curing shed above the harbour. Now it would be more remarked on if I didn't call on her than if I did.

I chapped on the shed door and went within. Caustic sulphur caught at my throat as Rosie Nicolson left the group of elderly women working at the boiling pots, stirring lines and nets with wooden paddles. Her work clothes were splashed and stained.

'Ootside,' she said, restrained.

We stood in the shed lee, in lemon-yellow sunlight. Over her shoulder the *Sonsie Quine* rocked by the pier. Rose had filled out in face and body, a girl no longer. That extraordinary bloom had gone. Doubtless I looked changed to her.

'So ye thought to leave wi'oot seeing me?' she said. 'Not very friendly, let alone *très gallant*.' Her eyes still had sea-depths I never saw elsewhere. 'How went the play?'

'Right coorse,' I said.

She laughed quietly. 'I'm a marrit woman with a bairn. I've seen it all.'

'I hope you've not seen the likes of yon shenanigans.'

'Now I am fair curious!'

Our eyes met, then parted. 'Things go brawlie in Embra,' I said eventually. 'My trade grows. When time allows, I meet wi poets and musicians.'

'Good, I'm glad!' she said. Her fingers on my arm were warm and rough. 'Will, I have often felt guilty for – you know. In case I . . .'

'There's nothing to rue,' I replied. 'Being sweet on you was my best education.'

'I'm so relieved,' she said, then looked away. The wind jiggled curls of brown hair across her cheek and ear. I watched, incapable of movement or thought. Her thick salt-stiffened hair, her lovely perishable being. I was going to have to say it. Then a toddler came round the corner, barefoot, broken crochet hook in her hand. 'Mam!'

Rose hunkered down, lifted the bairn easily into her arms. 'This is Lucy.'

'So it is,' I replied. 'Pleased to meet you again, lucky Lucy.' The bairn laughed at me, hid her face in her mother's neck. 'I brought ye a couple o fairings,' I said. 'Flemish ribbons for your hair.' I proffered them, newly bought in Merkit Street. Blue for her eyes, green because she favoured it.

'I canna accept yon,' Rose said. 'I'm a marrit woman.'

'Then take them for Lucy. I will be her godfather, if that is still your wish.'

Lucy was already reaching for them. Rose hesitated. Perhaps she was calculating how she might explain such fineries. I reached into my coat, took out the tan calfskin-bound book. 'Ovid,' I said. As she stared down at it, I hastily clarified. 'It is not *Amores* or anything unsuitable. This is *Heroides* or "Heroines".'

'I havena entirely forgot my Grammar, Will. You needna translate.'

'This book is less well kent,' I said. 'The poems are letters from women of history and myth, that have been put aside, scorned or misrepresented. I thought it might appeal.'

Lines set in by her mouth. The bairn chuckled merrily, still clutching the ribbons. 'You think I hae time for such fripperies?'

'Rose, you have the best mind I have e'er met. Dinna waste it.'

'Best, including my brither's?' Perhaps she was smiling?

'He is better read, no doubt,' I conceded. 'But he doesnae run as deep.'

'Better intellect than George Buchanan?' She was definitely smiling now.

'That might be going too far, but Buchanan is old and his time has passed. Yours is but beginning.' I thrust the book into her hand, which closed around it automatically as a sea anemone round its morsel. 'You can find the time.'

Now she truly looked at me. 'So you and Ovid hope tae rescue me from life as a fishwife?'

Words spilled from my mouth like fish from a net. 'None but yersel can do that, my dear. Be the best-read fishwife ever!' My heart's purse was filled by her laughter. 'I must awa,' I said. 'My skipper wants to be round Fifeness by nightfall.'

Her lips turned perilously close to mine. 'I'll find the time,' she murmured. 'Thank ye.'

'Thank gowf!' I said, and stepped back. 'Your brother and I got lucky on the Links.'

She studied me head to foot. 'Being the trader suits you, Will. You seem . . . bigger.'

'Ach, it's just the shoes,' I replied. Touched my bonnet to her.

'Dinna be a stranger,' she said, then turned for the curing shed, the bairn looking back at me over her shoulder. 'Guid shoes they are too!' came on the breeze.

I HURRIED ALONG THE pier, feeling all at sea and I hadn't even boarded yet. She had felt guilty! She acknowledged something once happened between us and she had not forgotten it.

I turned to face the pier and clambered backwards down the ladder onto the deck.

'Sweetheart in every port,' Captain Wandhaver said cheerily. 'You took your time.'

'She is but the sister of a friend,' I replied. 'Whit are we hanging round here for?'

Ropes unhitched, the sheets tightened, the foresail filled. Without fuss and with no little skill the *Sonsie Quine* navigated the narrow harbour mouth at the full tide. Then up with the main, and course set two points off Fifeness. Only then did I let myself look back. She was not there, but the toddler Lucy stood outside the curing shed, blue and green Flemish ribbons streaming from her fist.

A stranger I must be.

CHAPTER 4

The Gudeman o Ballengeich

IN OUR MEETINGS OF poets, musicians and scriveners-for-hire, Embra gentry mingled with scholars and enthusiasts. Some wag cried us *The Castalian Band*, though we drank more claret than we did Apollo's Castalian Springs of inspiration.

We were united by the pleasure we took in well-crafted poetry and songs. I like to think that our true devotion was not to attaining a royal pension, but to making and sharing something high, fine and lasting. It was our protest against the low times we were born into.

When I left St Andrews to make my way in Embra, John Drummond of Hawthornden was my connection to that world. Drummond was minor gentry, at the fringe of the small Court starting to gather about our boy King. He was bright and high-spirited, devoid of pomposity. I enjoyed his company, as did my sister Susannah. We played gowf. We exchanged hand-written poems, loaned much-thumbed books. He played the lute with a light and merry touch.

In the Canongait one afternoon in March he introduced me to Lindores the epigrammist and Stewart of Baldyneiss. It turned out we shared a passion for both Dante and our own makars Henrysoun and Dunbar. Enthused, we left the street for Ma Dunsyre's howff, where we drank hot chocolate enriched with brandy, and began flyting, quoting and chirruping like speugs about a dripping tap.

That afternoon acquired consequence in the form of an older man in a dusty blue coat, lop-sided brown hair, and a wide selection of facial warts. As he stood scowling at the door I thought him a hefty laird's son, but Drummond jumped up and clasped him like a brother.

'Sandy! I thought you were still warring in the Low Countries!'

The man grunted. 'Only as metaphor.'

'How goes the world with you, *mon ami?*'

His reply was both ironic and heartfelt.

'*I that in health was and gladnes, Am trublit now with great sicknes, And feebled with infirmitie.*'

To which we chorused back to as one: '*Timor mortis conturbat me!*'

The new arrival scowled with pleasure. 'So good Dunbar is fifty years deid and not forgotten yet.' He sat down among us, gestured for drink. We shifted our chairs and he became the head of the table. I stared at him, that pugnacious set of shoulders, a voice I had heard somewhere.

'Will, you hae not met my friend Alexander Montgomerie?' enquired Drummond. So this was the leading makar of our time, skilled in metrics and at adapting our Scots tongue to French verse.

'William Fowler, sir.' I held out my hand. I had him now, glimpsed emerging from our back door into the shadow of the vennel, in that same blue coat, same throaty Western Borders voice as he bade goodbye to whoever.

We would-be makars began to meet informally, when time allowed. The Hudson brothers joined our group, with their lute and viols, willing to play the old songs and drouthy to try out their new compositions. They already possessed what we all dreamed of: a paid position in the renascent Court, as *Masters of Music*.

Gentry and commoners, sharing youth, education and a wish to advance poetry and ourselves, at our meetings we excitedly exchanged fair copies of our latest attempts, read aloud verse from Ronsard and his younger rival Du Bartas. We relaxed with songs of drink and death (Scottish) or hopeless yearning (French, Italian). We were, I think, in equal measures pretentious, ambitious and sincere.

We became all the more so the first time Jamie Saxt joined us, stumbling through the doorway behind two guards, blushing furiously. He hesitated before me, then nodded. '*Nel mezzo del camin!*' he said loudly. When he spoke about Poesie in a hasty stammer, wiping his mouth with the back of his hand, it was with good sense and some knowledge. When he recited from memory Dunbar's bleak *Poem in Winter*, it was with feeling and eloquent restraint. At times, towards the end of the afternoon with drink taken and song to the fore, we forgot who he was. Perhaps he did too, for a while.

In time he abruptly rose, waved to the guards, hesitated. We too groped for the etiquette here. Kiss his hand? Kneel? Bow? He beat his palm to his heart, and was gone.

OUR BOY KING LIKED to slip in the back way at Dunsyre's, and to be greeted as one among fellow practitioners. He used his grand-father James V's pseudonym, *The Gudeman o Ballengeich*, or just *Ballengeich*. He aye had the same two guards, handsome muscular young thugs with smirks long as a whaup's beak. They would come in first, take a quick look round, hand on swords, then nod and let their master in, await, then escort him home when we were done. It seemed they had all been schooled together at Stirling Castle, and were trusted completely.

We were told not to speak of his visits. I mentioned them only to my mother, hoping to impress. I see now that was unwise of me. She opined that such interest in the arts suggested the growing lad was moving towards his mother's Faith.

I also reported his attendances to George Buchanan at Kennedy Close. 'Hairmless' was his verdict, before turning back to his opus (that is how books get written, by such turning back). And harmless our meetings were, till that morning John Drummond of Haw-thornden appeared at my workshop.

For the most part History goes by us like the breeze, lightly brush-ing at our sleeve as if *Come along! Come along!* We notice in the distance it is bending the corn, and observe on the high road it has shaped trees to the east. News comes to us days later of armies meeting, a royal birth, an execution, the plague in another city. We meet in the street, talk about it, then pass on to our more pressing interests of the day – our sick child, a ship arriving with new merchandise, the by-law from the Council setting the hours for the water pumps, the cutting of silver content in our coins, that attractive smile across the street . . .

For we of little consequence, our small affairs are big enough. The distant commotion in a stand of trees, or a man who once ran our lives glimpsed stepping up onto the scaffold, these are usually as close as we get to the blast.

But once, twice, maybe four times in this little life, there comes an overheard phrase, an ambivalent look, a casual request, and these are the first puffs before the storm of History hits us. And so it was that day, as I was minding my business in my workshop warehouse, kneeling over a jar of French lacquer, brush in hand.

'Still putting a gloss on the things of this world?'

I looked up to see John Drummond. I think it embarrassed both of us for him to see me on my knees varnishing. I handed my brush to my assistant young James Budge and greeted him.

'You might sprush yourself up for our Poesie meeting later, Will,' he said.

'You dinna approve my breeks?'

'They were surely a bargain, and well darned,' he replied. He lowered his voice. 'The Gudeman will be attending, keen to read his latest Ode in the French manner.'

I collected my wits. '*Très bien*,' I said.

Drummond's hand on my arm as Budge inspected the drying

lacquer. 'Usual conditions,' he said quietly. 'He wants no fuss or flummery. And keep this quiet.'

'Siccar as the grave,' I said.

I CROUCHED BY THE workshop's sole window, shining up my buckles, already in my best hose. I was thinking to take a fair copy of my latest *Tarantula of Love* sonnets to present to Jamie Saxt, when a shadow fell across my lap.

I got off my knees and greeted Alexander Montgomerie. This was the first time he had called at my place of work.

'Change in venue the nicht,' he said. 'The Auld Tower in the Lawnmerkit. You ken *Ballengeich* is coming?'

'Aye,' I said. 'No fuss, and best behaviour.'

He nodded, then hesitated. 'Your mother asks that you might leave early and call on her,' he said. 'She has some business to discuss wi you.'

I stared at the closing door. It was by-ordinar, the late change in venue. My mother's request had been delivered with something like apology. As Montgomerie had turned away, I'd caught a curtailed twitch of his fingers as he signed the Cross to himself.

I gave my buckles a final polish, told the capable Budge to lock up when he'd finished, then went to find the man who ought to hear about this.

GEORGE BUCHANAN LOOKED UP from his table, peeved at my interruption. 'I come about the Swallowgait conduit,' I said: my code words. He carefully set down his quill.

'John, will you fetch me the twa books on the table at my lodging?'

Geddes went reluctantly, leaving the two of us alone. I told my patron about our intended congregation of poets that latter afternoon. He nodded. I added that there had been a late change of venue, no reason given.

He frowned at that. 'Anything else by-ordinar?'

I hesitated. Montgomerie, though endlessly grumpy, was a true poet. *Come, my Children Dere* would make a stone weep and be a better stone for it. His religion was his business. His connection to my mother was mine.

'A feeling, no more,' I said. '*Timor mortis conturbat me.*'

THE AULD TOWER WAS off a vennel at the soggy end of the Lawnmerkit, more shambling coaching inn than tower. I met John Stewart of Baldyneiss on the narrow stair. I asked if Montgomerie was already present. 'Of course,' he said. 'It is a special afternoon.'

I could hear two lutes flirting as we came along the upper passage a row of dark oak doors. Ever since The Skelpit Dug, upper rooms in unfamiliar hostelries made my bowels churn. Then Montgomerie's unexpectedly tender voice:

'*No state on Earth stands siccar, As with the wind waves the wicker . . .*'

'I will have to leave early,' Stewart said quickly, then he lifted the latch and we went in to join the company.

The guard appeared, glaring round at us. Then the Gudeman o Ballengeich poked his head round the door. He rather sweetly waved a sheaf of manuscripts by way of greeting. We quietly stamped our applause. He blushed, sat down amid our company.

I expected the usual second guard, but none came. The sole guard got bored of standing up for Poetry. He sat on the boards by the door, and gradually his head dropped as we discussed projects of translation. Jamie Saxt stuttered that it was essential for our country to have the Holy Book in our own tongue for all to read. When he had control of the Exchequer, he would see to it. In the meantime we should look to render our own Scots versions of Petrarch, Dante and Du Bartas. How else were we to keep abreast of new developments in the Continent? He intended to invite Ronsard, the greatest of the French poets, to the Court, through his former tutor, Master Buchanan.

As you would expect of impecunious poets, there was great enthusiasm for the project of translation, its particular problems and challenges and costs! Did one replicate the metre, when it did not sit well with Scots? How to render different sounds and images and figurative expressions? How faithful could one be and still retain the poetry?

Montgomerie huffed and puffed, grew red, and finally banged his fist on the table and shouted, 'We seek not Fidelity but Correspondence and Equivalence!'

The guard scrambled from his slumbers, hand on hilt. The King giggled and signed him down. More drink and chocolate were sent for. Two of our number excused themselves to take a pipe, the King being strongly opposed to that weed. A message came, the Gudeman o Ballengeich read it, beckoned to the guard, spoke softly and the man left, leaving the King unguarded.

Stewart of Baldyneiss made his apologies and left also. The light was failing outside the narrow window. I sat on, as Buchanan had instructed, my heart whuddering.

Low voices on the stairs. Heavy boots along the passageway. A grue ran through me. I'd known this before and it had not ended well. Surely Buchanan would have acted on my intelligence. Or had I been mistaken in him?

Loud bang on the door, a long feathered hat flourished, then in came a tall man with a long, thin, fair moustache and a fine rapier in his hand. He bowed low to Jamie Saxt. Behind him stood a more muscular specimen with pike and pistol.

'We have come to escort you hame, Your Majesty.'

The Gudeman o Ballengeich looked peeved. 'So soon? I have yet to recite my Ode.'

'These are our orders, from the Council, sir. The Ambassador has arrived early and must be spoken with this evening.' The thin man held out a round plaque. Jamie Saxt glanced, nodded, sighed, accepting its authority.

We all stood as the King stood. He left, followed closely by the two new guards. I glanced at Montgomerie, who I thought was struggling to appear surprised by this development.

There was a silence as we listened to the boots fade on the stair. The Hudson brothers hastily bagged their instruments, drained their brandy and made ready to leave.

A pistol shot banged in the courtyard below. Then shouts, another report, a demented squealing that ended abruptly. A door slammed. I felt giddy, it was all too familiar. Then boots running up the stair, the door was thrown open. Four armed men hurried us all off down the winding stair, pushed us out into the street. But not before we saw the bodies being dragged away, a long, thin, pale moustache trailing on the cobbles, smell of blood and powder in the night air.

Of the Gudeman there was no sign. '*No state on Earth stands siccar*,' Montgomerie grunted, then hurried off with the Humes.

THAT WAS THE LAST time the *Gudeman o Ballengeich* appeared at one of our meetings in town. Any further sessions he attended were in Holyrude, where the guards outnumbered the poets, the King was a touch more formal, and the atmosphere never so free and fervent.

I wonder still how the storm of History would have veered had I not reported my misgivings to Buchanan that afternoon. I wonder if that kerfuffle was one of Bishop Leslie's plots, got up quickly after hearing from my mother about the Castalian Band meeting. And I wonder yet about the allegiance of Alexander Montgomerie, long gone though his work remains.

JOHN GEDDES CAME NEXT morning to my workshop, wanting the word about last night's stushie. I gave him little, other than that the poetry was good, the songs better, and the end of the evening was as unexpected as it was frightening. I could not say more.

'These poetry evenings are getting o'er lively,' I concluded. 'I will confine myself to trading.'

He looked hard at me. I smiled back guilelessly. 'You and I are on our own, my friend,' he said. 'We have no rank or fortune, and must live by our wits at the fringe of the Court. Folk such as us must have a patron.'

'Master Buchanan is an ally,' I replied.

'Perhaps, but he is out of favour.' I did not say this might not be entirely the case. 'Anyway, he is old.' Geddes stood closer to me, tuned his voice to the tones of sincerity. 'I offer this advice from fellow-feeling: you would do well to find a more coming man.'

'You have such a one?' I asked.

He nodded. 'Several. Ye can't have o'er many patrons!'

John Geddes shook his head as he left, as if in despair at my naivety, or perhaps he suspected I had withheld, as the times demanded of so many of us.

IN HIS KENNEDY CLOSE lodgings later that day, George Buchanan told me the plot had been not murder but kidnap, to secure the King in different hands and so help him return to the Old Faith.

Unfortunately those directly involved had been killed, so nothing could be proved higher up.

'Ye ken nothing against Montgomerie?' he asked, staring into my face.

'I know he is our finest poet,' I replied. 'We end each meeting singing *Come, my Children Dere* wi the Hudsons, and we are all the better for it.'

He examined me closely as though I were a forged letter. 'I am gladdened you remain so loyal to Poesie,' he said, very dry. 'Our divisions will not be healed in my lifetime. And maybe not in yours,' he added softly. He handed me a small purse. 'Oh, and best not be seen wi Stewart of Baldyneiss. It seems he serves another cause.'

> *Our plaisance here is all vainglory,*
> *This false warld is but transitory,*
> *The fleshe is brittle, the Fiend is slee;*
> *Timor mortis conturbat me.*

I WALKED HOME WITH Dunbar's *Lament for the Makars* murmuring in my head. I went via the High Street while it was still light, keeping away from the wynds and close-ends, my best friend the blade sheathed within my doublet.

CHAPTER 5

A Guid Sharp Cut

I SAT IN THE SANCTUARY of the Doo-Cot, catching up on paperwork. To my right, the Virgin stood in her niche, pink and gold and smiling smugly. The smell of ink, that dark and pungent rot, soothed me. It was good to know again the movement of hand across page, as though quill were the whole bird moving across pale sky.

I glanced up at the cubbyhole that had lately contained my mother's correspondence and dealings with John Leslie, Bishop of Ross. Had his visit led to the attempt to take control of the King? Had she burned the correspondence, or locked it away? I heard George Buchanan murmur, *Our divisions will not be healed in my lifetime. And maybe not in yours.*

I filed away the Tam Anderson contract and receipts in the slot by the unicorn carving. I did my figures on the return to date, then the likely return on the next tranche. The latest devaluation of the currency was the talk of the Lawnmerkit traders, who now complained greatly about Morton, who had once been their man for ending the war and for the stability he brought.

Things were shifting in our country, I could feel it like the deck of the *Sonsie Quine* unsteady under my feet. Skipper Lindsay pronouncing his malisoun on Morton. Buchanan in the dimness under the Swallowgait arch, telling me I had been recruited. The foiled attempt to take possession of Jamie Saxt. Lucky Lucy with ribbons whirling from her fist, the bairn that could never be mine . . .

THUD THUD THUD. Spilled ink and my hammering heart. Some madman was banging at the door as though life depended on being answered. I blotted, listened. Susannah was shouting, *Will, get your arse doon here!*

I hurried down the spiral stair, and there stood young Walter Scott of Branxholme and Buccleuch, in fine green doublet and black hide riding coat, booted and spurred.

'Good to see where a man bides! Are ye going to ask me in?'

WE SAT IN THE Doo-Cot. Scott told me he had come from Stirling, after witnessing the assize on Arthur Hamilton of Myreton. Most of the Hamiltons had fled in time, their strongholds confiscated on Morton's authority, but the Earl of Bothwell's men had picked up Arthur struggling with his horse in a bog.

'Arthur was not the sharpest arrow in the quiver,' Scott said. 'When you've got to get out, you don't swither and moan. You go!'

'So he is gone?'

Scott peered into his glass. 'Very gone.' He drank. 'One less who would kill me.'

'That is a hard accountancy.'

He shrugged. 'I suppose it is.'

I could just about picture Arthur Hamilton. A thin-haired, morose man, the boo of the litter. A memory of once seeing him outside St Salvator's, squinting up at the sun, light glinting on his oversized scabbard. *Whaur next?* he had exclaimed, flushed with drink. Well, he'd ken now what came next, if anything.

'What did they charge him with?'

'The usual – part and parcel of the shooting of Regent Moray at Linlithgow, back in 'seventy.' He wiped crumbs from his ruddy moustache. 'They hanged Archbishop Hamilton for his part in it – hanged like a commoner, despite his office and nobility! The Hamiltons have never forgiven that insult.'

'Christian forgiveness in these parts is scarce as snow in June.'

Scott laughed. 'What's Christ got to do wi it?' He said Bothwell had got himself onto the panel for the assize, his forces having arrested Arthur Hamilton. As the judges retired to consider their verdict, the scaffold platform was already being made in the street outside. When he was sentenced, Arthur Hamilton cried out, *It wisna me!*, then burst into tears. They gave him an hour with a recusant priest.

'Yon was merciful, considering,' Scott commented. 'We pleaded successfully for his cousin James to be excused sentence, being of such unsound mind even his brothers keep him locked up.'

The rain had stopped as Arthur Hamilton was led out of the

Tolbooth to the scaffold. Not greiting now, but resolved. 'I don't know what the priest had said to him,' Scott told his wine glass, 'but I wouldn't mind some of it. Hamilton looked about him almost wi pleasure. He nodded to the executioner, then knelt. I was impressed.' Scott's knee stopped jumping. 'I looked away, but heard the sound.'

'At least he made a good end,' I muttered, remembering that sound.

'You and your damnable Stoics!' Scott cried, abruptly het up. 'Why spend time rehearsing your end? Dying is a very small part of a life, and being dead is no part at all.' His eyes snagged on the secretively smiling Virgin. 'I take no pleasure in judicial killings. Odds are it will one day be me.'

Let me add this to my understanding of him. 'And Bothwell?'

'He watched. He said, *It was a guid cutting. The blade was sharp and the aim true.*'

'Sweet Jesus!' I put my glass aside. 'Does he think himself immortal?'

'Probably! It gives him power and abandon. It also makes one question his judgement.'

'*Don't be under him when he falls?*'

Scott looked sharply at me. 'Exactly. They say I am bold, but Bothwell is rash. Many confuse the two.'

He said Bothwell's reward for helping return the desired verdict was the custodianship of the Hamiltons' Myreton stronghold. Thus does one ascend. He would be seeking to have that verified by the

Law Lords. That decision would be a measure of the degree of Morton's restored influence.

'With the Hamiltons routed and Atholl dead, surely Morton's power is not in doubt?'

Scott yawned, stretched like one of his great lurchers. '*He* thinks it is not. But will my great-uncle live see his gardens green next year?' He jumped to his feet, paced round the room, peered at the cubbyholes with their documents. 'So this is your mother's armoury?'

I stared at him, then at the stuffed boxes, my own and hers. 'Aye, very like,' I replied.

Scott smacked his hands together. 'You still have yon crossbow? Let's go shoot!'

WE WENT DOWN THE Pleasance towards Holyrude Park, Scott with my crossbow across his shoulder like the Cross itself, me with a full quiver. Folk glanced as we passed, for Scott had something about him, with his head high and long hair dark red as autumnal bracken.

'You ken my father once rode wi the Hamiltons? They were with the Queen's Party in the raid on Stirling, when Regent Lennox was shot.' He stopped at the archway into the practice park where the butts were set. Scott seemed raised, chatty, and I wondered when he would broach why he had called on me. 'They couldna all get away after, because my father had already seized and carried off all the horses of the town.'

'A Borderer to the core!'

'Exactly!' We went on to the butts and introduced ourselves to the attendant, took off our coats. 'At seventeen, my faither was leading three thousand men raiding into England! Captain of Newark Castle!' Scott cranked up the crossbow then squinted at me. 'How can I live up to such a man?'

'By not dying young?' I suggested, handing him an arrow-bolt.

'Very good! I will live longer than he! Secure my knighthood, then in time become Lord Scott of Buccleuch. Have children who marry well!'

And he did, he did all that.

He raised the crossbow to his shoulder, sighted, released the catch. The bolt clipped the edge of the butt, then toppled into the grass. Scott held out his hand and I passed him another bolt. Recalling the stymie incident on the Links, I was struck by this new self-control.

'Think ye to marry well, Will?'

I stifled Rose's bright eye, her mouth on mine. 'I fear my mother has someone in mind.'

Scott chuckled. 'I fear my mother does too! She may well be right.'

'But what of the heart's choice?'

Scott fitted the bolt, squinted across at me. 'What's the heart got to do wi it?'

He pulled the catch. The bolt hissed out, missed the butt completely. He swore quietly, then passed me the crossbow. I cranked it up, aimed, released.

'Outer bullseye!' Scott cried. 'Can ye do it again?'

I did it again, clipped the inner this time. Scott looked impressed. My third bolt lodged dead centre.

'Man!' Scott exclaimed. 'You are truly good!'

'I'm not bad,' I conceded. 'There are folk much better. I once came third at the St Andrews medal.'

'Have you ever shot for real? At boar or man?'

'Never,' I admitted.

'Until you do, skills are shadow-play, and this bow but a toy.'

Scott held out his hand for the crossbow and walked closer to the target butt. He cranked up, plucked a bolt from the quiver, sighted and shot. This time he hit the fringe. He handed back the weapon.

'Not my talent, it appears! I favour a pistol, then my sword and a dirk in the other hand for close quarters.'

That terrible room in The Skelpit Dug, those dying men. A long pale moustache lying bloodstained on the cobbles. 'I have had enough of close quarters.'

'And you acquitted yourself well! Nicolson too was handy, for all his philosophy.'

There it was again, that pleasure at praise, no matter what for. 'I survived,' I said modestly.

'And two folk who wanted to kill us died. That is a good result in my book.'

'Your book is o'er short and bloody for me.'

I intended it as witticism, but Scott grasped my crossbow. 'I will not have you judge me, Fowler! I have a title, two strongholds, lands and beasts, kin and retainers who depend on me, and many who want to take it all. You have little to defend, and those who might want it use but the pen and the Law.'

I jerked away the crossbow and wound it up. I steadied myself, squinted along the sight. 'So my best defence is a modest existence in trade.'

I shot another bull, not so hard at this range. It would have been a lot harder had the butt been running me with rapier and dirk. Scott put his hand on my arm. 'Yet I think you want much more,' he said softly.

It was as if Scott's words punched a hole in an ornate false wall, to reveal a whole other room beyond. I yearned for adventure but was feart of the unknown. I wanted advancement yet recoiled from the means. I wanted to be a gentleman, or at least my children to be, yet was resigned to being a burgess at best. I wanted to complete *The Tarantula of Love* and amaze everyone, including myself, yet trading walled me off from writing. I had lost the only woman for me, and was half-ways prepared to marry another.

Walter Scott forced me to know myself. I would aye fear and thank him for it. At our final goodbye days in Antwerp, he let drop all bravado as he spoke again of the men he had killed, summoning them up one by one. *Do you think I will burn forever?* he asked me. 'I think you will pish on the flames of Hell,' I replied. He gripped my arm as his pain rose. *Ach well. We had some fun, did we not, from Perth to Padua.*

Back then, still young and unmarked, we walked forward together and plucked my bolts from the butt.

'Come wi me to Branxholme,' Scott said, casual-like. 'I ride out to restore twenty-seven cobs reived from me last winter. I have a use for your bow skills. It will give you mair to write about than unrequited love!'

'I don't think I'm that desperate for new material,' I replied. Here at last was the purpose of his visit.

'I have also invited Nicolson,' Scott continued. 'And at Branxholme I have a barnful of items needing traded into cash.' I hesitated, he smiled guilelessly. 'There will be plenty of us on the ploy, and I'll make sure you're tucked awa near the back.'

I hesitated, felt grasped in a hot wind. 'I'm o'er busy in Embra,' I said, without conviction.

'Adventure! Good business! Quines! Are you feart?'

'What do you want Tom for?' I prevaricated.

'Nicolson is a handy man. He will tutor my siblings. Between times he can teach me some Humanities and save us on University fees! Oh, and George Buchanan sends his regards.'

'*Buchanan?*'

'We met by chance on my way here.' Scott smiled slightly, not fussed whether I believed him. He stretched his arms out wide, looked up at the Crags, blood-red rock in the late sun. 'He suggests you write a ballad about our adventure!'

'Ballads are poor stuff.'

'And they sell like scones warm off the griddle! Write it anonymously, if you wish.' He dropped his arms. 'Besides,' he said soberly, 'you and Nicolson are the only folk near my age that I ken and can trust. Come wi me and live a little!'

'Just how little is what worries me,' I gurned, but I was as good as gone.

CHAPTER 6

A Ride Out

TOM NICOLSON WAS WAITING by the gates into Branxholme, clutching his staff. I dismounted slowly, numb from the two-day ride. Scott and his followers went into the courtyard, leaving us together.

My friend had cut his hair short, and shaven clean. But still the same eyes, intensely staring at the world and beyond it.

'You look more monk than scholar.'

Nicolson shrugged. 'I suppose I am one, Faith apart.'

'And the celibacy?'

'Seldom a problem wi me,' Tom said peaceably. 'You'll be sorry to hear Mags is marrit and awa, but Annie is braw as ever and keen to make your re-acquaintance.'

I managed a smile. At home in Embra, the Mitchisons had become regular visitors, and sometimes I felt myself a butt waiting to receive its Fate as the bow is cranked. Marianne was a capable, level-headed, practical young woman who accepted the world as it was. She promised good sense, competence and children.

'How did Scott persuade you to come?'

'He settled my fees for the term. All he asks is some tutoring for himself and his twa brothers and sister. I can carry on my Averroes studies in the upper tower room. I'm bedding down there.'

I looked up at the east tower. 'It's no made of ivory, but might as well be. Are you riding out with us?'

'He insists on it. Says I'll be kept siccar at the back.'

'He said the same to me.'

'Hey, *mes amis*! *Venez manger!* Come and get chawed in!'

Scott and Bothwell leaning out the great window, waving and calling on us.

'Are ye feart?' Tom asked quietly as we went in.

'*Bien sûr*. Yet it will be an adventure to tell our children when we are old and full of lies.'

Nicolson reached down to grasp my shoulder. 'I have learned this much from Averroes and Montaigne – our Stoic masters spend o'er much attention to making a good death, and not enough to living beforehand.'

I felt those words lodge, quivering, somewhere near my heart. Despite everything, they remain there still.

LADY MARGARET DOUGLAS SCOTT sat at the head of the long table, her eldest son on her right. Bothwell came in late, hesitated, then took the heavy chair at the far end. Other kinsmen took up the places. Annie's wrist brushed the back of my neck as she leaned across to serve me.

Lady Margaret raised her glass. 'To the King, and Regent Morton! To our learned young visitors, each with their talent. May all profit by your time here!'

Another who doesn't take her eye off the prize, I thought as the wine warmed my thrapple. *We are here to be of use.* The man on my left jogged my elbow. 'You the new bowman, pal?'

'I suppose,' I said. 'Though I'm really a trader in furnishings.'

The man grunted. He was older than me, weathered, with pale raised scars across the fist that clutched his glass. 'Name's Morgan,' he said. 'I've been tellt to mak sure ye dinna get killed.'

'Good luck wi that,' I managed. He grunted, speared beef into his maw, chomped and drank. 'Have you many other bowmen in your party?' I asked.

'We had three guid ains.' Morgan looked into the distance, nodded. 'Just you now.'

We said little for the rest of the meal.

BRANXHOLME CASTLE COORIED WITHIN its courtyard and outer defences, bounded by the chattering burn and the home farm, a world in itself. It was now high summer. Kye fattened in the fields, oats and barley swished in the winds as men, carts and cob horses came along the track from Hawick to bed down in the stables. They brought provisions, greaves and spurs, metal-enforced jacks, leather and iron helmets.

Pikes leaned up glinting against walls. Within the cellars, pistols and hackbuts, powder and shot were laid out, divvied up and stowed. Kinsmen, retainers and messengers arrived, were taken within to be instructed by Bothwell and Scott.

The pantries filled with dried meat and the reivers' favoured hard cheese and sweetmeats sealed in twists of waxed paper. Small leather flasks of brandy and wine.

With stomach fluttery and tight, I tried to focus on the contents of the big barn where Annie and I had once pleasured. It had filled up considerably since then, with furniture and furnishings, fine pewter and plate. Tactless to enquire the provenance.

Supervised by Margaret Douglas's steward, I made three lists: standard stuff to be taken to Dumfries; high-value destined for Glesga to be sold or as security against loans; specialist ecclesiastical items to be handled by my mother.

It had become my practice with a special deal to hold one piece back, as a reminder. My hand alighted on an ink pot of yellow and green jade, with a silver-hinged lid and attached quill-holder. By the inscription, probably made in Byzantium or Izmir. It sits now on this table, battered but enduring, breathing the workaday air of Spitalfields.

'This for myself,' I said.

The steward looked closely at it. 'Clear it with Her Ladyship.'

We finished up as the sun swelled red over the hills. The steward left. I stood checking my lists against the items. For a couple of hours I had not thought about the impending raid. A shadow fell across my knees.

'I hae till sunset,' Annie said. 'For auld lang syne.'

She closed the door, slid the bar across, as I gallantly spread my jerkin on the hay.

ON THE THIRD EVENING, after eating, Bothwell had slipped away with Lady Margaret. None of us made mention of it as Walter Scott led Tom and I up the Gowrie Tower and onto the roof. He clambered onto the bale-fire stack and pulled us up.

The evening was warm and still, unlocateable laverocks dribbled song from abune. Trees, fields in all directions, the burn blethering in its glen. It was extraordinarily peaceful, yet we stood above a castle stapped with weaponry and purposeful men. Scott pointed at mauve masses on the southern horizon.

'They came from Carlisle in my grandfather's time,' he said. 'Henry's army, on a *rough wooing*. They burned us out, killed the garrison, ravaged the women, then went on for Glesga, did the same there. It took us a generation to rebuild.' He frowned, swayed on the loose pile of signal firewood. 'My father gave it a lot of thought. He told me, *It taks an army to stop an army, and we havena had one since Flodden*. He was not a quick thinker, but he got there.'

I leaned over the parapet, feeling slightly sick at the thought of what lay ahead.

'This is scarcely an army,' Nicolson said.

'Exactly! You take two thousand men into England in winter, and you find three thousand waiting for you every time.' Scott laughed. 'We will gang in summer wi thirty-odd men – you twa being the oddest! – and nobody pays us heed till o'er late. Trust me.'

Tom and I looked at each other. 'We have entrusted our lives to you,' I said.

'As have aa these folk down there in the yaird!' Scott replied. 'You think that doesna weigh wi me?'

We stood in silence on the roof-top amid the luminous summer gloaming. An owl enquired *Why, Who?* from the woods across the river.

'This is a lot of stushie and lives risked, just to get twenty-seven horses back fae the Carletons,' Nicolson said.

Scott gripped my friend and spoke into his face.

'*It is. Not. About. The. Horses.*' Nicolson flinched, but held his ground. 'Never was, never is.'

A fine title for a ballad, I thought as we descended in silence. I could see it on the broadsheet fresh off the press:

Buccleuch's Summer Raid,

Or

Not about the Horses

NEXT EVENING IN THE courtyard, all readying for the gang. Some were silent and pale, others like Scott and Bothwell were flushed as bairns going to a feast. These ploys were what they lived for and by.

I was fitted into a metal-sewn jack that came down past my knees. 'Aye, you'll no be running awa fast in yon!' Morgan cracked.

'Anyone shoots at me, I'm off,' I said.

He clapped me on the shoulder. 'Ye'll be awright, son! You're wi me!'

I managed, 'Aye, that's what worries me,' though struggling not to boke with nerves. Leather helmet. Riding boots. Gauntlets. Annie handed up my food-wrap as I eased into the saddle. 'Come hame safe,' she said quietly. 'But yon was the last time. I'm getting marrit efter the hairst.'

In quick succession, like a flight of arrows loosed by skilled archers, I felt regret, then relief, then glad for her.

The stockade gates were opened and Francis Stewart, Earl of Bothwell, rode out at the head of his gang. He planned to cause a rumpus in the Western March and so distract from Scott's raid. He looked splendid as he galloped into the simmerdim.

(For a while Bothwell would become Admiral of the Fleet, at which he was strikingly *out of his depth*. He was impassioned but not serious, except perhaps about the four sons and four daughters he somehow found time to sire with Lady Margaret. I smile faintly now, remembering him, though in life he was best enjoyed at a distance.)

THE STOCKADE WAS QUIETER now. I counted twenty-two mounted men, not including myself and Nicolson. I fitted my crossbow into its saddle harness. Looped the quiver with the specially prepared bolts over one shoulder. The tarry stink twitched in my nose. I had somehow assumed this was never going to happen, that I would get sick or come to my senses.

Morgan jostled his cob alongside me, dark eyes glittering, beard flowing over his throat-guard. Rapier on hanger, dirk on hip, brace of pistols, he looked what he was: a battle-hardened Border reiver.

'Stick close tae me, son,' he said. 'Ye'll be tellt when to do yer stuff.'

Walter Scott stepped out from the Castle door, slipping something within his jack. Head down in some private thought, he looked very young, and for a moment I glimpsed the weight he carried. Then his head came up, he flowed up onto his barrel-chested cob, pushed back his long flaming hair. He looked at us, secured each man by eye.

'Let's gang reiving!' he yelled. The gates were opened and we rode out with the setting sun monstrous over our shoulders.

'Did you mark what Buccleuch put away as he came out the door?' Nicolson said as we forded the burn that marked the end of Buccleuch lands. 'A comb! I kid you not.'

I laughed. 'Our lad aims to be a legend in his own lifetime. The hair matters. You ken he wants me to a write a ballad about this raid?'

'It's not about the horses?'

'*Never was, never is!*' we chorused, then rode on. Self-belief and flaming hair will make men follow, though it will not bring them all back.

WINTER WAS THE FAVOURED reiving season: long dark nights, ground frozen hard on the secret trails through woods, harvest long-secured, horse and kye helpfully gathered together in paddock and barn. But Scott, being canny and contrary, chose to gang in high summer: ground dry, the woods full-screening green, beasts grazing far from the strongholds.

And the question of numbers: a few hundred hard-riding men at any season soon had the bale-fires burning, signalling from one glen to the next: *Here comes trouble!* But Scott chose a small force, discreet and casual, with arms stowed away within saddles and under cloaks as we left his heartland. And we rode a distance back from the Border, thus avoiding strongholds, Warden's patrols, and inspection points.

We cantered steadily through the Debatable Lands in the luminous grey of summer night. Above the headwaters of the Tweed we stumbled on a tinklers' encampment in a hollow, watch-fire burning low, and its dogs set off our gang's dogs. A dozen travelling men scrambled to stand half-dressed with crossbows and swords.

Scott raised his hand companionably, wished them good health and a dry night. He said his party were Douglas men, going to reinforce the garrison at Hermitage, in the King's name. He shared out brandy, admired their dogs. He leaned down from the saddle to shake hands with their main man, exchanged an unheard joke, then our party trotted on.

'They believed him!' Nicolson said quietly.

'It's the hair,' I replied. 'They might not have believed him, but they could see he is somebody.'

WE FORDED TWO MORE burns, and were now deep in Crozier and Kemp lands. Though it was getting lighter, the farms and fields were empty and still. Away on the horizon, watch-fires burned low on a couple of hilltops and on one dark keep. The fighting men had been called away to take on Bothwell's force, further to the east.

Below Wauchope, our gang took a break to eat and drink. Voices low, conversation practical, low-key, as if another day's work. Which in a way it was. The outliers came back through the woods, leading four unsaddled shires and a couple of yearlings, lightly haltered. Morgan went round them carefully, inspected teeth, ears, feet, for markings and condition.

'Crozier horses,' he said quietly.

'Na, they smell o'er sweet for that,' someone said. Soft laughter.

IT WAS STILL EARLY morning as we threaded through a narrow wooded pass then came out above a dale. A bonnie place. Peaceful. A solid farm hall, some outlying byres, sheep in the outer fields. An old keep off to the side. At the centre, two large thatched stable barns.

Our gang grouped within the trees and began to count the men and women at work in the garden and paddocks. I dismounted, lifted my crossbow from its hanger. I unslung the bulky quiver, checked the flights were still well set.

Walter Scott did not force me to leave Embra to accompany his raid. Seduced me, perhaps, with his talk of ballads and adventure. In truth, I was seduceable. Were I sworn to Marianne Mitchison, there would be none of this. Had I been with Rose, there would have been no need of it.

But as it was, I was crouched behind a hedge somewhere in the English West March, wide-awake and clear-sighted. I watched my scrivening hand select the strongest, straightest tarry bolt.

'Time spent in reconnaissance is seldom wasted,' Scott murmured in my left ear. 'My cobs and shires are in yon stables.'

I looked through the bushes at the thatched stables. Must be a full hundred paces. I had practised this over and over at Branxholme. The tree-tops were unmoving, which helped. Still, it was a long shot. I cranked up, fitted the tarred bolt. *All else is shadow-play.*

'Ready,' I said. Curiously enough, I was.

On my right, Morgan conjured his tinderbox and lit a fuse-flame. He leaned across and put flame to tar. The arrow flared. I nestled the haft to my shoulder, steadied my elbow on the branch, waited till the flame had well caught. Pigeons were crooning in the woods as I raised the bow, sighted, released.

The bolt fizzed through the grey morning, dropped and lodged into the bottom of the stable thatch. Flickers of flames. The first shouts from around the farm as I cranked the bow again. Morgan passed the next fiery bolt. I aimed a bittie higher.

The second burning bolt lodged smack into the thatch. The third one landed close by it. The flames met and smoke rose.

Buccleuch's gloved hand gripped my shoulder. 'Weel done. Bide here.'

Then the gang rode full-tilt into the dale. The women and bairns ran for the keep and shut the door. The few men and lads were torn between frantically opening the stable doors and defending themselves against on-coming horsemen. One carbine shot from Morgan and the tallest defender fell backwards in the yard. Surrounded by horsemen, the other farmers dropped their staves and dirks, and waited for whatever was coming to them.

Walter Scott ran to the stables, jerked the doors open, and grey cobs streamed out into the smoke-filled yard. His grooms dashed around with halters. I saw movement by the burn off to the left, then two men hurrying away up a track to the next glen. Too late to stop them.

The remaining defenders were herded into a thatched byre. The door was jammed closed. The shot man lay twitching in the yard. The main stables were now blazing, making the air quiver over the dale. Sick at heart, I watched as Morgan approached the byre with his lit fuse.

Scott's hand descended. The fuse was tramped out in the yard, the byre and its occupants left intact. Within minutes our gang was back by the woods, with the haltered cobs and one wild-eyed boy with hands tied. A woman appeared at the door of the keep, waved her arms, then ran screaming to the fallen man.

'On to Greendale!' Scott cried and we rode up by the Blackwater, then down into the next valley.

IN GREENDALE THE HORSES were in the paddock, but this time the defenders were ready for us. They had a carbine, and one of the Scott groom lads cried out and slumped face down onto his horse. Scott turned and rode straight at the marksman, who struggled to reload, fumbled fatally, and the lance spun him to the ground. The other defenders retreated to the peel tower and barred themselves in. Shots from the roof made our men back off and regroup.

'Fire it?' Morgan suggested.

Scott considered. I felt sick. I had reached my limits.

'I want my horses, not a blood-feud. Let's awa hame.'

We strapped the lanced man – who to everyone's surprise was not dead yet, just bleeding and cursing softly – to one of the horses, then hurried about the paddock just out of range of the pistols, rounded up the remaining cobs. Then with our two hostages for good behaviour, we set off on the long wearisome ride back through the narrow wooded glens for the Border and Branxholme.

Wabbit and dumfounert yet strangely awake, I roughed out the ballad in my head as we rode: '*Bold Buccleuch's Summer Raid, or Not About the Horses*', in the old metrics, rhymed *abab*. Nothing fancy called for.

It fell upon the summer time
When nights are brief and light
That Branxholme crossed the Borderline
Wi men of vir and might

AT SOME POINT I must have fallen asleep in the saddle, for Tom Nicolson's grab woke me. During a pause in the woods, I made myself eat hard cheese and pastry, washed down with brandy. I kept seeing my lit arrows thudding into the thatch, felt the flare of triumph, then the nausea when the man flipped over as he was lanced. The short cry of the groom boy.

A hand tightened on my shoulder, Walter Scott's breath at my ear. 'Weel done, my trusty fiere.' By the standards of the time, perhaps it was. But then again, the times were dreadful.

I just nodded and stepped back up onto my cob, aching in every part. Tom Nicolson rode beside me, eyes fixed on some distant thought.

AS EVENING CAME, WE finally emerged from the mosses of the headwaters of the Tweed. At the inn there we released the two hostages, the boy silent and furious-eyed, the man with his leg-wound tightly bound, pale but likely to live.

As our gang made down into Teviotdale, relaxing now on home ground, the young groom toppled from the horse we had secured him to. Scott crouched over him, put his hand on the boy's forehead, looked briefly at a loss. His lips moved but I couldn't hear what Scott was saying. A prayer, a curse, a blessing?

He lifted the dead boy, and with Morgan's help carefully tied him across his horse. The others stood in silence, looking at the ground as their cobs shifted. Some took the opportunity to eat and drink. A few crossed themselves, old habits dying hard. The boy now lay across his cob like two sacks of flour, skinny arse sticking up in the air, brown hair straggling down over his face.

Scott came over to me. 'He was Peter Crawfurd, from our home farm. His name goes in the ballad.'

We saddled up and rode on the last miles, with Buccleuch's twenty-seven horses, plus some extra shires for interest. Everything was returned that was owed. Our loss gave it weight.

> *'Pete Crawfurd took a mortal wound,*
> *Fell frae his cob wi'oot a soun,*
> *His mither will him long bewail,*
> *Noo he sleeps sound in Teviotdale.'*

'NOT QUITE THE *Aeneid*,' Nicolson commented beside me as I recited. 'But it will do the job.'

'My best review yet!' I said.

Then we came over the brae and looked again on familiar hills and Branxholme cooried within. It was done.

NEXT EVENING TOM AND I found Scott in the stables, checking over his restored horses. He read through my drafted ballad, then handed it back.

'Chant it out for me.'

So my ballad had its first airing in among sweet-smelling horses, rather than a howff thick with wine and tobacco. Scott frowned down at the straw as he listened intently.

'Braw,' he said at the end. 'And the boy is in it. Good.'

'You got your horses back, with interest.'

'Aye, the word will have gone out that they cannot take the piss o me. And my followers will better follow.'

Nicolson rapped his staff on the stone floor. 'I've been thinking,' he said. '*It's not about the horses, but what is riding on them.*'

Scott stared at him, then at his grey cobs. Considered. 'Ye have it!' He laughed with delight. 'So yon's what scholars are good for!'

'Phrase-maker,' I muttered to Nicolson, but he had nailed the shoe to the hoof.

BACK IN EMBRA I would have the pleasure of lifting my ballad fresh from the press and smelling of ink. I nailed a copy above the table in my Lawnmerkit storehouse, and liked to say it was the only poetry I was ever paid hard cash for. It assuages me to think Peter Crawfurd will be remembered in a ballad – only his name and that he died on a small raid to retrieve some horses, but that is more than most of us can expect.

And Tom Nicolson spoke true. It was always about reputation, the ghost riders that persist long after we and our horses have left the dale.

CHAPTER 7

Arrival of a Manly Daffodil

O N THE 8TH OF September 1579, Esmé Stewart, Sixth Seigneur of Aubigny, was ushered into Leith harbour on a warm backing wind. Folk said he stood at the prow like a figurehead made flesh, radiant in a green coat parted to reveal the dazzling yellows and deeper green worn beneath. He was tall, slim yet strong-shouldered, thirty-seven and in his prime. He walked down the gangplank with hands raised, smiling at all. He tipped the captain with the last of his purse.

'I would so appreciate it if you would have my trunk and baggages delivered. And I thank you for a most skilful passage from Dieppe.'

The captain stammered, stunned by those cornflower-blue eyes. 'Sir, I wish you a profitable time among us.'

Esmé Stewart smiled. The sun flashed in his face, lingered in the opulent waves of his red-brown hair. He put his hand gently, intimately, on the captain's shoulder.

'I feel certain of it, *mon cher*,' he said.

Witnesses said the captain – a hardened, battered piece of teak – blushed like a maid. He offered to find a carriage, but Esmé Stewart announced his pleasure was to walk through the wonders of Leith, up the High Street and on to his lodgings in Anchor Close by the Castle.

Some sniggered as he passed through the docks, a few shook Calvinist heads at such magnificence. But no man or woman could ignore the new arrival as he strode up the Leith Walk track, not a *sou* in his purse, with modest yet absolute assurance, towards his destiny.

Allow an old man his flourishes! It was a very fine arrival.

I HAD JUST RETURNED home from my warehouse, with oily hands and hose marked by the clart of the street. Stepping over the ghost of my father's blood, I looked up to see a vision in green and yellow clasping my mother.

She untangled herself. Her face was flushed, her eyes shining.

'William, this is a loyal friend from the old days. The Duc d'Aubigny.'

The vision smiled. His bow was French but his voice was melodious Scots. '*Enchanté*. Please cry me Esmé.' I hesitatingly held out my smeary hand. Esmé Stewart clasped it unhesitatingly, looked me in the eye. 'I so enjoyed your recent verse, *mon ami*. *Upon this firth, as on the seas of love, My beaten barque with waltring waves tossed sore* . . . Petrarch in Scots sonnet form – who'd have thought it!'

Aghast and flattered, I stammered 'Where did you read this?'

'Your mother copied it in a letter! She is very proud of your abilities.'

'She is?'

'*Absolument*. I have no doubt you will achieve great things.'

Esmé Stewart had a skilful right arm, a wide education, astonishing looks and a quick brain, yet his greatest asset was apparent sincerity. That smile, that warm voice, those approving eyes – I wished to resist him but found I could not.

My mother laughed. 'We shall all achieve great things!'

She took Esmé Stewart's arm and led him into the Counting House. A shake of her head for me, who went down to the kitchen to clean myself up and arrange for hot chocolate to be taken up. His trunks arrived and were installed in the guest bedroom.

In the kitchen I sipped chocolate and let our new lodger's charm wear off. *Loyal friend* – in my mother's world that signified Catholic. I half-listened to my sister's praises of John Drummond of Hawthornden, whose parents were still some distance from agreeing a match with the daughter of a wad-wyfe, however prosperous.

I heard my mother's footsteps go down the stair to the cellar where she kept her hard cash in a lead-lined cubbyhole behind panelling. A few minutes later she returned, almost skipped back into the Counting House. I heard the Bishop of Ross announce himself, then his steps up the stair, and a number of things came clear.

The conference in the Counting House went on past the noon cannon from the Castle, then the Bishop of Ross left quietly, out the back way. Our new arrival stayed on – apparently he was going to lodge with us for a while.

That morning Embra had received more than an exotic visitor. Esmé Stewart was a scratch from a prepared blade, about to enter the bloodstream of the body politic.

'AT COURT IT IS love at first sight,' Bothwell exclaimed. 'They're aa infatuated with our Esmé, or fake to be.'

In the back room of Burdie's tavern, he poured himself another brandy. Well set in the inglenook chair, Scott of Buccleuch seemed amused. 'You'll still be his second favourite.'

'I'll no be second to any man!'

'I have observed Esmé Stewart.' Scott leaned forward, his right knee quivering. 'You will never compete with our new arrival. In addition to being part-French, stunning, elegant and well versed in *belles lettres*, I'd say he shares inclinations with our young King.'

I looked up at that. 'But he has five children.'

Scott and Bothwell spoke as one. '*So?*'

'I bow to your sophistication, gentlemen' I said. 'Our guest is indeed devastating.'

'Admit you were attracted.' Scott grinned.

'I wanted him to think well of me,' I conceded.

It was the talk of Embra. The boy King was spellbound. He stared at Esmé like a young chick at a chalk line. He fondled. He took him by the crook of the arm. He likewise embraced young

Captain James Stewart, who had arrived from France but days later, who also seemed in thrall to Esmé.

Over-excited and hectic, Jamie Saxt had paraded his new favourites as they rode to the woods around Holyrude. He then called the Privy Council and announced that, with their invaluable advice, he was going to assume personal rule. The ruling triumvirate would step down as of now.

Bothwell said that in the Council room, the colour had drained from Regent Morton's meaty face. When Argyll and Morton began to protest, Esmé Stewart murmured in the King's ear. The boy sniggered and whispered back, stroked his inner thigh. Morton collected himself and bowed respectfully, but if looks could kill, the Duc d'Aubigny would have been drawn and quartered on the spot.

'There is a change in the wind,' Scott murmured. 'We must tack wi it.'

He called for the best wine in the tavern – which wasn't saying much, Burdie's being a dreadful hole, though discreet – and we got down to what in men is called *sharing intelligence* and among women merely *gossip*.

I admitted Esmé was staying with us for a few days. 'You and your mother had best both bar your private chambers at night,' Bothwell sniggered.

'They are just old friends,' I protested.

'I bet they are.'

I said nothing about where Esmé's finance was coming from, nor the conference with the Bishop of Ross. I still had not settled what

I would tell Buchanan. I could not get my mother in trouble. Esmé Stewart brought colour and music and poetry to our dour city. I had nothing against him except, perhaps, his cause.

Life as a conduit is seldom clear-flowing.

HOURS LATER, WE THREE swayed up the precipitous wynd from the Grassmerkit, our caterwauling voices echoing up the ancient walls. *I've travelled this wide warld all over / And now to anither I'll go.* We had all seen parents, brothers or sisters die. We kenned that fell visitor waited round any corner, yet could not believe He waited for us. We were young and could sing in His face. *When I'm deid and laid out on the counter / The ladies will aa want tae know!*

Still singing and panting, we emerged onto the High Street. The moon was brilliant on the frosted setts, on the disintegrating flesh of last month's heads of the Irvine brothers, spiked on the Tolbooth wall.

Two men stepped from the shadows. I turned to see two more come up behind us.

'Hand o'er yer benisons, lads.'

Three long dirks, one weighted cudgel. In quick reply: Buccleuch's short sword, Bothwell's rapier. I drew out my father's dirk.

The four robbers hesitated. A fifth stood in the shadow of the wynd. Bothwell smiled happily, cocked his head to the left, not a good sign.

Scott of Buccleuch stepped forward. 'I hae killed eight men in my few years.' He spoke calmly. 'Tonight I can make a round dozen.' His sword tip ticked one side to the other, like a moonlit pendulum. 'Decide while ye can, my bonnies.'

A pause, then the men were gone clattering down the close. We put away our weapons, Bothwell muttering his disappointment.

'Was that political?' I asked shakily.

'I doubt it,' Scott said. 'Just after our purses.'

'They woulda been disappointed in mine,' I managed. 'I spent my last groat back there.'

'At least you didna piss yourself this time,' Bothwell said. 'We'll mak a fighter of you yet.'

Just the same, they escorted me to the entry of Anchor Close. I bade them goodnight and let myself in quietly. I stood in the hallway. It was not fully dark, on account of light round the sides of the Counting House door. Laughter. My mother and Esmé Stewart. Drink taken by the sound of it.

I hesitated at the door, wanting to join them, tell of my evening and the confrontation by St Giles. Then other sounds, muffled squeaks and thumps. Rising gasps that had not been heard in the house since my father's time.

I turned away, made my way up the stair to bed by feel alone.

I SET UP SLEEPING quarters in my workshop off the Lawnmerkit. 'And about time,' Marianne Mitchison said as she helped hang heavy Flemish brocades to mark my new private space from the business premises. 'There are bonnie houses up on Abbeyhill, gin ye can afford it.'

I nodded. My head ached from brandy and wine the night before. It was indeed time to grow up and put such gaudy nights behind me. 'So I hear.'

'Dinna push the man,' old Mitchison said from the door. 'He'll be wanting to grow his business first. Is that not right?'

Subtle negotiation between the families had been going on some time. The Mitchisons would bring solid mercantile status to Janet Fockhart's enterprises and questionable French connections. Each head of family believed they were doing the other a favour.

'I'm considering moving from furnishings to spices,' I said. 'The snuffs are going like hot scones aff the griddle.'

Mitchison looked unconvinced. 'Spices are risky as they are profitable, son. Folk will aye want furniture and gee-gaws, same way they aye need coffins and time-pieces.'

'Risk high, gain all,' I muttered, though in truth that philosophy was more of Bothwell or Esmé Stewart than my own.

Mitchison shrugged. 'I was young aince,' he said. 'I grew out of it, as you will if you're spared.' He looked at his daughter. 'I'll see you back at the hoose. Nae hurry.'

Then he was gone, leaving us to the French couch. Each understood what was on offer. Marianne took my hand, entwined her cool fingers through mine. She sat on the couch and drew me down by her. 'You ken how far we can go, Will?'

'The Canongait but not the Palace?'

She smiled a little at that. 'Aye,' she said. 'I'll see you right.'

With an ache I couldn't quite place, I bent to kiss her practical lips.

AT THE DOOR ONTO the street, she turned back to me. 'Dinna worry,' she said. 'You can do business, hae bairns, prosper and keep the poesie as a hobby.'

I watched her go on up the High Street, determined and capable. There comes a time to put youthful things aside. Rosie Nicolson would have said the same, only her eyes and her meaning would have been so, so different.

AS WINTER SET RIGID the cart tracks in the Lawnmerkit, I noted my mother was lending money with fresh vigour. She was lending to the Court, which had come to new life with Esmé and James Stewart's arrival, and with Jamie Saxt's formal reception into the city and the palace of Holyrude. New clothes, new tapestries and robes, more candles, more entertainments. Music and masques and recitals, though restricted to Holyrude to spare the Kirk's feelings. Dancing! All directed by Esmé Stewart, the weathercock and the new wind.

It all cost money and it generated money. The loans went out and would come back with interest. The Kirk was borrowing too, finally making good the cleansed kirks, and building parish schools, training and even paying ministers, not all of them Calvinists. The Town Council borrowed to make fit public courts, tolbooths, parks and streets. Now decoration and beauty did not seem such bad things, except to the those to whom Fancy would aye stink of Popery.

Though he remained a regular visitor, especially towards the day's end, Esmé Stewart had moved out of Anchor Close to fine lodgings in the Canongait, in easy reach of Holyrude and the ardent King. Through that winter, Esmé was everywhere in Embra. He was Spring come early. Seeing him walk out in green and yellow, some wit had cried him *The Daffodil*.

'That may be apt,' my mother said with relish as we walked through the Grassmerkit, 'But he is a *manly* daffodil.'

She was much revived these days, singing French *chansons* to herself, happy even. And why not? Business was booming and – so she believed – Catholic Restoration was imminent, this year or the next.

A manly daffodil! So be it. None of my business. No point reporting to Buchanan what he already knew. Business was now my business, and the risky spices-and-snuffs venture excited me. With money I could hold my own among the merchants. My father would have approved. The Mitchisons would approve. The Nicolsons would see what they had missed.

A manly daffodil sprung up / And tossed his bonnie head . . . I sensed a flattering Satire coming on, that would amuse the Castalian Band. Perhaps Jamie Saxt would hear of it and approve. It could even be a Masque! One day there might be a commission, a post, a salary!

At my premises I went straight to my quarters, drew the curtain and sat down by the lamp, smoothed out paper and stirred the ink.

Through the Parks and by the sea
Wheree'er the bonnie King rode out . . .

A WHEEN OF BLETHERS, meaningless trotting measures! I thought of remembered lips and truly great verse, all that meant all to me, both so far out of my reach. Outside a pair of horses went clacking by over the setts. I listened to one go off to the Fleshmerkit, the other towards the White Horse Inn. That was it, wasn't it? I was one who aye swithered atween two horses, the merchant and the makar.

That was the truth of it. So why not make the problem the topic?

I sat in a dwam, between my orderly ledgers and the scored-out page. Perhaps the course of one's life is made by the particular manner in which we never quite resolve ourselves.

I teased out the quill's feather. I could feel a set of oppositional tropes coming on.

CHAPTER 8

A Death in the Family

A S REAL, NON-SATIRICAL DAFFODILS began to flare along the woods and roads, I was stirred to go to Fife on business. This time I rode on my elderly shire horse Bucephalus. It seemed more mature and dignified than the lurching *Sonsie Quine*.

With me came two laden pack-ponies, and a covered cart of assorted goods driven by my lad. James Budge cared for business but was also cheery, adaptable and handy with pistol, cudgel and dirk. There were many hungry people living outwith the Law in the caves along the coast. My crossbow was in its leather hanger, my father's blade rubbed on my skin. Only the poor travelled unprotected.

I spent a night with Walter Scott's kinsmen in their lodge by Dysart harbour, catching up on news of Bothwell and Scott, currently harrying the English Marches. This seemed an odd way of putting themselves forward for one or the other to be appointed King's Warden of the Western March, but the current wisdom was *It taks a reiver tae rule a reiver*. I gathered George Buchanan approved of Buccleuch. *High politics*, he had murmured. *You will understand in time*.

The following day I met with the Fife lairds at Tam Anderson's solid house of Cauldhame by Wemyss, complete with doo-cot, ice-house, nearby coal mine and salt-pans laid by the sea. The lairds were doing well in the Baltic trade, and were ready to acquire embroidered tapestries, silver candlesticks, inlaid snuff-boxes and tobacco jars that I had brought. Though clearly not gentry myself, I felt easy among the lairds, for they were not grand, and we had shared student days. They were practical men, unashamed of commerce.

The talk there was all of Esmé Stewart. The King had just made him Earl of Lennox, gifting the title of the exiled Hamiltons, and hung him with jewels of our former Queen Mary. Esmé was now in the Privy Council. His protégé Captain James Stewart had been made Captain of the Guard, in charge of the King's security.

'Earl of Lennox? More Lord o the Bedchamber, by what I hear,' Lindores declared, to much sniggering.

Morton still appeared at Court but was seldom with the King. He was not the power he had been. Then there was Skipper Lindsay's malediction that Morton would not see another spring. A drunkard's ravings, or an uncanny prophecy?

'Morton's still the man,' Torrance declared over wine. 'He'll be back. Who is this Esmé Stewart but the King's passing fancy?'

'And he's Catholic!' shouted Cunningham of Ceres.

'Ah, but the King is giving him instruction in the Faith,' Torrance retorted. 'True, Fowler?'

'Last time I saw him,' I said carefully, 'the new Earl of Lennox was purchasing a vernacular Bible at the King's printer.'

'A man dressed like yon can never be a Protestant!' Cunningham slurred.

I caught Tam Laird Anderson's eye. I believed he still kept the Old Faith, but cannily, privately. Perhaps his time was coming. That evening I felt all was in flux, and it wasn't just the claret. I tried to concentrate, to remember for my report to George Buchanan.

'We hae had our Reformation,' Torrance said wearily. 'Can we really be arsed doing it all over again?'

I RODE INTO ST Andrews by the West Port, settled up at the Tolbooth for my remaining goods, then on towards the ruined Cathedral. I took my time, noticing how yet more of Blackfriars had melted away, and its gardens were being farmed now. The faces looked less starved but still wary. A few glanced at me, then nodded recognition.

Strange to return thus, as a sound man of business. The excited boy still stirred in me but was smoored under good clothing. I called in on the printer to check my broadsheet Reiving Ballad was still available.

'Sold oot a while back,' James Spaven said. 'Snaw aff a dyke!'

'You'll be getting more in?'

'Na, it is last year's news. Had there been scenes of ravishment or slaughter, it might have sold on longer.'

Still, I treated myself to a calfskin-bound Robert Henrysoun.

Budge waited outside in the street, winking at lassies and whistling *The Yellow Burd o Lesmagow*. I sent him on to the inn to make good the horses, feeling siccar now, and in any case most of my settlements were held as promissory notes, to be cashed back in Embra.

I went by Merkitgait, and bargained for fresh silk ribbons for Lucy, yellow and green as was the new fashion. Then I walked through well-kenned streets to St Leonard's. The Hebdomadar spied me coming across the courtyard, frowned, held up his podgy hand.

'Tutor Nicolson isna at his classes.'

'You ken where he is?'

The Hebdomadar gave me a sombre look.

'At hame, of course.'

There was something akin to compassion in the man's face. Impatient and uneasy, I hurried back past the Cathedral and turned into the narrowness of Fishertown. Past the cellar where once Tom and I had stashed the Dean's church goods. And then . . .

The Nicolson cottage windows were like eyes that had been put out, hidden with black cloth. From the door latch a wooden cross swung to and fro in the breeze. I hammered on the door. It opened on Mother Nicolson, more stout and more bent than ever.

She clutched my arm. 'He is gane!' she wailed. 'Gane! And but twenty-four!'

I grued to my core even as I protested. 'How?' I said. 'He was well when he last wrote me!'

Mother Nicolson looked up, her lined face damp and puzzled.

'Wrote you?' she said. Then I saw Tom behind her, spindly and pale as a snowdrop.

'John Gourlay drowned yestreen off Fifeness,' he said straight off. 'You'd best come within.'

I went into the room where I had spent my happiest hours. Today grief reigned. Silence and tears, the bitterest withheld. From the back room, cowled in black and her face blank, Rose emerged with Lucy in her arms, and my ambitions and defences slumped like a bairn's sandcastle in a rising tide.

THE KIRK WAS NEAR-FULL with fisher folk – Gourlays, Nicolsons, Watsons and Moncrieffs. I saw Bella Muir put her black-gloved hand gently on her enemy's shoulder. The service was short and to the point. *A man is deid, it is God's will. Praise the Lord.* Gourlay's name was said but once. Knox and the Calvinist wing of the Kirk did not approve of elevating the dead. Their virtues, successes and lovable qualities were earthly things of no account.

I stood back from the lave. I was not family. I was not of the fisher folk to whom this had happened many times before and would again. They took their grief like salt, to toughen and help them last. I watched Rose, silent, with her kin. Tom stayed close, stooping down, holding her arm. One of the Gourlay twins carried toddler Lucy.

Rose stared incredulously as the minister spoke of God's infinite mercy. Her lips parted and she seemed about to speak. Her brother tightened his grip on her arm and somehow they got through to the end.

James Melville was waiting in the queue outside the kirk. He and Tom nodded awkwardly to each other, then Melville leaned down.

'I am so sorry, Rose. He was a good man. It is a great loss.'

Rose nodded. 'Thank you,' she managed.

Behind them, Nathaniel Pow spoke up. 'The Lord giveth and the Lord taketh away,' he intoned. 'We praise His infinite wisdom.'

Rose's head came up. Her face was blotched, her eyes dark. 'This is too much,' she whispered.

Her brother gripped her. '*Rose.*'

She shook all over. 'The Lord has naethin to do wi it!' she cried.

'She is in grief,' Tom said hastily. 'She knows not what she says.'

'She kens fine!' Bella called.

Pow glared Bella down. 'She is a grieving widow in need of pity and instruction.'

Tom grabbed his sister, pulled her into his chest. 'Wheesht, Rosie. Wheesht now.' He stared at the crowd. 'Thank you for your attendance,' he said formally. 'It is greatly appreciated by both our families. Now my sister must lay her man to rest.'

He began to limp forward. People parted. Rose clung to him, then they walked away from the crowd of shocked mourners, on to the waiting slot of dark Fife earth.

I glanced across the graveside at Tom Nicolson. Tom grimaced, then looked down again. I understood what had just happened was very bad. *The Lord has naethin to do wi it*. It was not so much the blasphemy – worse things were said in private, among family or trusted friends, drink taken – but where it was said. At the door of the kirk. In front of three ministers. In earshot of many. It was a wonder she had not been struck down.

Only grief excused her, to some. Pow looked raptly at Rose as she released the handful of earth onto her husband's plain kist.

TWO DAYS ON, I walked with Tom and Rose out onto the East Sands. The sea was flat and dazzling in the low sun, the sand coarse yellow. When Lucy tired, I picked her up and carried her cooried warm in my arms. She had her father's dark brows and eyes, but the look of quick intelligence was all her mother's. I felt the warmth and weight of her, her breath puffing on my latest moustache.

We spoke little as we walked. Rose kept looking out by Kinkell Point where her man's boat had couped. She would flinch away, then stare again. The low sun picked out a crease I had not seen before, folded from the corner of her mouth down towards her chin.

I also saw that her remarkable mind, her beliefs or lack of them, were of no use whatsoever to her. She was not a vision of girlish loveliness, nor the seed-pearl for a sonnet. She was just Rose Nicolson, mother and widow, cleverer than most but still born to suffer and endure.

As I stared at the side of her face, she turned as though alerted. She gave me a brief thoughtless smile, our eyes met. Then she looked down and away towards Kinkell.

I saw myself taking her aside, heard my tender, ardent, fitting words as I proposed our lives together. We would live in Embra by my trade, or in Dunino as I taught and we raised Lucy and she wrote out her thoughts for another and better age. In time, bairns of our own, everything! Why not?

I caught my breath at the rightness of it. Then I looked across at Rose in the clear Fife light, and saw water shimmering on her eyes, and was appalled at myself. My awful tastelessness, her man but days dead.

I loved her, of course I did. But now was the time to love her better. I could help practically, at a distance. I must go back to my world, leave her to hers.

Lucy protested in my arms, and I put her down. We all watched her zig-zagging out ahead. Rosie stumbled and Tom grabbed her hand. The back of her other hand knocked against mine. Then she took my hand, clasped it firmly, and we three walked together, and for a while all was complete as we walked through dazzling light.

A group of townsfolk was coming our way. I released her hand. Murmurs of condolence, and a few hard glances coming my way. It was time to go home. My being here was not helping, whatever fanciful notions had strayed across my mind.

AT THE EAST PORT, the Gourlay twins Marjorie and Ellie clutched Lucy, ready to lead Rose back to her married home.

'You will be in my thoughts and prayers,' I said to her last thing.

'Prayers are a waste o breath,' she replied flatly. 'And thoughts are jist thochts, however fond.'

'Well,' I said uncomfortably, disconcerted by her eyes, her muffled rage. I clasped her hand, leaned closer to kiss her cheek. 'Ca canny, my dear,' I said into her ear.

'Yon's the last I said to him. *Ca canny.*' She looked out by Kinkell Point. 'He went out on a blowsy day to bring the creels in. Stupid, stupid man.' Then she was gone amidst the Gourlays.

'Better you leave soon,' Nicolson said. 'There has been talk about you twa in the past. She has lost her best protection.'

I nodded. 'I hope there'll be no more outbursts like yon at the kirk.'

'She is not in her right mind. She loved him well.'

For a moment I saw John Gourlay again, running over from the futeball on the West Sands, a dour man ablaze with energy and happiness. Of course she had loved him well.

I reached into my coat, pulled out the green and yellow-gold ribbons. 'Gie these to Lucy at a better time,' I said. 'I'll send money as I may.'

I squeezed my friend's arm and set off back to the town to find Budge and the horses. Time to go home and back to trade and occasional writings. The rest was but tormenting fancy.

CHAPTER 9

A Short Cut

MARCH TURNED BACK TO winter, harder than a Calvinist's heart. The freeze on the Nor Loch below the Castle had skaters out again, with braziers and stalls. Marianne was set on going, but I had more urgent business that day. An opportunity had arisen to invest in the biggest spice shipment – two entire boatloads – ever destined for Scotland, but at that point I had little savings. All I held were promissory notes and bills of goods yet to be delivered, and the consortium insisted on hard cash.

So I left Marianne to go off with her pals, picked my way carefully up the iced-over setts to the top of the High Street and into our close. Mother let me in with a sardonic *Hello, stranger*. No sign of Monseigneur Esmé. I did not ask and she did not say.

I admitted I had come on business. She nodded and let me in to the Counting House. A fire smouldered low in the grate, for coal from Fife was very poor that year. We huddled close to the stove, both happed in fur, the moth-eaten ermine stole from student days wound round my neck, my feet numb.

I made my pitch for a cash loan for the spices shipment, stated the interest I could offer her. She listened without comment, alert but weary, like her fire was smoored under ashes.

'I cannot do it,' she said after I'd finished. 'Not the whole sum. Even if I thought it wise, my cash has gone out.'

I rubbed a gloved hand across my face, tired of myself. 'No matter,' I said and started to get up.

'Stay awhile,' she said abruptly. 'I've scarcely seen ye.'

She heated wine and brought spiced biscuits. I poked the fire into some life. She lit the candle before the Virgin, signalling business was over, and we settled into talk.

Perhaps it was the shared brutal cold of the season, but this time felt like a truce in our undeclared struggle. She talked of Esmé's progress in Court. The King's Protestantism was proving intransigent, surrounded as he was by Reformers, and Esmé was even taking instruction from that eager youth. She went on to confide that he would soon declare as a Protestant, and take his place among the leaders of the Lords of the Congregation.

Mais c'est ne pas vrai! she whispered fervently. She had seen his letter to the Guises stating he remained in his heart committed to the True Faith. The rest was just politics. 'Sometimes one has to offer folk what they need to hear. It is necessary insincerity, in a sincere cause. You ken how it is.'

I nodded. I kenned. She poked the fire and stared into the pulsing glow. 'I hear a friend of yours has lost her man,' she said at last. 'That is hard, I know.' Nothing much I could say to that, so I just grunted. 'And she has a bairn?'

'A wee lassie.' The weight of Lucy against my chest as we walked on the sands, her breath sweet and warm on my face.

'Not one of yours?'

I stared at her. 'No! Absolutely not.'

'But you wish she was.' It was not a question.

'*If wishes were fishes, men would swim free,*' I replied.

It was one of my father's sayings, and for a moment he was in the Doo-Cot with us, sorting through his papers, chuntering happily to himself. My mother glanced at where he used to sit. Her mouth softened. 'Doubtless the fisher girl will soon find another among her own kind.'

The sympathy due a young widow would soon wear off. Rose was far too clever. Her brother was peculiar. Her father was absent, and a Catholic Hielander to boot. She talked aloud to herself as she worked at the nets. And now her outburst at the door of the kirk.

'No doubt,' I said quietly.

'The Mitchison girl has good sense and child-bearing hips,' Mother said. 'She will give you heirs aplenty.' The fire sighed, or perhaps I did. She cracked her knuckles one by one, grimacing with each release. 'Will, it takes more than one more generation to become gentry. Your fancy friends are well and good, but not to be relied on. The Court may find use for you, but you are not one of them.'

'If Susannah marries Drummond of Hawthornden, she will be gentry.'

She waved her hand. 'Puff! Your sister has no intention of raising us up behind her.'

I knew it to be true. As for my friends in the Castalian Band, when we met as makars we would flyte and drink, plan new ventures and recite as equals, even Jamie Saxt – but come evening, the gentry would go one way and the rest of us returned to our tradesmen's dwellings. In the end we were men for hire. Scott and Bothwell were about the Court by right of birth. If the wind changed, they would be executed. We would merely be hanged.

'Oh well,' I said. '*Ambition is a tarantula that stings sair.*'

'You should ken,' she retorted. 'You keep stirring it from its sleep.'

I laughed, for she was quoting one of my own lines. And perhaps on account of the freezing day outside, the closeness as we cooried in by the poor fire, maybe even the shade of her husband and my father, for a while she talked openly to me.

As I sat, she revealed the Bishop of Ross's grand scheme. Esmé would soon publicly declare as Protestant. The King could then promote him from Earl to Duke of Lennox – the attainted title of the exiled Hamiltons – and he would befriend both the remaining Catholic lords who knew his heart, and the Protestant Lords of the Congregation. Morton would be sidelined. James Stewart, another in the True Faith, would become Captain of the Guards.

Mother was flushed in the dimness, her voice hoarse with excitation.

'Esmé proposes to take our young King to Spain on a great adventure. Away from the Reformers, amid the power and beauty and wealth of our Church, he will revert to his mother's Faith. He will be married to the Spanish infanta. He will return, well financed, to help restore our Queen Mary to the English throne, with Spanish and French troops led by Captain James Stewart.'

This sounded raving to me, yet my mother's voice was steady. I had no doubt the letters had been written, the plans being made. She truly believed it possible. Then again, she truly believed that consecrated wafers were the flesh of Christ.

'Why would our King agree to this?'

'Ambition, what else? The proposal is that he remain King of Scotland, perhaps as joint ruler with his mother. But he would be made heir to Mary for the English throne, and in time rule *both* Kingdoms. That desire is already in his heart, fanned by Esmé. Surely that would be a good?'

I thought about it, remembering the ruinous Borderlands, the dying Peter Crawfurd. Some were happy for the reiving wars to continue. Others, like Buccleuch, had hinted they had a solution in mind. Uniting two Kingdoms could be it. But under a Catholic monarch? Really?

'And tell me, mother, how many would die for this peace to come about?'

She more or less threw me out.

THE DAY WAS BRUTAL cold as I left Kincardine. My shire cart horse Bucephalus plodded behind on the iron-hard rutted lanes, saddle packs laden down with goods that had once been the Abbey's. The Laird needed cash to start a new coal pit, and reminders of the Old Faith were in demand again. Budge was making other deliveries about the Lothians, so on this trip I was alone. The winter landscape was empty save for a couple of distant packmen making their carry towards Stirling Brig.

I plodded on, still burdened by my mother's confidences. It seemed more wishful thinking than plan. Was that the will of the people, that we return to the Old Faith? I truly did not know, for so many kept their own council, while others feinted this way and that. Those who cared really cared. But the lave, what did they wish for, other than a quiet life?

If the Catholic Restoration went ahead, there would be no quiet life for a long, long time. Would things be better at the end of it? Uniting the Kingdoms! It was dizzying to contemplate.

I plodded on at the side of my steaming, lumbering beast, flexing my numb hands within their gloves. *I must report this to Buchanan. I cannot. She is my mother.*

So where does my loyalty lie? With my dead father or living mother? Or to myself, whoever that is? Can I fairly judge my mother's Church, when I was born in the year of its banishment, then educated entirely under the Reform?

I trudged, thought-laden, by fields of neeps and frozen tattie-banks. Bucephalus raised his tail, farted monstrously, then lumbered on. He did his day's darg, then rested, was fed, watered and groomed. I rather envied him.

I whistled till my teeth ached from the cold. By Tom Nicolson's latest letter, Rose had taken ill in her breathing and perhaps in her mind. Pow had taken to calling at her cottage to bring her the peace of the Lord. The bairn Lucy was mostly in care of the Gourlay twins.

Lord lift my burdens. May my spice ships come home safely. Bide wi me.

The track came down to the river, where ice was solid, snowed-over right to the far side. A path had been tramped across the ice. The packmen were testing it, staves in hand.

It was a mighty short cut. The next possible crossing was Stirling Brig, best part of a day further upriver. If I crossed here, I could be in the Black Bull in Linlithgow before dark. Embra the next day, and finally unload my gear. Within days I would be solvent again. When my ships came in, I could send money to Tom, for an apothecary for Rose and cash for Lucy. I might even take it to them myself. Why not?

The packmen had made their decision and set out on the path across the Forth, moving steadily against an iron-grey sky.

I watched them dwindle. The snow and ice were still, soundless. I crouched to look more closely at the track across, and made out several hoof prints that had melted into the ice and then re-frozen. There were grooves from a cart's wheels.

I hesitated. Bucephalus was a big beast, his load substantial. I looked upriver, towards Stirling. The clouds were darkening. My horse looked at me from huge brown eyes. He was elderly and biddable.

I took the reins, twisted them round my arm, then led off onto the ice.

HALF-WAYS ACROSS, I FELT tiny, exposed and alone. The packmen were ants, picking their way up the far shore. One stopped and waved, seemed to point. Some kind of encouragement, or warning.

The horse's shod hooves had clanged on the ice like muffled hammers. Now the tone of that impact seemed to change, become more hollow. I looked round at my beast. His head was up, his bulging brown eyes rolled. Increasingly uneasy, I looked back from whence we had come, then at the distance ahead. We must be two-thirds over.

No choice. I jerked the reins, the great head came down and Bucephalus moved on.

Maybe the current was faster near the bank, making the ice thinner. It now seemed to flex slightly under our weight. The packmen had stopped at the top of the brae and were looking back at us. I could see pale blobs of faces under their cowls. Then, quite slowly, the ice folded in.

I was thrown sideways, onto solid ice. My horse shrieked as he fell back the other way. More ice collapsed and my beast began to slide back into water dark as the grave. The reins tightened and began to pull me off my shelf. Bucephalus was now fully in, his great head up, legs slowly churning dark water. His eyes rolled to me. The current was dragging him under the ice.

The reins were tangled round my arm. I plucked out Dad's knife with my free hand and hacked frantically at the leather straps. Finally the leather reins ripped apart. I fell forward and Bucephalus sank away from me. Flared muzzle, brown eyes, twisted reins bubbling in the water. Then nothing but ice and empty dark water. In the distance, the packmen came running down the brae, one unslinging a rope from his shoulders.

TWO DAYS LATER, MITCHISON stopped me at the Embra Lawn-merkit, his face even more dolorous than usual. He said he had come from Leith with ill news. Two ships carrying spices had been caught in storms off Berwick and gone down with all hands. And their cargo with them.

The pavement split under my shoes. I felt myself sliding away. 'Both ships?' I managed.

'Aye. You paid up front?'

I had, of course. The consortium had demanded it as condition of the better price. I gripped the door to my premises. Gone. All gone, near on two years' striving and dreaming, and a blameless, trusting beast with it.

Mitchison put his gloved paw on my shoulder. 'I am richt sorry, lad,' he said. 'Such things happen when you are in a hurry. I heard ye took a short cut across the Forth?'

'Lost the lot,' I said. 'Pack-horse and all.'

Mitchison leaned in closer. 'I have tellt Marianne we shall hold off the nuptials till you have recovered the business. Ye understand me?'

'Full well,' I said.

I went inside my storehouse, looked at my few remaining goods. I sat on the blue velvet couch, clasped my hands, stared down at my filthy shoes. '*Ruin*,' I said quietly. '*So be it.*'

A brisk knocking on my warehouse door. Esmé Stewart glided in, gorgeous in modish plaid and bonnet, beard trimmed to a fine point. He swiftly sat beside me, clasped my hands fervently in his.

'*Oh, mon cher ami!*' he said. 'I am so sorry at your losses, so thankful you are still alive!'

His concern was irresistible. I nodded and found myself telling the story of my crossing above Kincardine. Esmé listened avidly. At the end he shook his head. 'That poor horse,' he said softly. 'Our dogs and horses trust us completely. It is heart-breaking when we fail them.'

Tears brightened his eyes. I swallowed. To be understood so deftly! Who could resist such a man? Not my mother, at any rate.

Esmé put his hand soothingly on my knee. 'You will recover and learn from this, my friend. I have great confidence in you.'

I nodded, blinking back tears. Took a long deep breath in, a longer breath out. Tried to change the subject. 'So, you are still taking instruction in the Reform from our King?'

'Yes indeed.' Esmé's long-fingered hand spread, smoothed the soft fabric above my knee. 'I am almost persuaded. It is strangely stirring and rejuvenating to change the outlook of a lifetime. You understand?'

I nodded, swallowed again. I felt the warmth of Esmé's hand, his tender concern. 'Aye,' I said at last. 'I myself have always been divided, though I incline towards my father's side.'

'Of course.' Esmé slipped his hand across my thigh, paused there for a long moment, then passed on to caress the velvet of the blue couch. 'This is very lovely,' Esmé said softly. 'Would you consider selling it to brighten my lodgings?'

'Why not?' I said. I jaloused Marianne Mitchison wouldn't be sharing the couch with me any time soon. 'Anything else here take your eye?'

Esmé looked at me and smiled like the sun. 'What I see is a young man greatly in need of a change of direction. Perhaps I can be of assistance.'

There was a price, of course. Esmé asked me, charmingly yet persistently, about Walter Scott, his mother Lady Margaret, and Bothwell. Where did their loyalties lie? I protested they did not confide in me.

'You have been a visitor at Branxholme, even shared in an illegal raid?' Did I imagine a hint of threat there? 'There are rewards for information on anything that relates to the King's security. You do care about that, don't you?'

'Of course, of course. *Bien sûr.*'

Damn them all. My name had gone out, and could not be recalled. I was in deep financial trouble, the Mitchisons had distanced themselves.

I had glimpsed my death in the dark waters of the Forth. Now I was being pulled apart by my various patrons.

'Let me open my heart to you,' Esmé said, breath warm in my ear. 'My friends do not seek to overthrow our King. Anything but! We ask only that he governs for all, not at the dictates of joyless fanatics in Kirk and Court. Some of them are quite mad, you know.'

He had a point. But just as mad were those who slaughtered the Huguenots, burned George Wishart with green wood to prolong his agonies. Still Esmé pressed. 'The Melville party wishes to reform the Universities and bring them under control, and put an end to free enquiry. And the pleasures of playing, of music and decoration, dancing, they would put an end to all that too.'

'They already have,' I muttered. 'There will be no more *Philotus*.'

'There you are! We believe in joy, free thought, and Arts. And good relations with our friends in France and Spain.'

'And Italy, and the absolute authority of the Pope? And the many corruptions of the Church?'

Esmé sighed. 'It is time you went to Paris to judge for yourself. I understand there are some legal and financial matters there that your mother cannot resolve. My apartment is yours, I will give you letters of introduction and defray your expenses.' He ruffled my hair. 'Young man, you need a change.'

I saw again the eyes of my Bucephalus bidding farewell. 'You're not wrong there.'

FOR EVERYTHING GIVEN, SOMETHING must be returned. For the gift of this present life, we owe our future death. More immediately, in return for the sanctuary of Paris and Esmé Stewart's apartment, I would study French commercial Law, with an eye to finally releasing the revenues from our Queen Mary's French estates. I guessed that some of that finance would be diverted to aid further plans for her Restoration.

After a sleepless night, I went to Buchanan and told him the circumstances under which I was leaving Embra for Paris, omitting only the conversation with my mother. I was awarded the name of Agent Bartholomew, in memory of the Massacre some ten years earlier.

George Buchanan added as I hesitated at his door, 'Doubtless Esmé Stewart has urged you to meet and cultivate certain people. Do so. And keep me informed. I need to know where his loyalty lies.'

'*Bien sûr*,' I said. He was right, of course, Esmé had given me a list of contacts. I lingered, waiting.

Buchanan looked at me. 'Loyalty is its own reward,' he said sternly.

There would be no purse. 'Of course,' I said.

His ancient claw gripped me fiercely at the elbow. '*Enjoy Paris. Avoid crowds. Know yourself.*' His lizard mouth pouted something like a smile. 'How I envy your youth and ignorance.'

I stepped out into the midden of the street, new chapter bound.

CHAPTER 10

Immanence in Paris

Paris! so strange, so different, so huge after Embra. The streets might be tense but they were not dour. Priests, friars and nuns everywhere, magnificent unruined churches, cathedrals and abbeys, all with acres of shimmering stained glass unbroken, paintings, frescoes, ornate altars and statues beyond number. What an expense of candles! Embra and St Andrews stood revealed as bleak ruined backwaters, no more than puddles.

The lectures and debates were in Latin of course, while the gossip and broadsheets were French. Montaigne's *Essais* were everywhere that year. It seemed he held to a traditional Catholicism, yet his mind was free, unpredictable, personal. He made me laugh and gasp. *Oh mighty man, that cannot make a bird or flea, yet creates gods by the dozen!* How did he get away with this? I doubted if he would have in Scotland.

I took Esmé Stewart's letter of recommendation and met Michel de Castelnau, soon to be appointed Ambassador in London. He was younger than I had expected, quick-witted, funny, indiscreet. At our first meeting we talked excitedly about Erasmus, the new optics, astronomy and astrology, the diverse merits of metre and syllabics in verse. As we parted he enquired after my mother's health and well-being.

At his dinner the following week, I sat between the poet Philip Sidney and a peppery, garrulous former monk, Giordano Bruno, both arguing with two Gascon poets. I supped astonishing soup as the volleys flew over my head. My mother's little jewelled crucifix was warm on its chain within my chemise. It felt like a *passe-partout* to this old world so new to me.

Later in the Île-de-France gardens, sharp-bearded Castelnau quizzed me about the current balance in Scotland between Kirk and Court and nobility. How was our boy King turning out? How much power did he have? When would he marry? Was there any likelihood of him sharing the throne with his mother? I blinked at that, made a joke to the effect no throne is that big.

'We have broken few windows compared to your land, but we have broken a great many more skulls!' Castelnau observed. He was not wrong. There were daily reports of riots and deaths. I stowed away a great deal about the weak French King, the power of Navarre, the partial, stalled Reform. Their struggle was nowhere near concluded. It made me fearful of my mother's dreams of counter-Reformation being enacted in my country.

Castelnau knew everyone and had a very fine cook who created ice creams of infinite colours and flavours, and held music recitals most Wednesdays. At one of these he suggested I continue to inform him of developments in Scotland once I was home. He hoped that through friends in the Law Courts, he would be able to facilitate the release of Queen Mary's revenues. He hinted gracefully at recompense for my time and expertise, but was vague about the detail. *And give my best regards to Monsieur Buchanan when you next write to him!*

I walked home, shaking my head. They used me and I used them and it seemed we all knew it. I was a murky conduit, where currents flowed both ways. Once in a while a useful person such as myself would be found floating down the Seine or the Thames or the Forth.

Still, it was pleasing to be regarded as worth cultivating, though not as profitable as one might imagine. Intelligence seemed to work more by exchange of favours, promissory notes so to speak, rather than coins in the hand. I would in time also discover that, however tangential one's role might be, it was impossible to quit.

Spying is too sharp-edged a word for it. Like so many other things in life – marriage, for instance – this was at heart an exchange, a trading of information, offers and rewards, giving and partial with-holdings. At best, once in a while one might glance into another's eyes and see a warmth amid the trade, glimpse the cause we are loyal to.

Wherever I go, I wrote to Tom Nicolson, *everyone believes they are doing the right thing. It is most confusing, and educative.*

SUMMER WAS ENDING, THE heat dying down in the streets as I slipped the patisseries into my valise. I walked across the wooden bridge onto the Île Saint-Louis with a sense of returning to home territory. The promise of warm custard pie followed, sweet and fragrant with egg and vanilla, overpowering the acrid drains in the passageways.

I emerged into sunlight and the little *jardin* at the end where the divided river was reunited. I went to the farthest promontory, where a fig tree dangled its leafy figurehead over the ship of the Île Saint-Louis. No one in sight, though I could hear singing from the nearest apartment. I pushed through the foliage, found my favourite branch. I hung up my valise by the strap, sat with feet dangling over the turbid river, leaned back to let sun into my face.

I unwrapped the paper bag and slowly tilted custard pie to my mouth. Crumble of warm pastry, soft custard coating my tongue, the sweet dissolve of vanilla. Sun on my eyelids, slow rush of the river, the little crucifix lifting and falling against my chest. Blissful solitude amid the great city.

Immanence. The word announced itself in me. Everything is transient, and everything is immanent. Was that what Rose Nicolson had meant, when she suggested there was always exactly the right amount of time for everything?

The purpose of Life is the enjoyment of it. How sweet is the Epicurean philosophy! And how unthinkable an outlook back in Scotland, where grim greybeards proclaimed *Life is a fallen state, a crawl across broken glass*. What did Rose believe now, convalescing amidst her griefs in that cold cottage by the sea, pestered by Nathaniel Pow?

I brushed the crumbs off my lap, licked the last traces of custard from my moustache. I had notes to write up from that morning's Civil Law lectures, my report to write for Buchanan, plus a document of facility to be lodged with Fuggers bank. Such is the relentless pace of our times!

Yet I let my hands drop to my lap, my head rest back on the branch. Sun on my eyelids, the rush of the waters below, vanilla lingering in my mouth. It is enough. The glass of my life was full again.

Despite the events later that day, that idle hour on the fig tree at the tip of the Île Saint-Louis would aye be Paris for me. My liver-spotted hand pauses on the table, an irresolute, diverse man scratching out the erratic hither and thither of his life. My cracked lips remember vanilla custard pastry, and I smile.

ESMÉ STEWART'S APARTMENT, UP the *allée* from the little park, was plain, dark and not extensive. However the Duc d'Aubigny presented himself in Embra, he was not a wealthy man. On the *rez-de-chaussée* lived Madame Elise, in the manner of my landlady at St Andrews, equally bulky and suspicious, though a much better cook. She claimed the Seigneur had bought the apartment for his mistress who had now left him for a bishop. Madame and their five children lived elsewhere. A manly daffodil indeed!

Madame Elise caught me on the stair. Was it true, she asked, that Monsieur Esmé had become an apostate? That he would be the next King of Scotland?

'Scarcely,' I replied, 'though they are cousins.' I hurried on up the stair.

I spread my lecture notes on the table by the small window. Latin was Latin everywhere, that was the point of it. It was comforting to be studying again. Civil Law was complex but (mostly) clear. My mother suspected the lawyers administering the revenues of our Scots Queen Mary's estates had been cheating and obstructing her for years, and it was becoming evident they were.

I closed my eyes, shivered. The dark grave of the river opening up, my horse's last look before he went under the ice. My fault, surely.

I jumped up, went to the window and looked out at the wind-harrowed Seine. I heard the Cathedral bells, summoning the faithful and faithless alike. Enough of Civil Law! Time for some spiritual elevation!

I SAT AT THE back of Notre-Dame, by a vast honey-coloured pillar, part-enchanted and part-repelled. Acres of stained glass, unbroken! Huge candles, the magnificent rood-screen, the saints in painted ranks, air thick with incense unwinding in speckled sunlight. The sumptuous, sweeping ecclesiastical robes of white, green, purple and gold. These giant frescoes of distant lands and Biblical scenes, dying Christs and chaste Marys. And the music from the choir, not intoning bleak Psalms but vaulted edifices of song, flying buttresses of Fancy, intricate curls of decoration and delight.

I couldn't think for the beauty of it all. Ah, but wasn't that the point? And with that notion, the bishop with his pointy hat and mitre, the robed priests, the tortured, exultant saints, even the soaring choir, seemed but an army of necromancers preying on my Reason, aided and abetted by music and incense. Who but wizards and fraudsters claim to change wafers to Christ's flesh, wine to His blood? The wealth and confusion of these churches after the sombre clarity of Reformed kirks. The complacent, soppy Virgins, more prevalent than our Lord!

I looked around at the faces, the elderly and the young, nodding along to the Latin few had been educated to understand. Within, my father murmured, *Are we here to worship the Church or worship God?*

When the congregation prepared to take Communion, I felt the tug of it, but could not join them. I sat aching for wine, for bread, for Salvation, but could not kneel for it. Like kissing and fondling with Marianne Mitchison on the blue velvet couch, for me this was all arousal and no consummation. Would that I believed Grace was given by these means, but the hard truth was I did not.

I left Notre-Dame that morning, as I used to leave Marianne, torn, aroused and unsatisfied. And so it was when I walked past the College of Navarre, saw the notice for a public disputation on Reason and the Articles of Faith, I pivoted and went in unknowingly to meet my Fate.

I stood off at the side in the crowded lecture hall. Many were students in the cowls of the college, others were just interested parties. A few priests loitered, several portly friars in both black and white habits. A crop of Sisters to the side, heads inclined towards each other like snowdrops. It still felt strange, almost unnatural, seeing them in public.

I listened, intrigued and stirred, as a lean speaker passionately set out the teachings of Erasmus the Humanist. That great scholar had brought the light of Reasoned research to the various versions of the Word of God, and revealed the thinkers that had come before, clearing away the cobwebs of centuries of superstition.

'Erasmus the apostate!' a harsh voice shouted from under his cowl. 'False religion!'

And something in my own unease and frustration, and loyalty to George Buchanan, made me cry out 'Nonsense, man!'

The cowled scholar turned and I stared at Claud Hamilton, his brother John, and their pet bullyboy, Billy Hay.

I hurried for the doorway but got blocked off. I pulled hands off my shoulder and squeezed out into the street. I bolted left, made a couple of turnings, then forgot where the river was from here. Shouts echoed down the college walls behind me. I took a side passage, jumped onto a cart and scrambled over an ornamental gate to drop into an orchard.

I ran through the trees but the gate at the far end was locked and the walls too high. I could hear yelling behind me, turned to see men coming over the wall. I felt the panic of the Huguenots who had died in this city, cut down in their thousands a couple of years before I had started at St Andrews.

I spotted a decrepit door to my left, smashed my shoulder through it. Back onto the streets, I ran for my life towards the Collège de Fortet where the administration should protect one of their own scholars.

I didn't make it. The Hamilton clan rounded the corner at the rue Prévert and clung on to me. They dragged me back towards Navarre, punching and kicking and throttling. Hay laid in with his cudgel. Citizens looked on. Some laughed as I shouted protest. My assailants dragged me into the lobby of Navarre, threw me down and began to kick in earnest. I felt my left arm crack, then a couple of boots smashed into my privates. Agony tore me up in strips.

'I'll settle ye, Fowler!' Claud Hamilton stood over me, slate-eyed. 'No commoner takes the piss o me!'

His heavy boot drew back. *Sic transit Gloria mundi.* Then steel clanged, much shouting, and then as through warped glass darkly, Francis Stewart the Earl of Bothwell grinning down.

'I HAVE HAD TO leave my country for my country's good,' Bothwell said, helping himself to a plate of pastries by my bedside. 'Lucky for you, eh?'

'May I enquire why?' I eased from one searing hip onto a fiery rib. Speech was a welcome distraction.

'You may! In the first place, there has been a misunderstanding about some horses in care of the Warden of the English March, Lord Scrope.'

It's not about the horses but what is riding on them. 'Was Walter Scott involved in this misunderstanding?'

'Certainly!' Bothwell swung his long shanks down from the bed. 'At the moment Wattie is sanctioned within Blackness Castle by the bonnie banks of Forth.'

'Sorry to hear that.'

'Ach, he will no be there long.' Bothwell bared his teeth, a grin of sorts. 'His imprisonment, like my exile, is mostly for show, to keep the English Queen in good temper. In a month or so a back door or an upper window will be left open.'

'And the second reason you are here?'

Bothwell swivelled and stared at me, quivering with excitement. 'It has happened at last!' He flung his arms wide, eyes sparking. 'All is changed at home! *Regent Morton stands accused of Treason.*'

From my childhood, James Douglas, Earl of Morton, had been the one solid and certain pillar of political life. Now he had given way. It was as though my pallet bed split like the ice near Kincardine.

Bothwell strode round the room, gesturing wildly as he relived his story. He had met the Privy Council as they spilled from the inner chamber in Holyrude. Minutes earlier, in front of the young King, Captain James Stewart had formally accused Morton of aiding and abetting the murder of the King's father, Lord Darnley, in Kirk o Fields, way back when. And he further accused Morton of conspiracy to overthrow our present beloved King. And for good measure, he threw in the killing of Rizzio – but who had not killed Rizzio? That wasn't the point!

I was becoming fearful of my visitor's excitement as he chomped grapes and spat pips around the room. The point was the Captain of the King's Guard had made the accusation, with full connivance of Esmé Stewart, in front of the boy King, not yet fourteen but in full command of his faculties if not of his physique. The boy had looked on with hungry eyes, gripping the arms of his chair, with his guards around him, and *said nothing*!

He just nodded, and that was enough. Ruthven and Mar and Argyll and the others had gaped while four guards straightway seized Morton and marched him from the chamber and out the back way, heading for the Tolbooth. He looked a dead man who had not yet grasped his passing.

The Privy Council broke up, honking and a-flurry like panicked geese. Esmé Stewart had taken Bothwell by the elbow and recommended he leave for France immediately. After all, Morton was his new wife's uncle, and he was tainted by association. *You may stay with William Fowler at my apartment on the Île Saint-Louis*, Esmé had murmured. *I will let you know when it is safe to return.*

'And thus my felicitous and timely arrival!' Bothwell crowed. 'Though I will of course lodge somewhere more salubrious than this.'

I lay back and looked at the ceiling. Thank the Lord for that. I always found Bothwell stimulating but alarmingly *de trop*.

'Did I mention I now have an heir?' Bothwell said, and scooped up the last pastry. 'James Patrick Francis Stewart.'

'Congratulations,' I said faintly, but Bothwell was already gone clattering down the stair. I heard him talking with Madame Elise, then the street door close, the bar thudded across. Relief.

I examined the ceiling. So Morton had fallen. I felt myself fluttering, then sinking, a leaf disturbed by the hooves of History as they thundered on towards whatever.

DAWN CAME AFTER A pain-wracked night, and the Earl of Bothwell was back again. His hair was wild, doublet buttoned askew, smelling of stale wine and woman's perfume as he laid an *assiette* of meat pies by my head.

'*Salut, mon vieux! Ça marche?*'

In reply I twisted and retched into the bowl. On the floor, the chamberpot brimmed with reddened pish. My balls throbbed mightily. There might never be heirs to whatever I still owned back home.

'Bastard Hamiltons,' I muttered. 'I will fit them proper.'

I rubbed my bruised chest. My mother's jewelled crucifix was gone forever, torn off somewhere in my flight and struggle. So be it.

Through the long night I had had time to consider my retaliation. I was a commoner, without position, and my business near broken. But I had a fine hand and a good command of Scots and Grammar. I had a patron in George Buchanan, and was not unknown in a small circle. From the safety of France, John and Claud Hamilton were clinging to their claims on their Scottish estates and titles. I would write a denunciation that would damage their case, detailing their attack on me, reviving memories of the massacre of the Huguenots, warning of the dangers of allowing such fanatics or their heirs back into the country.

Through the pain-wracked hours, I had distracted myself with constructing methodical arguments and rhetorical devices, exposing the Hamiltons' apostasy in France, their continued adherence to the Papish Faith, arguing that they were heretics, plotters and traitors: the full cannonade. I'd concentrate my fire on the older brother, the heir.

'If you can bring me paper and ink,' I said, 'I will put my convalescence to good use.'

'Surely,' Bothwell said. 'Any enemy of the Hamiltons is a fiere o mine.' He drummed on his thighs and stood, ready for the off again, like a boat just kissing shore. 'You will need a patron, *petit* Fowler, to pay the printer and help in the Court. A patron who appreciates a flattering dedication, and could do with some secretarial help! I will soon have the Hawick parsonage in my gift.'

We looked at each other. I had already suspected that Bothwell was scarcely literate. He didn't have to be. Lawyers and scribes did that for him. Now he wanted to buy a general-purpose writer.

'I would be honoured, my lord,' I said. Muffling a groan, I leaned forward and extended my hand.

(And indeed Bothwell, that volatile and unpredictable man, did come good with the Hawick parsonage, which would prove a helpful sinecure in straitened times. One cannot have enough patrons, lest they drop you or die.)

FOR A WEEK I continued to pee bloodily. Gradually red became pink became clear. My left elbow would never quite straighten. On raw afternoons my chest still aches from those broken ribs. Yet I could say – and did all too often in my later years – 'My enemies have aided me more than my friends ever could.'

There is some truth in it. My pamphlet *Ane Answer to the calumnious letter and erroneous propositions of an apostate named John Hamilton*, written to distract from chronic pain over a few weeks in Esmé Stewart's dank apartment on the Île Saint-Louis, printed in the Netherbow in Embra by Robert Lekprewick, would establish me in a way my poetry never did. I dedicated it to the Earl of Bothwell, who had posted two of his men outside the apartment against the return of the Hamiltons – as if Madame Elise were not enough to repel boarders! – and called by most days with custard tarts, gossip and helpful suggestions.

Finally I showed Bothwell my manuscript title page with its flattering dedication. 'Please read it out,' Bothwell said. 'My eyes are tired and the light is poor.' I did so. 'Excellent,' Bothwell said carelessly, picking pastry from his new-trimmed beard. 'My bad news is the Earl of Morton escaped custody in Stirling Castle. The good news is Captain Stewart and his Guards overtook him, and he is now secured within Dumbarton Castle.'

So we could go home soon, before we both got plump on pastries? Apparently not. The situation was very fluid. Powerful enemies like Ruthven and Mar were still in the Privy Council. There was talk of the King being pressed by Esmé to jaunt to Spain, to return with a

swarthy bride and Spanish troops. Bothwell confessed such manoeu-
vrings bored him, but Scott – who had duly escaped Blackness, and
was now lying low – had written to insist it was not yet safe to return.

Bothwell thumped down onto the chair and chewed his fingernails.
He looked so cast down that I gently suggested he must miss his
wife and new son at Branxholme. 'Indeed,' Bothwell said. 'It is too
much to bear. At home the ground is dry and firm. It is the season
for reiving, and we are stuck here!'

At times it was hard to tell if Bothwell was joking or just a creature unconstrained by self-knowledge. I had come to look forward
to his daily visits, but was equally relieved when he left for whatever
diversions the city might offer.

Alone again, I set about revising *Ane Answer*, preparatory to
making a fair and final copy for Lekprewick the Embra printer. The
promise of publication – paid for by Bothwell – helped distract me
from the raw itching under my bandages, and the ache down below.

A WARM APRIL WIND ploughed bright furrows across the Seine as
Bothwell accompanied me along the banks of Île Saint-Louis, past
the timber yards and the slaughterhouse. Two bodyguards followed.
Bothwell could be rash and impetuous but he was not entirely foolish
– we were both self-declared Protestants, and the Hamiltons and
their followers remained in the city.

Bothwell was in high good humour, happily decapitating nettles
with his sword. News had come that Captain James Stewart had

been made Earl of Arran, taking over the title from James Hamilton, who had gone completely insane – even by that family's standards! – many years earlier. Despite his enemies' efforts, Scott of Buccleuch had managed to distance himself from the imprisoned Morton who was awaiting his assize. Scott's letter of today concluded the time was right to come home.

Bothwell hurried away from the door of Esmé's apartment, lustily singing *Jeannie o Prestonpans*, scabbard glinting in the sun. I watched him cross the bridge and disappear into the city. I had absorbed enough French Civil Law to help sort out my mother's affairs. Castelnau had been confirmed as French Ambassador to London, and had invited me to call on him there to 'exchange news'. And my pamphlet was fit to be printed and promoted. Tom Nicolson's latest letter suggested all was not well with Rose. Time to go home.

I walked to the tip of the Île Saint-Louis to say farewell to the city. I did not climb into the fig tree – that manoeuvre was still too painful – but stood clasping a branch, staring at the water gliding by below. The wee jewelled crucifix, my *passe-partout*, was gone. No Immanence today, only that poorer yet more enduring thing, the memory of it.

CHAPTER 11

Of Death and the Maiden

THE HARBOUR AIR WAS sour with pumped bilges, the houses small and ill-made after Paris, but the clear light of the north-east was all mine as I stepped ashore at Leith. I could once again understand the undercurrents beneath words, the coarse rasp of sarcasm and the lighter file of irony. My people, my kind, however cantankerous and divided.

Bothwell had left the ship at Berwick, heading back to his new bairn and whatever ploys for excitement and advancement awaited. 'A patron of the finer arts!' he had cried, louping onto his post horse. 'Who'd have thought it?'

As I put the latch key to my storehouse by the Lawnmerkit, a hefty hand descended on my shoulder. 'Man, ye look an awfy mess,' Mitchison said.

This was what passed for affection in these parts. 'I hoped a spread nose brought character to my features,' I replied.

'If ruination were character, lad, Embra would be the bonniest city in the land.'

Marianne hurried across the street, beaming, kissed me on the cheek. 'Grand to see you, Will! My, but you look terrible.'

'You should see the other men,' I responded, smiling. I had forgotten she cared for me, even as she worked to make me the man she wanted me to be.

While she hung on to my arm, Mitchison congratulated me on my forthcoming pamphlet. 'But you'll be back to build up the business, Will?'

'See how it goes,' I replied.

Then James Budge came down the close to greet me. 'You could use yer neb for a corkscrew,' my young assistant observed.

'I would have missed your ready wit, had ye any,' I responded. I excused myself to the Mitchisons, then went with Budge into my near-empty storehouse to discuss where we went from here.

MY NEXT CALL WAS on Lekprewick in the Netherbow. The premises smelled thrillingly of ink and paper. That round-shouldered, black-palmed craftsman glanced at me, grunted, 'Yer pamphlet will be late, friend.'

'No matter. I trust you to set it better than any in Embra,' I replied. This truculent man had been printing for the Reform for twenty years, setting the Psalms in the vernacular, and a slew of ballads, broadsides, sermons and proclamations. His works were pinned haphazardly to walls and shelves, but they were well done.

'I'll need payment in advance,' Lekprewick warned. I produced Bothwell's money and the printer near-smiled. 'This pamphlet will raise a stushie among the ungodly,' he said with relish. 'I bar my door at night, and I suggest ye do the same, patron or no.'

FINALLY I BRUSHED MY hair, sprushed up and made the climb to the High Street and up towards the Castle. Outside Anchor Close I looked out over Fife, the Firth and the green Lomond hills, then down to the Canongait and the distant masts of Leith. I minded my first setting out for St Andrews, a world ago. Once in a while that boy still keeked out of my eyes, but it was time – way past time – to become my own man.

Because Mother had long been a supporter of the Catholic Hamiltons, I had always equivocated when their names came up. Now I was about to denounce them in print as apostates and enemies of our New Jerusalem. Doubtless she would have heard about my forthcoming pamphlet, for Embra produced rumour like the Low Countries did cloth.

I passed through the close, braced myself, then knocked.

She looked ready to slam the door on the prodigal son. Sister Susannah darted forward, hugged me, exclaimed at my still swollen features, my poor bent nose. She opened my shirt and nearly fainted at the bruising. My mother went pale and was unusually silent as we ate.

Later, we went into the Counting House. Two new carvings of St Francis had been set on the walls, and the room now smelled more of incense than old papers. My mother poured the claret. We looked at each other.

'They beat you sair, son,' she said, 'I am sorry for that. But I must ask you to withdraw this pamphlet. Can you not see our cause hangs in the balance?'

I looked down into my red wine and for a moment was back again in Notre-Dame, those dazzling windows, the seductions of incense and candle, the thrilling choir inviting the soul to Heaven. Also the illiteracy, poverty and street mobs, the wealth, power and majesty of the Church. The memory of George Buchanan in the Swallowgait, enlisting me to a cause as real as it was indefinable.

'No,' I said. 'It is too late to withdraw. I cannot change in this.'

In that small chamber we looked at each other across a great divide.

'*C'est comme ça*,' she said at last. 'I had hoped you might find yourself in France.'

'And I did,' I replied, and knew it true.

She put her glass aside, and when she looked at me again, all the shutters had closed, like on hot afternoons in Paris. This separation of sympathies would be final.

'So,' she said briskly. 'Tell me how our affairs stand. Who is holding back the estate revenues, and where can we find them?'

'The problem is now not Paris,' I said. 'It is in London. If I go there to sort it out, it will have to be as a partner, not as your courier.'

She raised her eyebrows. I raised mine in return.

'What of your trading business?' she asked.

'I'm going into partnership with young Budge, so there will be time to spare for London. I am diversifying.'

'And the Mitchison lass? Are you diversifying with her?'

'*Comme çi, comme ça*,' I replied, wagging my hand in Parisian mode. 'We will see. I'm not sure they'd have me.'

When I left, I looked back from the door as she bent over at a draft contract, her eyes not what they were. Is this being grown-up at last, I wondered, this living on an island sized for one?

Then as I made his way down the stair a contrary thought announced itself: *It may be time to marry cannily, after all.*

SOON ENOUGH, ON A warm May morning in 1581, after much to-and-froing with Lekprewick, I finally held *Ane Answer to the calumnious letter and erroneous propositions of an apostate named John Hamilton*, still warm in my hands. Never mind the quality, feel the weight of fifty copies!

I had some bound, and walked round the town with a satchel, distributing them to friends and rivals alike. I called on George Buchanan, who wearily raised his antique head from his History of Scotland. He put a reading glass to his better eye and scanned my first pages while Geddes waited for the verdict.

'Good lad,' Buchanan said as he put aside the lens. 'So you have come down on one side at last.'

'I suppose I have,' I replied uneasily.

'*Suppose* is strong enough for a true scholar,' Buchanan commented. 'Leave conviction to the fanatics.'

'But you are convinced, sir, are you not?' John Geddes interjected. 'Of the teaching of Calvin?'

George Buchanan stared at him through milky eyes. He spread his hand, the knuckles lumpy and cadaver-white as candlewax.

'I suppose,' he replied, with a thin smile. 'Yet in my other ear aye hear Erasmus.'

IN THE DAYS TO come, I found what I thought an act of private retaliation had confirmed and promoted me in the Protestant cause. In the High Street and Lawnmerkit and the Canongait, sombre men hailed me as one of their own. After all, I had taken a beating for the Reform. My good father would have been proud! I politely declined their invitations to speak in the kirk debates, on the grounds I was a poet and trader, no preacher or theologian.

Esmé Stewart hailed me at the archery field below the Salisbury Crags, wearing a magnificent green casque around his head, though he had otherwise toned down his display. I gave him two copies of *Ane Answer*.

'I hope my rhetorical arguments do not give offence, sir,' I said diffidently.

'Not at all!' Esmé cried. 'Every day I am more of a Reformist!' His voice carried like a public announcement. Was that a hint of a wink? 'I shall make sure this is read in *the most exulted circles*. Now come to my lodgings and give me news of Paris.'

THE MORTON ASSIZE WAS hurried through at the end of May. To a crowded temporary court behind the Tolbooth, surrounded by his King's Guard, Captain James Stewart read out the charges – primarily complicity in the killing of our former Queen's husband, Lord Darnley, in Kirk o Fields, November 1564. The prosecution admitted Morton had not actually been in Edinburgh in the early hours of that morning when the old house blew up. Nor was he the one who tracked down the dazed Darnley and garrotted him in his nightshirt – this, the father of our King! Beloved uncle of our esteemed Esmé Stewart!

Instead Captain Stewart read out the signed admission of the Earl of Morton, that he had been told about the plot in advance. His convenient absence on the night was a sure sign of guilt. Morton protested that at the time he was not permitted to be within ten miles of Edinburgh.

No matter. He knew about it in advance. That was enough. And in the case of the Queen's secretary, David Rizzio, it was accepted that Morton's had been the first blade in. The prosecution did not linger on Rizzio's murder because half the nobility of Scotland, including the soon-to-be martyred Darnley, had been in on it.

After the briefest adjournment, the Lords returned the verdict: Guilty of Complicity to Treasonous murder. The sentence: hanging, followed by drawing of the entrails and then quartering. Esmé Stewart, all in black that day, smiled courteously and made a slight bow across the court at Morton.

Amid the stir Captain James Stewart announced that our gracious and merciful King had commuted the sentence to . . . beheading, by the device known as *The Maiden*, ordered for Embra at Morton's own commendation.

Morton bowed his head. He knew how the world worked, he who had worked it so often. Skipper Lindsay's prophecy had been only a couple of months out.

THE DAY OF EXECUTION was muffled by a chilly haar off the estuary. I combed my hair and moustache, checked myself in the keeking-glass. Still a bit wispy, but getting there.

In the High Street, people were murmurous as flies on a cowpat. The very stones of the city seemed to hum. I had known this before on execution days, a kind of dirty excitement in the air as the crowd gathered around the Tolbooth. The stage had been erected during the night. Peering past heads, I saw the Maiden up there. It looked like the frame to a hefty door.

As I watched, a bare-headed man in black bent his back and winched up a dull-glinting blade and tied it off. The door was now open through which James Douglas, 4th Earl of Morton, would pass into Eternity.

'Fine day for it!' Bothwell said at my side, making me jump.

Behind him was Walter Scott, another inch taller and sombre in Reform black, his red hair tied back with a green ribbon, Esmé Stewart's colours. Canny man.

'I did not think executions were to your taste,' I said, trying to be worldly.

'They make my blood run cold,' Scott retorted. 'But I have to be seen to be here, approving the verdict. Otherwise I shall be marked down as a threat. My mother is upset, for she cared for Uncle Morton.'

'As surely did you?'

Scott stared at me. 'He acted as a kinsman should,' he said coldly. 'Nothing more nor less, though he made sure to benefit by it. It was a habit of his, and he is paying dearly for it now.'

A murmur swept through the crowd like a wave breaking through shingle. Up through the haar in the High Street, under escort of the King's Guards led by Captain James Stewart, stumbling on foot and manacled, came the former Regent Morton. His head was high on his hefty neck. Behind him, vernacular Bibles in hand, came the leading Kirk men and the town Provost. I looked away, ashamed to be there, and so glimpsed how as Morton stepped onto the stage, with his foot the executioner pushed a battered wicker basket alongside the Maiden.

That practised gesture did it for me. I turned away and hurried homewards through the crowd. As I turned into the Lawnmerkit I heard silence, as though the entire city held its breath. Then a clanging thud. For a moment, hush. Then the roar.

I had a burning in my throat. I closed my eyes but still saw a worn boot easing the wicker basket into place, could not stop imagining the rest.

Morton's head would remain for months, blurring and disintegrating, on the highest spike of the Tolbooth. Folk glanced up at it in passing, spat or bowed their heads. Ministers used it to preach against greed and worldly striving.

The end of Morton was the lifting of a sluice gate. The great wheel began to turn again. A fortnight later, Jamie Saxt formally assumed personal rule, with the aid of the Council. Whatever came next, the age of the Regents was over.

THIRTY YEARS ON, TRYING to write the fall of Morton, that is what I see again: a scuffed boot pushing a wicker basket alongside the Maiden. Whatever happened to my fine shoes I loved so long ago? Were they ruined when I went through the ice near Kincardine? Did I discard them in Paris, judge them outdated for dinner at Castelnau's with Sidney the poet and Giordano Bruno, that self-proclaimed genius so lacking in commonsense?

I look under the table at my shapeless fur-lined baffies. Who knows where one's pride goes? My secretarial hand with its fine tremble resumes scrieving the years of my formation. Dip and scratch. Somewhere the executioner still eases a basket into place, ready for the head.

CHAPTER 12

Flight of a Necromancer

THE NOTE WAS HANDED over at my warehouse door, and I instantly knew the erratic scrawl. I paid the rider then sat beneath the skylight. I paused, broke the seal.

> *Come now. Rose is in trouble deep. PS Funds if possible. PPS Coin not promissory. N.*

SOMETIMES LIFE PIVOTS ON its heel, and one must follow. I left Budge to burnish a carving that may or may not have come from the Papal Court, and hastily packed for St Andrews.

MY FRIEND AND I sat in silence on the cliff-top near the Bishop's Castle, looking out over the gurly sea. How to reconnect our worlds? 'How fares the University?' I asked at last.

Tom Nicolson shrugged. 'We pretend to teach. The students pretend to study. The college pretends to pay us.' He considered the empty cowrie shell between his fingers. 'On good days I might believe we are a brave ship of scholars navigating the sea of learning.'

'Even Dean Jarvie?'

'Dean Jarvie long ago ceased to believe in anything.' Tom Nicolson held the shell closer and peered into the vacancy within. 'Where think you came this defunct creature in the Great Chain of Being?'

Then I was back with Rosie, among the nets on a day when she had plumpness in her cheeks and sport in her eyes. *And what does this ladder lean agin?*

'Tell me how it has come to this.'

Nicolson tossed up the shell, then swung at it violently with his staff. The fragments of the shell blew away in the wind out to sea. 'I had not wanted to burden you,' he said. 'Now I must.'

He told me that after her outburst at the funeral, Rose spoke little to anyone, even family. She took a fever and lay for days on her marriage-bed. She refused to leave the cottage she had shared with her husband. It was isolated, cold and dreary. The Gourlay twins Marjorie and Ellie would come and light the stove, bring soup and medicines bought with my Embra money, clean up the little girl. Next day the stove would be out, wee Lucy found wandering about clutching a blanket.

The Gourlays removed Lucy to their cottage. Rose spoke even less after that. Between bouts of gasping for breath as she talked Latin to the air. Her middle sister Peggie moved in to look after her, though she had to leave to clean and do laundry at the Provost's house. Tom came by when he could, trying to cheer his sister with gossip of the college.

One day he found a copy of Ovid's *Heroides* under the settle, looked without comment at the inscription: *To RN, heroine to my mind, your steadfast WF*. He opened it at random and began to read aloud the plaint of Medusa to her vanished lover. '*Tush! Pish!*' Rose muttered. '*Whit kind of sorceress lets her man leave for the sea?*'

So he carried on reading *Heroides*, a poem a visit. The beauty and wit of the verse made its complaints and losses bearable, and the doings of goddesses, witches, warrior women and heroines, seemed to entertain Rose.

'*Ochone, ochone!*' she groaned in mockery. '*He is only anither god wha undone you!*' She learned Penelope's plaint by heart, and wept with her at Ulysses' long absence, the lonely marriage-bed and those absurd, pushy suitors. '*Whit do ye expect when ye marry a sailor!*' she muttered. On the occasion when Achilles replied in his defence, she sat up and swore like the fishwife she was, then asked for more tattie broth.

She recovered somewhat. She said she was going back to work on her Johnny's nets and creels, to make them good to sell. And that's where the Gourlays found her some days later, kneeling by the nets on the Green in steady rain, knife in one hand, spindle in the other, staring helplessly at the rents and remnants.

After a long pause, his long hair blowing like demented spiders crawling over his skull, Tom Nicolson continued his telling, determined that I understood the whole circumstance.

He said Nathaniel Pow was the last son of a brutish tenant farmer up at Grange. He was a poor crittur, wi a lang neb and a bright skelly eye. His father cried him *the boo*, meaning the runt of a litter, not expected to survive. But he did, in part through his doting mother's care and prayers. She died when he had some eight years, and his sister Muriel reluctantly looked after him.

The boy found some refuge in the kirk, hiding there from his father's hard hand. He did jobs about the place and helped restore the fabric after the Reform. He did well at the school. He followed around another clever outsider chiel – Rosie – though she was more interested in her brother's learning.

Pow's Faith quickened in the shadows of the kirk. He took comfort in the promise that the first shall be last and the last shall be first. At St Mary's College he was drawn to James Melville, that popular, hearty, good-looking young man. Melville encouraged or at least tolerated him.

When he first stood to talk in disputations, and then later in the college chapel, Pow found he could command attention through his fervour. A student wit cried him *the corbie* for his beaky nose below black hair, the dark glistening eyes and harsh voice, and that by-name stuck. Corbie Pow, stomping along ungainly after the errant flock of the town.

Though his hero James Melville spoke of a loving God, Pow brooded on Satan. He glimpsed the De'il in the hypocrisies of the town, the casual cruelties of his father, the mockeries of the fish girls. He glimpsed the De'il in the kirk and in his own heart. He tried to save the fisher girls but sensed more kinship in the brightness of eye and troubling intelligence of Rose Nicolson. Even when the Satan within her repelled his attempts to oust Him, even when she married Johnny Gourlay, Pow did not abandon her.

Then Gourlay died and the poor girl was desperate and alone and outcast, crying out blasphemies in her grief. He would defend her. He would bring her back to the light.

Pow became a devoted visitor on the afternoons when she was alone. He defended her to the Presbytery, saying grief for her husband had let the De'il in. She needed sympathy, kindness and human company. On his pitiful stipend he brought Rose wee treats, a warm bed-bonnet, hot spice drinks and salves to ease her chest. In return he only asked that she listen as he read Scripture.

One dark afternoon she sat up in bed in her shift with her dead husband's coat about her shoulders, listening intently. When Pow read selected texts urging submission to the will of God, she murmured, '*Christians and Musilmen surely agree on this.*' Pow patiently said he had heard this was so, yet the Musilmen were mistaken pagans. '*Yet my brother tells me they too laud the Christ.*' Pow replied there was little benefit in studying false religions. One might as well throw the door open and invite the De'il in! '*Surely Reason can keep the Horned One at bay?*' Rose muttered.

Pow leaned closer, his pale cheeks flushed. 'Faith, only Faith can do that!'

'And the Musilman's Faith, it also keeps the De'il at bay?'

'You mock me, woman?'

'Man, I take you very seriously.'

He clasped her hand between his and stared fervently into her eyes. 'Come out, come out o there,' he intoned. 'In the Lord's name, leave this good woman! Let her be! Gie her peace!'

Her eyes brightened like sodden ground stepped on. Tears ran down her cheeks. In his exultation Nathaniel Pow felt his powers rise. He knelt on the bed and clasped her face between his hands.

'Come oot o there!' he crooned. 'Let in the light!'

She tried to sit up. His hands slipped from her face onto Gourlay's parting coat. She leaned back with a low gasp. His hand went inside, clasped her thundering heart.

'Be gone, Satan!' he cried. 'Let in the Christ!' His fingers tightened round her breast and for a long moment Corbie Pow and Rose stared at each other.

She shrieked and whipped her hand across his face. He fell back, grabbing at her. His hands tightened on her throat as she clawed for his eyes. The Watson girls would testify they were on their way to the harbour when they heard shouting and shrieking. A moment later Pow rushed out, wild and bleeding around his staring eyes.

'I came to exorcise the De'il and He attacked me!'

The minister ran off, hands clasped to his head, leaving the lassies hesitating outside the Gourlay door. When cross-examined as to what they did next, they admitted they did not go in. Why not? *'We were feart what we might find within.'*

By his sister Muriel's testimony at the hearing, Pow came home bloody. She cleaned and salved his face. He said he had been visiting the Nicolson lass with Christian intentions and she had misunderstood. '*The De'il is surely in that hoose.*'

To calm down, he went to the garden to dig up tatties. His sister had watched him flailing about with the fork in an awful state. She heard a cry, ran out to see him clutch his shin and topple over.

She stated that he greited a long while on his knees in the garden. Finally he came in, had his tea, then went to bed early. The next morning he asked Muriel to keep this to herself while he prayed for guidance.

Came the Sabbath, Pow looked *awfy no weel*. Pale as death he was, limping, shivering and in a sweat, two livid wounds beside his eyes. The elder helped him up into the pulpit. He swayed and stood gripping the lectern to sustain himself. He looked out over the congregation, put his hand on the Bible, opened his mouth, then collapsed.

He died that night in delirium.

AS TOM NICOLSON TOLD his tale on the cliff-top, I began to grasp the peril Rose was in. The charges had been laid against her as before, Nicolson said, but now with new vigour and more weight of evidence. Surely witchcraft and necromancy had killed Corbie Pow. The venom from her nails had killed him. She had been heard muttering spells at the nets as her man went to sea.

The kirk had lost one of its own. They could not have ministers assaulted while visiting parishioners. This time they were better organised. They came to Gourlay's cottage with scribe and witnesses, laid it before Maclehose the magistrate. Rose remained near-silent but for asserting she had been startled by Pow's attempted exorcism and believed she was defending herself.

This time James Melville did not speak for Rose. She was taken to the town gaol, awaiting a second hearing. In the morning, Tom had argued for her release to her family's care in the meantime. She was plainly unwell and ailing. Pow had more likely died from the fork wound on his shin. The Kirk would be held responsible if she died before trial.

Bail granted, subject to someone putting it up in cash. Rose Nicolson would be confined to the Nicolson cottage.

'Ye hae the money, Will?'

'Aye.'

I had borrowed from Mitchison, using some vague excuse he no doubt saw through. Tom clasped my arm fervently. 'They hae witnesses saying Rose muttered spells and curses aloud,' he said in disgust. 'She was reciting Latin, mostly your damn *Heroides*! The Muirs have got it in for her, and even the Gourlays aren't sure. They have lost their lad, and the twins say his drowning was caused by spells.'

'Do they really believe that?'

Nicolson tore up heather in the gathering dark. 'They are full of pain and pain will find its outlet.'

A whistle carried on the wind. The youngest Nicolson cousin

came running from the end of Fisher Row. Panting, he told us that Rose had been returned hame, awaiting a second hearing. We must come.

When I put my arms about her, I felt the hard bones of her spine. She who had been so vigorous at her work and in her thoughts, now looked insubstantial and lost.

The rest of the family looked on as she thanked me for standing bail. I stammered she was most welcome. It was as if we were business acquaintances. I stayed for supper but had no opportunity for private word with her. Twice her eyes snagged on mine, then she looked down to pick at her herring and tatties.

THE SECOND HEARING WAS held in Court. I had to wait outside with other non-family. I hailed James Melville, who came over reluctantly from a group of elders. He was now Principal of St Mary's College, a young man of great influence, but he flatly said he could not speak in favour of Rose. His uncle would not stand for it. Besides, one of the Kirk's ministers was dead, possibly at her hands.

'But surely you do not believe in supernatural forces!' I cried.

'I do not,' Melville said, his eyes on the ground. To most Reformists, the supernatural meant superstition and Popery. 'But I do believe in natural ones.'

'What does that mean?'

'Take a look round. What do you see?'

'I see elders and ministers and many over-excited onlookers.'

Melville nodded sombrely. 'What has happened between you and Nicolson?' I blurted. 'You were such friends.'

Melville stared at me, his big handsome face pale. 'He did not say?'

'No, nothing.'

'Then there let it rest.'

The courtroom door opened. Rose appeared behind the magistrates, held up by Tom's arm.

'*Witch!*' Bella Muir shrieked. 'Ye drooned puir Johnny!'

'Ye poisoned Chaplain Pow!' one of the Theology students shouted.

The Gourlays stood apart, uncommitted, the twins holding Lucy. Tom looked across at me and shook his head. Our lawyer shrugged some kind of apology. James Melville hurried away down the vennel and I knew there'd be no help from that quarter.

The hearing found for a trial in the High Court in Embra, on the charges of witchcraft, heresy and necromancy. There had been attempts at witchcraft prosecutions in Angus and the Mearns a decade earlier, but they had collapsed. Though many believed there were witches, spells and curses, *Demonic Pact* was theologically dubious. It was too close to the Old Church's claims to turn water to wine, wafer to Christ's flesh, a written Indulgence into Salvation.

But times were changing. Morton had been a moderating secular force but he was gone. Across the land, many folk were anxious and near-starving after another brutal winter, the town councils were low on tolls, and the recent intake of Kirk ministers was poorly trained and credulous. Sightings of Auld Nick, the Maister, Himself, the Horned Yin, the *De'il*, were on the increase, usually at country crossroads, lonely farmyards and outside pubs.

The lawyer cheered up as he handed me his fee note, and pointed out that bail conditions were unchanged. Rose Nicolson could bide at her family's home, but the Presbytery was resolved to have the house watched at all times.

TOM AND I WALKED out the West Sands, heads down into the rain and wind.

'It's damnable James Melville will not speak for her,' I said, exasperated. 'Whatever happened between you two?'

Nicolson leaned on his staff and looked out to sea where one wave after another poised, then fell. 'Drink had been taken,' he said at last. 'I made a gesture of affection that was perhaps misunderstood.'

I felt understanding release in me. 'Ah, that was unfortunate.'

'It canna be helped.'

I looked at my friend anew. He stared out sternly at the waters, his hair writhing in the snell wind. 'I suppose not,' I replied uncertainly.

A wild yell from behind. We turned to see a familiar horseman skitter down the dunes, then gallop towards us, cloak flying behind, fur cap pulled low over his red hair.

'Aye, ye suppose rightly,' Tom Nicolson said. 'So I wrote for a man who owes me much.'

'Cannily done,' I said. 'I don't question your judgement, Tom, or your nature.'

For a moment we looked each other in the eye, then turned to greet Scott of Buccleuch, sliding from the saddle.

WHEN DARKNESS CAME AND the gale abated, Tom lit the lamp and hung coarse blankets over the little windows to front and rear. Outside, numb Reformers muttered and regretted their night-shift surveillance. I peeked round the curtain and saw them as a darker dark, with the pale bones of the Cathedral glimmering behind them. Tom went into the back room with a coil of rope over his shoulder.

Old Mother Nicolson, the sisters, the two boys, slept or pretended to sleep, all cooried on pallets in the front room. I watched them, thinking of the many afternoons of food and laughter, affection and learning I had passed here. Though I was not one of them, they had accepted me. They had given warmth and food and laughter, without calculation.

Tom Nicolson emerged from the back room. 'She asks for you,' he said quietly. 'The tide has twa hours to run.'

We looked at each other by the yellow flare of the creusie lamp.

'You are sure of this?'

'I trust ye.'

I went in to the room where she lay. By candlelight, I pulled off my boots and laid myself down by her, the soft mass of a bolster atween us.

'Mither insisted on the divide,' Rose said, and giggled. For a moment she sounded a girl again. I turned on my side, reached an arm over the bolster and found her.

IN WHAT TIME REMAINED to us, we spoke little of the future. We talked instead of the podgy wee scholar boy on his bollard and the sturdy barefoot fisher girl (*'Sturdy! You mean short-legged?'*) at the nets. 'It was your eyes,' I whispered. 'There was a sea in them. I yearned to swim there.'

I felt her mouth twitch under my fingers as she smiled. 'You,' she said. 'Oh, you.' For a while she was silent. Her lips grazed across my fingertips. 'What think ye, now I am a necromancer and mother unfit for her daughter?'

'That you are the most remarkable mind I have known.'

'Much good it has done me.'

'And that I love you more and better.'

I heard a small gasp, then she drew my fingers between her lips. My heart leapt over the bolster, though my body did not.

WHEN ALL ELSE HAS gone, those few hours remain with me: the sea murmurous outside, her lips passing across my fingertips as though they were rosary beads. The candle wavered while she spoke out her mind.

'In the days when I could still make and mend, maist of it was dull and cheerless work. Numb fingers, sair back, neck stiff and belly rumbling!

Sometimes in company but many times on my ain. How such as you and I yearn to be alane when in company, and in company when alane!'

I lay on the other side of the bolster, her words my sole mooring to the world. *'Yet there were other times,'* she continued, speaking carefully as one reciting a final testament. *'There were days on the Green, wi the sea flashing and the wind about my shoulders, when I thought: how curious! I am doing this work while watching masel doing it. My hands mak and mend, and I see them do so. I came to know we are twa-fold, keeking within and keeking without. We witness our life even as we live it.'*

I felt she was speaking out her mind as never before, though there seemed o'er much farewell in it.

'Yon witness is the hairt of aa my kenning,' she said, firm and low.

'You mean your immortal soul?' I asked of the candlelight. *'Perhaps,'* she said. *'It is aye with me.'* Her fingers shifted on my wrist to where my pulse bobbled. *'In any case, it is not Time-bound.'*

For a moment I was sitting again in the fig tree on the Île Saint-Louis, dangling my feet over the Seine where the currents divide and conjoin.

She chuckled quietly. *'My brither the philosopher gets lost in the detail! We are audience to our play.'*

'Even Bella Muir?' I asked.

'E'en Corbie Pow, rest his soul.'

Silence but for the sea thrashing on rocks below the Castle. Was her ship in place, riding at anchor? 'What undid those good days?' I asked.

She laughed – a catch in the breath, no more. '*Life! I couldna live on a dream, nor be a scholar like you and Tom, nor teach scholars. It seems the mair I enquire, the less peace of mind I hae. So I married a man I fancied well, and had our bairn. I tended her and my man's gear and was mostly o'er busy to ponder. Then my Johnny went out on a blowsy day chasing siller to better us, and I lost him and was lost in turn. Lost to my bairn, lost to masel.*'

'*The world gets its way,*' she continued after a long silence, '*and nae cogitation changes that.*'

'And now, my dear? How are you now?'

A silence so lengthy I thought she slept. At last her fingers stirred across my palm. '*I must leave my bairn. But I hae recovered myself again, and for that I thank you, who have aye understood me.*'

Understood? I nearly laughed. 'I have tried to be your friend,' was what I said, and then silence but for the sea outside.

'*Let us just lie here for the time we hae,*' she said at last, low and tender, '*and mind how we once met on the Green, near-bairns, wi the bright day aa about us.*'

We lay a long while, the candle flickering yellow, hands clasped across the bolster, minding.

'Rose, was there a time I might have won ye?' Straightway I regretted speiring. Her teeth, softened by lips, closed on my thumb.

'*Aince. Twice, maybe. Had you or I been bolder! After the funeral when we walked the Sands wi Tom. Had ye pressed, that day I'd hae taen Lucy and gone wi ye, whatever iithers might hae thought.*'

'So I was not mistaken?' Her hand uncurled on mine, lay slack.

'*There was a time, Will.*' My eyes prickled in the dark. '*There wis a time and it has passed. I see a tree half-green and half on fire. It can yet be made richt . . .*'

I propped myself up on one elbow and studied her face as she slept, to fix her always in my mind.

TOM CHAPPED ON THE door and woke us. It was time to go.

'The guard are still out front,' Tom murmured as he tied the rope to the bed rail. 'Freezing their shrunken willies aff.'

He eased the little window open, and one by one we crawled through. We stood in the garden out back, the wind wrassling among the pea-sticks and tatties. The rope twitched where it went over. Our man below was in place.

'You first,' Tom whispered to his sister. 'Like when we were bairns.'

She nodded, then grasped the rope and stepped backwards off the cliff.

'There goes your bail,' Tom murmured.

'Worth every groat,' I said. 'She must not stand trial in Embra.' Soon the rope slackened. I grasped it and stepped back into nothing.

ON THE ROCKY SHORE, the dark form of Scott of Buccleuch grasped the tender and tried to hold it off the rocks. Some way off I could hear a sail flapping. Rose held her brother. She hesitated, then clasped Buccleuch. Finally she held me by the elbows of my outstretched arms.

'Thank you.' Her lips were cold but soft on mine. '*Goodbye, true friend.*'

She stepped into the boat, was steadied by a silent man at the oars, then sat at the back. A final glimmer of her face and they were gone into the swell.

We three stood in silence, till a low whistle came through the night, then the faint thud of an anchor dragged on deck. The barque was off and heading out of Scottish jurisdiction. Then Nicolson clasped Buccleuch's hand. 'Thank ye.'

'I have been indebted to ye since the Skelpit Dug,' Scott replied. 'Consider it squared. The Cistercian Sisters by Coldstream will give her shelter.'

He scrambled off into the darkness towards the Bishop's Castle. Tom and I stood alone on the wind-scoured beach as first light opened along the horizon.

'Her *Goodbye* sounded final,' I said at last.

My friend hesitated. 'It's jist a mode of speech,' he said. 'The Gourlays will keep Lucy for the while, till times change and my sister recovers. That was their price.' He abruptly turned away from the sea and grasped the rope. 'You go wi Buccleuch. I'll face the music.'

'You are tone deaf,' I replied. 'You'll need me wi you.'

Tom stared, then nodded. 'Thank ye,' he said. 'This knot will ne'er be untied.' Then he began climbing up the rope back to their cottage.

I stood below, brooding on the things Rose Nicolson had said. There had been a time, I had not been mistaken. And that time had passed. My mind protested, my heart kenned it.

True friend? Yes, I could be that. I had hoped to be much more. How often I had imagined a night with her, delighting and tormenting myself. I had not thought to be given so little and so much.

The rope from above stopped twitching. Her ship would be soon be crossing the Firth for North Berwick, then England. That she of all people was to be staying with nuns, in a country that still permitted such! She would have to learn forbearance.

I almost smiled as I clasped the rope, then started hauling myself up.

CHAPTER 13

A Grand Entry into St Andrews

THERE WAS A GREAT to-do when the witch Rose Nicolson vanished overnight. Some said she had flown off with the De'il. Days of hard questioning and threats followed, but our student days had trained us in resilience in debate, and our sworn statements made no mention of Buccleuch's part. Nicolson and I were charged with abetting her escape to an unknown destination. The bail on Rose was forfeited, leaving me skint again. We were taken from the Sheriff Court to the Tolbooth and were incarcerated to the cheers and jeers of a small crowd.

Days passed in that chill, piss-haunted room. John Geddes visited us, all the way from Embra, with an armful of blankets, fresh pork pie, two lamps and a new *essai* by Michel de Montaigne from Buchanan. Whatever my reservations about Geddes, for this thoughtfulness I have aye been grateful.

Finally Buccleuch and Bothwell were let into our the cell, laughing freely and dispensing jokes and sweetmeats. Bothwell paced up and down, counting strides, four each way.

'It is somewhat bigger than the grave!' he cried. 'Never fear, your patron will get you out of here. Are you not the author of *Ane Answer to John Hamilton*, beloved of Reformers?'

Buccleuch sat silently on the bench, one riding boot crossed elegantly across his knee. He had filled out, these last months, as much in gravitas as muscle. Walter Scott of Branxholme and Buccleuch had learned to consider, to respond rather than react.

'Rose is siccar,' he said eventually. 'But the authorities have learned she is with the Hospitaller nuns of the Priory of St Mary. Our Kirk has persuaded the courts to apply for extradition.'

'Pish!' Bothwell said. 'That will never happen!'

'There is every chance,' Scott said. 'Corbie Pow had a cousin who is godson to Lord Scrope, Warden of the English Western March. Scrope is my enemy on account of some horses and various insults, and he knows I had some hand in this. He will prick me if he can.'

'But has he jurisdiction outside the Western March?'

'No.' Buccleuch frowned down at the earthen floor. 'But his cousin Ludovic is Warden of the Eastern March, and the Priory is in his bailliedom.'

'Are the cousins close?'

'Close to Scrope!' Bothwell laughed scornfully. 'None can bear him.'

'Lord Scrope is no joke,' Scott countered. 'He has men, money, and his Queen's support.'

'How are relations between the Kingdoms at the moment?' I asked.

Buccleuch and Bothwell looked at each other. The latter shrugged and went back to pacing the cell. Confinement did not suit his energies.

'Not good, save that they are both still Protestant,' Scott said. 'Our King has a strong claim to succession, as does his mother, and Queen Bess kens it. And she is not pleased at the fall of Morton, whom she regarded as her man here.'

'Well, then!' Bothwell cried. 'She will refuse a request for extradition.'

'Maybe,' said Buccleuch. 'Maybe not. She is well-advised and subtle.'

'Can you not petition the King?' Nicolson said. 'Ask for this extradition to be dropped?'

Scott laughed quietly. 'You overestimate my position,' he said. 'Bothwell and I suffer from our kinship to Morton. We are only just hanging on.' He looked up to me. 'You still have access to Esmé Stewart?'

'Some,' I said. 'But he kens my mother does not approve my friendship with Rose.'

'Surely it is time to defy your mother?'

'I have done so. Surely it is time you defied yours?'

Scott's hand twitched to his sword. Bothwell stopped pacing. Scott sat back against the wall, keeping his eyes drilled on mine. 'I have dispatched men for less,' he said. 'But you lent me your dirk when I was a boy.' His hand came off the hilt and I breathed again. Bothwell resumed pacing. Scott chuckled. 'Right enough, our mothers are a monstrous regimen – but they are usually right.'

'That's my wife you're talking about!' Bothwell cried. 'Enough of this – I have an appointment on the Links.' He reached into his satchel. 'I near-forgot – a wee fairing for you,' and handed me a packet of snuff.

'Thank you,' I said. 'I have been craving this.'

'You want to wean yourself off it – yon dangerous stuff,' Bothwell said in all seriousness, then hurried off to play gowf.

(That hectic man hurled himself through life like a bluebottle trapped in a window, seeing where he wanted to be, baffled and enraged at being unable to get there. After many raids, insurrections, plots and pleas to his first cousin Jamie Saxt, he would declare as a Catholic. This did not save him from penury in Italian exile, where he finally buzzed into silence.)

OUR CELL WAS QUIET after Bothwell's departure. Then Walter Scott smacked his knees, stood up, put his arm round my shoulder. 'Write to Esmé Stewart, plead against the extradition,' he said. 'I will contact the Hospitallers and assure them of my support.' He gripped Nicolson's elbow. 'I will do what I can. Your sister is a bonnie fighter, and I would not like to see her persecuted.'

'I thank you,' Nicolson said, looking him in the eye. 'I am forever in your debt.'

The gaoler opened the door, then the two young gallants were gone into the world outside. I opened the packet, took a big pinch of snuff, sniffed deep, then dropped my shoulders in relief. 'I'm sure it will be alright,' I said.

Tom made no reply. I picked up the *Essay on the Importance of Travel* and began to read aloud Montaigne's observations of the differing practices of drinking, thanking, greeting and parting between men and women in different lands. 'I don't get it,' Tom said impatiently a couple of pages in. 'He doesn't know where he is going wi this!'

'Who does, except in the ideal worlds of Law and Religion?' I replied.

I had another pinch of snuff, sneezed explosively. Felt better. Felt almost at ease, for a man in a cell, imprisoned by others' certainties. I allowed myself to think again of Rose, her fingers moving over mine across the bolster. *A tree half-green and half on fire . . .*

I went back to Montaigne's essay. I looked for its conclusion, but naturally there was none.

IN THE MORNING, A letter was pushed through our grille, stained, crumpled and smelling faintly of fish. Rose wrote that she had recurring fevers and weakness in breathing, but was settled among the Sisters. She would be given board in return for teaching Grammar to the younger novices.

I sense dawn amid sunset. In defeat lies our victory. Pray not for me!
'You understand this?' Tom asked. 'Is she still disturbed?'

'She said something of this on our last night,' I said. 'It is not Philosophy such as you or I were taught.'

'For sure she dwells in anither country,' Tom said. 'Yet we may meet again some day.'

Our cell door opened on John Geddes, smirking away. 'Bail is granted, my bonnie lads!'

Our lawyer loitered by the Tolbooth gate. He said we were still bound to the town awaiting a further application, then presented his fee note. I wrote him a promissory, then Tom Nicolson and I walked out into the world, full as always to the brim.

Tom lurched off to teach his classes. I headed for the West Bow, for word was our Jamie Saxt was due to progress through St Andrews, en route to an extraordinary Privy Council meeting in Perth. It was rumoured much might turn on that, and so it proved.

A CROWD OF TOWNSFOLK were gathering as I settled on a ruined column of Blackfriars Priory. First the sound of hooves, then voices, then winding into the narrow port came the procession of King, nobility, gentry and clergy, to be followed by the pikers, swordsmen and crossbow men. Around me, farmers assessed the horses, boys exclaimed at the pistols and arquebuses, the merchants noted the gear. Tailors studied cloaks and Scots bonnets and French wide-collared embroidered doublets.

It was agreed the King was not much to look at. He lurched on his mount, waved a shaky gloved hand. He was but a boy erratically grown, with short legs and a large head on a thin neck, a wispy ginger fuzz on his upper lip. Nevertheless, as ever he hung on.

His immediate escort far outshone him. Esmé Stewart sported a green coat with black ermine cuffs and collar, knee-length boots, set off with a charcoal tweed bonnet with a pheasant plume held in place by a silver clasp and green peridots winking in the sun. Smiling pleasantly, modestly, he looked around with interest and approval. His French doublet was unbuttoned just enough to display a simple Kirk-approved wooden cross worn at his chest. He sat elegant and easy on his mount, reins in one pale blue gloved hand, every inch a man who had just been made Duke of Lennox.

St Andrews had never seen the like of him. Folk stood or paused midway across South Street. A group of truant laddies perched up in the ruins of Blackfriars gaped in awe, a few sniggered.

Then the crowd's attention turned to the man immediately behind the King, riding a powerful black stallion, pistols on his belt and sword upright in hand: Captain James Stewart, newly made Earl of Arran, glaring, muscular, in dark red hose and otherwise all in black. Dark beard trimmed to a chisel end, he was flanked by his King's Guards, his head turning and turning, looking for assassins in the crowd.

He flicked his reins and came up alongside Esmé and the boy King, jostling into position. I was looking at an old, old story: the protégé turned rival. With Morton gone, two men now shared power. That had a history of working.

Behind them rode much of the old aristocracy – the Earl of Mar, Argyll, Lord Lindsay, the Master of Glamis, faces I kenned from

Embra. In their midst rode William Ruthven, made Earl of Gowrie the week before, as the King exercised his prerogative. This group did not smile or wave, but looked preoccupied, even sullen.

Straggling behind them through Swallowgait followed assorted courtiers, physicians, tailors, secretaries, makers of masques. Also a couple of squalling pipers and a toothless man strumming his lute with a happy, vacant expression. Behind them, grimly disapproving such frivolity, walked James Melville and his group of Kirk elders in black. Behind them at a fast trot came the Earl of Bothwell, rakish and dishevelled as though he had just sprung out of someone's bed, along with his Hepburn cousins looking eagerly around for foes.

I leaned back against the ruined apse and watched them all go by. It was the onset of a new age, one of colour and fashion, the King visible and out and about, if not convincingly in charge. Yet there was a stubborn force in how he clung on, and alertness as he turned to look adoringly at Esmé, who said something and the King gave a high excited yelp.

Esmé saw me, raised his hand with an elegant flourish, and I could not but be thrilled and wave back enthusiastically. Jamie Saxt picked out my movement at the edge of the crowd. His cumbersome head turned, and for a moment his black eyes settled on me, and he peered, frowned as he tried to remember. Then he nodded, with his right hand made a gesture of writing on air, then he made a remark to Esmé and the two of them exchanged a smile, rode on.

Vanity, vanity, truly all is vanity under the sun. How easily we are gratified when momentarily half-recognised by the high heid yins of this world!

The procession moved on towards the Bishop's Castle. The crowd was already dispersing, to buy fish, make a profit or settle a bairn. *Leaves churned by the passing hooves of History, then settling again.* I should note the image, though probably wouldn't. It returns to me now, too late to do anything but add to this page.

Then a familiar figure came at a fast canter through the West Port: Walter Scott of Buccleuch. I threw up my hand. Scott saw me, slowed, hesitated, then rode on to follow where the power lay.

THE BLOOD HAS BEEN scrubbed from the stage. The money has all been spent. The fine shoes have gone, who knows where or when. A procession once came through St Andrews on a summer morn, halted, then moved on.

The mill wheel turns, the grinding stone rumbles against the fixed one, and the husks blow away in the wind. Love and memory remain, to hurt us into life.

CHAPTER 14

The Ruthven Conspiracy

R UMOUR SHOWERED DOWN UPON St Andrews, thick and fast as a flight of English arrows. The Privy Council meeting in Perth had been quarrelsome. Apparently Esmé Stewart and James Stewart, Captain of the Guard, had erupted into furious argument, each accusing the other of corruption, nepotism and flagrant disrespect. Gowrie, the Lord Treasurer, announced the country had fallen into great debt from the recent spending at Court and it had to stop. He himself was owed near on forty thousand pounds Scots! The Melvillian elders of the Kirk agreed, and allied themselves with the old nobility that had been sidelined these last months. And Jamie Saxt? It was agreed he had looked sulky and nervous. He was but a boy, more pawn than King.

The meeting had broken up, unresolved. Esmé Stewart hurried back to the security of Embra. The King had stayed on to hunt the Forest of Atholl with his young companions. It was believed James

Stewart, Earl of Arran, had taken a huff and gone to Forres with his Guards.

It was all distant thunder so far as I was concerned, compared to Rose Nicolson's health and security. I was anxious to have my bail restrictions lifted, then get back to Embra. Then go to see her in Northumbria? *Had ye been bolder . . .*

Such was my intent. Instead, Fate brought an impatient rapping at the Nicolson cottage door. I opened it on George Buchanan, thin and pale as Death itself.

'You're wanted elsewhere, lad,' Buchanan wheezed as he lowered himself onto the chair. 'There has been a changing of the guards. Ye'll need a satchel of writing materials.'

This didn't suit my plans at all. 'I cannot leave St Andrews till I'm free from bail conditions,' I protested.

Buchanan handed me certification, freshly scribed, wax still warm. 'Well, you're free now.' He coughed and gasped, chest heaving. He looked to be nearing his end, but then he had for some years. 'They have taken our King at last. You are needed.'

Who can resist those words? To be needed. It seemed I was bound for Ruthven Castle, on a mission whose true nature I would grasp too late.

WHILE I MADE PREPARATIONS to go, Buchanan revived enough to brief me. After the Privy Council broke up in disarray, he had been too unwell to ride further than Ruthven's castle,

Huntingtower. The fifteen-year-old King had opted to enjoy a day's hawking nearby, with a small youthful entourage. In the latter afternoon they were thinking to ride on to Newburgh when they were hailed by William Ruthven, the new Earl of Gowrie. Gowrie invited them to a night's hospitality in Huntingtower, promising entertainments, song and dance from some high-spirited lads. He was quite insistent.

With a dramatist's flourish, Buchanan told me Jamie Saxt ate nervously at Huntingtower, without the King's Guard at his back. His few companions were taken to bed down elsewhere. Next morning, Buchanan had risen from his sick-bed to find the hall filled with armed men, among them Thomas Lyon, the Master of Glamis, a bear cloak about his brawny shoulders. Buchanan met the King at breakfast and heard him stammer thanks to Gowrie for his hospitality, but now he must be on the road to Embra.

Lyon loomed over. 'Na,' he said bluntly. 'Ye maun bide whiles.'

'Why for?' the King asked.

'I'll show ye for why.'

Lyon dragged the King over to the window and pointed. Outside in the courtyard and in the parkland stood several hundred armed men.

A dozen *soi-disant* Lord Enterprisers then entered the Huntingtower hall, led by the Earl of Mar. Buchanan kenned them all: an impressive collection of passed-over men. Mar declared they had a letter of Supplication calling for the dismissal and banishment of Esmé Stewart, the so-called Duke of Lennox, and Captain James

Stewart, the supposed Earl of Arran. They had the full support of
the Kirk in this.

Jamie Saxt stamped his foot. 'Never! *Jamais!*'

Buchanan paused for breath. His fretful bronchia rattled like side-
drums. 'They read out the full Supplication again. Our lad sits and
listens, hand over his eyes. When it is done, the young King looks
up, seemingly calm. He has heard their complaints, and will consider
the matter in Embra. He makes to leave, but at the doorway Glamis
puts his mighty leg across the way. *It's no expedient*, Glamis says in
his coarse manner. *Ye sign the Banishment in this place.*'

Buchanan looked up at me, wiped his lips with shaking hand.
'The King burst into tears,' he said. 'To which Glamis said, *Better a
bairn greits than bearded men die.*'

That contemptuous remark went out and is quoted to this day,
long outlasting the man who made it. I was shocked at the disrespect,
though perhaps the brute Glamis had a point.

'I believe the King will sign, sooner or later,' Buchanan concluded.
'I am low with ague and heart-fever, and the Court secretary has taken
unwell. I said I'd send you in his place. You can take shorthand, help
draft the proclamations, then make fair copies to go out to the Burghs.'

'Why not John Geddes?' I protested. 'He's more senior, and able.'

'Nobody trusts Geddes. They trust you, on account of *Ane Answer*.'

'But my Lord Esmé has men at command! So does the Earl of
Arran, and the rest of the King's supporters. Surely there will be war!'

'We must hope not,' Buchanan said quietly. 'The Catholic cause
has overplayed its hand. This must end.'

He looked up at me, a flame in his ancient eyes. Who was I speaking to here – the Humanist or the Calvinist Presbyterian? I wanted no part in this. I wanted to be on a ship south to Northumbria, not riding north into an uprising.

'We wish the King no harm,' Buchanan insisted. 'You think Scotland would be better wi his mother on the throne? Jamie Saxt is the best of a bad lot.' He almost chuckled. 'After all, I moulded him myself! You are near his age, and can be a comfort and assistance to him. When there, *use your initiative*.'

'If I maun go, I maun go,' I muttered, frustrated, fearful and excited.

I RODE NORTH FOR Huntingtower with two men assigned for my protection. They rode one on either side and I felt myself a steer escorted to market. The day was warm, the corn grown high, a world away from the iron day when I had gone through the ice above Kincardine. My life had been loitering, now it was headlong. My eyes stung from the stour of the road, thinking of Rose sick in England, and of our boy King, greiting in Huntingtower. How am I to mend this rent and ruinous world? With what spindle and flick of my scrieving hand?

We crossed the Tay below Elcho Castle. On the far bank armed horsemen rode from the trees. They surrounded us, took us to a dell where a violent, unpredictable man got to his feet. James Stewart, newly Earl of Arran, was a Captain of the Guards the world over.

Young Walter Scott would kill to defend himself, though he might preface it with a witticism and tell his tale of regret later, but I believed there was no limit to the Earl of Arran's ambition and ruthlessness.

He stared at me. I tried not to look at the hairs growing from the warts patterning his throat. He was said to be sensitive about them.

'You are to Huntingtower on business?' he said. 'So are we.' He smiled, not kindly. 'You are Buchanan's lacquey?'

I protested I was a stand-in scrivener, the King's secretary having taken ill. His black eyes chilled my soul.

'Very ill, by what I hear. And you are also Esmé Stewart's bum-boy?'

'Monseigneur Esmé does business with my mother, Janet Fock-hart,' I protested.

The Earl of Arran raised his eyebrows at that. 'As do we all – to her advantage. You come wi us.'

He signed to our captors and we rode on for Huntingtower.

BY THE FOLD OF a dale, a company of foot soldiers waited, some bloodied. Arran spoke with them, then turned and beckoned to me.

'You. Wi me. They hold my brother.'

It seemed troops led by his brother to attack Huntingtower had been driven off by the Earl of Mar's men. Arran's brother had been wounded and taken within the walls. I expected Arran would ride south to gather reinforcements among Esmé Stewart and the other Association lords loyal to the King.

Not so. An hour later I was one of four horsemen cautiously approaching Huntingtower, which rose stark and bleak against the light. James Stewart, Earl of Arran, rode up front, unhesitating as a hundred horsemen and foot soldiers advanced to meet us. It was insanely bold, gambling everything on his kinship with Gowrie.

The great doors creaked open. We entered the courtyard and I heard the doors being barred behind us, a thudding *clonk*. What was Buchanan thinking of, sending me here? James Stewart jumped from his mount to meet the men who strode out from the castle: Glamis, Gowrie, Atholl – the key conspirators.

Straightaway the Master of Glamis seized Arran by the throat. Then Gowrie intervened, protested; Atholl seemed to agree. Glamis reluctantly let go his prey, and the four men went within to share the mysterious councils of the high heid yins.

I WAS TOLD TO make myself available for scrivening, and taken to a small chamber with a plain table and south light, some papers and a battered Tyndale Bible.

'So the usual secretary is unwell?' I asked.

'Indisposed,' the valet muttered, setting out candles, vellum, string and sealing wax. He was a short, wide man, with a Nordland accent and a dirk glinting on his hip. 'Taking a lang rest.'

He left me alone there with bread, cheese and watered wine. A yellowed casque lay under the bench. I set it on my head for warmth.

I wondered where my predecessor was resting – within the castle, or below ground?

Eventually I opened the Bible and settled down to reading Ecclesiastes. What would be, would be. For the rest of the afternoon, I remained strangely calm.

IT WAS DARK WHEN I was taken up the stairs into a long main chamber. Jamie Saxt sat twisted in a too-big chair, with the chief Lord Enterprisers towering over him. The King looked up, seemed puzzled to see me, then some thought moved within his eyes. He nodded, raised his hand in acknowledgement, then let it fall on his lap.

'We will now agree on the Proclamation dismissing Esmé Stewart, the *soi-disant* Duke of Lennox, from all offices, and commanding his exile forthwith.' This from Ruthven. Jamie Saxt whimpered as if whipped. 'There will be a codicil, stating that His Majesty issues this Proclamation on his own free will, and has chosen to stay within the protection of the Lord Enterprisers.'

The boy King wriggled in his chair, muttered '*Pish!*' under his breath. Glamis's massive hand clamped down on his shoulder. James Stewart, Earl of Arran, stood at the window, looking out into the night without expression. It seemed his gamble had paid off, for now at least.

I roughed out a draft Proclamation at their dictation. Some of these men were illiterate, though highly skilled at fighting and plotting; others were as educated as I. But none had a practised hand or could speedwrite, the skill Burne had bequeathed me.

So I scratched, deleted, rewrote and blotted. From time to time, Jamie Saxt sobbed. At others, he muttered, '*Treason, Treason.*' Ruthven was consoling and mostly respectful. Glamis was openly contemptuous. Atholl and the others moved away to muttered conference at the far end of the chamber. Melville's staunch Presbyterians went off to pray for their New Jerusalem. As ever, they mattered, but not as much as they wished. Positions had hardened in our divided nation, and now only a theocracy would satisfy them.

There seemed more nervousness than exultation in that room. I wondered at men who took such risks. Ambition, yes. Principle, sometimes. Survival of themselves and their family, always. And some, some truly believed, and these fanatics dismayed me more than any.

I was at the heart of a coup, but would it hold? In the towns, few would believe the King's Proclamation was of his own free will. Though associations to free His Majesty had just been declared as Treason, that did not make it so. Esmé was still a power. Surely in Embra, Stirling and Glesga, he and the Lords Huntly, Argyll, Montrose, Home, Seton, Maxwell, would be organising. Atween them, the Association held the bulk of the great castles and estates, with many, many followers. Another civil war becoming more and more likely.

Ruthven took my fair copy of the Proclamation, unrolled the parchment before Jamie Saxt. 'For your signature and ring, Your Majesty.'

'Shan't,' he said petulantly. '*Jamais.*'

Glamis growled, stepped forward with his hammer fist raised. Gowrie prevented him. The Earl of Arran got to his feet.

'Let us sleep and reflect,' he said. 'We will talk again with His Majesty in the morn.'

It was agreed, for the night was well advanced. The King was escorted up the stair, glaring at his protectors. James Stewart seized me by the elbow.

'Make four fair copies of the Proclamation for signing the morn.' I looked away from the hairy moles at his throat. 'I will explain the facts of life to this stripling King. Sooner or later, he will sign Esmé Stewart's banishment.'

I went off to my improvised study, called for a fire and some good candles, and once my hand was steady, settled down to work. As I wrote my best enlarged secretarial, I was aware these words would be announced in the main towns of our country. My biggest audience! Would this proclamation lead to war, or avert it? Dare I invoice for this labour?

Eventually I lay on a pallet, under some rough hides. The creusie lamp flickered dim yellow, smelling of fish oil. I thought of Rose sick in her convent cell in Northumbria. This new ascendancy of the Calvinists must make her extradition more likely. And I thought of Jamie Saxt, his quick look to me as he had left the room, some fixity of purpose in those dark eyes, even as the tears dried on his face.

I would use my initiative, if opportunity arose.

MY PROCLAMATIONS FOR THE banishment of Esmé Stewart, Duke of Lennox, were signed and sealed towards afternoon of the next day. The signature was shaky but recognisably the King's. Who knows what had gone on in his chamber? What veiled threats, what hollow assurances?

There was now a stir in the castle, and among the forces camped outside. It seemed the King was to be moved to Perth, where they could hold him more securely. From the upper window I watched James Stewart, Earl of Arran, shake hands with the Lords, then ride south to meet up with his Guard. I saw those Lords look on after his departure, then turn to each other, talking closely. They were neither stupid nor impetuous, those men, even those who could not read. First Esmé, then deal later with the Captain of the Guards before he dealt with them.

The Master of Glamis, greasy with sweat though the morn was chill, pinioned my shoulder as I cleaned my writing kit. 'Anither wee scrieving job for you, laddie. Trust me, and keep yer mooth shut.'

I packed my satchel and apprehensively followed his man through the narrow dank passages. As Nicol Burne used to say, I'd conjugate a leprous ferret afore I trusted Glamis.

JAMIE SAXT LOOKED UP as I was shown into the cloak room where they had lodged him. He looked pale, red-eyed, shivering constantly.

'Ah yes,' he said loudly, 'Secretary Fowler. I wish you to take some personal letters at my dictation. My hands have cramped.'

I bowed, and laid out the contents of my satchel. For all his shivering, those red-rimmed eyes were steady. The guard hesitated, then found a stool and sat at the window, watching the action in the courtyard below. After all, I was the author of *Ane Answer*, approved by George Buchanan and the Kirk, seen in the company of James Melville.

I took the King's dictation, assuring friends of his safety and well being. He added another note, for George Buchanan, enquiring after his health *for auld lang syne*. As the seals cooled, we talked of Alexander Montgomerie, sighed over his lovely song *Come, my Children Dere*. The guard had grown bored of us, and was now leaning out the window waving down into the courtyard. Jamie Saxt slipped two sealed letters from his doublet, whence they went into mine. *For my love*, he whispered.

Back in my room, I barred the door and secured the secret letters down my hose, one on the inside of each thigh. Then I picked up my satchel with the other letters, made for the hall and the way out, trying to walk normally. Though my skin crawled at everyone I passed, no one paid any attention to me.

At the main doors, two gatekeepers jumped forth and barred the way. I explained I was Secretary Fowler and had permission to leave with private letters from the King. While one man went off to check, I stood by the other, looking at the ground, then up at the free sky. The two hidden letters burned against my thighs.

The guard came back into the courtyard with William Ruthven, Earl of Gowrie, and pointed across at me. Ruthven glanced, nodded.

'Search yon satchel and his person.'

They opened my satchel, took out the King's letters. I held out my arms and let them rummage inside my cloak and doublet, shivering the while. I dropped my arms and waited for a further search and my doom.

'Ach, send him on his way,' Ruthven called. He smiled, briefly. 'He's *hairmless*.'

CHAPTER 15

Ane Tragedie of the Phoenix

EMBRA CRAWLED AND STUNG like a poked hive. Head down, I made my way through the vennels to Esmé Stewart's lodging. There, even the guards had guards. I was pinned to the wall with a sword at my vitals while they searched me for weapons. Esmé stuck his head out of an upper window and bawled for me to come up.

The secret letters I had brought shook in his hand. His buttons were uneven, his colour was high. He could not sit still but paced the room, glancing down at the street below.

'The Proclamation was read at the Tolbooth, and again at Holyrude,' he said. 'They would banish me, though few believe it is the King's will. Tell me all you witnessed at Huntingtower.'

Half-way through my account, he interrupted me, apologised for his manners and called for hot chocolate. Then he questioned me closely about the position of James Stewart among the gathering.

'He is Captain of Guards without a King to guard!' he exclaimed.

'How long can he last?' Nevertheless, Esmé couldn't stay away from the window, even as he assured me an Association had been formed in the City to free the King. Huntly, Argyll, Montrose, the Lords Home, Seton, Maxwell, were reviewing their forces at Brunt's Field.

'I do not have many followers,' Esmé confessed, 'having not lived long in this country. 'Friends say I should withdraw to Dumbarton for my safety.'

I made some sympathetic noise. I heard again Buccleuch's mother a world ago, as we had left Branxholme: *Take care not to back a horse that will not stay the race.*

Esmé checked the seal of the first letter I had brought. 'This is the King's private letter?' he speired. 'Written without his captors' knowledge?'

'Aye, surely,' I said. 'He passed it to me secretly, then I smuggled it out within my hose, at great personal risk.'

He almost smiled as he held the letter to his nose. 'And thigh-fragrant it is,' he murmured. He slit the seal with his knife, unfolded the paper and read once, twice. Then he slumped onto the window seat and read again, lips bloodless as they moved.

'He begs me to leave Embra, for my own safety.'

With shaking hand, he ripped open the second note. I watched him as he read, and felt sorrow at the droop of his head to his chest. I had felt awe, attraction, irritation towards this manly daffodil who had sprung so brightly into our midst. Now I knew pity at his withering.

There was commotion outside, a stushie of shouting, hoof-clatter, steel and oaths. We went to the window. A dozen or so of the King's

Guards on muscular horses were grouped up on the High Street, looking down the close. They stared impassively as Esmé's men waved their pistols and pikes. At last their leader twitched his reins, made a casually obscene gesture, and they set off down towards Holyrude.

Esmé held the second letter close to his face, and I realised this perfect specimen was short-sighted. 'This was written later the same day,' he said quietly. 'My friend and master says the situation has worsened. He begs me to save myself. He says if I love him at all, I should return to France. These look like tears, don't you think?'

He waved the paper in front of me. 'I can believe it,' I said hesitatingly. 'He was indeed red-eyed.'

'He now believes my cause is broken beyond repair,' Esmé said, his voice low and hoarse. 'He begs me to return to Paris. *C'est fini.*'

LATER THAT DAY I witnessed Esmé Stewart ride through Tollcross with some forty followers, bound for his castle in Dumbarton. The guards set by the Association waved him through, not hostile but ready to see the last of him. The cause of freeing the King from the Gowrie conspirators would continue without the Duc d'Aubigny. He had never quite been one of them.

I watched the riders dwindle into the west, then hurried to report to George Buchanan. I went by the meadows where the harvest had been taken in my absence, scrunched with pleasure across the autumn stubble towards Kennedy Close. It was a fine crisp afternoon, the trees turning, some already shedding as Esmé had been shed. As I approached Buchanan's lodging, I anticipated praise and I hoped to be paid for my mission.

The main door was part-open. I hurried up the familiar stair and at Buchanan's door walked into John Geddes with arms full of papers. He stared at me, red-eyed, in high colour, drink taken though it was not yet noon. Behind him I saw the empty table, the quills scattered on the blotter, the old grey-blue cloak hooked over the cathedra chair.

'The master is dead,' Geddes said. 'We must secure his books.'

TWO DAYS LATER I stood among the crowd at the Tolbooth and heard the latest Proclamation. Esmé Stewart the traitor was to leave the Kingdom, forever. Support for him was treasonous. Even as we listened, a counter-Proclamation was nailed up to affirm that the King was being held against his will by the Ruthven conspirators. A band of ultra-Protestants made to tear it down, and a rammie ensued. Sick at heart, I hurried away to a more pressing appointment.

We interred George Buchanan, Humanist, scholar, writer, Calvinist of sorts, in Greyfriars kirkyard, the small rain settling on our shoulders. Only a few notables were present, including both Andrew and James Melville, the town Provost, and Lekprewick the printer with black kerchief and stained thumbs. The King was guarded in Perth. The nobility were busy drilling their forces up at Brunt's

Field. The wind was strong, and shredded the few words said. Beside me, John Geddes wept silently. My heart hung low and heavy like a stuffed purse that could not open.

Walter Scott's arm weighed on my shoulder. 'You have lost a patron,' he said.

'We have lost much more,' I muttered. 'He was the greatest scholar and teacher of our times.'

I felt shallow-rooted, as if the wind could lay me flat. My father, Nicol Burne, Regent Morton, and now George Buchanan. The great oaks that once sheltered us had been cleared.

'You remain his man?'

'I suppose I do,' I replied. I was no Calvinist, and favoured Montaigne over Melville, but since an afternoon in St Andrews Swallowgait, something in me had been sworn to Buchanan.

'Quite right,' Scott said. 'Still, you will need a new patron. Come tell me over brandy about your doings at Huntingtower. I hear you have been busy.'

His voice was kindly, though this was more command than offer. Even as they shovelled down the dirt, the contest among the living went on. I followed Scott to Ma Broon's rancid howff, kicking the earth from my once-fine shoes.

UNDER CLOSE QUESTIONING, I recounted my mission to Huntingtower, quite proud of my daring, saddened by its outcome, though Esmé's cause was not mine. He listened, rubbing goblet to lip.

'You truly think you smuggled out those letters?' he murmured after I concluded.

'Certainly! If they'd caught me . . .' I put my hand round my throat, tilted my head to the hanged man.

Buccleuch sipped. 'There was no likelihood of that. Who sent ye to Huntingtower?'

'George Buchanan himself!'

'And who permitted ye to leave that fell place?'

'Ruthven, the Earl of Gowrie.'

'And in what cause are Ruthven and Buchanan united?'

I hesitated. 'The Reform,' I admitted. 'The Protestant ascendancy.'

Then I saw what Scott saw. I had been chosen to go to Huntingtower, as someone with enough acquaintance of the King to be trusted by him. Someone Esmé Stewart trusted enough to believe my assurances that these private notes from Jamie Saxt were sincerely meant. As they were. Those tears had been real.

'Aye, you did the job for them,' Scott said. His smile was brief but sympathetic. 'It achieved their ends. The erstwhile Duke of Lennox has left the field. I hear he is in Rothesay now, down to twenty men.'

I had thought I had been daring, but I had only done what I was supposed to do. I stared down into my glass at the lees gathered at the bottom. Walter Scott gripped my sleeve with a hand some said had already killed twenty men.

'Never ye mind,' he said. 'They will deal with our Captain of the Guard in due course. As they will wi Gowrie and his crew.

Our King is canny for his years. He is no Presbyterian and will insist on being head of the Reform Kirk. I do not doubt he rejects Catholic alliances and this nonsense about sharing the throne wi his mother.'

'What do you aim to do?' I asked, sensing a rare moment of candour.

He tilted his powerful hand this way and that, a gull side-slipping the wind. For a moment I saw again the resourceful boy on the *Sonsie Quine*, heading below decks with my father's dirk. 'Whatever is necessary,' he said. 'I will follow Jamie Saxt. He has another throne in mind, gin he can hold on to his own.'

'Unite the Kingdoms?' I exclaimed incredulously. When all was said and done, Scotland was a small, impoverished and desperately riven country.

'Queen Bess has no heirs and will not now,' Scott replied. 'Only uniting the Kingdoms will end the Border wars that ruined my family.'

He balanced his glass on his thigh and stared down at it. Walter Scott of Branxholme and Buccleuch was born far above me, and by his boldness and cunning had risen further, and was minded to go yet higher. I was but a useful scrivener, a leaf whirled in his passing. I believed he was also, when circumstance allowed, my friend.

'So that is your final destination.'

'Aye. London.'

The word sounded like a heavy bell struck, summoning the faithful to worship their ambition. In time I would go too, though I never truly flourished there.

'If we are spared,' I said, for want of anything else. My father's phrase, humble before God and the powers that be.

Buccleuch's hand closed over mine. 'You mean if we are clever, bold and blessed to see more years of miracles and wonder!'

He laughed, and was the bold boy again as he raised his glass. I raised mine, thinking of Esmé Stewart in his pomp, his beauty and dash and his lost cause. And of subtle George Buchanan, who to the end believed in the limited power of kings. 'To miracles and wonder,' I said, and we drank.

'Speaking of miracles and wonder,' he murmured, and leaned closer. 'Rose Nicolson.' My heart was thundering already. 'My cousin the Chief Justice has told me that with the Kirk's current ascendancy, an extradition request will go to the English Privy Council.'

'Surely it will not be granted?'

Scott looked at me direct, eyes blue-green like coloured glass. 'The English Queen was well-pleased at the putting down of the Catholic attempt. There is every chance her minister Walsinghame will sign the extradition.'

'We must get her out!' I rose to my feet, wild with agitation.

His hand firmly pulled me down. '*No*. The roads are much too dangerous for the likes of you. My cousin Magnus holds the estate of the Coldstream nunnery, and I have personal business with him. I shall go see how she fares, and judge what can best be done. You shall hear from me.'

I tearfully thanked him for his care. After all, it was a minor affair to him, though it meant the world to me.

'No matter,' he said. 'The Nicolson woman has twice my boldness and ten times my brains. Besides, she is particular to you, and I maun help if I am to be your friend and patron.'

I held out my hand and we shook on it before parting. I would be duty-bound to be his, if required. And I would be required. Friendship with men like Walter Scott of Buccleuch never came unalloyed with service.

I TRIED TO WORK on at my Lawnmerkit premises, the door double-bolted, with a new keeking-panel to check visitors. One afternoon I admitted Mitchison and his daughter. He looked round my near-empty premises without comment beyond *Aye, aye*. Marianne looked bonnie, but carried herself cautiously, like a full glass.

'I see you still have the blue couch,' she murmured. 'Does naebody want it?'

'Plenty want it,' I replied. 'But it may come in handy yet.'

We looked at each other till we both took a redder on the cheeks. 'You never know,' she said softly.

Her father circled back to us, having checked out my limited stock. 'The snuff trade?' he enquired.

'Snuffed out,' I replied, and got a wee laugh from Marianne.

'Aye, stick to what you ken best,' Mitchison said. '*The supply may not aye be available.*'

He took his daughter by the arm and led her away, message delivered.

A band of lads bold with cudgels came whooping down the close. Budge closed and bolted the door just in time. We heard them beating on the oak. *'Esmé's nonce!'* Laughter and shouts, fading towards the Grassmerkit.

Scott had been right, this was no time to journey into Northumbria. Yet every hour my thoughts kept returning, frantic as a hound scraping at the door, to one who dwelt there.

AS DAYS PASSED WITHOUT word from Scott or Rose, I formally made James Budge my partner and we tried to rebuild the business. But trade was slack in fine furnishings. Deep in debt, the Court lacked money to pay for acquisitions. Prosperous folk wetted their finger and held it aloft, waiting to ken the airt of the wind.

I heard Esmé Stewart had left Dumbarton and drifted round Rothesay, Callandar, even overnighting in Blackness Castle, with steadily diminishing retinue. They said he was ragged, reduced to sleeping in stables. Winter was coming, but still he had not left the country.

It was dark and I was alone when the messenger rapped on my door. I checked through the keek-hole, then laid back the bolts. He had come from my mother who begged me to attend her now. The lad had passes for the Watch, issued by the Association, in case we were stopped.

We went through the back lanes and wynds unmolested, cautiously passing other small groups of moving darkness. We groped upwards and finally emerged at the top of the High Street. We stood in the shadows till the moon foundered, then hurried across the glinting granite setts, the haft of father's dirk nudging my ribs.

A soft tap on that familiar door, then it scraped open. We slipped in, the door was speedily barred. The creusie light wavered in my sister's hand, her lips cool on my cheek. The lifelong-known smell of her. I stepped around where my father's blood had spread, and went on up the winding stair.

They were alone in the Doo-Cot, Esmé Stewart and my mother. Esmé wore a rough cloak and torn coarse britches, his face bruised, mud on his collar and hair in disarray. Mother's face was tallow-yellow as she bent over her cash box. 'I need your signature as witness,' she informed me.

So the Catholic Restoration project ended as it had begun, with cash and credit notes. This time there was no laughter, no fine wine and flirtation and toasts to a glorious future. I tried to cheer with talk of Paris and patisseries, but failure clung like mould to the walls of that room. When they withdrew to the window to talk quietly, I stared at the empty cubby that had once held Bishop Leslie's papers, to the left of the Gates of Hell. Word was the bishop was confined in Banff, his high schemes dinged doon.

The end came quickly. Esmé embraced my mother, to my *Au revoir* responded *Adieu*, then was gone into the night.

He had swept into Leith on a warm backing wind, penniless but magnificent, and he left under darkness with an apologetic backwards wave of the hand. He was heading for London, then

Dover, then Paris. He would not be stopped. Even his own party wanted him gone.

Our stripling King went on to pen a fine, bitter poem, *Ane Tragedie of the Phoenix*, on the theme of beauty killed by envy. *First love, as greatest God above the rest* . . . My mother never smiled again, not in her eyes. When news soon came of Esmé's death in Paris – poison or broken heart, take your pick – her face was lumpen and still as spilled candlewax come dawn.

CHAPTER 16

Desperate Remedies

WHEN THE NOTE CAME, its text occupied less space than the magnificent insignia, the one I had first set eyes on as a boy, and had worked at for weeks to imitate the billowing sails and flying shrouds of that stately $\mathcal{B}$.

> *Extradition papers for RN will be received shortly. The Nicolson lass is sick and asking for you. Ride with the Warrant Officers if you desire private speech with her. Desperate times, desperate remedies.* $\mathcal{B}$.

SCOTT WAS MY PATRON, and she the great hope of my life. I sent Budge to arrange a post horse, my heart rat-a-tatting like the drummer of a Hieland regiment.

I CLATTERED OVER THE cobbles down into the White Horse Inn stables by Holyrude. Two high-mounted, scarlet-uniformed officers of the Law scowled haughtily around at a world waiting to be arrested.

'William Fowler?' the one with the squared-off beard demanded.

'The same,' I replied.

'I am Lieutenant Cluny.' He pointed a white-gloved finger at the one with the unconvincing moustache. 'This is McPhail.'

'*Enchanté*,' I said, suppressing a nervous smirk.

McPhail glared at me. 'We are bound for Coldstream, to execute an order for the extraction of the necromancer Rose Nicolson.'

'The *alleged* necromancer.'

'You may not ride ahead, and do not get left behind,' Cluny stated. 'We go now.'

Having established they did not like me and I did not like them, I followed them for Northumbria. The remorseless jolting speed with which we travelled, hour after hour till nightfall, added to the nausea lodged in my gut.

We overnighted in a lodge by the Tweed. I did not sleep much, thinking of her ill in the Priory Hospital, wondering how her trial might go once we returned to Embra. I was up early, quietly scoffed bread and cheese in the dawn. I saddled up my fresh post horse, slipped the tether. A heavy hand clapped my shoulder.

'Leaving us, laddie?'

'I just thought to get a start,' I assured Cluny. 'My horse is not the peer of yours. I do not wish to hold you up.' In truth, I had hoped to get there before them, to have some private time with Rose.

No chance. I was in the rear as we hit the coastal road, and remained there, sick at heart, for the remainder of the ride.

WE FORDED THE RIVER above Coldstream, from where I could see the square tower of the Abbey by the centre. The Flodden dead lay buried there, the chief graveyard of our nation's hopes. Once across, we were in England. It did not look or smell so different. Then we followed directions on towards the Hospital. It lay below the headland, not so far from Eyemouth where Rose had once worked in better days.

A small chapel, dwelling quarters, high walls, gardens glimpsed through the gates. Three nuns worked among the vegetables. They glanced when we came by, then ignored us as though in their world we did not count. A low building, off on the seaward side, must be the Hospital. It was a lonesome place, set apart for reasons of health.

The wind sighed in the little bell tower. At its base, a stone statue of the Mother and Child, faded but miraculously complete. Knox's cleansing sermons had not come this far.

Wearily, I slipped down from my mount and tottered a little. I leaned my forehead on the saddle, offering up a silent prayer. Cluny sat erect, sword in one hand, his Papers of Authority in the other. McPhail masticated, spat.

A shout on the wind, and round the corner of the convent garden came Walter Scott. He plodded head-down towards us, bare-headed and sombre. He stopped an arm's length off and studied the three of us. No greeting, no salutation. The wind tugged at his coat, his long fiery hair flayed around him.

'Here is the good news, Master Fowler,' he said, quite formal. 'You are now freed of all charges relating to Rose Nicolson's escape.'

'Pleased to hear that,' I said, my relief moderated by unease.

Scott fixed his eyes on his boots. Then he raised his head and looked at me alone. 'Here is the reason why,' he said quietly. 'Rose Nicolson is dead. We buried her yesterday.'

Some words register instantly, before their import arrives, as lightning ahead of thunder. The Officers looked at each other, their jaws open like a corpse's before binding.

Scott took me by the arm and led us into a little cemetery. I smelled fresh earth in the morning air. A dark mound lay in the corner. The few crosses nearby were of wood, most faded and aslant, the inscriptions burnt on with a poker. That seemed so humble and pitiful, a stone would weep.

Scott's voice came from afar, like the sea. I hung on to his words as to a rope above a great drop. I feared what would happen when he stopped speaking.

He was recounting the last afternoon he had talked with Rose in her cell, when she was feverish and weak, but lucid. She had asked after her daughter Lucy, her brother and her friend Will Fowler. She said she was resolved to accept the extradition when it came, and to make herself over to the will of God and the mercy of the Kirk.

'That doesn't sound like her at all,' I managed.

The Prioress had ghosted up behind. 'Perhaps our prayers were answered,' she said. 'It does happen, whatever you might think. In her last days, she returned to God.'

Prioress Hoppringill had a smooth, doughy face, and bright, sharp eyes that turned on me. How I loathed her complacency, the plump fingers fiddling with her damn beads.

'Then she said she was tired and had to rest, and closed her een,' Scott said. 'When I returned next day, the Mother here told me she had passed.'

'God rest her soul,' the Prioress murmured. 'The fever takes suddenly, and she left us that night for a better world.'

'And you saw her?' I managed.

Scott looked out at sea as though the answer lay there. 'Aye,' he said quietly. 'I did that.'

'How seemed she?'

Scott stared at me. 'Well . . . deid. Ye ken.'

'Peaceful?'

'Aye, at peace.'

I spread my hand across my face and wept shameless as a bairn.

'Let him be a while,' I heard Scott say to the Warrant Officers. I found myself kneeling on damp earth.

'This is not possible,' I said. 'It's just not.' Scott knelt by me, hand gripping my shoulder. 'She cannot die without my seeing her.'

Scott leaned so near I smelled cheese on his breath. 'I'm afraid she can. There was not time enough to wait for you or her Eyemouth relations afore the interment. On account of concerns about infection, you understand.' He hesitated. 'I will pay for her plot and memorial stane. They await your inscription.'

He put his arms under my oxters and hauled me upright. I felt my chest would crack.

'Come awa, freend,' Scott said softly, in tone of the Borders, not the Court. His heart's voice, perhaps.

'It's not possible,' I groaned. 'She canni just go from us.'

Scott took a firmer grip on me. 'I expect the Warrant Officers will ride hame the morn.' He looked to them as they stood, embarrassed and uncertain.

Cluny cleared his throat and spat. 'What a long ride for nothing.'

It took Scott and the Prioress – a strikingly muscular woman – to prise my hand from his throat.

WE WERE TAKEN TO the room where Rose Nicolson had lived out her last days on Earth. The narrow bed was stripped, the room was empty save for wash-bowl, praying stool and wooden crucifix. The small window over the bed looked aslant at the sea. Behind the shutter lay a book. Ovid's *Heroides*.

I picked it up and quit that dreadful room.

Prioress Hoppringill left us with a nod and a sharp glance. Scott and I watched the Warrant Officers ride back for Coldstream and the inn there. They would come for me the morn, and we would ride back to Embra together. We watched till they turned the corner and went out of sight.

Scott sighed long, as if expelling the sins of the world. 'Let us go for a daunder,' he said. 'They take good care of your mount here.' What was the point in a walk? What was the point in anything? He nodded, though I had not spoken. 'There's another wee harbour over the hill, and a better inn. The Groat and Compass. You'll like it.'

Scott and I spoke little as we walked the way, myself with over-night bag across my shoulder. I felt like an ox who has received the spike but has not yet dropped. Rose's death stuck in my head, a bolt of incoherence. 'It is not possible,' I kept muttering. 'It is not right.'

He keeked sideways at me, sympathetic yet resolute. 'No,' he said. 'It is not.' Then later, as we approached the solitary dwelling above the harbour, a yellow lamp in its window, he added, 'They have unexpectedly fine fare here.'

Scott rapped on the door, a quick triple-knock. I heard the bar slide back. Scott stood aside, gestured me to enter. Then the world slipped as though we were at sea. Rose Nicolson stood within, pale and drawn but very much alive.

'THERE WAS NO OPPORTUNITY to warn you,' Scott apologised. 'The Warrant Officers had to witness and believe, as you did.'

Rose reached across the table and gripped my hand. 'I am awfy sorry,' she said. 'This seemed the only way.'

'It is a great joy,' I said, looking into her eyes. Dark blue, deep as the North Sea. 'Had I known, I'd have brought more gear for the journey. When do we leave?'

Scott coughed. 'There is a two-master in the harbour. The Prioress insists it must be gone by first light. It carries wool for Bruges, an agent of my mother will be waiting there.'

'Your mother?' I said wonderingly.

'Mistress Gourlay is bound for Padua,' Scott said. 'She will be safe in our collegiate convent. A new name, and a new calling! The previous tutor and librarian drowned in the Arno.'

I remembered Lady Margaret in her room in Branxholme, sipping that herby wine as she talked of Padua and their family interests there. 'I can still taste that wine,' I said. 'So rich, so heady! Italy! The land and language of the divine Dante! *Molto bene!* It will suit us well.'

Her hand stroked my brow, my cheek, lingered briefly on my lips. 'No, my dear friend,' she said quietly. 'I travel alone.'

Walter Scott got to his feet. 'I will leave you two to talk,' he said. 'The barque sails before dawn.'

I SAT BY HER side for hours and tried to make that woman my wife. I offered everything I had, admittedly not that much. But I had skills and hopes. I had languages and a fair hand. I could teach. I could trade.

To all my reasoning she listened and said no. 'I am not what I was,' she insisted. 'I am no longer your sweetheart fisher lass.'

'You said there were two occasions when you might have been,' I said. 'What was the other?'

She looked down at her palms, as though examining the lines of her life. 'Afore I was marrit,' she said low. 'The day you gave me the queer stane and looked on me with love. John and I had been at odds whiles, and I doubted. You mind that day?'

'I mind it,' I managed.

'Had we not been interrupted,' she murmured. 'Had ye been bolder, or I mair flighty . . .'

It is more torment than consolation to know it might have been. 'So you are no longer a mother?' I asked harshly.

She winced, looked away. 'No longer,' she said, very low. 'Lucy will be better off among the Gourlays and her ain folk. Of this I am sure.'

'But can you flourish outwith Fife?' I protested. 'What will you do without your people?'

When she looked me in the eye, I saw her face was thinner from illness, and more than that, from purification of purpose. 'I will teach in the convent,' she said, calm as the night outside. 'I will read and I will learn. The Order has connections to the poet Veronica Franco in Venice. How I long to talk with her and her ilk!'

I stared at her. 'But she is a courtesan!'

Rose laughed quietly. 'Doubtless she has kenned the pleasures of the flesh! And doubtless she has a patron – but so, I understand, do you?'

'It is a regrettable necessity,' I admitted.

'Franco has a place and position, and she can hold her own in any company. There are others! Have you read of Gaspara Stampa? They are *poets*, Will. Their letters are printed and widely read. Your friend Montaigne recognises them! Can you imagine that in the land of Knox?'

I had not seen her so animate in a long time. 'But a convent?' I said. 'Have you become a Believer?'

'Scarcely,' she replied drily. 'Though doubtless the Sisters hope I will become so! I shall nod meekly, say my orisons and stay out of trouble, and in return I can live the life of the mind. My life, Will! Do you no want that for me?'

I shaded my eyes with my hand. It hurt to look at her radiance. 'Of course,' I said. 'But I also want you.'

She looked back at me. The night went still around us. She stroked the back of my hand – her fingertips were still rough – and I like to think I saw more than sympathy in her eyes.

'Yon ship has sailed,' she murmured at last, to herself as much as to me. 'You reasonably expect children and an heir. That is no longer for me.' She put her fingers to my lips as I protested. 'Will, you are sae dear to me, but you ken well I am not the mate you need.'

'I love you,' I protested. '*Ti amo. Je t'aime. M'eudail, a graidh.*'

She smiled at my use of her father's tongue. 'You are right,' she replied. 'Love takes many forms. Let this be ours.'

She put the fingers that had touched my mouth to her own lips, and kissed them, all the while looking into my eyes. I would never be closer to another in this world.

Scott chapped on the door, entered, and looked at us questioningly. Rose nodded firmly, then I did too. 'Good,' he said. '*Desperate
times, desperate remedies.*'

We ate bread, cheese and beef with our hands, standing, washed
down with brandy. Scott pushed a purse across the table to her 'Take
it,' he insisted. 'I owe Master Fowler more than this, on account of
the *Sonsie Quine*.'

She looked questioningly at me, at him. 'It happened lang syne,'
I said, and broke off a hunk of bread and cheese.

Scott turned all his attention on her. For a long moment they
looked each other in the eye, and I wondered what had passed between
them these last days. 'Auld Scotia will have to get by without you,'
he said respectfully. 'She will be the poorer for it.'

She looked straight back at him, then slipped the purse within
her cloak. 'I dinni doubt that,' she said. A small grin, a flash of her
earlier self.

'But you'll be back some day?' said I. 'When times are fit?'

She ate the last of the cheese, drained the cup. 'The arrow has left
the bow, naebody kens how far it will fly.' She tightened her cloak.
'In five hunner years they may be fit.'

BY LANTERN WE WENT down to the harbour, Scott tactfully up
ahead. Rose had one bag of her necessities. I passed her *Heroides*.
'You'll be needing this,' I said. 'Live up to it.' She held me close.
How thin she had become! 'I pray we may meet again.'

'We have never parted,' she replied, then stepped down into the dark.

The sails were raised, a pale shimmer and thwack as the sheets tightened, then they were gone on the pre-dawn breeze, heading south.

'ALRIGHT!' SCOTT SAID. 'LET us get up the road. The Warrant Officers await. Ye maun go to Embra and St Andrews and put this sorry story out.' I groaned, watching her cutter lean through the first light. 'Our remarkable friend has gone her way,' he said. 'Let her go.'

'Sic is the world?'

'Aye,' he chuckled, 'so it is.' He blew out the lantern as we walked up the brae from The Groat and Compass. 'I think you have business pending in London?' he asked, casual-like.

'Aye. Financial matters, long-standing.'

'You should go soon. Secretary Walsinghame would speak wi you.'

I had not imagined Scott's contacts went so far. 'But Walsinghame sounds dreadful!'

Scott clapped me on the shoulder. 'There, there. He but wishes to enlist you.'

'I'd rather be enlisted by a tarantula.'

'You will be of more service to him free than in the Tower. He is not like Bothwell or our Captain of the Guards – he is a rational man. Your choice, of course!'

Threat and opportunity, hand in glove as ever.

Warrant Officers Cluny and McPhail were waiting outside the small Hospital, their horses pawing for the Embra road. The Prioress came out and bade us farewell. She said she would make sure Sister Rose's grave was kept clean. As she handed me the reins of my post horse, I swear Mother Hoppringill winked.

CHAPTER 17

The End of an Old Song

THE RUTHVEN PLOT FALTERED. Come spring, the King would escape his captors in St Andrews. Gowrie was accused, found guilty of kidnap, then pardoned. He tried to make another comeback. This time he was speedily condemned, drawn and quartered, the bloody works.

And James Stewart, Earl of Arran, former Captain of Guards? He returned to Court and was for a couple of years useful to Jamie Saxt in pushing back the Calvinist wing of the Kirk. Then he shot a man too many – son of the Earl of Bedford, no less; bad mistake. Despite passionate pleas in the King's chambers, he was forced from the Privy Council. He retired to his estate in Ayrshire for some nine years, till Regent Morton's surviving nephew rode into the orchard and shot him point blank. *An act of great patience and some Justice*, the Judge pronounced before passing sentence.

Walter Scott had grown from wild boy to seasoned reiver to one who could stand back and consider. In time he would become Sir Walter, finally Lord Buccleuch. When our Jamie Saxt became James I of England, and the Court moved south, he prospered there as I did not.

Tom Nicolson cut his hair close as a monk, became a chaste, fierce scholar, a beacon on the rocks, his heart iron-caged following his sister's departure. And I would carry on trading with the world, veering when the wind did: merchant, financier, occasional poet and useful servant of my various patrons. To be pensioned off with 2,000 acres of Ulster bog! My pen shakes, a reed in that gale of indignity.

I had seen Rose Nicolson grow from witty quine to thinker of dangerous thoughts to married woman and mother, to outcast kneeling in the rain before rents she could no longer mend. Then she was gone, to Padua and the circumscribed freedom of a convent library. Our letters were secret and few. Her public correspondence continues to circulate. I come across it here and there. She has not disappointed.

Rose Gourlay née Nicolson

1560–1582

She lived regarded and died regretted

IN ST ANDREWS JOHN Geddes shook his head at my draft for her memorial stone. 'The Kirk Session will remove it within the week.

Better to save yon for the Coldstream kirkyard.' He looked at me keenly. 'She remains there, yes?'

I pictured the earth mound, the empty cell, how I had felt in those moments. With that in mind I could look a suspicious man in the eye. 'She is not bound anywhere save Eternity,' I said hoarsely. He seemed to accept that.

He was right, of course, a second memorial stone was a daft notion. Yet I wanted to leave some marker to Rose in the town where I had known her. In two days I would be sailing south on business, London being as good a place as any for a man who wished to cease to be himself.

I shook hands with Geddes, thanked him for his advice, and bade him *adieu*.

'*Au revoir*,' he said. 'Translation and forgery are a small world. We shall work together again.'

Translation was nothing like forgery, I retorted. He smiled at that. 'Letters of political import, or Plutarch rendered into Scots, share but one aim!' He leaned closer, his breath stale wine. '*Producing conviction in those who wish to believe.*' He laughed. 'How else are folk like you and I to live, but with our adaptable hand?'

Geddes's laugh was that of someone who had sold himself to the world and now wanted it back but knew it was too late. As I went to meet Tom Nicolson, I recognised that murky laughter as my own.

'IN BETTER DAYS, WE did night-business in this toun,' Tom whispered. 'Let us do so again, in her name.'

He handed to me something cold, irregular and heavy. As the moon rose above the Cathedral's ruined Night Stairs, I turned the queer rock in my hands. Certainly not sandstone, granite, slate, nor basalt. It was time-worn, the lettering round the base foreign to me. The carved figure was some sort of beast.

I tilted it better to the moonlight, made out legs, perhaps a horn, a disc in the sky. Something projecting from the beast's side. It made me shiver, like an old song plainly sung.

'What in the Lord's name is this?' I asked Tom.

He took it reverently from my hand. 'The last of the Culdees gave it me, to do with it what I saw fit.'

'This is surely pagan!'

'It is, but the Prior couldni bring himself to destroy it. He said those who built the first church found it in a cleft by the old well.'

All rock is old, sculpture can be strange, but this was older and stranger than anything I had seen. I thought it might be a sky-stone, not of our world.

'This is the bull, son of the sun god,' he said softly. 'Sacrificed that his blood might let us live again. *Mithras*. His cult is recorded in Pliny, though our masters would rather we forget.'

I looked at the stone and now made out the kneeling bull, the lance, the sun in the sky. Sacrifice and healing. I looked up at Tom in the moon-shadow, his eyes overflowing with tears without shame.

'It is wondrous,' I said. 'Like herself, wondrous and lost to our world.'

DOWN IN THE UNDERGROUND chamber, I made up mortar as my father had once shown me. With a marlin-spike Tom enlarged a crack in the wall opposite the Virgin. As the cistern trembled, the creusie lamp threw his hand into shadow-play. I saw there Rose working at the nets on the Green, her eyes shining as she talked beyond my understanding.

'All that is by-ordinar is doomed,' I muttered.

Tom ran his hand along the little ledge he had created. 'We'll be alright, then!' he said. 'Her life will be far from us, but it is her ain. Best we can do is remember her as she was. What is scholarship but close remembering?'

I silently laid down a base layer of mortar, set the sculpture on it, then built up the sides. It was now flush to the wall. In a few hours it would be solid set. You would have to look carefully before you noticed it at all.

We knelt for a while, alone in our thoughts, joined in our hearts. Finally Tom blew out the lamp and we groped the few steps up into a cold dawning. We slid the stone across. I picked up my satchel and we left that place.

'Perhaps one day I shall see her in Padua,' he said as we walked down the brae towards the harbour. 'Till then, I will light her lamp on High Days and Holy Days'

'I will light a candle to her wherever it is allowed,' I replied. And I have done so, through all the years, as if it were my religion.

THE *Sonsie Quine* RUBBED and groaned against the harbour wall. The morning was brisk and the airt of the wind apt for bearing south. Now there was only leaving.

We shook hands. I clamped my other hand on his arm, to steady us both. Lanyards rattled all along the inner harbour, seabirds clashed above our heads as we said inadequate parting words. We would write letters, our lives would continue, at some point we would meet again. Tom would give me accounts of Lucy as she grew among the Gourlays. I would send funds for her when possible, along with veiled news of my life of a conduit.

My nose in his smelly cloak, the heave of his chest. When he released me, we stared in silence down where long weeds stirred in the current.

'So,' he said, trying to be lichtsome, 'you can now proceed from Purgatory to Paradise?'

'With Beatrice gone? No chance.'

'It's just a book,' he said, 'however divine.'

'Sic are we,' I said bitterly, staring down at the dark fronds. 'Weed attached to our bit rock, believing that with all this swirling and wavering we must be getting somewhere.'

He inclined his head, as in thought or prayer, then looked at me with swollen eyes. 'For all that, Will, we serve to mark tide's turn.'

I awaited something from the Stoics, perhaps reassurance I was dear to him, or that Rose had indeed cared for me. 'Go weel and cannily, my friend,' he said. 'Flourish in London, then come hame. We may yet see better days.'

With that he turned to limp up the brae to give his morning lectures on St Anselm, with a discreet side-serving of Averroes. As his stick tapped into faintness, I felt myself cut loose on the pier, with a satchel of papers, quills and inks, letters of introduction and a scrimshaw snuff-case.

I truly believed my life, the part that mattered most to me, was over. My early Formation, that time of freshest joys and pains, shaping all that follows, was done.

What remained for me was habit, vain ambition, and necessity. I would likely marry Marianne Mitchison if she would have me, produce children and an heir, write in whatever manner was fashionable until it went out of fashion. I would continue to be a hidden conduit, part of the sewage system that runs between the houses of the great. I would trade furniture and furnishings, and in time become a burgess like my father, and all the while my heart would wizen like untended leather.

I foresaw it all, or so I thought. The Reform would sink unevenly into the peat bog of my country's soul, a great edifice erected on insufficient piling. I had been a tiny part of its history, a twig, a buried leaf that once had known the breeze.

I stooped to pass my satchel to Jan Wandhaver, then turned inward to climb down onto the ever-shifting deck.

EPILOGUE

SUM QUOD ERIS   FUI QUOD ES
I am as you will be   *I was as you are*

I FIRST ENCOUNTERED THIS INSCRIPTION in the kirkyards of my youth, and it comes back to me now as I conclude. Such Latinate gloom, so very Scottish!

Yet at its back come bright memories of the World, the joyous appetites and pleasures of the senses. Mutton stew wolfed down with coarse bread in a sunlit doorway; Rose's deep blue eyes above the drying lines as she mends nets and opens my mind; gulls wheeling overhead as she and Tom and I walk the East Sands hand in hand; straddling a fig tree above where the Seine divides; brandy warm and sweet on my lips while Nicol Burne intones, *Nel mezzo del camin di nostra vita* . . .

For all the deaths, pains and losses of those years, what comes to me now is laughter, returning like tide across the sands. Laughter of Tom and Rose flyting, of Buccleuch and Auchterlone as we played on the Links, my goddaughter Lucy birling in blue pinafore, loving voices across the table in Fishertown, the roar in

Branxholme Hall when we feasted after our raid, glad to still be alive.

SUM QUOD ERIS indeed. Yet the hours are sweet while they remain. Put down these pages, friend, and look on the world. Let gladness rise like a laverock abune the May.

Full many a time the Archer slacks his bow
That afterhand it may the stronger be.

(*Ane Tragedie of the Phoenix*, Jamie Saxt)
WF

Scots Guide

aa *all*

aathing *everything*

aboot *about*

abune *above, overhead*

affrichted *frightened*

agin *against*

agley *askew*

ahint *behind*

ain *own*

aince *once*

airm *arm*

airt *direction, as of wind*

alane *alone*

anither *another*

atween *between*

awa *away*

awfy *awful/ly, very*

aye *yes, always, forever*

baffie *golf club*

baffies *slippers*

bairn *child*

besom *broom*

birl *turn, whirl*

blate *shy, diffident*

blootered *drunk*

boke *vomit, throw up*

bonnie *pretty, fine*

boo *runt of a litter*

brae *hill, slope*

braisant *brazen, bold*

braw *fine, good*

brawlie *will*

brig *bridge*

brither *brother*

buik *book*

bunnet *bonnet*

by-ordinar *unusual, extraordinary*

ca' canny *be cautious, go carefully*

cauld *cold*

canny *careful/ly, shrewd/ly, prudent, skillfully*

carlin *old woman, witch*

chap *knock, strike, as on door*

chiel *child*

clart *dirt, muck*

cleek *golf club*

clootie *cloth, rag*

clype on *inform on*

coory, cooried *snuggle/d, embrace/d*

corbie *hoodie crow*

crabbit *ill-tempered*

creel *basket, trap for crab or lobster*

creusie lamp *simple oil lamp*

cry *call, name*

dae *do*

daftie *fool, idiot*

darg *day's work*

daunder *stroll*

the De'il *the Devil*

didna/ didni, dinna/ dinni, disna / disni *didn't, don't, doesn't*

dinged doon *knocked over*

dirk *dagger*

dominie *schoolteacher*

doo-cot *dovecote*

doolie *melancholy*

drave *seasonal shoal (of fish); drive (of cattle)*

dreich *grim, severe, dull, desolate*

drookit *soaking wet*

drouthy *thirsty*

dug *dog*

dumfounert *dumbfounded*

dunt *hit, blow*

dwam *trance, day-dream*

een *eyes*

Embra *Edinburgh*

fae *from*

fairing *gift, reward, dues*

fairlies *wonders, things of beauty*

faither *father*

fash *fuss*

feart *afraid*

featherie ball *early golf ball of hide stuffed with feathers*

fecht *fight*

fiere *close friend, loyal companion*

flyte *a contest of mutual abuse, esp. between poets*

fou *mad, drunk*

fousty *dry, fusty*

freen *friend*

futeball *football*

gemme *game*

gie *give*

gin *if, would*

glaikit *foolish*

goonie *gown*

gowf golf

gowk *fool*

greit *cry, weep*

grue *shiver with fear, terror, repulsion*

guid *good*

guff *smell, reek*

gurly *stormy*

haar *a sea-mist*

hae *have*

hairm, hairmless *harm, harmless*

hairst *harvest*

haiver, haivers! *talk nonsense, nonsense!*

hame *home*

happed *wrapped*

haud *hold*

Hebdomadar *university supervsor*

heid *head*

Hieland *Highland*

high heid yin *senior leader, boss*

hirple *hobble, limp*

hoose *house*

howff *shelter, tavern*

hunner *hundred*

isna *isn't*

jalouse *intuit, suspect*

keek *peep, glance*

keek-hole *peep-hole*

keeking-glass *looking-glass*

ken *know*

kirk *church*

kist *chest, trunk*

kye *cattle*

lang syne *old times*

lave *remainder*

laverock *lark*

lichtsome *light-hearted*

lift *sky*

loup *leap, jump, bound*

lug *ear*

lum *chimney*

mair *more*

maist *most*

makar *poet, maker*

malisoun *curse*

marrit *married*

masel *myself*

mashie niblick *golf club, about 7 iron*

maun *must*

May *hawthorn, esp. in blossom*

merkit *market*

mither *mother*

mony *many*

muckle *much*

muir *moor*

nane *none*

neb *nose*

neuk *nook, corner*

no *not*

ochone *alas (Gaelic)*

onytime *anytime*

oxters *armpits*

peel tower *fortified tower*

paps *hills, vaguely breast-shaped*

pooch *pouch, pocket*

puir *poor*

quine *female, young woman; also queen*

rammie *fight, brawl*

richt *right*

reiver *robber, marauder, rustler*

rug *tug*

saft *soft*

sair *sore*

scrieve *write*

setts *paving stones*

scunner *disgust, loathing, repelled by, bored*

sea maws *seagulls*

shoogly *wobbly*

sic *thus, such*

siccar *safe, reliable, certain*

siller *silver*

simmerdim *long twilight of Northern summer*

skeely *skilful*

skelly *squint*

skelp *beat, strike*

skint *penniless*

sleekit *crafty, sly, cunning*

smoor *smother*

snaw *snow*

snell *biting, bitter*

sonsie *plump, agreeable; also lucky (from Gaelic* sonas: *fortune)*

speir *ask, enquire*

speug *sparrow*

sprush *spruce, smart*

stane *stone*

stapped *stuffed*

stoor *dust*

stot *spring, bounce*

stoup *tankard, mug*

stravaig *wander*

stushie *disturbance, fracas, fuss*

swithered *be uncertain, in doubt*

tae *to*

tak tent *pay attention, be careful*

tellt *told*

thocht *thought*

thon *that*

thrapple *throat*

thrawn *contrary, obstinate*

toun *town*

tousie-headed *with hair disordered or wild*

trig *spruce, tidy*

twa *two*

twa-three *a few*

uncanny *unearthly*

verra *very*

wabbit *very tired, exhausted*

wad-wyfe *female moneylender*

wan *one*

waur *worse*

weel *well*

weskit *waistcoat*

wha *who*

whaup *curlew*

whaur *where*

wheen *small amount, several*

whin *gorse, scrubland*

wheesht *calm down, be quiet*

wi' *with*

wi'oot *without*

wis *was*

wynd *alley, narrow lane*

yersel *yourself*

yestreen *yesterday evening*

ACKNOWLEDGEMENTS

MY SPECIAL THANKS GO to Andrew Dorward, for his enthusiastic historical tours of the town of his birth and of Edinburgh; Peter Dorward, for his key suggestion that allowed this book to grow; Ron Butlin, for his insightful readings and our many years of shared endeavours; and Lesley Glaister, for her lasting patience, support and literary acumen.

In St Andrews, the enthusiasm, kindly hospitality and generously shared historical perspectives of Margaret Beckett, Linda Dunbar and Dr Bess Rhodes, were a great help in the early stages of this book. I am further grateful to Alessandra Patrina of the University of Padua, for drawing my attention to her work on Walter Scott of Buccleuch and the early life of William Fowler, and to Allison Steenson, who showed me around the Hawthornden archive.

Sarah Dunnigan's *Eros and Poetry at the Court of Mary Queen of Scots and James VI* (Palgrave Macmillan, 2002), Billy Kay's

'Diplomats and Double Agents' (Radio Scotland, 2015), and Jane Dawson's fine *John Knox* (Yale University Press, 2015) have all greatly enlarged my understanding and sympathies. *Humanism and Calvinism: Andrew Melville and the universities of Scotland* by Steven Reid, clarified for me the underlying issues in the struggles between Church, State, the Crown, Town Councils, for control of the universities in this time.

The instincts, guidance and long-time support of my agent Georgina Capel and my editor Jon Riley have made this writing life possible. Thank you so much.